THE FALLEN

THE
FALLEN

ACE ATKINS

RANDOM HOUSE
LARGE PRINT

Copyright © 2017 Ace Atkins

Penguin supports copyright. Copyright fuels creativity, encourages diverse voices, promotes free speech, and creates a vibrant culture. Thank you for buying an authorized edition of this book and for complying with copyright laws by not reproducing, scanning, or distributing any part of it in any form without permission. You are supporting writers and allowing Penguin to continue to publish books for every reader.

All rights reserved.
Published in the United States of America by Random House Large Print in association with G. P. Putnam's Sons, an imprint of Penguin Random House LLC, New York.

COVER DESIGN by Kaitlin Kall
FRONT COVER IMAGES: (cars) Robert Warren / Getty Images; (stack of bills) CSA-Archive / Getty Images
BACK COVER IMAGE: (safe) CSA-Archive / Getty Images

The Library of Congress has established a Cataloging-in-Publication record for this title.

ISBN: 978-1-5247-7832-3

www.randomhouse.com/largeprint

FIRST LARGE PRINT EDITION

Printed in the United States of America

10 9 8 7 6 5 4 3 2 1

This Large Print edition published in accord with the standards of the N.A.V.H.

There are no one hundred percent heroes.

—John D. MacDonald

Every night you'll be told where to meet if surrounded by a superior force.

—Rogers' Rangers Standing Order No. 13

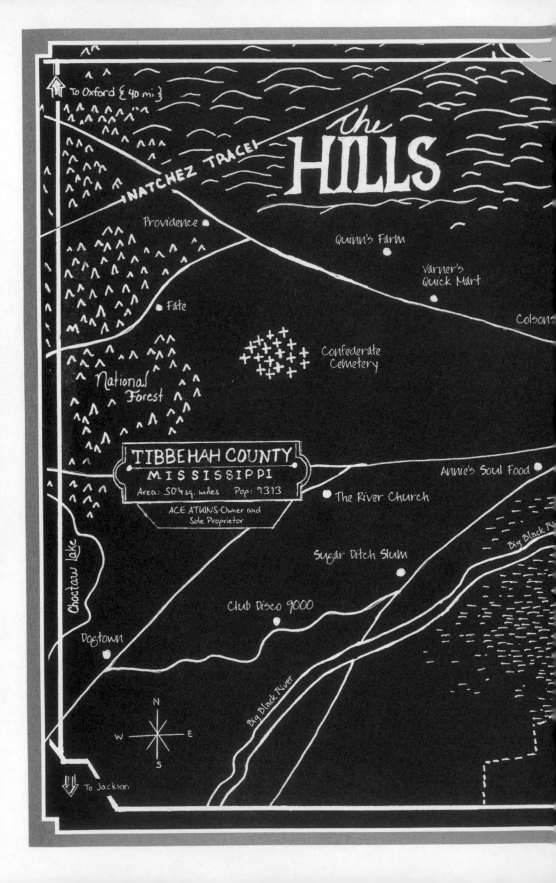

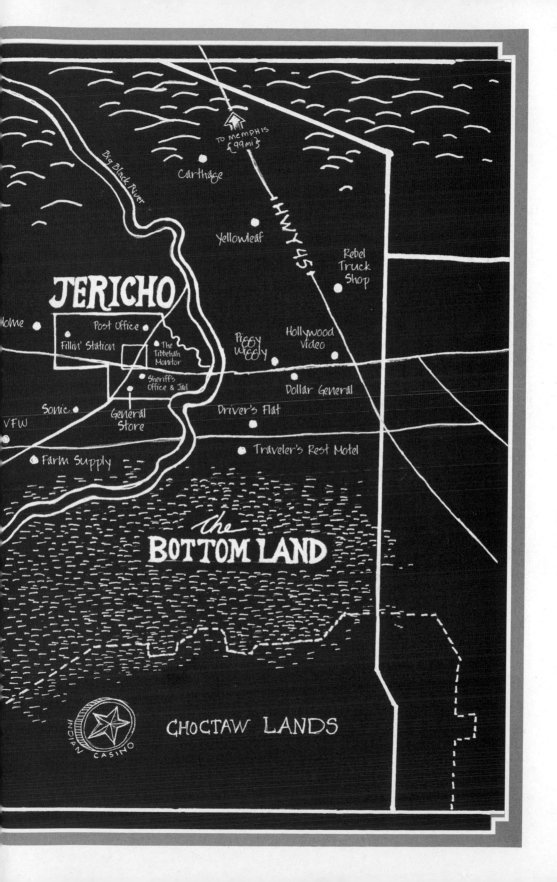

1

"I guess I got the idea about the time I got fired from the Ford dealership," Rick Wilcox said. "Some big-money swinging dick had hired me to motivate the sales staff, pep talks and all that bullshit, and do a bunch of commercials. To be honest, I didn't like the whole thing. He wanted me to dress up in combat gear and read this corny as hell line while I saluted the viewer. It made me want to puke."

"What was the line?" Opie asked.

"Christ, Ope," Wilcox said. "Why do you want to know all of this? I mean, right now? At this very moment? I find it highly inappropriate."

Wilcox looked at his watch. Nearly five minutes to the Walmart delivery, the mission, and the action. He and Opie sat up front in the white Ford van, smoking Marlboro Reds just like they had back in all those mud-slapped Zamindawar compounds. Cord was in back loading the AR-15s they'd modified, duct-taping the magazines back-to-back for easy loading. The guns were untraceable. The van stolen. They'd picked it off that morning at the Oak Court Mall in Memphis, switching the plates taken off a similar model.

"You got me into this, least you can tell me how it all happened," Ope said. "If you hadn't noticed, we're knee-deep in Shit City."

"Well, what if I don't want to talk about it?"

"You brought it up," Opie said. "You said it was the reason you and Crissley got into it. Since she has no fucking clue what we're doing, she wanted you to go back and beg for your old job."

"She was pissed," Wilcox said. "She thought she was going to get a cherry-red Mustang out of the deal."

"So what's the line?"

"Come on, buddy."

"Why the hell not?"

"OK, OK," Wilcox said. "You really want to know? So I'm dressed in my cammies and salute the camera and say, 'At Big T Southaven Ford, we never leave a customer behind.' The fat-ass sales guys look to me and salute back. Then a flag unfurls out of my ass and the band strikes up 'God Bless America.'"

"Damn," Opie said. "You're right. That fucking sucks. Humiliating. Are you even allowed to wear your uniform? I mean, isn't that against regulations?"

"I didn't wear my dress blues," Wilcox said. "Just some utilities. And a helmet. They made me wear a fucking helmet. It was something from World War II."

"What about your medals?"

"They wanted me to wear them, but I told them hell no. I mean, I do have a speck of dignity somewhere I forgot. I'd run out of money. It's not like winning a Silver Star led to some financial reward. I figured, if anything, it might help jump-start my country music career, but you know how that turned out."

"I thought you sounded great," Opie said. "Kind of like a more hard-edged Kenny Chesney."

"That hurts, Ope," Wilcox said. "You know how much I hate that bald-ass pussy. If I hear that song 'Me and Tequila' one more time, I'm going to blow my fucking brains out."

Opie, freckle-faced and jug-eared, grinned. That was the one thing about Ope, he could drive you crazy with his diarrhea mouth, but, damn, if he wasn't game for walking into hell itself with a positive attitude. He was the kind of guy who'd make jokes while you were tiptoeing though the poppy fields waiting for an IED to blow off your dick. "I remember how you hated that song when you found me down in Florida."

"Find you, hell," Wilcox said. "I fucking rescued you."

"Rescued me from pouring cocktails for women in bikinis," Opie said. "Tough gig."

"You were picking up trash on the beach and living with your grandpa," Wilcox said. "Those women all over you were cashing their Social Security checks."

Jonas Cord moved up between the two front seats of the van and looked out the windshield. They'd done a week of recon last month, hours of laying out the plan on maps, timing every mile, and stashing the Kawasakis. The only thing they couldn't have predicted was the damn rain. Great falling sheets of it between where they'd parked and the target. Jonas, hard, muscular, and absolutely humorless, leaned up between them and said, "Can't see shit."

"Life ain't all blueberries and paper airplanes," Wilcox said. "We say we're going to take the hill, we take the hill. I don't care if we're ass-deep in hailstones or a monsoon."

"Well, we got a monsoon."

"Spring showers," Wilcox said, "bring spring pussy."

"They're late," Cord said.

"Two minutes," Wilcox said. "Get your panties out of a twist."

"What if it's longer?"

"Then we adapt," Wilcox said. "Adjust. Overcome. Clint Eastwood shit. Have you forgotten everything you've learned, Sergeant?"

Cord grinned and disappeared into the back of the van. A minute later, a big gray armored truck rolled up in front of the Jericho First National Bank and idled there with its headlights shining bright on the entrance, red taillights glowing. When the guard stepped out into the rain and reached for the big sacks, Cord hit the timer on his watch.

"Did you see his commercial?" Opie said.

"Yeah, I saw it," Cord said. "Also saw him open up for a Jimmy Buffett tribute band at the dog track in West Memphis. I'd say I've seen too much."

"How was it?"

"He had one good song," Cord said. "Real tear-jerker about coming home from war and finding out Momma didn't know his name."

"That one was true."

Opie and Cord didn't say anything, knowing they'd gone one place that a Marine just couldn't tread. Talking about another Marine's momma. After all, there were tattoos for that and everything. As American as apple pie and a gallon of milk. Cord handed him and Opie a couple of rubber masks to cover their faces—Donald J. Trump—and two AR-15s, locked and jacked with double-dick magazines. Cord would stay behind the wheel, he and Opie would run into the bank and make a large withdrawal.

"This looks like a nice town," Opie said, sliding the Trump mask over his face and pulling the rifle's charging pin. "White lights in those trees on the Square. A big gazebo. Should we feel bad?"

"Nope," Wilcox said. "Life isn't fair. Look at you guys and look at me. It should be a crime that I got to be born so damn good-looking."

Wilcox checked his watch and put on his mask, remembering last time it had been Yoda, and before that Santa Claus. He liked Trump better. It'd scare the crap out of folks and would also make the news. Wilcox loved making the news. The Trump Bandits. He could see it now.

The guard appeared back outside the bank and crawled up front with the driver. Two minutes later, they were gone and the diversion well in motion. A little tight but manageable. A minute later, they heard the sirens. A cop car passed, and then two more headed toward Highway 45. It almost looked like a parade.

Wilcox and Opie got out of the van and walked together in the rain. Both carried their guns in big black canvas bags. The rubbery latex mask caught in a puckered gesture, yellow fake hair flapping in the wind.

Inside, Wilcox pulled out the weapon, shot at the ceiling, and shouted, "Anyone moves and I'll grab 'em by the pussy."

———

Earlier that morning, Quinn Colson sat in a back booth of the Fillin' Station diner finishing his third cup of coffee. He signaled the waitress, Miss Mary, for a refill right before Boom Kimbrough walked through the door and took off his jacket. He'd known Boom for most of his life, the two growing up together and hunting and fishing all over Tibbehah County. Boom still did his fair share of hunting, coming in that morning dressed in an orange vest, even though he'd had his right arm blown off six years ago while serving in the Guard in Iraq. He now wore a bright silver prosthetic device that Boom bragged was good for just about any job except wiping his ass.

Mary refilled the coffee and noticed Boom. She walked back toward the kitchen for his morning sausage biscuits and tall Mountain Dew without being asked.

"I saw that big-ass tom," Boom said. "So close, hearing that **gobble gobble** call. But, man, he knew I was around. Got spooked and flew back into the woods."

"He'll be back."

"You coming on or going off?"

"On," Quinn said. "Lillie's off today. Spending time with her kid."

"She still pissed at you?"

"Why?" Quinn said. "She's the one who wanted me to run. After a woman takes out a local hero, there's nowhere else for her to go but down."

"This county wouldn't have elected a woman anyway," Boom said. "Men don't have the nuts. A woman like Lillie Virgil scared the shit out of them. She talks straight and tells the truth."

"Too qualified," Quinn said. The previous fall, the acting sheriff, Lillie Virgil, had charged the longtime football coach with molesting kids and the whole town blamed her for the fallout instead of the coach. The locals didn't make a hell of a lot of sense. But Lillie told Quinn that if he didn't step up and take her place, everything they'd worked for would turn to shit.

"And they settle for your broke-down ass."

Quinn saluted him with the coffee mug and leaned back as Miss Mary slid two sausage biscuits in front of Boom. The woman had been waiting tables at the Fillin' Station since Quinn was a kid, back when his Uncle Hamp had been sheriff and received visitors every morning at the same booth. More business getting done at the diner than at the office where Quinn had been sheriff for nearly five years, except for a year or so when he had been voted out of office. He was dressed in a stiff khaki uniform shirt, crisp Levi's, and polished cowboy boots. His Beretta 9mm rested on his belt and his uncle's rancher coat hung by the front door.

"Listen," Boom said. "I don't want to cause no trouble. But ever since the first of the year, Old Man Skinner been riding my ass. He wants me gone from the County Barn and he wants to put in his own people."

"Where'd you hear that?"

"From Skinner," Boom said. "That motherfucker been shitting on everything since he took over the county supervisors. You know what he was like before he retired and said he was out of the life, letting Stagg run things. He's too old and too mean to do Jericho any good."

"Don't tell him that," Quinn said. "First of the year, Skinner announced to the supervisors and county employees that he intended to make Tibbehah a more godly place. Just like it'd been when he was a boy. Leaving out the parts about the Klan, killings, and moonshine wars. But that's exactly the kind of horseshit people around here believe and trust."

"And how'd you get elected?"

"Nobody else wanted the job," Quinn said. "Including Lillie, if she was really honest about it."

"How's your momma and them?"

"Fine."

"Daddy?"

"Hadn't heard a word since he shagged ass."

"Ophelia?"

Quinn drank some coffee and watched Boom

shove most of an entire biscuit in his mouth and chew. He watched him eat, not wanting to discuss a good woman who'd been a terrible match for him. Boom knowing full well that Ophelia Bundren had once thrown a steak knife at Quinn's head, barely missing. With his damn family and county politics, he'd had enough crazy in his life.

"How about we go look for that big-ass tom this weekend and not speak a word about women or politics?" Quinn said. "Later, I need to burn a brush pile before the weather turns. We can smoke some cigars and tell lies."

The Fillin' Station was packed that morning with farmers, fancy town women, camo-covered hunters, and glad-handing local politicians. Three old men sat at the closest table, all in tall-crowned ball caps, smoking cigarettes and downing cheap coffee. One of them muttering something about "goddamn China," bringing to mind the late Mr. Jim, who'd run the barbershop, and Judge Blanton, who fiddled with local affairs until his untimely death. The diner had been a gas station well before Quinn was born, the linoleum floor unchanged, propane heaters glowing a bright orange against the walls under endless rows of framed hometown heroes and yellowing news. Somewhere up there, young Quinn had survived ten days in the National Forest, his father had jumped a dozen Ford Pintos, and sometime in recent memory he'd graduated Ranger training and gotten a Purple Heart in Iraq. All that was now as yellowed as the rest.

"Will you talk to Skinner?"

Quinn nodded.

"We still on for supper at Miss Jean's?"

Quinn nodded again. "Fried chicken," he said. "And collard greens."

"It's good to have you back, man."

Quinn nodded. He drank some coffee and listened to the men talk about how things used to be better when they were young.

Boom leaned toward Quinn and said, "Not for my people."

"Y'all weren't happy working the cotton fields at gunpoint?"

"I think Skinner will do everything in his power to turn back the clock."

"He's too old," Quinn said. "It won't last. Nobody can stop how far things have gone."

"Evil don't die," Boom said. "Least with Johnny Stagg, you knew where you stood."

"How about we not talk about Stagg, either?"

"No Stagg," Boom said. "No Ophelia. Times do change."

"If you ask my sister, she'll say it's all part of God's divine plan," Quinn said.

"But you don't believe it?"

"How about you ask me when we both get old?"

"Too late," Boom said. "That clock sure is a bitch."

Quinn rubbed his weathered, lean face. Damn, if he wasn't coming up on forty and no one had bothered to tell him.

"Please don't kill me," said Mr. Berryhill, bank president and, according to the plaques on his wall, a two-time Jericho Citizen of the Year. "I think you broke my nose."

"You do as I say," Wilcox said, "and I give you my word of honor, I won't shoot your dick off."

Mr. Berryhill nodded in total agreement. Damn, it must've been a sight to see for those two women at the teller counter, the woman at the front desk, and those three folks—two men and another woman—waiting in line. Two Donald J. Trumps rushing in from the rain and flashing assault rifles as soon as they walked in the door, commanding attention and respect. Berryhill hid under his desk, Wilcox having to pull his fat ass out by the belt and rush him into the lobby. Opie stood on the teller counter yelling out orders, keeping watch over the front and back doors. Wilcox pushed Berryhill through all six of the drawers, two of them empty, as an aged black woman, the loan officer, kept on crying out to Sweet Baby Jesus.

"Jesus is playing golf today," Wilcox said. "Don't you see it's raining?"

"Sixty seconds," Opie said, high up on the counter, roving his AR-15 over the folks lying facedown on the tile floor. On a grease board by the drive-thru someone had written **Beautiful things happen when you distance yourself from negativity**. Eight cameras placed in various corners recorded every move and gesture.

"Open the cage."

"I can't," Berryhill said. "It's on a timer."

"Sir," Wilcox said. "Do you or do you not value your dick?"

Wilcox pressed the muzzle hard into the fat man's crotch. Berryhill nodded again in complete agreement and moved toward the accordion gate shielding the big safe. He reached into his pocket for a key ring and selected a gold one with shaking hands. Opie tossed Wilcox a second black sack and said, "Fifty seconds."

The gate was pushed open and Wilcox rushed inside, leaving Opie to make sure Berryhill kept his hands to himself. Wilcox had never seen so much damn money, neatly bundled and stacked on a stainless steel table by the deposit boxes. All that beautiful cash fresh from Walmart's big Presidents' Day sale. Wilcox snatched them up in his arms, cramming it all into the black sack, finding more stacks of twenties and hundreds on a second shelf and even more on a second table. "Thirty seconds," Opie said.

There was a peace and calmness when you did what you've been trained to do. It was like entering a warm bath, everything smooth and fluid. All that bullshit with pills and booze and therapy didn't matter jack shit right now. Controlled chaos. Speed and violence. Once a Marine, always a Marine.

"Fifteen," Opie said.

Wilcox had nothing but time. He could breathe easy, see everything. He finished up with the bag, zipped it shut, and dragged it out—so damn heavy—into the lobby. Opie had a gun on the neat group of prisoners, telling them all to shut the fuck up. "Get down," he yelled. "I said get the fuck down."

A gray-bearded mountain man in a fringe coat had gotten up to his knees, without being asked, holding his empty hands away from his body. "Gentlemen," he said. "Let's all think about this for one moment. 'Every prudent man dealeth with knowledge: but a fool layeth open his folly.'"

The old man turned to Wilcox, smiling with an uneven row of brown teeth, arms outstretched and jacket fringe hanging loose like a honky-tonk Jesus. Wilcox looked to Opie, Opie shaking his head, and Wilcox turned back and punched the man square in the gut with the butt of the AR-15. The man fell to the floor on his back, sucking at the air.

"Time," Opie said. They rushed out the door to where Cord had backed up the van, rear doors flung open. Wilcox grabbed one handle of the heavy duffel and Opie grabbed the other. The bag from the teller drawers was much lighter and Wilcox easily tossed it into the van and slammed the doors shut.

Cord mashed the accelerator, and, from the passenger seat, Wilcox turned back to where Opie had pulled off his mask, already into the heavier bag, rummaging through fat bundles and laughing like crazy.

"Better than cookies and milk," Wilcox said.

"I hate milk," Cord said, driving slow, with purpose, away from the bank and heading around the town square. "I don't drink it."

"Well," Wilcox said, "you should. It's fucking delicious."

2

Sometime around two, Quinn got the call that Fannie Hathcock had beaten the shit out of one of her patrons with a sixteen-ounce hammer. His dispatcher, Cleotha, was very specific about the size of the hammer, saying that Fannie had made the call herself and seemed proud of her accomplishment. "Attempted robbery?" Quinn said into the radio.

"Looks like a truck driver couldn't keep it in his pants."

"Ten-four," Quinn said, rolling away from a call up in Yellow Leaf and back down to Jericho to the Rebel Truck Stop and the refurbished Booby Trap, which the new owner had christened Vienna's Place. Even the updated metal siding, new cursive neon, and fancy antique bar shipped in from Kansas City couldn't change that Vienna's was a low-rent high-way titty bar. The billboards all along 45 promised THE FINEST SOUTHERN BELLES, COLD BEER, and HOT FUN. Not to mention the live advertisements on CB, letting all the truckers know which of their favorite dancers were working and the daily drink specials.

A big sign outside promised 2 FOR 1 BUD-WEISERS and HAPPY HOUR LAP DANCES $20. Just outside, he spotted one of his deputies, Reggie Caruthers, speaking with a man holding a towel to his head. The towel was a bloody mess and the man leaned on the fender of the patrol car, Reggie speaking in patient tones, the man saying he had absolutely no idea what came over the crazy bitch. The guy was redneck skinny, with a patchy black beard and long, stringy hair. One of his eyes was swollen, and his nose swollen and twisted. His bloody T-shirt read BORN TO PARTY, FORCED TO WORK.

"She just up and hit you?" Reggie said, nodding over at Quinn.

"I was watching Cinnamon working the pole," the man said. "She loves that song 'A-Yo' by Lady Gaga. You know, the one got that hook about the mirror on the ceiling?"

"No, sir," Reggie said. "I got no idea what you're talking about."

Quinn liked Reggie. Lillie had hired him when she'd been acting sheriff. He was smart and direct.

Black, medium-sized, mid-twenties, with four years in the service with the 10th Mountain Division. Good new blood in an aging department, now that Ike McCaslin had retired. Someone Quinn would've hired himself.

"I gave Cinnamon two bucks," the man said. "Maybe it wasn't enough."

"Are you sure you didn't try and touch her?" Reggie said. "Or say something inappropriate?"

"What can you say inappropriate to a stripper?" the man said. "Those girls have heard it all and seen it all. You say, 'Nice titties,' and that'll just put a real shine on their day."

Quinn knew the man but didn't. He looked familiar, like someone he'd seen in the jail a few times for public drunk but not for anything that sent him to court. He looked away as Quinn studied his face, the white towel nearly soaked through with blood.

"Man says Fannie coldcocked him," Reggie said.

"With a hammer," Quinn said.

"Sixteen-ounce," the man said. "Goddamn framing hammer. Made by Stanley, 'cause I seen the yellow on it when she swung it a second time."

"How'd you know it was sixteen ounces?"

"'Cause I'm a damn roofer, Sheriff," he said. "I put that metal on your home place up in Fate."

"Charlie Ray?"

"Yes, sir," he said. "Guess you didn't recognize me with one of my eyes snapped shut. Jesus, Sheriff. You need to do something about this woman. I realize we ain't at the First Baptist Church, but, Good Lord Almighty, you can't just walk up to a man and start trying to knock his fucking brains out while Lady Gaga is on."

"Yeah," Quinn said. "That doesn't seem right."

Reggie looked to Quinn and shrugged. He'd been taking notes in a little book and he slipped it into the back pocket of his uniform.

"Miss Hathcock?" Quinn said.

"Inside," Reggie said.

"You spoken to her?"

Reggie shook his head. "No, sir," he said. "She asked for you personal."

"Terrific," Quinn said, walking through the front door, out of the sun and into the darkness and the smoke, the only light coming from colored patterns on the raised stages and the neon signs along the handcrafted wooden bar. Quinn had always liked the bar, thought it was a nice touch, like something you'd see in Deadwood or Dodge City, looking oddly at home in Tibbehah County, Mississippi.

The naked girls kept dancing. Behind the bar, a black kid named Ordeen kept on pouring beer. Quinn just made out the curvy shadow of Fannie Hathcock, staring down from the catwalk outside her office, and the faint orange prick of light coming from her cigarillo.

Quinn nodded to Ordeen and headed up the steps.

He found Fannie sitting behind her desk, alligator-hide pumps up on it and the long, thin brown cigar in hand. The desk cluttered with papers, a sixteen-ounce Stanley framing hammer placed at its edge.

"Thought we'd been over this," Quinn said.

"You said, 'without provocation,'" Fannie said, spewing smoke from the side of her mouth. "That dumb bastard had it coming."

They followed the county road until it stopped cold at orange traffic drums and NO TRESPASSING signs. A cattle gate swung closed between a couple of 4×4s, showing where the gravel road ended and private property began. The windshield wipers cleared the glass, revealing what lay beyond the dead end.

"Too easy," Cord said.

"You call that easy?" Wilcox said. "I call that perfect execution and timing. In and out in ninety fucking seconds."

"All this rain," Cord said. "They could track us. Maybe we should keep driving?"

"Nobody's gonna find this van for a long time," Wilcox said. "Damn road's been closed for years."

Opie got out, kicked open the cattle gate, and Wilcox got behind the wheel and pulled on through. After closing the gate behind them, Opie jumped back in and they rode on until they spotted the old barn and drove inside and killed the engine. Rain drummed on the tin roof, headlights shining into the kicked-up dust and grit and the Kawasakis where they'd hid them under a brown tarp.

"If they connect us," Cord said, "it could put my friend in some real trouble."

"From what you told me, that bitch is used to trouble," Wilcox said. "Besides, with all this god-damn rain coming down, the tracks will be gone. We can ditch the bikes a couple klicks from the cars and hump it on in. By the time we head out, roadblocks will be down and we can roll on back to Memphis."

Cord nodded, and the three men divided the cash and packed it in rucksacks, with their discarded clothes and the Trump masks. Once they got to the switch cars, they'd burn everything but the money.

"This woman must be **some** friend," Wilcox said. "How the fuck did she get those cars?"

"Didn't ask," Cord said. "Don't want to know."

Opie leaned into the handlebars, looking like he had something on his mind. Wilcox zipped up his new jacket and stared at him, letting him know to get on with whatever was bothering him.

"How much do you think we got?" Opie asked.

"At least a hundred grand," Wilcox said. "Maybe more."

"Getting close," Opie said.

"Yep."

"That's good," Opie said, grinning. "Right?"

"I guess."

"If you don't care, then why do it?"

"For the good ole American life," Wilcox said. "For the money, for the glory, and for the fun. Mainly for the money."

"You said you didn't give a damn about the money," Opie said.

"Don't listen to me," Wilcox said. "My ex-wife always told me I was full of shit."

Opie shrugged and tugged on his helmet, rucksack packed tight with the money, tip of the rifle sticking out the top. He kick-started the motorcycle and turned north, looking back to Cord and Wilcox, waiting for them to follow. As they rode together, the engines sounded like a buzz saw ripping through the trees.

"I know you don't care for this place and would be damn happy if the county closed us down once and for all," Fannie Hathcock said. "But I can't stand for some dumbass redneck to walk into my bar and start feeling up my girls. I know the law. I know what we're doing is legal. And my girls have every right to be as protected as some Sunday school teacher with locked knees."

"Why'd you hit him with a hammer, Fannie?" Quinn said.

Fannie tapped her cigarette and shrugged a bit. "Maybe because he wouldn't listen," she said. "I got a problem with men like that. Or maybe because my girl was scared and I worried she'd get hurt. I was doing some repairs and it was the only thing I could use on him."

"That's not what Charlie Ray said."

"Charlie Ray is a crazy-ass meth head," Fannie said. "I have witnesses. He was unhinged. You think any judge around here is going to believe what that man says? I don't think he has two teeth left inside his whole head."

Fannie was a fine-looking woman, somewhere on the young side of forty, with a lot of red hair, good teeth, and a body some said rivaled the great Blaze Starr. Quinn hadn't had much dealings with her, as her arrival in the county had come while he was in Afghanistan. But since he'd been back, Vienna's had been a frequent call for disturbances, assaults, and allegations of prostitution. Fannie leaned forward, the top of her red silk blouse showing a good amount of white freckled skin and black bra, and said, "Are you fucking with me? Or are you going to arrest me?"

"All these witnesses also happen to be your employees?" Quinn said.

"Does it matter?"

"And they'll say Charlie Ray just got up and went crazy, trying to attack Miss Cinnamon."

"Exactly."

Quinn shook his head. Fannie leaned back, touching a loose button on her blouse, before pushing forward a big fat humidor with a lot of gold filigree. "Help yourself."

"No, thank you."

"Goddamn, don't be a such a Boy Scout, Quinn," she said. "I have to protect my girls. I'm not asking for anything special. I thought you were one of the few locals who had a little bit of common sense."

"I prefer my own," Quinn said, tapping at the two Undercrowns he kept in his right-hand shirt pocket. He crossed his leg at the knee, kicking up his spit-polished Lucchese with its square toe. He nodded at her, waiting for her to explain herself like any normal person might under the circumstances.

"Talk to anyone you like," Fannie said, waving her hand down toward the bar. "They'll tell you what they saw."

"You could have killed him."

"Damn it, he was gripping my girl like she was a fucking bowling ball."

Quinn shook his head, the room getting thick with Fannie's smoke.

"Didn't expect to see you," Fannie said. "Thought it would be Lillie again. I do believe that woman has some kind of special problem with me."

"Just doing her job."

"She staying on with the department?"

"Assistant sheriff."

"She didn't offer that to you when you got run off."

Quinn shrugged. "I didn't care to stay on."

"And now you give a shit?"

"You've got me for the next four years, whether you like it or not."

Fannie sucked on the cigarette, the red silk top straining at low buttons, before she spewed more smoke from the corner of her mouth. She tipped the ash and leaned back into her spinning chair, her eyes darting over for a second to the yellow hammer at the edge of the desk. Some dried blood flecked on the claw.

"Lillie, that tight-ass Skinner, and now you," Fannie said. "I never thought you'd jump on that goddamn moral bandwagon, Quinn. I always thought you to be your own man, too smart for all this dick wagging from the Baptist pulpit."

"Doesn't take a moralist to keep you from knocking a man's brains out."

"Cinnamon feared for her safety," Fannie said. "I look after these girls. That's my moral vision."

Quinn shook his head, standing up, reaching for his walkie-talkie to let Reggie know that he'd be taking in Fannie Hathcock himself and charging her with aggravated assault. But before he got the mic halfway from his belt, Cleotha came over the dispatch channel, so flustered she forgot to use the radio code, and just shouted out that the First National Bank had been robbed by two men, last seen heading north in a Ford Econoline van with Tennessee plates.

Fannie looked to Quinn, smiling big. He nodded back and headed toward the door.

"Were you really thinking of arresting me?" Fannie said. "No judge in north Mississippi would fault me for what I did."

"That's because most judges in north Mississippi are your best customers," Quinn said, heading to the catwalk and down the steps.

"Quinn?"

He turned.

"Don't get wet on the way out."

3

"**Holy shit, did I pick the wrong day to take off or what,**" Lillie Virgil said. "Two shitbirds in Donald Trump masks robbing the First National? That one guy shooting into the ceiling and yelling, 'Anyone moves and I'll grab 'em by the pussy.' **Damn.** You have to admit, Quinn, these guys may be some bad mother-fuckers, but they got style."

"I knew you'd like it, Lil."

Lillie Virgil—all nearly six feet, one hundred and fifty pounds of her—leaned against a file cabinet in the SO meeting room while Quinn assembled the interviews and queued up the bank video. She'd brought in a sack of hamburgers and two tall cof-fees from the Fillin' Station and set them on the conference table. Lillie, curly brown hair tamed in a bun that poked from the back of her TIBBEHAH COUNTY ball cap, had showered and was in uniform in less than thirty minutes after getting the call from dispatch.

"Of course I like it," Lillie said. "I spent all goddamn night running down Robert Earl Hicks for violating his restraining order. Not only did he slap Autumn for taking a couple of his Luke Bryan CDs but he beat the dog shit out of her daddy for saying she had the right. So by the time I find him sipping on an Oreo Peanut Butter milk shake at the Sonic, he's facing not only the violation but two new assault charges and a failure to appear in Tishomingo County for public urination."

"And how does that make things better?" Quinn said.

"Because this is something I can own," Lillie said. "I got into law enforcement to track down the bad guys, not take out the fucking garbage. I'm sick of being in the waste management business. Maybe I just appreciate a higher class of criminal. Running down bank robbers is something I can be proud of."

Lillie had on her jeans, lace-up work boots, and a shiny green SO coat with a black Sherpa collar. Her face was freshly scrubbed and her nails cut to the quick. Since Quinn was first elected, Lillie had been his guide and mentor in law enforcement, often reminding him the objective was to keep order, not blow shit up. Before coming home to take care of her dying mother, she'd spent nearly six years with Memphis PD, and, before that, she'd been a star shooter on the Ole Miss Rifle Team.

Most folks in Tibbehah found her odd, a straight-talking tomboy with low tolerance for bullshit. For Quinn, he couldn't have found a better partner in keeping order in a sometimes lawless county.

She reached into the sack for a hamburger and took a seat at the conference table. Quinn punched up the bank video and turned around the laptop so they both could see it.

"We can't keep it," Quinn said. "It'll go federal."

"Feds got too much on their plate dealing with homeland security, terrorism, and all that," Lillie said. "Didn't you clue into that shit over in Afghanistan? Unless this thing is an epidemic, we're stuck running down these fuckwads. Just how much did they get anyway?"

"One hundred and ninety-two thousand dollars," Quinn said. "Give or take a buck or two."

"That's a lot for the First National."

"Walmart had just dropped off the morning receipts," Quinn said. "Big Presidents' Day sale."

"Anyone spotted that van yet?"

"Nope," Quinn said. "Highway patrol has 45 cut off in both directions. We have roadblocks set up on nearly every road leaving the county. We got

Kenny, Art, and Reggie on patrol, and a few folks over from Choctaw County. I called up the boys at Jericho PD, too."

"Those fucking morons?" Lillie said. "God help us."

"I'll take what I can get."

"There's no way these turds are still in town," Lillie said. "These guys are smart, like I said, have some style. They'd have dumped that van, gotten a couple getaway cars, and are miles away from here."

"Sounds like you admire them."

"We haven't had a bank robbery in Jericho since Gowrie five years ago," Lillie said. "We got too many damn crooks cornholing this town from the inside. Outsiders are an exotic animal."

"You didn't have to come straight in," Quinn said. "Plenty more to do tonight on the night shift."

"And let you have all the fun?" Lillie said. "Fuck that, Sheriff. I got my aunt to come on over and look after Rose. How about I go back and talk to Mr. Berryhill some more? I never liked that son of a bitch. I kind of want to ask him what it was like having his dick in jeopardy. Truth be known, that fat bastard probably would need a magnifying glass to find it."

"We got plenty of interviews," Quinn said. "I talked to every person in that bank personal. Now I'm looking at any type of surveillance that might have seen them before. Gas stations. Maybe these guys fueled up before. Or after."

"Doubt it," Lillie said. "They're not from around here."

"How can you be sure?"

"Because they're smart."

"Do I detect some type of contempt for Tibbehah County?"

"Tell me you don't shower after a long day."

Quinn pulled up a chair to the conference table and pressed PLAY on the laptop. Everything he needed from the robbery, every single camera, each angle, already uploaded and downloaded. He'd watched it four times already. Good quality, not grainy at all, but not telling them much, either. Images were in black-and-white. One of the men, the one who'd knocked Chester on his ass, stood about six feet. He was white, judging from the skin tone on the back of his neck. He spoke fast and sure, not a bit of an accent. The other guy was white, too. He stood a few inches shorter than the first man. The way they worked as a team, it was clear that the taller man was in charge.

The shorter man glanced back and forth at the big man for hand gestures and sometimes commands on what to do next. The quick entry, the checking of corners, the speed and precision, was familiar as hell.

"Hmm," Lillie said. "I know what you're thinking."

"Did you add bacon and pickles on that burger?" Quinn said. "I haven't eaten since breakfast."

"Not that," she said. "You think these shitbirds

are pros. They move like Army folks. You see what they're carrying. The way they work the room."

Quinn nodded. "I can reach out to the Feds," Quinn said. "See if this all seems familiar to them, too."

"Just don't let them spoil our fun."

"I'll let you know when to assemble the posse," Quinn said. "In the meantime, let's find that white van."

Lillie reached into the sack and slid a hamburger wrapped in foil over to him. "Cheese, bacon, and pickles."

"How could I ever doubt you, Lillie Virgil?"

Lillie smiled, took a bite of her burger, and swallowed. "By the way, you need to call your sister back," she said. "She's been making a lot of noise about those two girls again."

"Not much we can do," Quinn said. "Looks like they're runaways."

"Not the way Caddy sees it."

"My sister and I seldom see the world the same way."

"Truer words were never spoken," Lillie said.

"It ain't much," Boom Kimbrough said. "But it might help out a few families. I grew too many plants this year."

"We'll take 'em," Caddy Colson said, reaching

into the bed of Boom's pickup truck for the big box of freshly picked collards. "We have a big dinner after the Sunday service. I'd like it if you'd stop by."

"You trying to save my broke-down ass?"

"I'm trying to feed your broke-down ass."

"Good to add some brown sugar to those greens," Boom said. "I always like that Creole seasoning with some cut-up country ham."

"Will do."

Boom smiled, reached in with his good hand and his prosthetic arm, and grabbed another box, following Caddy into the barn. The barn being the core of The River, a nonprofit she'd started with a man named Jamey Dixon a few years ago. It was more than just an informal place for folks to worship who'd given up on mainstream churches in Tibbehah. The River was an outreach program for the abused women, neglected kids, and families with nowhere else to go. They kept a food bank, a few small cabins for shelter, and offered a good sermon and even better music on Wednesdays and Sundays. As usual, they were running about two thousand dollars over budget.

Caddy was dressed in threadbare Levi's and one of Jamey's flannel cowboy shirts, which had gotten more worn and frayed since his death. She placed the box of greens on one of the hay bales where folks sat during the service and thanked Boom for his thoughtfulness.

"I hate seeing shit going to waste."

"You're a good man."

Boom ran his good hand over the splotchy beard on his dark face, scars from a long-ago IED marking his ears and neck, and smiled. "Took a while to get there."

"I tell folks I walked through hell to find heaven."

"I ain't found heaven yet," Boom said. "But I promise to go to church every Sunday when I get old. I'll play the tambourine and take up the collection. Get that ole-time religion."

"Good place to meet women."

"Women who want to set me right?" Boom asked.

"You still seeing that social worker down in Eupora?"

"Naw," he said. "I guess me and Quinn are a lot alike. We got some bad luck."

"Quinn makes his own luck."

"You got to admit Ophelia Bundren was a piece of work."

Caddy smiled, "Can't disagree with you there. The girl threw a damn steak knife at my brother and he still got her back in bed. What's that say about Quinn?"

Boom laughed, both of them heading back out to his battered GMC truck. He reached into the passenger's side and opened the glove compartment. He handed Caddy a white envelope and told her that he admired all she did and that he was sorry he hadn't been able to make a contribution earlier.

"The greens are enough."

"Like I said," Boom said. "Ain't much."

Caddy didn't take the envelope. Boom pushed it toward her. "Take it now before my ass is unemployed."

"You quitting?"

"Old Man Skinner wants to fire my ass," he said. "He wants his own people running the County Barn."

"That's dumb," she said. "You're the best mechanic in town."

"Hell," he said, "I know."

"And you've done a hell of a job."

"I know that, too," he said. "Sometimes makes me wonder why we all stay on in this goddamn place. What those Catholics call purgatory."

Caddy shook her head, giving him a big hug. He smelled of a hard day's work and cigarettes like her late Uncle Hamp. She felt the cool steel of Boom's hand on her back. "Didn't someone say 'home is the place where they have to take you in'?"

"Figure lots of folks said that."

"This place took me back in," Caddy said. "And now I got a chance to even things up."

Boom nodded, moving toward the driver's side of the truck. Caddy wrapped her arms around herself, watching him get in and crank the engine.

"You seen Quinn?" she asked through the open window.

"Sure," he said. "Had breakfast with him this morning."

"He won't call me back."

"Been busy," Boom said. "Or hadn't you heard?"

Caddy shook her head.

"First National got robbed," he said. "Doubt he and Lillie will get much sleep tonight."

"Crap."

"Something I can help you with?"

Caddy shook her head. "Worried about a couple girls who came to The River last month," Caddy said. "One of them doesn't have a family. Other one's momma is a hot mess. Girls are only fifteen. Can't get a damn straight answer."

"Maybe the girls ran away."

"That's what her momma said," Caddy said. "And Quinn. But I think something bad's happened."

"Why?"

"I've been on the same road," Caddy said. "We were into a lot of the same bad shit. The girls wanted to get straight, but there was a lot against them. They wouldn't have left without seeing me first."

"Fifteen, huh?"

Caddy nodded.

"They black or white?"

"Black and Mexican."

Boom nodded. "Who are their people?"

"One of the girls is an Odom," Caddy said. "The

other wasn't from from around here. Her family was migrants coming through at sweet potato time."

"Jericho ain't their home."

"And no one wanted to take them in."

"Except you."

"Maybe that's why I can't let this thing go."

"I'll ask around," Boom said. "Shit, you know all us black folks know each other?"

"I heard that."

"'Cept for the Colsons," Boom said. "Y'all are OK, for some white folks."

They rode the Kawasakis for an hour or so through the National Forest until they came to a path marked with NO TRESPASSING signs tacked on a few scraggly pines. Cord lifted a hand and pointed down the path, Wilcox and Opie following him down the deer trail, which descended into a small valley to a clearing dotted with a couple of Quonset huts and a big metal warehouse. As they rode closer, Wilcox could see the busted old tarmac Cord had told him about, saying the place had been an airfield during World War II and then been a place to smuggle in grass back in the seventies and eighties. When he'd asked what it was used for now, Cord just shook his head and said, "I don't want to know, brother."

They zipped down into the valley, the money stash

fat on Wilcox's back, taking a final turn onto the cracked tarmac filled with dead weeds. Cord headed fast down the path, bucking up and down on his seat, heading toward the big shed and the huts, where he'd said they'd have supplies and switch cars waiting.

They were soaked and covered in mud after the ride. Wilcox could taste the dirt in his mouth and spit on the ground before lighting up a Marlboro.

"How the fuck did you find this place?"

"Never been here before in my life," Cord said.

"I like it," Opie said. "Reminds me of that **Scooby-Doo** episode where they run into the space pilot. You know, the one with the glowing skull head? It was laughing like hell the whole time."

Wilcox took off the backpack and tossed it at his feet. He reached for his rifle, pulled the charging handle, and took in a good three-sixty of the place. He couldn't see any cars or any sign of life. The only sound came from soft rain hitting the gravel and tin roofs. With the cigarette bobbing between his lips, he told Opie and Cord to go on and clear the buildings.

"Shit, man," Cord said. "Don't bite the hand that feeds you."

"I don't know these people," Wilcox said. "And I ain't hungry."

He nodded at Opie, who moved toward the metal building, which looked like a cotton gin or warehouse, no windows, a loading platform out front, with a couple of nasty-ass sofas and whiskey barrels cut in half with dead plants inside. Wilcox followed Opie up onto the platform and into the warehouse, knowing if there was trouble, Cord would have their six.

Inside, the warehouse was completely empty except for a few crates and broken chairs. There was an office and two bathrooms, which were both empty, too.

Wilcox and Opie moved back onto the loading platform, ARs sweeping the area, almost like they expected fucking hadji to start firing from some goddamn murder hole in the hills. Vacant buildings and quiet open spots always worried the crap out of him. When you could hear the fucking wind, that's usually when the shit was about to rain on your ass.

"Cord say we were sleeping here?" Opie said.

"That he did."

"Cool," Opie said. "We've slept in a lot worse."

"No goats," Wilcox said. "I'm so fucking tired of goats. All that piss and shit in those compounds. That fucking smell."

"I knew some guys who got so horny, they talked about screwing one."

"I ate a few," Wilcox said. "Better for eating than fucking."

"But would you?"

"Screw a goat?"

"Yeah."

"Damn, Ope," Wilcox said. "You are a gentleman and a philosopher."

Somewhere between the big metal building and the smaller huts, Wilcox heard Cord talking and maybe even Cord laughing. Cord never laughed, so it sounded strange as hell to him, until he heard the woman, too. Cord was a different guy around women. He smiled. He laughed. He softened up a hell of a lot. Wilcox didn't lower his weapon but kept his eyes on the doors and open spaces, up into the young pines planted up on the hills, turning back once and twice to watch for a flicker of movement in the big valley around them. But when he got to Cord and the woman, he stopped cold.

The woman, a curvy redhead in a khaki trench coat and carrying a black umbrella, turned to look at him. She had pale skin, a very red full mouth, and some of the biggest tits he'd ever seen in his life. She had a sweet smell to her, like some really fine flowers left too long in the heat.

"Be careful with that thing," the woman said. "It just might go off."

Wilcox smiled, lowered the rifle. "How about you take off that raincoat and we'll see what happens?"

The woman didn't smile at Wilcox. Women always smiled at him.

"Keys are in three cars," the woman said. "They're

nothing to look at. Some real junkers. But everything works. They'll get you to where you need to go."

"How's it look in town?" Cord asked.

"Like shit," she said. "I definitely wouldn't leave until tomorrow. The highway has a roadblock and the sheriff's office has extra folks in from three counties."

"Where do we sleep?"

"That hut to the left has cots," she said. "I brought in some barbecue plates for you and a cooler of beer. I don't run a fucking B and B, but it'll get you fed and not too drunk."

Wilcox nodded. "You look even better than Cord said."

"Does it matter how I look?" she asked.

"Sure as hell doesn't hurt."

The woman still didn't smile, eyes keeping on Cord, as if Wilcox was just some kind of damn background noise. Opie stood away from them, keeping watch on the valley, listening and watching, making sure they hadn't been set up.

"If you don't need anything else," the woman said, "I'll be on my way."

Wilcox could not quit staring at the woman. She was a little bit older than he normally liked, but she had a way about her—her slow, careful gestures and sleepy eyes—that made him think she sure as hell knew what she was doing. He patted his jacket pocket for his cigarettes, shaking loose the last one in the pack.

"You have any smokes?" he said.

"No," she said. "But the girls probably do."

"Girls?" Wilcox said.

Opie turned back from watching the valley and raised his eyebrows up and down. Opie was interested at the first mention that women might be around.

The redheaded woman edged her chin to the Quonset hut behind her. "I don't have any heaters," she said. "Might get cold. Easier to bring along some company."

"How about you, baby?" Wilcox said. "I bet you could keep me warm. Those big ole titties pressed against me could make it feel like Tahiti under the covers."

Cord turned his eyes on Wilcox, eyes narrowing, and swallowing just a bit. Wilcox grinned, now knowing one goddamn thing that could make Jonas Cord into a true and authentic human being: some redheaded tail. This woman must be some piece. She stared at him, giving him a long, hard look, her left eye twitching just a bit.

"You couldn't afford what I have," the woman said.

"I'm not so sure about that," he said. "We're pretty well set at the moment."

The woman flicked her green eyes over him, not smiling, not reacting a bit, just a slight nod of the head. She followed Cord off around back of the hut, knowing Cord had promised to deliver a nice little cut of the action in exchange for a little help.

"Did that woman say she'd brought some girls?" Opie asked.

"When's the last time you've been laid, Ope?"

Opie looked up, closing one eye, giving it some real serious mental energy. He shrugged. "Not really sure," he said. "Does a goat count?"

"Girls," Wilcox said. "Funny how they're always around when you're flush."

"Women do like bad boys."

Wilcox popped the last cigarette in his mouth and grinned at Opie. "Oh, we're not that bad," he said. "We're American folk heroes in the making."

Opie looked uneasy at him, dropping the weapon down beside his leg and scratching his neck with his free hand. "Didn't you always say you never wanted to be a hero because all real heroes are dead?"

Wilcox snorted smoke out his nose. "Yeah?" he said. "That sounds like me. Profound as hell."

4

"Damn, you're sentimental," Quinn said. "Picking this spot for a meet."

"I'm sick of the Oxford office," the man Quinn once knew as Jon Ringold said. Jon Ringold was Jon Holliday, federal agent, now that he was no longer undercover in Johnny Stagg's organization. "Wanted to get out, breathe a little. Besides, I missed this view. This place definitely puts things in perspective."

The men stood shoulder to shoulder, looking across the rolling mounds built by the Choctaws eons ago, just off the Natchez Trace in the far northeast corner of Tibbehah County. Quinn had parked the Big Green Machine by the small viewing area at dawn, only two cars passing since he arrived. The sun had just started to rise as Holliday pulled up in a black Chevy Tahoe with tinted windows and government plates. The rain slowed to a soft patter, dripping down the trees' bare branches, small patches of earth just turning green.

"Time?" Quinn asked.

"Sure," he said. "Time, war, your place in this world. White folks in these parts are a relatively new phenomenon, although most will tell you their folks have been here forever. People don't understand the concept of forever. Forever doesn't exist."

"You have been in the office too long," Quinn said, handing Holliday a cigar. It was a nice Undercrown from Drew Estates, the kind he'd been smoking most of the winter, after he came back on as sheriff. A maduro, wrapped tight, with a nice long burn.

"Haven't worked bank robberies in a while," Holliday said, biting off the end and lighting it. "Did some undercover work with a chop shop up in Southaven, drug dealers on the Coast, and then the time I was with Stagg. How is that piece of shit anyway?"

"I wouldn't know," Quinn said. "And don't care. I haven't visited him since the trial. Hopefully, he won't be back for a long while. Federal prison suits him."

"Tibbehah must be lot less colorful without Stagg."

"You'd think," Quinn said. "But we've had our share of problems."

"I heard about the coach," he said. "And the burning girl."

"And now we got three men getting away with two hundred grand," Quinn said. "Not much for Memphis. But a lot for us. Lillie believes shit rolls downhill and we'll have to work it."

"You sure it was just three?"

"Two guys robbed the bank," he said. "And a driver."

"Carrying assault rifles."

"Hard to tell the type with video," Quinn said, nodding, "but damn sure if they didn't look like cut-down AR-15s to me."

"And these gentlemen moved fast," Holliday said. "Bust in the door, quick and hard, shooting up the place a little."

"Fired a shot into the ceiling," Quinn said. "Wore gloves and Halloween masks."

"Working the room like a two-man team," Holliday said, tapping the end of the cigar on the edge of a picnic table. "Over and under, clearing corners, kicking ass and taking names. Almost like they knew what they were doing. And had done it a hell of a lot of times."

"Yep."

"White guys," Holliday said. "One about six foot and the other a short guy. Both of them quick and mean. The tall guy thinking he's funny. Always saying something clever."

"Donald Trump masks," Quinn said. "Funny as

an ass ache. Damn, you Feds sure are on the ball. Sounds like you know these turds."

Holliday pulled on the cigar and let out a steady stream of smoke. It was strange seeing him now without the bushy Moses beard and nearly shaved head. Quinn wasn't sure he'd have even recognized Holliday on the street. He wondered if he really had those sleeve tattoos or the Feds knew how to fake those, too.

"Yes, sir," Holliday said. "We know them. Looking at maybe eight banks last fall. Three so far this year, including that job in Jericho."

"Know much about them?"

"Only that we're pretty sure they're pros," Holliday said. "If you weren't in law enforcement, I might suspect you as the main dude. You're about the same height, have similar training, and move in the same way."

"Or you," Quinn said.

"Or me," Holliday said. "Yeah, we know these guys. What scares me about these assholes is that if they fuck up, something goes wrong, and they could end up quickly and effectively shooting a lot of people."

"I can get you the video," Quinn said. "All the interviews we did with customers, tellers, the bank president who they threatened."

"They promise to kill him?"

"Nope," Quinn said. "They had empathy. Only threatened to shoot his dick off."

"In my book, that's worse than killing," he said.

"What do we do now?"

"Keep vigilant?"

"Ha."

"They'll screw up," Holliday said. "They always do. Someone they pissed off will step forward. An angry girlfriend, a partner they'll screw over. We'll keep looking."

"You got most of north Mississippi," Quinn said. "I'll do my best in Tibbehah County. But unless they come back—"

"They'll think you're an easy touch," he said. "They'll want to come back for more."

"Appreciate the vote of confidence."

"Maybe they worked with someone local?"

"Don't know why they'd need it," Quinn said. "I bet they're a hundred miles from here."

"Maybe," Holliday said, extending his hand. "But keep an eye out. All sorts of shit keeps folks from running too far. Usually it's booze, drugs, or women."

Wilcox was still drunk. And tired. He'd screwed some girl twice before passing out. A cute little blonde with a pug nose and lots of freckles. She thought he was real funny, laughing too much, the friend of

Cord telling these girls they were some businessmen up from New Orleans. When she'd asked what kind of work he did, he couldn't resist saying, "Banking," and just left it that. She seemed impressed with that. And impressed with the six hundred bucks he tipped her. He left the money under the tequila bottle and took the Mexican blanket with him outside to watch the sun rise.

Opie was sound asleep, cuddled up on the floor with some skinny black girl, talking a lot but being smart and telling her only about their time in the service. He told her a lot about his machine gun. He talked more about that damn gun than he did his own family.

Wilcox draped the big blanket around his bare shoulders, wearing just blue jeans and boots now, and walked out onto the tarmac to smoke a cigarette and watch the dawn. He could taste the tequila and cigarettes on his tongue and smell that vanilla perfume from the stripper. She'd been sweet to him, liking his tattoos. And the bullet scars even more. A couple of times Opie had called him Sarge, which made him look like somebody to the girl. They'd used fake names, fake places they lived, and fake stories of meeting up with the girls again.

Halfway through a cigarette, the pug-nosed girl, who went by the name of Tiffany Nicole, came outside and sat beside him. He offered her a bit of the blanket, as she was still wearing a white leather bikini top with her white leather chaps. The fringe blowing in the wind.

"Aren't you cold?"

"Nope."

"We drank a mess of tequila," Tiffany Nicole said. "Lord, my head hurts. I found a handful of lime slices in my panties."

Wilcox grinned. He placed his hand around her shoulder, no reason to kick her loose yet. They were both professionals, doing what they did best.

"Will I see you again?"

"Nope," Wilcox said. "But thanks for a good time last night."

"I figured," she said. "You didn't have to tip me like that. Miss Fannie paid us fine to come out here. She and that friend of yours are close. I think they're sweet on each other."

"You don't say . . ."

"I seen him a few times at the club," she said. "He goes up into her office. Nobody goes up there. It's like some kind of fucking birdcage. She can look down on the stages, see us working the pole, and back in the VIP room she has cameras. You don't steal from Fannie Hathcock. No one messes with that woman."

"Fannie Hathcock?"

"Yes, sir."

"That's a hell of a name," he said. "She owns the club where y'all work?"

"Vienna's Place," she said, beaming. "Best strip club south of Memphis on Highway 45. Prettiest girls in the whole state of Mississippi. Cold beer. Hot women. Haven't you seen the billboards?"

"Your momma must be proud."

"Excuse me?" she said.

He put a hand on the young girl's skinned-up knee. "Don't be falling in love with a rascal like me."

Tiffany Nicole turned up her pug nose and smiled. "You're no rascal," she said. "You treated me real nice."

"You call that nice?"

"You didn't dog-cuss me," she said. "Or make me do any of that sick stuff. My ex used to like to put cigarettes out on my legs."

"Jesus Christ."

"It's true," she said, pulling up her skirt to show little puckered scars on her legs. "Can't blame him. He didn't grow up real good."

Wilcox stood up, the blanket drawing off the girl, keeping it high on his shoulders as he walked onto the tarmac and into the morning light. He could use a shower and a shave, a decent breakfast with lots of bacon and home fries. Black coffee and more cigarettes. Keep moving. Don't stop.

"Can I ask you something?"

He looked to the girl, teeth chattering and arms wrapped around her bare waist. Last night, he hadn't noticed all the makeup she wore. All that eyeliner and lipstick a damn mess on her face now.

51

"Who are y'all, really?"

"I told you."

"Bankers?" she said. "Doing some turkey hunting?"

"Gobble gobble."

"I don't know anyone shoots turkeys with AR-15s," she said. "My daddy just had a twelve-gauge loaded with Winchester Double X. It kicks like a damn mule but puts out a real tight shot."

"What else did you see?" Wilcox said, walking up on her. The wind kicking up that blanket behind his back like a superhero cape. He snatched her quick and pulled her in close to see if she was lying.

"Nothing," she said. "Nothing. Goddamn. Hey. You're hurting my arm."

"Why were you looking through our stuff?"

"I wasn't," she said. "But I saw y'all's guns. Just trying to give you some friendly hunting advice. My daddy said a rich man loves his gear but don't know shit about hunting. I guess that's true."

Wilcox felt that old familiar rage coming up in him, teeth grinding, blood in his face, but he let go of her arm. He felt into his pockets for the pack of cigarettes he'd gotten off that black girl last night. Goddamn Kools with a filter tip.

"Listen, this thing I'm doing," she said. "Working for Miss Fannie. It's just temporary."

Wilcox looked at her, cupping his hand around the cigarette to light it. "No," he said. "No, it's not. People don't change. You are who you are. You keep on being that person your whole goddamn life until you die. I hate to piss all over your rose garden, but the sooner you know these things, the better. You working that pole didn't just start yesterday."

"Everybody has a purpose," she said.

"And yours is working that pole."

"You're mean as shit," she said. "You're a mean man. You know that?"

"You bet," Wilcox said. "And if I hear you running your mouth about me or my associates drinking and screwing with y'all over here, I'll find you. Keep what happened out here to yourself."

"My daddy said even the worst kind of people started out with souls," she said. "Now I'm thinking he was full of shit."

"Go with that," Wilcox said, turning his back to her. "That'll do you a world of good, Tiffany Nicole. Or whatever the fuck your name is."

"I appreciate you meeting me for breakfast, Mr. Skinner," Fannie Hathcock said. "I didn't want to leave things like the last time. I figured with a new year and all, there was a way to straighten out our relationship."

Skinner nodded, fiddling with the rim of his coffee cup, his pale blue eyes looking her over. "We don't have a relationship, Miss Hathcock," he said. "And I don't think we ever will."

Fannie nodded, really, really starting to hate this old son of a bitch, but knowing if she wanted to continue to do business in this godforsaken county, she'd have to play nice. She put on her best smile, leaned forward into the corner booth of the Rebel Truck Stop, and placed a hand on his liver-spotted arm. "I don't believe that," she said. "I think we can be friends."

Skinner didn't answer. He just looked at her, neither smiling nor frowning. From time to time, he flicked his eyes around the truck stop café to look for anyone he might know, seeing him and the Jezebel of north Mississippi meeting up over a plate of grits and eggs. She thought of the little breakfast as a peace offering, make nice with the new guard kind of thing.

"I didn't expect to ever hold office again," Skinner said. "I done my time with the supervisors and in public service with the state. I retired to spend more time with my family, my grandkids, and now two great-grandkids. I have sixty head of cattle. A nice little bass pond. Kids call me Pop Pop."

"I know those grandbabies are just beautiful," Fannie said, but thinking if those kids looked anything like Skinner, they'd have bald heads, little potbelly stomachs, and humps on their backs. He was a tall man, thin of frame, with parchment-like skin and clear blue eyes. Every time she'd ever seen him, he wore a pearl-gray Stetson like LBJ, and kept a pack of cigarettes in his right-hand pocket. He was slow to speak and fast to pass judgment. He'd run on a platform to clean up Tibbehah County and restore morals to the place where he'd grown up. He'd called Vienna's Place a den of iniquity that he'd shut down in his first year in office.

"You have any children, Miss Hathcock?"

"I don't."

"Hard to be a woman running a business," he said. "Particularly the kind of business you run."

"You mean hospitality?" she said. "Folks come up from Jackson, down from Memphis. We're famous throughout the Mid-South. We make folks feel good. Send them down the road with a smile on their face."

"More like 'infamous,'" he said. "Having a brothel in Tibbehah County isn't exactly something to crow about."

Fannie dropped the smile. The plate of bacon and eggs in front of him remained untouched, as did the little bowl of grits and side of Louisiana Hot Sauce he'd requested. Steam lifted off the coffee, ice water on the side. What did you have to do to please this goddamn fossil?

"I don't run a brothel," she said. "Never have. Are you making public statements that there is prostitution going on inside Vienna's? Because if you are, that's something perhaps you can discuss with my attorney. That's slander, sir. I run a legal business."

"I know what you offer inside that barn of yours," Skinner said. "Not much different from what I saw growing up on a farm with the livestock and such. The real deals happen across the street at the Golden Cherry, where you board those miscreants on motorcycles and rent rooms out by the hour. We're both adults here. This kind of thing has gone on far too long for any decent Christian to stomach."

"Is that what this is about?" she said. "Christian values? Or money?"

"The way I was raised, everything is about values," he said. "Decency. People doing hard work for an honest dollar. When I got away from a public life, I had a hard time stomaching what Stagg had done to this county. I tried to fight it but lost. When he finally had to pay for what he done, I thought a new day had arrived."

"And then I showed up."

"Not too long after," Skinner said. "But you don't have the roots that Mr. Stagg had. Heck, you're not even from around here."

"I grew up in Biloxi," she said. "I paid my dues. And I would expect some folks around here to be grateful for us bringing some life into this little derelict town."

Skinner reached for a slice of bacon, crumbling it into the steaming grits, a little pool of butter on top. He dashed in enough hot sauce to choke a mule and stuffed a big spoonful into his mouth. She waited for him to chew, Fannie reaching for her coffee and taking a long sip, trying to control herself.

"The Skinner family settled this land," he said. "We cleared out the red man, invested in the land, started businesses that are still thriving today. We all took a hit when folks took their business to Mexico and over there in China. They didn't leave us with much. This may look like a 'derelict town' to a woman of your means, with your silk dresses and thousand-dollar purses. But we got something around here you may not have found on the Coast."

"And what's that, Mr. Skinner?"

"Old-fashioned values," he said. "Respect for our country and a Christian way of life. You think I want my little granddaughters to see your girls flashing a big wad of money because they show off their ninnies to some smelly truckers?"

"Lots of money comes this way," she said. "You shut us down and you might as well board up most of Jericho."

"I don't see it that way," he said. "This is a new era in Tibbehah County. I want to see things like they were when I was a boy. You went to church, said your prayers, and saluted the flag. About the most exciting thing that happened was two-for-one day at the soda fountain on the Square."

"Maybe I should dress up my girls like bobby-soxers," Fannie said. "Poodle skirts. Saddle oxford shoes. How would that work for you, sir?"

"Doesn't work that way," Skinner said, reaching for another mouthful, making Fannie wait until he filled his craw with more hot grits. "You got a nice spot here at the Rebel. I'd advise you to put your energies here. Work on bringing back the chicken-fried steak to the menu. I miss it. I don't have to do a thing but get the sheriff to enforce the laws already on the books and your nasty peep show and the Golden Cherry gets fumigated and burned to the damn ground."

"I don't like bullies," Fannie said. "And I don't like threats. Bigger folks than you have threatened me before, running off with their fucking peckers between their legs."

Skinner swallowed, working on the eggs now. He chewed and then drank a little coffee, thoughtful and smiling, like a two-bit preacher about to make a point on Easter Sunday.

"Your crude talk and slick friends down on the Coast don't mean a thing to me," Skinner said. "I'm putting y'all on notice."

He reached behind him for his wallet and Fannie shook her head, saying it was on the house.

"Nope," he said. "Not anymore." He stood up, reached for his white Stetson, and pulled it down on his bald head. He tossed down five bucks, leaving a nickel tip. Fannie didn't move, looking up at him before he left.

"Everyone has a weak spot," she said.

"'My grace is sufficient for thee,'" Skinner said, "'for my strength is made perfect in weakness.'"

Fannie studied him as he nodded at her, smug in his perfection. "I think I read that scrawled above a urinal once," she said. "Thanks for the tip."

5

"Grandma is going to shit her pants when she sees what we got," said Caddy's son Jason, who was now nine, as he walked from the woods with Quinn.

"Nope," Quinn said. "Your grandmother is going to shit her pants if she hears you talking like that. She already thinks hanging out with me and Miss Lillie is getting you into trouble at school."

"Sorry, Uncle Quinn," Jason said. "But look at this son of a bitch. Four beards. I bet this bastard weights fifty pounds."

"If it weighs fifty pounds, you'll have a world record," Quinn said. "But it's big. You made a helluva shot."

"He never knew what hit him," he said, coming out of the path and moving toward Quinn's farmhouse up on the hill. "What makes them so damn stupid?"

"He thought we were a mate," Quinn said. "It's all how you call him."

"Looking for a mate makes you stupid?"

Quinn pulled Jason's ball cap down in his eyes, holding the big turkey they'd harvested by its feet, and said, "You bet."

As they got closer to his farmhouse, Quinn saw his mother's car parked out front, not thrilled about it, as he hadn't seen or spoken to Jean Colson since Christmas. Jean had emptied nearly a box of white zinfandel before letting Quinn know exactly how she felt about him putting up their family farm for collateral on a land deal set in motion by Quinn's dad, her ex-husband. Jason Colson was a once-famous stuntman who'd leave his family every so often to work with Lee Majors on **The Fall Guy** in L.A. and on some show in Boston called **Spenser: For Hire**. Nobody could jump from a second-story window or run down the street on fire like Quinn's dad. Family life seemed to be the only thing that scared him. He left for good when Quinn was twelve.

Jean was up on the front porch of the big tin-roofed farmhouse, waiting to take Jason, who was out of school for a teacher workday, for the rest of the day. He'd picked the boy up that morning at The River, thinking they'd have a nice walk in the woods, not expecting to have any luck. But there was that tom, moving straight into the clearing, feathers splayed, beards on full display, thinking that the calls Quinn had made were some beautiful music. Jason pulled the bow, took careful aim, breathing right, and made the shot.

"About time," Jean said. "I've been waiting almost an hour. And my keys don't work. Since when did you change the locks?"

"I changed them last fall when I got home," Quinn said. "Someone broke in while I was in Afghanistan. Remember?"

"I remember," she said. "Probably your daddy. That would be just the thing he'd do while everyone was looking. Didn't he leave a bunch of crap when he ran off this last time?"

"He did."

"I see you haven't hauled off his trailer yet," Jean said. "I wouldn't think twice about it. The position he put us all in. We're lucky we got out of that mess or this farm would belong to someone else."

"That would never happen."

"No," she said. "Not now."

Jason bounded up onto the porch with his bow, pointing at the turkey in Quinn's hand, "I shot it," he said. "I got him just like Uncle Quinn and Mr. Boom taught me."

"Uncle Quinn sure is fun," Jean said. "Only when he's not. He teaching you any more of those dirty words?"

"No, ma'am," Jason said. "I promise. Can you cook him for us? Like you did last time."

"Uncle Quinn will have to dress him for us," Jean said. "I don't care for all that blood, guts, and feathers."

Quinn smiled at his mother and finally she smiled back. Hondo sniffed at the turkey, happy to haul off the bird for a big meal if no one was looking. The cattle dog looked up at Quinn, tilting his head up, staring with those two different colored eyes.

"You better lock up Hondo," Jean said. "He's licking his chops."

Quinn opened up the house, everyone following, including Hondo, and left the dead bird on a table on the front porch. They moved into the kitchen, where Jason handed Quinn his bow, and he set it in the homemade rack by the back door beside four of his own. It was a nice one, a Mission Ballistic, easy to carry and draw, nice and fitted to a kid Jason's size.

Quinn scooped out some dog food for Hondo and pulled out an old blue pot to make coffee. Jean sat down at the kitchen table, setting down her purse and letting out a lot of breath as she sat. Over the holidays she'd put on a lot of weight, quitting smoking about the time his father had run off again. She was in her mid-sixties now, reminding Quinn more and more of his grandmother, wrinkles around her eyes and mouth, hair now dyed a light brown.

"Everyone in town is talking about the bank," Jean

said. "It gave Mr. Berryhill a real scare. He said one of those robbers put a gun right between his eyes."

"It was actually pointed somewhere else," Quinn said.

"Have they been caught?"

"Nope."

"You expect they will?"

"We're working on it," Quinn said. "We hoped to find the van they used. No one saw them after they left Jericho. They pretty much disappeared."

"I do business there," Jean said. "I've been banking there for more than twenty years. Your uncle, too. They held the note on this farm at one time."

Quinn added some coffee to the percolator and sat it on the gas stove flame. He leaned back against the farm sink and reached for the half-finished cigar in his pocket. Quinn pulled out his Zippo and started to light it.

"Do you mind?" Jean said.

Quinn placed the cigar back in his pocket.

"I expected you'd be working today," Jean said. "On account of the robbery and all."

"We patrolled until late last night," Quinn said. "Reviewed evidence and searched for the getaway vehicle. I had a meeting with a federal agent I know this morning. There isn't a hell of a lot we can do besides interview witnesses and watch surveillance tape. These guys were good."

"Jason," Jean said. "Would you go outside and bring in a grocery bag I left in the backseat?"

"You brought me supper?" Quinn asked.

"You can't live on the damn Fillin' Station and Sonic."

"Boom and I were coming over Sunday night."

"So you can't eat good today?"

The coffee started to percolate, and Quinn sat down as Jason left the room. He was a tall, strong kid with the handsome features of his grandfather and the light brown skin of a father he'd never known or Caddy had ever mentioned. He had on some Carhartt pants and farm-and-ranch boots, with a Memphis Redbirds cap.

"Let's not fight anymore," Jean said.

"I'm not fighting."

"I'm not mad."

"Could have fooled me."

"It's just your daddy," Jean said. "Well, you know, it's just your daddy. That man loves taking risks, especially when it involves other folks."

Quinn nodded. The kitchen taking on a nice, pleasant smell of coffee and the faint odor of cigars and bacon. Skillets hung on the wall, along with framed movie posters of **Seven Men From Now**, **Track of the Cat**, and **Support Your Local Sheriff**, this last one given to him by Lillie as a little joke between them.

"I saw Ophelia yesterday at Ms. Vaughn's service," she said. "She did a beautiful job. Ms. Vaughn looked better than she did when she was alive. She really made her cheekbones stand out and tucked up that saggy neck of hers."

"She has a way with dead people," Quinn said. "She just has some issues with the living."

"You sound like your sister."

"Ophelia is a strange woman," Quinn said. "We shouldn't have tried to make it work again."

"I invited her to Sunday dinner."

"Shit, Mom."

Jean held up the flat of her hand and told him to please be quiet for one goddamn second.

"And where does Jason learn his language?"

"This is a big empty house," Jean said. "And I'm tired of bringing you casseroles, washing your socks. You been out of the service now for more than five years."

"I wash my own socks," Quinn said. "And I'm not big on casseroles. I have a freezer filled with enough meat to last me two years."

"Cigars, whiskey, and game," Jean said. "That's how you like to live? Like some kind of Mississippi river rat?"

"Exactly."

"And never get married?" she said. "I've been alone for a good long while and there is absolutely no pleasure in it. Don't be like your Uncle Hamp. You see what happened to him?"

"Maybe I prefer to be alone."

Jean didn't answer. She stood up, took two mugs from the cupboard, and set them down on the table. As she poured the coffee, she looked directly at her son and said, "Dinner's at six. Don't be late."

Mingo poured a drink for Fannie at the grand old bar right before the rush started, all those truckers headed back from Mobile, frat boys from State and Ole Miss, and the horny creeps from the surrounding five counties. Fannie rested her head against her hand, stirring the ice with the other and thinking on her conversation with Skinner. Mingo had been with her so long, he saw there was some kind of distress and asked if everything was OK.

"It's worse than I thought," she said. "Skinner doesn't want a cut. He wants us gone."

"He can't do that."

"He sure as shit can try," Fannie said. "He says Tibbehah already has laws against this place, but no one thought to enforce them with Stagg running the county. Skinner can start making the girls dance with fucking cancan skirts and lace-up boots. Far as I can tell, he doesn't drink, screw, or cheat."

"What does he do?"

"He says he likes to go to church and fish," Fannie said. "Said his grandkids call him Pop Pop."

"Pop Pop?"

"I know," Fannie said. "Isn't that the most country as cornbread shit you ever heard? Real **Hee Haw** crap. I bet his brats are just as ugly as him."

"That man wants, or needs, something."

Fannie nodded, taking a sip of her drink, half grenadine and half gin, with crushed cherries, lime, and an orange slice.

"Back on the Rez," Mingo said, "when I was a kid, you used to tell me that men only wanted three things."

"Damn straight," Fannie said. "That's all the holes available to them."

"Not that," Mingo said. "What motivates them."

"Money, sex, power?"

"You said, 'Accomplishment, association, or power.'"

"Did I say that?"

"Yes, ma'am."

"I must have read that garbage in **Cosmo**," Fannie said, tasting the cocktail. "I don't think Skinner is big on personal achievement outside the confines of this shithole. So it's either association or power?"

"Or association as a means to get power."

"Damn, you **do** listen to me, kid," Fannie said. "I'm impressed. But I don't think that bastard came out from the retirement home to build something.

I think he's working for someone. He's a goddamn tool. Man wouldn't have an original thought if I struck him in the forehead with my hammer."

"Maybe fronting for Johnny Stagg while he's in prison?" Mingo said, leaning into the bar, resting his elbows on that polished onyx. "You ever think about that?"

"No," Fannie said. "He genuinely hates that crooked son of a bitch. Skinner espouses morality. He started quoting Bible verses, talking about the good old days when an ice cream float tasted better than a shot of jack and pussy pie."

"Was there ever a time like that?"

Fannie smiled and plucked a cherry from the ice. "Not since Eve ate that apple."

Mingo looked down at her glass. "Want another?"

Fannie looked at her watch, a thin silver art deco Hamilton that belonged to her grandmother, the original and true Vienna. "You know I do, kid," Fannie said. "Since when do I like to run this place sober?"

"Thanks for taking Jason hunting this morning," Caddy said. "He's so proud of himself he's about to burst."

"He should be," Quinn said. "That's one hell of a bird. Did you see it?"

"What do you think?" Caddy said. "Momma

took pictures. And Jason's been wearing a turkey feather in his ball cap all day. He's telling his buddies it weighed fifty pounds and flew into the sky like a damn dragon."

"He's a good hunter," Quinn said. "I helped call in that tom, but Jason did everything else. He can quiet himself as well as any adult, steadying the breath before the shot. I've never seen anything like it."

"Well," Caddy said, "you're a good uncle. I was worried what things were going to be like when Dad left. You know how close those two got? But I'll be honest, I don't think Jason misses him a bit. All that bullshit about how much he loved his grandson. Why the hell do we fall for it every damn time?"

"Because he's our dad and we love him despite him being a professional fuckup."

Caddy nodded at the naked truth of it all. She looked around Quinn's office at all his unpacked boxes and bare walls, not doing much of an update since he took over again at the first of the year. The only bit of decorating he'd done is tack an American flag he'd brought home from his last tour with the Ranger Regiment behind his desk. He'd been meaning to put up a few pictures of him and his Uncle Hamp when Hamp had been sheriff. Maybe a picture of him and Jason on their first big deer hunt. All the photos of him and Anna Lee Stevens could stay in the damn box.

"Anything new with Tamika Odum and Ana Maria Mata?"

Quinn shook his head. "Lillie spoke to Tamika's mother," he said. "She said the girl had been having some trouble with drugs and boys and then just ran away. We couldn't find anything on Ana Maria. Her family moved on without her."

"Those girls were making some real progress," Caddy said. "They wouldn't have left without telling me."

"We've posted them as missing," Quinn said. "I can't put out an AMBER Alert because no one saw them abducted. Did you see the bills I put up around town?"

Caddy nodded, scooting onto the edge of Quinn's desk. Quinn offered her some coffee, but she declined, looking like she had more that she wanted to discuss than the two missing girls. Quinn reached for the thermos he'd filled up this morning and poured coffee into his mug. Steam rose from the mug as he cracked an office window and fired up the rest of his cigar.

"I can help you straighten up this office," Caddy said, looking around the bare room. "Make it seem more respectable."

"Every time I get comfortable, someone wants to vote me out."

"Isn't that every public official?"

"Or the village idiot."

"I don't think this county is dumb enough to make the same mistake twice."

Quinn eyed her, getting the cigar tip glowing red. He set it at the edge of a large Arturo Fuente ashtray and leaned back in his wooden chair. "You want to rethink that statement?"

"Well, they're stuck with you for the next four years," Caddy said. "So you might as well hang some pictures, put up a hunting calendar, and set your guns back in the rack."

"I moved the guns to the jail," Quinn said. "I only keep my shotgun and my sidearm here in the office or in the truck."

Caddy kept on looking uneasy, not looking her brother the eye, just talking for the sake of talking, keeping him going until she got to the point. Quinn lifted the cigar again and took a puff, the room filling with smoke. She finally looked back at him through the thick haze, back from wherever she'd gone.

"I think they're dead."

"Oh, hell," Quinn said. "You don't know that."

"No," she said. "But I sure as hell can feel it. I didn't tell you this, but I'm pretty sure Ana Maria was selling herself at the camp. She never told me exactly, but she hinted around plenty about her boy-friends. Tamika was a sweet girl but a bad girl, you know? She got in a lot of trouble in school before she got expelled. Got off on how far she'd push things

72

with boys. She didn't have any shame or any pride. The attention was just something to give her self-worth. Really twisted stuff for a girl that young."

"I'm glad to check back at the migrant camp," Quinn said. "But picking season is over. Not many folks still around. You know any of the Odums?"

"No," Caddy said. "But Boom does. He's asking around."

Quinn nodded. He watched Caddy, dressed as always in bootcut Levi's and some cowboy shirt of Jamey Dixon's. He'd once brought up that she might want to wear something smaller to fit her and he really caught hell for it. There was something about wearing a dead man's clothes that brought his sister some comfort.

"Glad you and Mom talked."

Quinn nodded.

"She's done saying her piece."

"Damn, I hope so."

"You shouldn't have gone behind her back on that land," Caddy said. "That farm really belongs to all of us. It always has. If you were to have lost it—"

"I wouldn't have lost it."

"But you trusted Daddy."

Quinn nodded.

"Same difference."

Quinn nodded again. Caddy stood, shoving her hands in her Levi's, shrugging her shoulders, rubbing her hand over the back of her neck. Still looking like a kid, with the short hair and freckled nose, those boy's clothes swallowing her up whole.

"See you at Mom's Sunday?" Quinn asked. He tapped the ash on his cigar as Lillie walked into the office, saying Samantha Adams spotted a white van yesterday shagging ass out by her property.

Caddy said hello to Lillie and nodded good-bye to Quinn, headed for the door.

"I'm not interrupting some kind of family squabble?" Lillie said. "This can wait."

"No squabble," Caddy said, passing her in the narrow doorway. "We got everything worked out just fine."

6

"I really appreciate you stopping by the dealership today," Tom "Big T" Bobo said. "It may not be much to you, but it sure gives our solutions experts a big lift."

"You mean the sales guys?" Wilcox said, walking with Big T down the rows of endless F-150s, American flags flapping on the light poles in the dusk. The light had turned a real funky orange-black, swarms of birds flitting back and forth, confused on where they're headed.

"Yeah," Big T said, tight and round as a bowling ball, in a blue Ford racing jacket. "You're no bullshitter. That's what these marketing guys up in Memphis told me to call them. That's why nobody works on a commission here. I don't sell nothing I wouldn't sell to my own momma."

Wilcox nodded, knowing the man's momma had been dead many years. He didn't say anything, too damn tired after being up nearly twenty-four hours straight, but he'd promised Big T he'd make it. Not to mention it was good to return to his routine and everyday work as a true, authentic American hero. Big T had fired him twice already but always asked him back.

"My daddy founded this dealership on Christian principles," Big T said, running a hand over each of the big trucks as if christening each and every one with his stubby little fingers. "You can see 'The Ten Commandments of Business' we live by right by the lavatories in back. My daddy thought that up. Thinking upon what God had set in stone and how we might apply those same values as salesmen."

"You mean solutions experts."

Big T stopped and grinned, placing a thoughtful hand over his double chin. "Sure," he said. "Sure, Rick. Of course things have changed a bit since the old days. I don't think Daddy could ever even imagine what all we've built here. Biggest Ford dealership in the Mid-South, an inventory of thousands. You can walk into Big T's and sell, trade, or buy within thirty minutes. How's that for a military operation?"

"Roger that."

"Y'all do everything with speed," Big T said, grinning, moving again, heading toward the big glass building. "Isn't that right? I saw a documentary about you Marine Recon boys on the Discovery Channel over Christmas out in Vail. One of the boys interviewed said the goal was to work a room like a damn scalded dog."

"Well," Wilcox said, slipping his hands into his pockets, getting a little cold wandering through the maze of inventory. "Not everything, Big T."

"Haw, haw," Big T said. "I hear you. I hear you. How's your friend Miss Crissley doing? Let me say, I'm a married man, but she's one of the best-looking little gals I've ever seen. Didn't you say she was a real beauty queen?"

"She was runner-up Miss Teen Mississippi," Wilcox said, lighting a Marlboro Red. "But she got the crown when the winner got herself into a little trouble."

Big T's eyebrows knitted together, stopping off at a big red Ford F-350 with tires about as tall as the man himself. "What happened?"

Wilcox shrugged his shoulders. "That girl was the star in a video shot on some Ole Miss football player's iPhone," he said. "Got lots of attention. Don't worry, though. She straightened up now and found God. But in the middle of all the teeth gnashing and tears, the crown went on to Crissley."

"Beautiful girl," Big T said. "Just beautiful. Biggest blue eyes I ever seen. And all that blonde hair.

Say, is she still interested in that cherry-red Shelby inside?"

"That's a lot of dough, Big T," Wilcox said, "to be spending on a woman."

"Could be a hell of an engagement gift," Big T said. "Put that ring on the car key ring. I've seen it before. Big engines and leather seats sure will make her frisky."

"I was married," Wilcox said.

"Divorced?"

"Sad thing."

"Kids?"

"Little boy," Wilcox said. "The absolute love of my life. Everything in my world is about that child. When I got home from my last tour, I promised I'd take good care of him. And I'm doing everything in my power to keep my word."

"Good man," Big T said, clasping his shoulder. They moved on toward the main office and the Ford Tough Café, where customers could have all the free burnt coffee and stale popcorn they wanted. Through the glass, Wilcox saw an older woman in pajama bottoms and a camouflage jacket eating a sack of popcorn and watching Fox News. "I knew you were a family man full of American values and vigor. I can't tell you how much we appreciate you being the spokesman for Big T Ford. My daddy sure would have liked you."

"And I know I would have liked him," Wilcox said,

thinking about the porky, bald-headed man in the brown suit and yellow tie in the oil painting in Big T's office. "He looked like a real straight shooter."

"I can tell you something, you sure are a lot better than the spokesman he had when I was a kid," Big T said, stopping by the big glass doors to the show-room, letting Wilcox finish up that Marlboro. "He was this B movie cowboy named Buddy McCoy, real famous in Memphis. When I was a boy, he hosted a cowboy show for kids. They'd show the Lone Ranger, Roy Rogers, and all that. He could ride, shoot. But he was about ten years past his prime, showing up drunk as a damn goat to do live shots back when the dealership was on Elvis Presley Boulevard. One time on live TV, he just closed his eyes and fell off his damn horse. I can't recall his horse's name. But that horse may have been more famous than him. You're not like Buddy at all. You're a real professional, Mr. Wilcox."

"Appreciate that, Big T," Wilcox said.

Big T looked at him, nodding, tears forming in his eyes. "Sometimes when I think what you boys have done for our country . . ."

Wilcox watched the man cry, tossed down the cigarette, and ground it out with his boot. He patted Big T's back to try to make him stop.

"Proud to serve."

Big T wiped his eyes, winked at him, and gave him a two-finger salute. "How'd you like to take that hot little Shelby home tonight? Now, you'll have to bring her back tomorrow. But might make a fun night for you and Miss Crissley."

"How fast is that car?"

"Zero to sixty in four-point-three seconds," Big T said. "Just the thing for a speed freak like you. Just bring her back in one piece."

"Oh, you can trust me," Wilcox said, smiling wide. "I never leave a customer behind."

"Welcome to Shift Change," Boom said, driving his truck slow past the rusted trailers and small houses held together with plywood, Visqueen, and duct tape. "One of the real bright spots in Tibbehah County. House on the right with the big porch is where they run the spade and poker games. Next door is sometimes a juke house, other times they run whores. You can get moonshine, weed, crank, pills. Stolen shit. You really sure you want to go in there?"

"You said Tamika and Ana Maria partied here?" Caddy said. "Right?"

"That's what I heard," Boom said. "I don't hang out here no more. This place ain't good for your soul. You end up in Shift Change because you done run out of luck."

"Who told you they'd seen the girls?"

"I promised not to say."

"And who runs all this?"

"Goddamn Cho Cho Porter."

"Never heard of her," she said. "Or him."

"Her," Boom said. "Whole lotta female. That's what folks call her, with the 'Goddamn' and everything. She ain't just any Cho Cho Porter. She's **Goddamn** Cho Cho. She thinks it means some real respect. Just don't get smart with her."

"Why's that?"

"Just wait," Boom said. "And you'll see."

"Why they call this place Shift Change?" Caddy said, looking out at the dozens of cars parked outside the house, black faces coming and going through a wide-open door. Rap music shaking from the back of trucks with bright chrome wheels. A yellow street sign reading SLOW. CHILDREN AT PLAY.

"Used to be the name of the grocery down the street," Boom said. "Burned up a long time ago. Most folks down this road are old. They can't do shit about Cho Cho. And if they try, she'll make their life hell."

"Spent most of my life in Tibbehah County," Caddy said. "Never heard of Goddamn Cho Cho Porter or the Shift Change."

"How 'bout you wait here for me?" Boom said.

"No way."

"Ain't your kind of place, Caddy Colson."

"Me and you both know that's not true," Caddy said. "This place looks like the Taj Mahal compared to places I've been. Would you like me to tell you a little about them?"

Boom turned off the motor, rubbing the stubble on his face in thought. His handsome profile shadowed and half lit from the dashboard. The radio playing some station out of Holly Springs, some of that stuff he liked. Chitlin Circuit soul. They sat there for a long while, just watching the comings and goings of the Shift Change. In the silence, he punched up his cigarette lighter with his steel hand. Caddy absently fingered the cross hung around her neck.

"I know you don't like to think about it," Caddy said. "But it doesn't bother me."

Boom didn't answer. He lit his cigarette and popped the lighter back in the dash. The cab filled with smoke.

"I coulda done something," Boom said. "With Quinn gone."

"You think you could've stopped me?"

"Yeah," he said. "If I hadn't been so damn fucked up myself."

"Nobody could've stopped me," Caddy said. "Not Quinn. Not you. Now we all got through it. And that's all there is to it."

Boom nodded and reached for the door handle, both of them getting out and heading toward the party house. A man on the porch eyed them, swinging off the railing and moving down the steps, a bottle in a brown wrapper in his hand. The guy was really young, just a teenager, looking stick-thin and jet-black in a big puffy coat and a flat-crowned base-ball cap. "Oh, hell no. Hell no."

Boom looked down at the kid.

"Ain't you the one-armed nigger works for the po-lice?" he said. "I seen you hanging out at the jail."

"No," Boom said. "I'm the one-armed nigger works for the sheriff's office. And I'm the one-armed nigger who fixes trucks and used to come here and party back when your momma was flat on her back. And I'd be glad to be that one-armed nigger who whipped your ass."

"Fuck you, man."

"Go on," Boom said. "Tell Cho Cho that Boom's here."

"Or what?"

"Or I'll pick up your young ass and see how far I can throw you," Boom said, showing off the hook on his hand. He flexed it and made the mechanism clamp with a tight click.

The kid moved. Boom made a motion with his chin at Caddy and shook his head, heading up the steps past the kid who'd tried to be tough. Caddy followed, brushing past the boy. Inside, folks were dancing and grinding in the dim blue light. Lots of cigarette and weed smoke, open bottles of cheap-ass vodka and jelly jars filled with homemade shine. A bright light shone from a back room, a big-ass woman nearly as wide as the doorway walking out. She had on a cheetah-print housecoat and was counting out cash with her hands.

"Shut up, shut up, shut up," the woman yelled. "Turn that shit off."

The rap stopped. Everything went silent. All eyes on Boom and Caddy.

"Boom Kimbrough," she said. "Goddamn you. I told you don't you ever show your black ass 'round here again."

"Couldn't we have gone somewhere else for a change?" Crissley asked. "I don't mean to complain, but Sammy Hagar's Red Rocker Bar and Grill doesn't exactly scream date night."

"I promised the manager I'd stop by," Wilcox said. "Maybe sing a song or two. You know how it goes. I have a lot of people asking me for a lot of favors. It's just part of the deal, baby."

"But couldn't we just have one night together?" she said. "Without old guys who want to hear your war stories, stinky car salesmen, or your Marine buddies."

"First off, my Marine buddies aren't up for debate," Wilcox said. "That's like you asking me to stop seeing my family."

"You hate your family."

"Second, those car salesmen aren't all stinky," he said. "Some of them are even a lot of fun. In fact, without knowing some stinking car salesmen, we couldn't be driving that cherry-red Shelby tonight."

"It's fun," Crissley said. "But it's not like we can keep it. Remember, renting something isn't the same as buying it."

"We talking cars, baby?" Wilcox said. "Or your cute little Disney princess ass?"

"See it the way you like," Crissley said. "But I'm the one who got all dressed up to come eat at the West Memphis dog track. What is this anyway?"

"Bacon-wrapped jalapeño poppers," Wilcox said. "And I ordered you a Waborita, named for Sammy's place in Baja, Cabo Wabo. You can read all about it on the back of the menu. I promise I'll take you there someday. The manager here actually met Sammy. He said that dude is stone-cold crazy."

Crissley reached for the blue drink and took a sip, making a squashed-up face far more critical than the damn drink deserved. She had on a sparkly black tank top, her face airbrushed to perfection, with dark-wine lips and lots of smoky blue eye shadow. The diamond earrings her daddy had given her were as big as bottle caps and the breasts her daddy had paid for filled out that tank top into a very nice D cup. Cheers to that perverted old coot.

"Is this comped?" she asked.

Wilcox nodded, taking a sip of a Coors Light. "Baby," he said. "Don't you want to hear me sing?"

Crissley straightened in her seat, patting at the

sides of her perfect blonde hair, sprayed and teased high and full. She looked around the open walls of the little restaurant inside the Southland dog track and casino, listening to the bells chirp and watching the bright lights flash. Endless red carpet for country folks walking around with quarters in to-go cups. She sighed.

"With all that money you cashed in for chips," she said, "they sure as hell should comp you. Why'd you bring so much anyway?"

"Just some cash from a few gigs," Wilcox said. "Figured we might play a little blackjack, maybe watch me sit in for a few rounds of poker."

"Last time I watched you play poker down in Tunica, we didn't sleep for three days straight," she said. "Please don't do that to me again. Please do what you need to do and then let's leave. Don't lose everything."

"What song?"

"Whattaya mean what song?" Crissley said. "You bring me out to the damn dog track and you better sing that song. You know, our song."

"I'd sell my soul just to see your face."

Crissley beamed. She placed her well-manicured hands together, giggling, Daddy's little girl, with those big ole Ds shaking.

"And I'd break my bones just to heal your pain."

"Lord, Rick," she said. "When so much bullshit

doesn't come out of your mouth, I remember that God gave you a gift."

Wilcox lifted a Coors Light her way and winked. "First song of the set," he said. "After, we can play a few games and I'll cash back out. I'll get the money returned in a check. Lot easier than cash."

"Things are really turning around," she said. "I remember you just singing for tips down on Beale Street when we met. And now people are just throwing money at you. Do you think we might be able to keep that Shelby just a little longer?"

"Maybe," he said. "But tonight, you drive."

"Are you kidding?"

"Nope," he said. "I'm a hell of a boyfriend. Besides, I plan to leave here so shit-faced drunk that you better take the wheel."

The waiter set down a Sammy's Rockin' Steak Burger for Wilcox and a Crabby Sammy sandwich for Crissley, as it appeared to be the healthiest thing on the menu. A crab cake with coleslaw slapped between a bun. Before the waitress left, Wilcox said he'd really like to try one of those I Can't Drive 55 iced teas.

"I don't get it," Crissley said. "Who the hell is Sammy Hagar?"

"A redheaded rock god who couldn't live by the rules."

"A personal hero?"

"Sure," Wilcox said. "We'll go with that. John Wayne, Ronald Reagan, and Sammy Hagar. That sounds just about perfect."

"I heard you got straight, Boom," Cho Cho said. "Right with the Lord. Come to the Cross. Ain't no more fucking, fighting, and drinking. What the hell you doing here?"

"We looking for someone," Boom said.

"And who's this skinny white girl?" Cho Cho asked. "Don't have no ass at all. This what happened to you? You get some white girl playing with your mind? What you need is Goddamn Cho Cho Porter to get you correct. When you hungry, you want some candy or a goddamn Whopper?"

"This is Caddy Colson," Boom said. "She runs The River up in Jericho. They're good folks. Help out a lot of people with a food pantry and ministry."

"Well, ain't that shit grand," Cho Cho said. "What the fuck do y'all want? 'Cause if you ain't come to get high, drink, or party, you lost as hell. I don't run no ministry."

"We're looking for two girls who like to party," Caddy said. "You know Tamika Odum? She's fifteen, maybe five feet tall. Light skin, long hair with a red streak in it? Runs with a little Mexican girl named Ana Maria?"

"You know how many folks come here to the

Change?" she said. "And you know how many damn Odums we got round here? Shit, half Tibbehah County's named Odum. Two motherfucking Odums smoking blunts in my kitchen right now. Y'all want something to eat? I got grilled cheese, hamburgers. Some fruit punch with likker in it."

"I heard she was friends with Kiara Pitts," Caddy said. "Do you know her?"

"Kiara?" Cho Cho said. "Ain't that the motherfucking girl cat on **The Lion King**? I watch that shit with my grandbabies. They just love that show. All those crazy cubs getting lost, getting into shit. Poking their noses around until they get bitch-slapped by a hyena. You know what I'm saying?"

"You know the girls, Cho Cho?" Boom said. "Or not? I ain't got time to play."

"No drinking, fucking, dancing, and now you ain't playing," Cho Cho said. "Ain't you the man, Boom Kimbrough. Come on to me, baby. Be good to Goddamn Cho Cho Porter and Goddamn Cho Cho be real good to your big black ass. How about you, white girl? You want to get high and party?"

Caddy shook her head, sticking her hands down in her jeans pockets. Everything in the room was too familiar, the burnt weed smell, the alcohol smell of people's breath, the booming bass music, and the lazy eyes following her wherever she went. She felt things get real small, tight in her chest, swallowing, trying to keep her footing, while Cho Cho stared at her.

"What's wrong wit her?" Cho Cho said.

"You help us," Boom said, "and I'll owe you. OK?"

Cho Cho, her big eyes glassy, moved on Boom, lifting the back of her hand up to his scarred face and chin, and said, "Oh, I sure as hell like that."

"The girls?"

"I don't fuck with any of that kiddie shit," Cho Cho said. "You need to be a grown-ass woman, you come in here. You better be a grown-ass woman if you want to get high. Get laid. I had my first when I was twelve motherfucking years old. I think that's some sick shit to do to a girl. My baby's daddy was old. Had kids, grandkids, himself. Yeah, I know them. But I don't like those girls in here. First, they gonna get themselves in trouble and then they gonna get Cho Cho's big ass in trouble. I told them whatever kind of business they doing with that freak, they keep it on the street."

Boom looked to Caddy, Caddy feeling that room twist and turn, music coming out of those speakers taking her back years ago into those broken apartment buildings, derelict projects. She felt those hands on her, being passed around, her mind separating from her body, like watching a damn movie, not feeling or worrying. Things just happening to her. She could've stuck a knife in her hand and she wouldn't have screamed.

"Girls getting pimped?" Boom said.

Cho Cho nodded.

"Who's that pimp?"

"You owe me, handsome."

"I said I would, woman."

"You know."

Boom gave her a hard, mean look. He plucked another cigarette into his mouth, reaching back into his jacket pocket for a Zippo and lighting it. "Yeah?"

"You gonna kill him this time?" Cho Cho said.

"He ain't worth going back to jail," Boom said. "But he sure as shit won't know what hit him. Come on, Caddy."

"What is it?" Caddy asked, swallowing, finding her feet. "What'd she say?"

"Goddamn Cho Cho gave us what we wanted."

7

"Still no sign of that van," Lillie said. "Samantha Adams is damn sure she saw it, though. At about the time it would have been shagging ass from downtown. We got three witnesses who saw it, too, heading north off the Square, moving in the direction of Yellow Leaf. I figured they would have hit 45 and been long gone. But if Ms. Adams is within a minute or two about the time, the roadblocks would have been set. They would've had to gone a different route."

Quinn was in the break room with Lillie, Lillie about to head off for the night and finally get home to her adopted daughter, Rose. A little Mexican girl she'd personally rescued from a child-trafficking ring run by a three-hundred-pound nightmare named Janet Torres. Lillie reached over Quinn to get a little bowl filled with sugar packs, ripping open three and dumping the packs into her tumbler, saying that Samantha Adams may be a busybody but she was a reliable busybody. She stomped her size-ten boot on top of a nearby seat to add emphasis to her point.

"Only two roads out from Yellow Leaf," Quinn said. "Unless they doubled back to the Square in a new car."

"Sure."

"Or maybe they didn't go anywhere," Lillie said. "Have you considered that? Maybe they ditched the van and roughed it or had locals who kept them hidden until everything got quiet."

"Crime lab folks didn't get much," Quinn said. "Robbers wore gloves with those stupid masks. Lab has a bullet and some photos of that mud they tracked in. Might be able to get a boot print. Looks like they were both wearing hiking boots, from the video."

"Guys who like Donald Trump and hunting," Lillie said. "Damn, that narrows it."

"Maybe they don't like Trump at all," Quinn said. "Maybe they think he's a complete soulless asshole and it's all a big joke."

"I ain't laughing," Lillie said. "You figure these bank robbers have a sense of humor?"

"Something like that," Quinn said. "Feds connect this one with ten more. So far, they've hit a few banks outside Memphis, two in northwest Alabama and then four in Mississippi. Holliday will let us know about the next one."

"We have five banks in Tibbehah," Lillie said. "We got six deputies. That leaves one of us to keep law and order while we keep watch. Assuming we work 'round the clock."

"They won't be back," Quinn said. "They switch up states, counties, each time. They've never gone back to the same county or town. Before the First National, they'd laid low for a few weeks. They're patient, good at choosing easy pickings."

"I never thought of them as stupid."

"These boys did the job quickly and effectively," Quinn said. "Every damn time less than ninety seconds."

"Hell, that's better than Patrick Swayze and those surfers," Lillie said. "You seen that movie **Point Break**?"

"Yeah, I saw it on cable one time," Quinn said. "But I always think about Swayze in **Road House**. What was his name, the guy who ripped out people's throats?"

"Dalton," Lillie said. "You're just like all the boys I know, can't help but watch a movie about fighting, titties, and monster trucks."

Mary Alice, now in her mid-sixties, gray-headed and big-bottomed, with half-glasses down on her nose, walked in. "Got two calls within the last two minutes from a woman over on Stovall Street," she said, hand on hip. "Says her house got broken into. Whoever it was is gone. But the woman's scared. Said things have been busted up real good."

"Send Kenny," Quinn said.

"Kenny's ten-seven," Mary Alice said.

"Reggie?"

"Domestic up in Carthage," Mary Alice said. "Dan Easley's drunk again. Says his wife hid the keys to his dump truck."

"I'll go," Quinn said. "What's the name of the woman with the burglary?"

"Powers," Mary Alice said. "Y'all know anyone named Powers? I sure as heck don't."

Lillie looked at Quinn and raised her eyebrows. "Signs and wonders, Mary Alice," she said. "New people in Tibbehah County."

Quinn smiled.

Lillie asked, "You want me to come with you?"

Quinn shook his head. "Get on home to Rose," he said. "Need you back here in the daylight to go hunt for that van. If what you're saying is right, it's got to be out there somewhere."

"I'm flattered," Fannie said. "You flew in just for me?"

"No, ma'am," Ray said. "Not that I wouldn't. You caught me straightening out some issues down in Tunica."

She and Ray sat together in his ninth-floor suite

at the Peabody in downtown Memphis surrounded by elegant if aging furniture, thick, billowy drapes, and satiny pillows. Ray had a drink cart brought up, with a nut bowl, fine cheeses, and meats. He was a class act, talking criminal activity over cocktails.

"You get things straight?" she asked.

"More or less," Ray said. Still good-looking after all these years. His salt-and-pepper hair and mustache had now grown to mostly salt. But he still had that dark Italian skin and those smiling eyes that crinkled at the corners. He looked like a country club playboy but had been a hell of an enforcer for Buster White back in the day.

"I half expected for Mr. White to come up with you."

"Mr. White doesn't leave the Coast too often," he said. "He's got a routine, family obligations."

And enemies in about every major city—women he owed alimony to and payoffs and men to whom he'd made big promises while doing the long stretch at Angola. Fannie couldn't imagine crawling out of a hellhole like that richer than before. But she'd always heard most of what Buster White had built had been done out of boredom down on The Farm. Grew his operation to three times its size, edging up into north Mississippi and west Alabama.

"So you got some Mississippi troubles, too?" Ray said.

Fannie nodded. She'd worn one of her favorite

dresses, a black off-the-shoulder, with some real fuck-me pumps, velvet, with killer heels. Not to mention the perfume. A dab of Chanel Gardenia right between her tits.

"I got a goddamn puritanical motherfucker riding my ass down in Jericho," Fannie said, tapping her bare leg, really wanting a cigarette. "He wants to shut me down and won't take cash or pussy to keep us open."

"That's trouble," Ray said, crossing his legs. He had a nice khaki suit on, it being a little early for khaki since it was well before Easter, but people who lived on the Coast really could give a shit. They were on their own time. "What's this asshole's name?"

"Skinner," Fannie said. "He runs the board of supervisors. Says he's going to make a motion to pull our liquor license and make damn sure every dancer is properly dressed and keeps their snatch shut as tight as a bear trap."

"I can't imagine any of those north Mississippi good ole boys immune to your charm."

Fannie smiled at him, tilting her head, red hair draping her bare shoulder. "I agree," she said. "But you're not some dickless prude."

"No, ma'am," Ray said. "I'm not. Just what would you like me to do?"

"I'm new to town," Fannie said. "I'd like to know more about Skinner. He fancies himself as a real insider in Jackson, lowering himself to run business in his hometown. I want to know who he fucked in the ass, how many times and how often he did it."

"Done," Ray said. "Nothing to it."

"Did you know you just get more handsome as you age?"

Ray grinned, stood up, showing a little bit of wear as he gripped a stiff right knee, and made his way to the drink cart. He fixed a drink for Fannie, her usual, and then a simple scotch and soda for himself with some Johnnie Walker Blue. He hobbled back to the couch and took a seat. Fannie recalled all the times they'd spent in bed. Ray, being twenty-five years her senior, had been sweet, kind, and giving. Taking his time, making sure she got hers, and always taking her out for a big steak dinner after. He was an old-school gentleman and it pained the damn hell out of her to see him becoming an old man.

"We have some problems, too," Ray said. "I know I can help you with yours. Maybe you help out with what we got?"

"Anything, Ray."

"First off," Ray said, holding up a finger, "can you stay for dinner?"

Fannie smiled.

"I went ahead and got us a table at Chez Phillipe downstairs," he said. "I recall you liking a good bloody steak."

"The bloodier, the better."

Ray smiled, took a breath, and looked at her a moment, almost making sure of what he was about to say next. Finally, he nodded, more to himself than to her. "Memphis has been kind of a clusterfuck since Bobby Campo and Stagg got taken down," he said. "Lots of blacks and wetbacks shooting each other. Those goddamn Mexicans now trying to cut us out of the equation. Of course you know those local boys, K-Bo and Shortbox."

"The Twins," Fannie said. "Last I heard, we were all one big happy family."

"They won't work with Mr. White," Ray said. "Not anymore. They buddied up with a new group of Mexes rolling in from Houston and New Orleans. And you know how that stands with Mr. White."

"I can imagine." Fannie leaned in from her seat, putting her hand on Ray's bony knee. "How can I help?"

"Well," Ray said. "Those Twins got a chicken-wings business and detail shop down on EP Boulevard. Lots of money being run through there."

"How much?"

"Jesus, Fannie," Ray said. "If I told you, you'd call me a goddamn liar."

"Try me."

Quinn left the engine running on the Big Green Machine and reached for his Maglite, heading up the walkway to the bungalow a few blocks off the

Square. It was one of those white houses he'd known since he'd been a boy, where old women had lived and died tending to their flower beds and little vegetable gardens. Most of the original Jericho houses fell on hard times in the eighties, few surviving, some being bulldozed, but a few had come back as of late. He had the lights shining up the path and onto the steps and the porch. No one coming out, a light on in the window. A tire swung slow from a giant oak in the front yard.

He knocked on the door and waited.

A young woman, maybe his age, maybe a little younger, opened the door. She had long reddish brown hair, pale green eyes, and pale skin peppered with a lot of freckles. The woman came up to Quinn's chin, standing there in blue jeans and an oversized gray sweatshirt cut wide at the neck. The shirt fell from her shoulder, an image on the front of Johnny Cash giving Nashville the finger. Standing there, looking pretty, while she held a twelve-gauge, broken open and loose, in her hands.

She had silver rings on her fingers, several rope bracelets on her right wrist, nails painted black on one hand and a bright blue on the other. The woman looked at Quinn from under the tangle of all that hair. "Don't worry," she said. "I took out the shells when I saw you drive up. Whoever did this is long gone. The dumb son of a bitch. Do you see the mess all over my house? My front door was wide open."

"Someone here with you?"

"Just me and my son," she said. "He's in his room. I'm trying to get him to sleep."

"And you're Miss Powers?"

"Maggie," she said, not smiling, eyeing Quinn as she turned sideways and let him walk inside the little house. "And you're the sheriff now."

"That's right."

Quinn introduced himself and Maggie smiled a little bit, setting the shotgun on the kitchen table and reaching for a bottle of beer. "Nice you answered the call," she said. "Didn't expect to see the county sheriff show up to a little break-in like this."

"Small department. We all put in time," Quinn said, looking around. "What'd they take?"

"Nothing," Maggie said.

"Nothing?"

She nodded, pulling the sweatshirt up over her bare shoulder, standing there in the middle of the room, which was a wreck of spilled books, DVDs, an overturned flat-screen TV, and cushions from the sofa tossed into the middle of the room. It was a pleasant room, with framed photographs and a half-dozen funky-looking paintings on the walls. The door to a greenish vintage refrigerator was open, a mess of food littering a black-and-white checker-board floor.

"You sure nothing's gone?" Quinn said.

"No," she said. "But my gun was right where I'd

hidden it. And my jewelry. I'm sure the TV is busted. Someone just ripped the whole thing off the wall. Why would someone go to all this trouble?"

"Got any enemies?" Quinn said.

Maggie Powers laughed and shook her head, staring at Quinn with those light green eyes. Quinn felt his mouth go a little dry, watching her, something so damn familiar about those eyes and those freckles, the way she stood there, with bare feet and face partially hidden by that long hair. He cocked his head and was about to say something when his radio squawked at his hip. He reached for it and turned down the volume.

"Does my ex count?" Maggie asked.

"You bet," Quinn said. "Divorced?"

"Almost," she said. "Thank God. All over but a few dashes of the pen."

"Y'all been getting into it?"

"We always get into it."

"Is this his style?"

"He doesn't have a style," Maggie said. "But he's not usually violent or abusive, if that's what you're asking. Mainly, he's just a self-absorbed asshole."

"Oh," Quinn said. "One of those."

"You got kids?"

Quinn shook his head. "I have a nephew."

"Married?" Maggie said.

"Nope."

Quinn had his hands on his hips, staring at Maggie Powers, trying to locate just where he knew the woman from. A long silence hung right there between them. She had really nice green eyes, so light they were nearly translucent, sharp and smart, looking straight through him.

"Goddamn you, Quinn Colson," she said. "Are you going to remember me or not? Don't hurt a girl's feelings."

"Maggie," he said. "Maggie Powers. Your grandmother lived here. You stayed with her during the summers. You came up from Biloxi?"

"Mobile," she said, running a hand through the long, draping hair like a comb, sweeping it from her face.

"Your daddy was a truck driver," Quinn said. "He used to let us come out and take a look at his rig when he dropped you off. He had a big Kenworth that had a funny name."

"The Blue Mule."

"Yes," Quinn said. "Had a big kicking mule on the mud flaps. He was a good guy."

"He's dead."

"I'm sorry."

"Don't be," Maggie said. "He's been gone a long time. I remember trailing you and your friends around at the baseball park and the town square. Your pretty little sister?"

"Caddy."

"And this real funny black kid," she said. "Y'all had dirt bikes. You'd jump them into the Black River."

"Boom."

"And that little blonde who wore dresses but loved to climb trees and follow y'all around," she said. "I remember how'd you sometimes hold hands down to the woods and talk to each other in little whispers. It was pretty cute."

Quinn nodded but didn't say Anna Lee's name, his mind coming back to the summers back in the eighties and early nineties, before high school, and before things got real and serious. Back when he'd been a local hell-raiser, and not a town hero or a military man, with plenty of rough edges and fear of absolutely nothing. Maggie Powers. Those freckles and that nice red mouth. He'd kissed her once but could not for the life of him remember when or under what circumstances. There had been a lot going on back then, slipping out, running wild, and a boy they'd all befriended who'd gone missing. A long time ago.

"Grannie left me the house," Maggie said. "We rented it for a while. But now, with the divorce, seemed like a good time. We'd been living in Nashville. Figured it was a good a time as any to see about the easy and slow-paced life in Tibbehah."

Quinn smiled. "Not as slow as you might hope."

"Crime?"

"Not much in town," Quinn said. "People on your street don't often lock their doors. But we have a little out in the county. I can search for prints on that front door handle, if you like, but most of the time we don't get a match."

"It could be my ex."

"You want me to talk to him?" Quinn said. "If he admits to being here, you could press charges."

Maggie shook her head. "The less I have to do with him, the better."

"Is he violent?"

"My ex-husband?" she said. "Yes. And no. Mainly, he's an asshole. And, boy, does that man like to drink. He might have stumbled through this house and not even remember it."

"I don't like the sound of that," Quinn said, reaching into his pocket for his card, writing his personal cell phone number on the back. "I'm on duty all night. Call if you need anything."

"Maggie," she said. "Maggie Powers. You won't forget me again?"

"No, ma'am," Quinn said. "I don't see that ever being a problem."

Maggie smiled at him, those pale eyes wandering over his face, and pulled the wide neck of the sweatshirt up off her freckled shoulder. "Damn. Doesn't it seem like we were just kids ourselves?"

8

"Damn," Opie said. "I like this car. Where'd you get it?"

"Borrowed it from the pre-owned lot at Big T's," Wilcox said, gunning the Challenger's Hemi motor. "Some douchebag just traded it in for a minivan."

"Hot damn," Opie said. "We could go from the bank to the highway in less than a minute."

"I'll steal something bigger," Wilcox said. "Some kind of SUV. Or another van. For the money and the guns."

Wilcox slowed down on Church Street and headed toward a big white bank set off from Flick's Amoco in the heart of Potts Camp, Mississippi. There wasn't a hell of a lot in Potts Camp. A truck stop, a barbecue joint, a mess of churches, a tanning salon, and two banks. The only bank Wilcox cared to see was the big bank, Potts Camp Federal. The men didn't speak as they passed the front doors and toured around the side by the window teller.

Wilcox nodded, tinted windows up, cab filled with cigarette smoke, and turned off from the bank and headed back toward the truck stop. It was past four o'clock and the day workers—the suckers—were cashing their Friday checks.

"Don't you want to see the inside?" Opie said.

"Don't ever show yourself on tape, that's god-damn amateur hour," Wilcox said. "Besides, you ever walked into a shithole bank that didn't look like every other one? Only a moron would overthink these things. We are trained, equipped, and ready to deal with hostiles within small spaces. These folks aren't hostile. Most of them are fat old ladies who piss their pants when you tell them to get down on their knees. Only thing you got to watch out for is the wild card. You know what I mean?"

"Like that crazy-ass coot down in Jericho?"

"Exactly," Wilcox said. "Every other motherfucker down here is carrying. And every motherfucker wants to be a stone-cold hero. We need to shut down that hero mode fast and hard. All the rest is easy. Anyone who takes more than ninety seconds in and out to rob a small target like this is a fucking disgrace."

"You think they really have good fried chicken at that truck stop?"

"Probably," Wilcox said. "But we're not stopping.

Every other asshole in this town knows each other. Just as soon as we'd sit down and wait for that chicken—and it may be the most delicious damn chicken you've ever tasted—someone is going to start asking questions. Where you from? What are you doing down here in Potts Camp? Are you all in the service? Because my idiot son jacked off on two tours in Afghanistan and came home to a parade."

"No fried chicken."

"No fried chicken, Ope," Wilcox said. "Soon as we get back to Memphis, let's go to Gibson's and get some donuts. We can study some maps, see the best way to hit that bank, and run for deep green cover."

"Nice to have a safe house."

"That was Cord's call," Wilcox said. "Only reason I agreed was because Tibbehah County was so damn landlocked. Only real way out of town was Highway 45. And I sure as hell didn't want to be Dukes of Hazzarding the back roads with those hick cops. Here, we got lots of options. Did you know Potts Camp backs straight up to the Holly Springs National Forest?"

Opie shook his head. Wilcox turned down onto Highway 78, gunning that big Hemi engine and taking that vehicle up to a hundred. Opie grinned like a damn kid in the passenger seat, the engine purring as he tapped the dash, wanting Wilcox to redline that motherfucker. But Wilcox took a breath, adrenaline flowing a bit, maybe a bit too much, and took his boot off the accelerator.

"What the hell, man?" Opie asked.

"Don't want to get busted by the nice guys."

"You mean the cops?"

"All cops think they're heroes," Wilcox said. "But, in reality, they freakin' suck. The nice guys of this world are really assholes. And the assholes, like us, are the ones doing the most good."

"And what are we doing that's good?"

Wilcox checked his profile in the rearview mirror, liking the close-cropped beard he'd been rocking lately, the square, lean jaw, the small, hard eyes.

"Making everyone feel alive."

"You're kidding."

"Tell me something, Opie," Wilcox said. "Do you or do you not feel like your boots are back on this planet now? Not like when you were picking up beer bottles down on Treasure Island and playing Jimmy Buffett songs for fat tourists from Cincinnati."

"I don't know," Ope said. "It was pretty relaxing."

"Relaxation only leads to death," Wilcox said. "That's what happens to people when they retire. They sit around and do nothing and pretty soon they stop giving a shit about everything. It's not getting old that leads men to getting limp dicks. It's when they stop giving a shit about life. This is life. This is purpose. The mission. The training. Keep that adrenaline flowing in your blood and that ding-dong will stay hard as a rock star."

Wilcox turned to Opie and, straight-faced, blew the smoke out of his nose.

"You're crazy," Opie said. "You do know that, Sarge?"

"That's what makes me an authentic genius," he said. "I'm just colorful as hell."

"Mom," Jason Colson said. "I need you to be really honest with me about something."

"Of course," Caddy said. "Anything."

It was after supper, and Jason sat on the floor near the television while Caddy lay on the couch, both watching the Avengers kill aliens while taking out most of downtown Manhattan. There was a lot of noise and violence, aliens on space bikes trying to take over the earth from a porthole from another dimension. Caddy was exhausted. She'd spent most of her day sorting and boxing donations of food and clothing, picking up Jason thirty minutes late from school. Caddy felt like hell about it.

"This is embarrassing," Jason said. "But I really need to know."

Caddy felt her heart flip a little, pushing herself up, planting her feet on the floor. "Is this about your granddad?" she said. "Because your granddad loves you very much. He just has some real problems with

110

saying good-bye. He fell on his head about a thousand times doing stunt work. You know, he didn't say a word to me or Uncle Quinn. He just packed up that cherry-red Firebird and said adios to this town. In his way, I think, he believed he was doing the right thing."

Jason just stared at her as Iron Man fell from the space portal, free-falling to earth without his jet propulsion. And then it was the damn Hulk—the brainless, muscular Hulk—who had the good goddamn sense to launch himself from a skyscraper and snatch Iron Man from the air and certain death.

"Is there really a Santa Claus?" Jason asked.

Caddy swallowed, flummoxed. "What's that, baby?"

"Kids in school were making fun of me," he said. "They said Santa was just your parents. But you and Grandma told me he comes to her house every year just like he did when you and Uncle Quinn were little. And Uncle Quinn always makes a big deal on how he has to work late on Christmas to help light the way for the reindeer. Is that just a bunch of bullshit, Momma?"

"Jason."

"Well, is it?"

"No," Caddy said, swallowing again. Taking a breath, thinking on it. "Well, I mean. Yes. You asked. You wanted me to be honest? Yes. It's not true. But it's not, altogether, bullshit."

"Isn't a lie bullshit?"

"Where do you learn to talk like that?"

"Uncle Quinn said it ain't cussing if Grandma and my teachers don't hear it," he said. "And Miss Lillie said the only folks offended by cussing are fat ladies in big hats who can't do their business on the toilet."

Caddy didn't speak, only nodded and blew out her breath. She looked at the television. All was right in the Avengers' universe. Iron Man was alive. Flat on his back, he opened his eyes and said he was hungry and wanted to go out for a shwarma. Whatever the hell a "shwarma" was, they wouldn't be getting them in north Mississippi for a long while.

"There is no Santa Claus," Caddy said. "It's for fun, to make children feel good and safe."

"Kind of like Jesus."

"Wait," Caddy said, now up on her bare feet. All the air washed from her lungs. "Wait. Wait. No. That's not the same. That's not the same at all, Jason Colson. One is a funny old man in a red hat who magically flies around and the other is a historical figure. Did you know there's more evidence that Jesus existed than there is for Alexander the Great or Julius Caesar?"

"Who's Caesar?"

"The man on the salad dressing," she said. "No, he's from a long time ago. Who's putting all these questions into your head? Is it Uncle Quinn? If

Uncle Quinn's bad-mouthing what I do again, I'm going to go over to the sheriff's office right now and tell him the way the world works."

"No," Jason said. "It's not Uncle Quinn. I've just been thinking on things. When it's quiet and I'm in the woods. Sometimes Uncle Quinn and I are hunting, but we don't talk for a long time. I just thought about what those kids were saying about Santa and it made sense. And I started thinking about all the stuff you and Jamey told me about Jesus. It kind of seemed like the same thing. Walking on water. Turning water into wine. Raising up a dead man. You know? It's all magic. And what I know now that I'm not a kid is that magic ain't real."

"It's not magic," she said. "It's divine. Jesus was the Son of God."

"But how did He know it?"

"He knew it."

"But He thought He had one father, Joseph," Jason said. "But turns out that God got His mother knocked up by herself."

"That's right."

"Joseph must've been mighty pissed."

"Jason," Caddy said. "It's called Immaculate Conception. She was filled with the Holy Spirit and made a baby."

"Like me?" Jason said, looking at her dead in the eye, really believing it. Not smarting off a bit. He seemed confused and curious at the same time. "The same way I was made?"

Caddy opened her mouth but closed it again fast. She reached for the remote control and turned off the television. For a moment, she could hear the wind outside, a thunderstorm expected overnight. The wind chimes on the back porch tinkled. She damn sure better be able to relay the concept of Jesus Christ to a nine-year-old boy. Although what had happened to her was far from immaculate.

"It's in the Bible," she said. "And if you have faith, you have to believe it's God's Word."

"But I don't have a daddy," he said. "That's true."

"You have a daddy."

"I do?" Jason said, smiling. Looking excited.

And there was quiet and sadness for a moment in the house. She nodded at him, feeling a heat spread through her chest. "He's nobody, though," she said. "Nobody that you ever need to meet. The Colson family is more family than most folks around here get in a lifetime."

"Why did Grandpa leave?"

Caddy wiped her face, tears feeling hot on the back of her hand. "Because he's weak," she said. "We're strong people. And I swear to you with all I am that Jesus Christ is real and that He loves you very much. That's all you need to know. Family and Him. And not to worry about another damn thing."

It was late, the dishes in the kitchen had stacked up, and there was a week's worth of laundry to do. They'd moved into the new little house last summer, their other house being sucked away in the big storm that hit town three years ago. Everything was a mess. Everything was chaos. Jason was growing faster than she could keep good clothes on his back. His feet were already larger than hers.

"Momma?"

Caddy looked to him.

"I believe you," he said. "It's just sometime Jesus sure makes you tired."

"I don't know how someone robbing a bank is your fault," Boom said. "You hadn't been back on the job but a couple months, and all these jawing assholes are the ones who wanted change after all you done for them."

"The **Tibbehah Monitor** says we had a slow response time," Quinn said. "Mr. Berryhill blamed us for answering that call out at Vienna's. He told Miss Mize it didn't take three deputies to work a scuffle at a beer joint."

"Making the point that you all were there to look at titties."

"Berryhill's just pissed about what happened to him," Quinn said. "He's back on his feet, thinking on things, and it's hard to take. Imagine being the chamber of commerce president and some guy in a Halloween mask threatens to blow your dick off?"

"Hard to imagine being chamber of commerce president."

"I don't think losing that van made us look great, either," Quinn said. "When I say that van vanished, I'm being honest. But it makes it look like we weren't running down every county road with the Choctaw sheriff's office and Jericho PD."

It was night, and Boom had asked Quinn to call if he got close to Sugar Ditch. An hour later, he found himself down by the Three-Way, which was actually a four-way stop now, but names didn't change easy in Tibbehah. A gas station, soul food restaurant, and scrapyard on three corners. An all-night laundromat on the newer fourth corner, windows steamed from the heat inside.

They sat at a picnic table, smoking cigars, under a large metal carport, a demo model on special sale for eight hundred dollars. Quinn had only seen it being used as a place for some of the Ditch's old men to gather or young men to play cards. The little building had become the unofficial meeting spot for black business in the district. Long as the Big Green Machine was parked out front, they'd have their privacy.

"Worked a break-in last night," Quinn said. "You remember a girl named Maggie Powers?"

"Nope," Boom said, shaking his head.

"She used to stay with her grandmother during the summers," Quinn said. "Back when we were kids. She used to run with us then. Real cute. Lots of freckles."

"Uh-huh."

"She just moved here," Quinn said. "And looks like her ex busted up her place. He didn't take anything, but he scared her good. She'd pulled a twelve-gauge from her closet and looked ready to use it."

"Momma Bear."

"You bet," Quinn said. "But I can't do a thing unless she wants to press charges."

"And she's not sure if it's her ex or not."

Boom was drinking a big bottle of Mountain Dew while Quinn drank coffee and smoked the rest of today's cigar. The tip glowed red in the darkness, the only other light coming from a sad little strand of blue Christmas lights strung along the carport. The smoke carried off into the warm wind blowing in a storm. Quinn's mind already back on Maggie Powers, recalling her skinny legs and scraped elbows climbing trees and running wild in the back creeks and endless woods. There was a little thunder in the distance, the smell of rain.

"She was good-looking," Boom said. "Wasn't she?"

"Why do you say that?"

"Why'd you bring her up?" Boom said. "You made a point of telling me about her freckles."

"I was trying to jog your memory," Quinn said.

117

"Sure, man," Boom said. "But she's married?"

"Divorced."

"No, you said 'about to be divorced,'" Boom said. "A big goddamn difference that ain't nobody needs to warn your ass about."

"That's why I have you," Quinn said. "To warn me. Because if I didn't have my own personal black Jiminy Cricket, I'd never get any advice from Jean. Or Caddy."

"Speaking of your sister . . ." Boom said.

Quinn tapped the cigar on the heel of his boot. "Those missing girls."

"Ana Maria and Tamika," he said. "Seems like their road winds up to Goddamn Cho Cho Porter and twists itself back around to Blue Daniels."

"Oh, shit," Quinn said.

"Problem is, no one seems to know where to find Blue Daniels."

Quinn reached for the cigar and took another puff. "How'd you get mixed up in all this mess with Caddy?" Quinn said.

"Girls been seen around Cho Cho's place," Boom said. "She knows I know Cho Cho and might get some answers better than the law."

"And did you?"

"Yeah," Boom said. "Blue Motherfucking Daniels. You know where he's at?"

"Blue ain't your friend," Quinn said. "Last time y'all got into it, you bit off his damn ear."

"Not the whole ear," Boom said, "just the lobe. You know, like Mike Tyson. But you tell me that the motherfucker didn't deserve it."

"Blue Daniels is a sick son of a bitch," Quinn said. "He's a damn triple-threat sex predator."

"OK," Boom said. "Tell me where I can find his ass."

Quinn didn't say anything. He just shook his head.

"Aw, c'mon, man."

"Jail," Quinn said. "I brought him in yesterday for parole violation. But I don't want you or Caddy going anywhere near the man."

"I can shake him loose better than you."

"I bet," Quinn said. "And what's he got to do with Ana Maria and Tamika?"

"Man was pimping them out right before they disappeared."

9

"You can't skimp on the buttermilk," Jean Colson said. "I mix it with just a little Louisiana Hot Sauce and always dip the chicken in the flour before it touches the milk. Fry it hot and quick. Do you see what I'm doing here, Quinn? Are you paying attention?"

"Yes, ma'am," Quinn said, standing in his mother's kitchen while "Burning Love" played in the next room. Fried chicken and Elvis being a way of life in the Colson family. "You know, I've been watching you do this since I could walk."

Jean liked to play Elvis loud while she cooked, converting little Jason to a fan at a young age. The poor kid having to lip-sync the song for the guests in the living room in a pair of gold sunglasses his grandmother got for him years ago. A lot of laughter and clapping, nearly as loud as the song, came from the living room. Jason seemed to enjoy it, lately billing himself as the ultimate Elvis tribute artist, half black and half white. Jean could not have been prouder.

"Now, I only made greens, peas, and cornbread," she said. "You told me to keep it simple and that's what I did. I don't want everyone thinking this is some kind of Fourth of July feast, although I did make two pies. Chocolate and lemon. You and Boom are going to fight over the chocolate because I only made one."

"I can't eat half a pie."

"Since when?"

"A kid eats a whole pie one time and the memory sticks with him forever."

"You see that oil?" Jean said. "Always use peanut oil and fry it hot as you can. Nobody likes soggy, greasy chicken. You want it crisp, only a few drops of oil when you pull it out."

"How long?"

"About fifteen minutes," Jean said, an authentic Graceland collectible apron tied around her neck and waist while she worked. So much Elvis shit in her kitchen, so little room. Back when he was a teenager, the Elvis collecting was fun. Now it had gotten out of hand. Elvis glasses. Elvis mugs. Elvis oven mitts. "You get the oil hot enough and you'll be sure to cook the chicken all the way through. While we wait—"

"You want me to be nice to Ophelia."

Jean looked up from the big silver pot where she was stirring a mix of collard, mustard, and turnip greens. "That's right," she said. "Do you think you can do that for me?"

"Yes, ma'am."

"Why do you say it like that?" Jean said. "All solemn. I invited her over here weeks ago, long before y'all broke up. And when I saw her at the funeral, I told her that I didn't care if you and her were no longer together, that she and I were still friends."

"Of course you did."

"There you go again, Quinn," Jean said. "Don't talk back to me. Don't talk like that to your momma. I will not be rude to that girl. She was good to you for a long time. And just because you and her don't see eye to eye sometimes doesn't mean that she's not welcome in my home."

"You can't forget I once ate a whole pie," Quinn said. "But you forget that Ophelia once threw a steak knife at me. That's not a big deal, right?"

"And what had you said to her?"

"It's fine," Quinn said. "It's fine. Glad she's here. I'll be polite. I'll give her some of my pie. But I'm not getting back together with that woman. It didn't work out and we've moved on."

"Hmm," Jean said, moving on from the pot of greens to the smaller pot of black-eyed peas, stirring and adding a little more salt and pepper. "Are you sure?"

"It was a mistake."

"How many pieces of chicken do you want?"

"Two," Quinn said. "Breast and a wing."

Someone switched up the records, and just when Quinn thought Elvis was finished, "The Wonder of You" blasted forth from the speakers. Jean hummed along to the sound of Elvis mixed with Jason's little voice, Jason trying to sound big and full to the dinner guests. Quinn peeked into the room, seeing the backs of Boom, Caddy, and Ophelia. Jason stood on top of Jean's coffee table, holding an imaginary microphone in his hand, gold glasses down over his eyes.

"You know you've screwed that boy up for life?" Quinn said.

"What kind of Southern boy doesn't know Elvis?"

"Most of them," Quinn said. "These days. Not many have grandmothers who actually saw him live."

"Meeting Elvis, seeing those shows, almost made the time I spent with your father worthwhile."

"Don't forget your kids," Quinn said. "Right?"

"That goes without saying, baby," Jean said. "Do you mind going on and setting the table? We're just about ready."

"I've always been curious about something," Quinn said.

Jean used a pair of tongs to place the fried chicken

on a large oval platter that had belonged to his grand-mother. She turned around and lifted off her apron, setting it on a kitchen chair.

"If Elvis had come on to you," Quinn said, "would you have left Dad?"

"You've got to be kidding," Jean said.

Quinn nodded, glad to hear it.

"In a damn New York second."

"Wait," Quinn said. "But did he? I mean, did Elvis ever come on to you?"

"Sometime you and me need to sit down and talk," she said. "There's so much about that time that's just a really wonderful blur. The Jungle Room. Vernon, George Klein, and the boys. Big talk. And so many guns. Now, take this chicken and get everyone set-tled down to dinner. And, do me a favor."

"Be polite to Ophelia."

"That's right," Jean said. "And do me one more favor and flip over that record. Put on 'Suspicious Minds.' I think that'll go just about perfect with the mood."

"Watch the hair," Fannie said.

Jonas Cord held her from behind, one hand up her Dolce & Gabbana dress while he kissed her neck. He'd been waiting for her in her room at the Golden Cherry. The room was dark and warm, humid after he'd just taken a shower, and smelling of aftershave. He was naked and ripped with muscle, ready to spring like a big crazy ape.

"And the dress, too," she said. "Be gentle with the dress, doll."

Cord took his free hand and unzipped her, slow and easy, the pink satin dropping from her shoulders, down her hips, and onto the green carpet. She stepped out of the dress as Jonas pulled her in to him, kissing her hard and pressing her big tits close. She wasn't wearing anything now but a lacy bra and panties, a pair of velvety pumps that climbed her ankles like a rose vine.

He moved his hand over her back, soft and slow, touching her gently.

"No," she said. "No. Don't be nice. Like this."

She gripped his hand and placed it on her meaty bottom, telling him to squeeze harder. "Smack it," she said. "Be rough. Be mean, soldier."

"You said—"

"I said don't mess my hair or tear my dress," she said. "But you know how I like it. Take the hill. Take the damn hill."

Jonas pushed Fannie down on the bed, pulling off her panties, Fannie up on her elbows, looking down at those gorgeous pumps still on her feet. The cars roared past the roadside motel, the neon flickering on the outline of the two golden cherries dangling from the sign. This room—her private room—being gutted, painted, and retooled into something out of a fifties **Vogue** magazine. Mid-century modern furniture, a big round bed with silk sheets. No one else used the room but her and Mingo when his girl was in town. And for the last six months, it had been her and this stocky, tough Marine.

He took it to her hard and fast, Fannie being the one who finished up on top, legs straddling him, while he lay flat on his back, gasping for air, and she slapped his face over and over. Right before she felt like things were going to all bust apart, she slapped him again, leaning down and biting his lower lip.

"Fannie," Cord said.

"Take the hill," Fannie said. "Damn you. Take the hill, Sergeant."

He did. And she followed. Fannie soon rolled off of him, forearm over her eyes, lying back in the sheets. She reached for her cigarillos and slim gold lighter.

"Ever think we might make love like normal people?" Cord asked. "Put on some slow music, dim the lights, and take it slow and easy."

"Nope."

"Why not?"

"Because I don't make love," Fannie said, clicking the flame and setting it to the tip of the cigarillo. She took a puff, reaching down with her free hand and untying the twirling straps of the pumps, kicking them loose onto the floor. "Be a sweetheart and do a search and rescue for my panties. I don't know where the hell they ended up."

Cord got out of bed and walked over by the door, snatching up the pair and tossing them onto the bed. He had all kinds of tattoos on his back of maps and guns, words in some weird language.

"You boys gonna take it easy for a while?" Fannie said.

Cord crawled back into bed, not bothering to cover himself up, plumping a pillow under his head, staring up at the twirling fan. "I'm not sure," he said. "Why?"

"Thought maybe that's why you came to see me."

"You know why I came to see you," he said. "Damn, Fannie. You bit the shit out of my lip. Am I bleeding?"

"Just a little," Fannie said. "Suck it up."

"One of Wilcox's buddies chopped up those cars," he said. "Their guts spread around half of Memphis."

"Doesn't matter," she said. "They couldn't touch me."

"Your buddies down on the Coast?"

"Mmm-hmm."

"Nice to have friends," he said.

"You boys must be pretty well set by now."

"I s'pose."

"Why not enjoy it?" Fannie asked, smoke scattering up into the fan's blades. "Take a vacation. Go down to the beach and spend some of all you got."

"That's not the point."

"How so, doll?"

"This ain't about the money."

"Everything's about the money, baby," she said. "Don't kid yourself. Why do you think I do what I do? You think I'd be dishing women and likker out down in Tibbehah County if it wasn't worth my damn time?"

"You got a stake," he said. "This is something we cooked up to keep from going crazy."

Fannie couldn't wrap her head around that one, turning over on her side, her breasts dropping against her prone forearm to the bed. She reached up and rested the ashtray on top of Cord's chest. "So let me get this straight," she said. "Y'all do this for fun?"

"It's more than fun," Cord said. "It's about keeping on running sharp. Sticking together as a unit. A family. Rick and I had some bad time of it when we got home. He was the one who came to me with this. And, I'll be goddamned, if that crazy motherfucker wasn't right."

"What about the kid?"

"Opie."

"Is that his real name?"

"Real as it gets," Cord said. Fannie ashed the tip of her cigarillo into the tray. Cord didn't move, just kept on fiddling with his lip, wiping the blood on the satin sheets.

"And none of y'all gives a shit about the money?"

"Did I tell you I was in AA before Rick found me?" Cord said. "Me. Sitting with a bunch of fucking losers, drinking coffee and smoking cigarettes. Eating cake and cookies, getting slow and fat. I was working security at a fucking shopping mall, busting black kids for stealing hundred-dollar sneakers. I wanted to fucking eat my gun."

"And this all works?"

"Running and gunning?" Cord said. "Sirens on our ass, ditching the cars, looking for new routes? Thinking and adapting with my brothers? Damn straight."

"You don't get bored?

"What do you mean?"

"Y'all boys are good at what you do," she said. "Maybe too good. Deputy Dawg and his crew here can't even find that van you used. Or know y'all headed out from the property up north."

"True."

"Wouldn't it be nice to face some resistance?"

"Without going to jail?" Cord said. "You get into some kind of shoot-out with cops and it's goddamn Butch and Sundance time. I'd rather not die in a Bon Jovi blaze of glory."

"I have something much better in mind for you," Fannie said, lifting herself up, draping her red hair down onto Cord's face, and pressing her lips and tits against him.

"What are you thinking?"

"I'd need to know that y'all boys would be up for the challenge."

"You know it."

"It's a test," she said. "A damn test of all tests."

Your mom said you'd eat half a pie," Ophelia Bundren said.

She and Quinn sat on his mother's back deck, the house still filled with laughter and more and more Elvis. The music had gone from serious and big seventies Elvis back to the sound tracks. Pretty much the way it always worked. The more boxed wine Jean Colson drank, the sillier Elvis's songs got. They were on to "Bossa Nova Baby" from **Fun in Acapulco**. If she drank way too much, it would all devolve into "Kissin' Cousins." "Kissin' Cousins" usually marked a turning point. Sometime after the second playing, Jean usually passed out cold.

"My mother is prone to exaggeration," Quinn said.

"Boom ate half a pie."

"Stick around and he'll eat the whole damn thing," Quinn said. "He outweighs me by a hundred pounds."

The deck had been rebuilt after the big storm,

restained the same deep red, and still facing a small rolling hill where Quinn used to play war. Quinn and Caddy's fort still up there somewhere, hidden in the pine trees. Jason's toys now mixed with his mother's and uncle's. Only last week, Jean found two buried G.I. Joes, missing since 1986.

Quinn took a last bite of pie and set down the plate and fork. Ophelia pulled her legs to her chest, chin resting on her knees. An odd, dark-headed girl with big dark eyes, she spoke in slow, serious ways. Even when she was trying to make a joke. Morticians didn't make a lot of jokes. She still had on her professional clothes, coming straight from work, a black pantsuit with black silk top, a name tag reading OPHELIA BUNDREN, SERVICE FACILITATOR.

"I shouldn't have come," she said.

"Of course you should."

"I wanted to talk to you face-to-face," she said. "No rumors. Not having to hear it from these gossip-obsessed folks in town."

Quinn looked at her. He took a deep breath.

"I'm seeing someone."

He nodded. He let out a long breath.

"Nice man," she said. "Lives in Tupelo. He sells medical equipment. Steady. Solid."

"No midnight patrols."

"Or gunfights," she said. "Or all those ups and downs."

"We've had a few."

"More than a few," Ophelia said. "I just don't think we're what each other needs."

"And what's that?"

"Push and pull," she said. "I push you away because you can't be around whenever I want you. And then I pull you back because nothing can change. You push me away because you don't like the tension but pull me back when you're feeling lonely. It was convenience. Something to do while you got straight with what happened to you and Anna Lee."

"It's complicated."

"Everything is."

Quinn smiled at her. She reached out her hand and squeezed it tight.

"Is he good to you?" Quinn said.

"Very," she said. "And he's never been married. Has a nice family. Good folks."

"But I bet they don't have Elvis fried-chicken parties."

"Nope," she said. "I'll definitely miss that."

"Ophelia," Quinn said. "I forgive you for throwing that steak knife into my wall."

Ophelia smiled at him. "Who said I was aiming at the wall?"

10

"I call bullshit," Wilcox said not five minutes after walking into Earnestine and Hazel's bar, watching Opie and Cord finish up their game of pool. Cord was solid-built, dependable, and tough as hell, but not worth a shit with a cue.

"No, man," Opie said. "It's true. This place is one of the most haunted spots in America."

"It looks about as haunted as my butthole," Wilcox said, lighting up a cigarette. He was still in his gym clothes, a little sweaty after finishing up a crossfit routine with Crissley. Crissley lived a few blocks over in Memphis on South Main Street in a brewery converted to loft apartments. She'd gone home to shower. He'd gone for a smoke and a couple of beers.

"It's true," Opie said. "You see that jukebox over there? Sometimes it has a mind of its own."

"Does it moan?" Wilcox said. "Or does it float?"

"It chooses the right song for the right moment." Opie motioned over to the bartender, back turned, flipping burgers and onions on the grill. "Go ask him. He said one time a woman walked in right after she'd signed her divorce papers and that song came on, 'D-I-V-O-R-C-E,' by Tammy Wynette. Like out of nowhere. No one slipped in a quarter, no one punched up that number."

The bar was all dim lights and scuffed floors within a stand-alone two-story brick building across the street from the train station. A red-and-green neon sign shone in a little oval window fronting Main.

"Another time, a guy came in and 'That Smell' started up," Opie said. "You know, Skynyrd?"

"Of course I know that song," Wilcox said. "That's like asking me if I know fucking 'Happy Birthday.'"

"Well," Opie said. "He'd just stepped out of a cab where a guy had just barfed. You just can't make that shit up. You know, 'that smell' because the barf stunk so bad?"

"If it plays 'Back in Black,' I'll believe it," Wilcox said, blowing out some smoke. "I got on a pair of black underwear at this very moment."

Cord leaned on his pool cue like it was a staff, grinning just a bit, not saying a thing but amused a bit by the shit talk between the two. Sometimes between real friends that was about as good as it got. If you can't fuck with a guy, then he's not really your buddy.

"I did two hundred push-ups and sit-ups," Wilcox said. "And you should've see Crissley. Christ on a stick. She puts a fifty-pound barbell between her legs for a pelvic thrust. I mean, I've been in some real hot spots before, but I believe that woman just might kill me."

"Wishful thinking," Cord said.

"He speaks," Wilcox said. "Are you going to try and knock a ball in? Or are you going to let Opie beat your ass?"

"Could you do any better?"

"Probably not," Wilcox said, drinking down half of his Pabst Blue Ribbon. The other boys drinking Pabst, too, as that shit was the house beer. Wilcox had been born and bred in Memphis, lived in east Memphis, and went to Christian Brothers, but sometimes the hipsters around here were too much. Cord and Opie bunking somewhere down in south Memphis at a crap hole apartment off Winchester Road. "So where's the fire? I just got invited to take a long, intimate shower with my woman, but instead I'm jawing with you two dicks."

"We need to talk," Cord said.

"We're talking."

"About a job."

Wilcox looked around the bar, no one except

some turquoise-haired chick making time with the bartender. The jukebox now playing a song called "Portland, Oregon" that held no special significance but probably meant a damn assload to that phantom in the machine.

"We've got a job," Wilcox said. "Tomorrow morning. Or have y'all forgot?"

"Sure," Cord said. "But what about after that? We talked about some places in north Alabama. But nothing's set."

Wilcox finished his beer, belched, and tipped the end toward Cord. "Initiative," he said. "I like your thinking. Where's this bank?"

"It's not a bank." Cord cut his eyes over at Opie.

Opie grinned. "Tell him, Cord," he said. "Better than any bank. Maybe enough to wrap up this whole damn mission."

"That would have to be a shit ton of money," Wilcox said. "Because this latest deployment won't be over for a while. Are you guys homesick? What is it, Ope? You missin' those saggy old broads doing tequila shots off your pecker?"

Cord walked off to the bar while he and Opie continued the unfinished game, Wilcox damn near catching up with Cord's shitty play. Cord returned with three cold PBRs and an ashtray for Wilcox. Wilcox set the ashtray on a barstool and waited to hear what kind of crazy shit these two had concocted. Wilcox had to remember he was the leader of this unit, one time overhearing these guys wanting to open up a goddamn Popsicle stand in New Orleans.

"Two bad motherfuckers with a drug house down on EP Boulevard," Cord said.

"OK."

"They control pretty much all the action around Memphis."

"I'm listening."

"Won't be like what we've been doing," Cord said. "These guys won't lay down. They shoot back. Got guards, dogs, all kind of bad shit waiting for us."

"Man," Wilcox said, drinking a little beer, mulling it over. "Don't sweet-talk me about it."

"Could be upwards of a dozen guys," he said. "They expect to be hit every minute. But the take would be a hell of a lot more than some cash drawers in Bumfuck, Mississippi."

"I like it," Wilcox said.

"It won't all be ours," Cord said. "But a good bit will."

"What do you say, Ope?" Wilcox asked.

Opie shrugged, thought about it for a second, and nodded. The jukebox went silent, then popped a forty-five on the platter, reloading with a solid snick. The horns started to blare the first bit of "Ring of Fire."

Wilcox laughed and nearly spilled his beer. "Well, well," he said. "I'll be goddamned."

"**You got my vote**," Maggie said. "Call the sheriff's office and get taken to the Sonic."

"I got voted out of office once," Quinn said. "It can't happen again."

"You do this for everyone?"

"You bet," Quinn said.

They sat on top of a metal table, drinking milk shakes and watching the cars come and go on each side of the drive-in. Quinn had gotten a big ice cream cone for Maggie's son, Brandon, a funny little blond kid who took a lot of interest riding in the Big Green Machine. Completely against protocol, he hit the light bar and the sirens as they headed into town. It was pretty easy to make friends with a kid when you wore a badge and drove a big truck.

"Brandon, you know Jason Colson?"

He shook his head.

"That's my nephew," Quinn said. "He's in third grade."

"The third graders are mean," he said. "They chase us around the playground. One of them threw a rock at me and I didn't even do nothing. Thanks for the ice cream."

Brandon ran off toward the plastic playground and began to climb to the top of the slide, turning back at the top to give a thumbs-up to his mom. Big night in Jericho. Not much else to do but hit the Sonic, cruise the Square, and maybe run the back roads with a six-pack, like Quinn and Boom had done all those years ago. Maggie had on her blue nurse scrubs, black Chucks, no socks, her hair twisted up on top of her head. Silver bracelets jingled on her wrists.

"You ever think you'd come back?" Maggie said.

Quinn lifted his eyes. "Nope."

"Why did you?"

"Unexpected circumstances," he said. "My uncle died. There was business to tend to."

"I heard," she said, looking happy and relaxed in the neon light, kicking her feet back and forth, sipping on a milk shake. "I'm sorry. I remember him coming into the Fillin' Station when I was a kid. He was a big man, larger than life. He sort of reminded me of John Wayne, with that hat and the rancher coat."

"He left me the coat," Quinn said. "And his farm."

"That must be nice," Maggie said. "I've started a little garden in the back of the house. My grannie had let the flower beds and garden go when she got sick. But I've been tilling them up over the winter, getting them ready for spring. I compost everything. Coffee grounds, eggshells."

"I don't do much farming," Quinn said. "I have cattle. And two horses my dad left at my place. It's too much work. I don't even ride."

"Why don't you tell him to take 'em back?" she said.

"I would," Quinn said, "if I could find him. Why don't y'all come out sometime? I have a little pond. Brandon could fish."

Maggie had a lot of freckles across her cheeks and nose and forehead. One of those girls who'd get a nice reddish golden glow in the summertime, but not until after they caught hell in the sun. "My ex won't take him fishing," she said. "He picks him up, takes him to Memphis, walks around the zoo, and then buys him a big stuffed animal. He puts in a few hours and acts like he's a goddamn hero."

"Supposed to be pretty next week," he said. "Y'all come on out."

Maggie colored a bit. "You barely know us."

"You think so?" Quinn said, smiling. "I've known you for years."

Maggie smiled back and glanced away with those really nice light green eyes. They didn't speak for a while, sitting with their shoulders not quite touching, watching her towheaded boy raise hell on the slide with a couple of other boys. The kid looked for a second like he might try to leap from the top stairs, and Maggie stood to stop him. But Brandon just turned around and laughed and went down the slide.

"Shit," Maggie said. "He really likes to screw with me. Too damn much like his father."

"Who watches him while you're at the hospital?"

"My neighbor," she said. "Nice old lady. She was

a friend of my grandmother. It's good for now. I really don't have any other options. I don't have family here, just meeting some friends. Night shift is hell."

Quinn nodded and didn't ask any more. He clasped his hands in front of him, swallowed, and said, "You want me to do anything about your ex?"

"No," she said. "But thank you. Probably just some kids messing around. Nothing was broken. Even the TV is OK."

Maggie's reddish brown hair fell a bit from her bun and she reached up and rewrapped it. He watched her lean, muscular arms and nice shoulders, the funky black and blue nail polish on each hand.

"You were always here for the summer," he said. "Like clockwork. And then you were just gone. I don't think I've seen you since I was sixteen."

She nodded. "That thing with the Taylor boy scared the crap out of my parents," she said. "My dad didn't want me up here anymore. And my grandmother knew I'd been friends with him. She never said, but I think she agreed."

"Nobody seems to know what really happened."

Maggie shook her head. "Nope," she said. "He just went into the woods one day with his rifle and his daddy found his body a few days later."

Quinn nodded. It had been the biggest thing in Tibbehah County since the time he'd been lost a few years before. The boy's death had been ruled a suicide, but his family and friends never believed it.

"I guess I don't have to tell you," Maggie said, nudging her knee into his, trying to lighten the mood, "'A Country Boy Can Survive.' Guess that couldn't have been easy."

"It was a lot more than just surviving."

Maggie tilted her head to watch Quinn. He didn't say anything, just looked into her eyes and studied her mouth, feeling good to be sitting next to this girl who'd just walked right out of his memory. And now they were drinking milk shakes and talking about things he hadn't thought about for years.

"I thought you were seeing one of the Bundrens who runs the funeral home?"

"I was."

"But not now?"

Quinn shook his head. "Since I got home, not much has worked out," he said. "Sometimes I think I do better alone."

"Oh, yeah?" Maggie said, tapping the brim of Quinn's cap down into his eyes. "Me, too. I've made too many mistakes. It's good just to be by yourself and make sense of things."

"That's a solid plan," Quinn said. "Don't you think?"

Caddy hopped up into Boom's truck and slammed the door.

"You sure you don't mind doing this?"

"Hell no," Boom said.

"Quinn said he'd handle it."

"Quinn can talk to Blue," Boom said. "But he can't reason with him. At least not legally. Your brother gets real touchy about that kind of shit."

Caddy took a deep breath and set her hands on her knees as Boom knocked the truck in gear and rolled away from The River. Maybe she could pray on it more, or wait for Quinn or Lillie to come up with something, but sometimes you had to take action. She knew what Boom was going to have to do and she had prayed on it. **For if any be a hearer of the Word, and not a doer, he is like unto a man beholding his natural face in a glass.**

"What are you thinking about, Caddy Colson?"

"I can come up with a dozen Bible verses of why I should do this. And a dozen more why I should have patience."

"Ain't no Bible verse about a man like Blue Daniels," Boom said. "At least not in the New Testament. He's a wicked, old-school motherfucker."

"You sure you know where he lives?"

"Well," Boom said. "I know where he stay at. He bailed out this morning. He won't go home, 'cause if he go to his place, he might wake up shot. He's staying with a woman named Dynasty Stewart. Dynasty's sick in the head. She's a thief. Can't stop stealing stuff. Goes over to Tupelo and spends all day working the Walmart and shopping mall. Can't leave Blue alone. Babies his ass."

"Just what did he do to you?"

"See," Boom said, "it went something like this. I beat his ass at spades one night down in the Ditch. Must've been three hundred dollars. Blue don't like to lose. That little motherfucker come up on me outside Club Disco with a goddamn butcher knife as big as your arm."

"And he cut you?"

"No," Boom said. "But he said he was gonna gut me like a fish. Told me if I gave him the keys to my truck, he'd let me go. So I took that knife out of his hands and rammed his goddamn head into the door. When I stop, you can still see the dents from that man's hard head."

"Then you let him go."

"Yeah," Boom said. "But Blue wouldn't quit. I had to leave him with a message not to fuck with me again. I was in no mood to be fucked with that night. You know how you get when you drink, not really seeing the world as it is but the way you want it to be?"

"I don't really remember," Caddy said. "I was a straight blackout drunk."

"I guess you'd call me a mean drunk," Boom said. "I bit that motherfucker's ear off and spit it into the woods. He must've found it 'cause next time I saw him, I saw it was all sewn back together like Frankenstein. But, man, he was pissed. Told me next time we locked horns, he was gonna shoot me."

"Were you scared?"

"Shit." Boom cut his eyes over at Caddy, turning off the Jericho Square and heading due south for Sugar Ditch, big hand on the wheel, cool breeze blowing through the cab. The whole cab smelling of cigarettes and pine air freshener that wasn't doing its job. Boom drove with his left hand, the right metal appendage down on the gear shift, working it as good, or probably better, than someone with two hands. He smoked as he drove. Caddy stayed quiet, starting to think this was a hell of a bad idea.

"I can talk to him," Caddy said. "You can stay out of it."

"You think he's a reasonable man?"

They slowed and turned off a country road, running down into Sugar Ditch proper, the shanties and shotgun cottages running along that foul little creek bed where the plumbing flowed, heaped with washing machines and car parts, trash, and debris. Place smelled so bad that some of the old-timers said it was almost sweet, giving the decaying district its name.

"I can try," Caddy said.

"No, ma'am," Boom said. "You asked for my help. And now you got it."

Boom drove on up to a little alcove off the dirt road and killed the lights, engine still running. Both of them watching a faded green trailer up on blocks, glowing in the moonlight.

"What now?" Caddy said.

Boom reached for the door handle with his good hand and looked to her. "I'd leave it running," Boom said. "If Blue comes out shooting, run over his ass."

11

"Don't worry, Ordeen," Fannie said, her red Italian boots kicked up on her glass desk. "I didn't call you up here to ream you out. I would've done that shit down on the floor. I called you up here to tell me a little more about your friends up in Memphis. The Twins."

"K-Bo and Shortbox?" Ordeen said. "They ain't my friends. I'm just the delivery boy, Miss Fannie. I work for you."

"And whatever we talk about in this office stays right here?"

"Yes, ma'am."

"Above all things, I appreciate loyalty," she said, reaching for her wooden box where she kept her cigarillos. "You're as smart and loyal as they come."

The stocky black kid nodded, dressed in black pants and a red T-shirt saying VIENNA'S PLACE, the silhouette of a curvy girl in white. A former high school football player who might've gone on to bigger things if he hadn't gotten mixed up with a football coach who preferred showering with children to winning games.

"Yes, ma'am," he said. "Appreciate that."

"You like those boys?"

Ordeen shook his head. "They mean as fuck," he said. "Just as soon put a bullet between your eyes as hug you. I ain't never turned my back on either of 'em. Not that I can tell which one's which."

"You've done real good since you came on with me," Fannie said, choosing one of the stubby cigarillos and lighting up. "You helped me run some stuff with those boys that I'm not real proud of."

Ordeen nodded, showing her he understood she was talking about those girls who sometimes came through Tibbehah and made their way up to Memphis or over to Atlanta. He was a good, tough kid who knew how to keep them in line while keeping his damn mouth shut.

"Mingo said you wanted to know how things look up there, around the wing shop and out back where they detail those cars."

"That's right," Fannie said, leaning back in her chair, cigarillo loose in her fingers. "The Twins have been down to Tibbehah, but I've never seen their

148

operation." Smoke trailed up into the swirling fan. Downstairs, the dance music pumped, shaking the office floor. It sounded like money.

"Not much to it," Ordeen said. "They got the restaurant out front called Wing Machine. Just a couple booths, not many places to sit. You order right there at the register. Those Twins make some mean wings. You better not go peepee after you done 'cause it will fucking tear you up."

"I'll try and remember," she said. "But what about the back room, facing the alley, where they run the detail shop?"

"Oh, that," Ordeen said. "Yeah, I been in there once with Nito. Twins don't like anyone in that place they don't know. That's where they keep their shit and the money. You try not to look around or nothing, keep your eyes straight on the boys even through there's a mountain of cash sitting right there on the table."

"Just sitting out in the open?"

"They got a counter," he said. "I figured they count it up and bundle it. I didn't ask no questions. Truth be known, I wanted to get the hell out of there. Being around that much cash makes me nervous as hell. Especially with what happened to Craig Houston."

"I thought the Mexicans cut off his head."

"They did," Ordeen said. "But it looked like the Twins were prepping in case they come back and finish them off, too."

"Lots of guns?"

"Hell yes," Ordeen said. "I mean, yes, ma'am. They got boys with rifles and shit, walking around like it's the Old West. K-Box wears two guns on his waist, just ready for that back door to bust open and, **pop-pop-pop**, start taking out his niggas."

"Could you draw it for me?"

"What do you mean?"

"Like this," Fannie said, leaning forward, the deep V-neck of her dress spilling open. Not thinking it was a bad thing to let the kid get a peek at the goodies stuffed in that lacy black bra. She pushed a pad of paper toward him and tossed him a pen. "Like a diagram. Where do the Twins usually work? And where are the doors out the back and into the wing shop?"

"Hard to remember, Miss Fannie."

"Try, Ordeen," she said. "Do your best."

"Yes, ma'am."

He started to draw, putting Xs in places for all the armed men he'd seen. There were a whole lot of Xs by the time he finished up. The bass music kept on pounding the floor beneath them as she took the pad of paper and studied what Ordeen had drawn. For a kid who didn't graduate high school, he had a real way with drawing. Maybe he could go to architecture school after he got tired of being a titty bar bouncer.

"What's that building there?"

"That's the detail shop," Ordeen said. "It's separate

150

from Wing Machine. The wings is just part of that building. It's in a strip mall, with a hair salon and another place sells cigarettes and bongs and shit. You want to get your car detailed, you roll around back into that metal building and they get started."

"You just roll on in?" Fannie said.

"Yes, ma'am," he said. "What are you thinking?"

"Don't ask questions."

"Yes, ma'am," Ordeen said, standing up.

"And don't mention this to anyone," Fannie said, blowing out some smoke. "Whatever happens to those Twins was of their own making. Nobody likes folks who are selfish. Nobody can just up and own Memphis. That's a good way to get your dick in the deep fryer."

Blue Daniels, or at least a man Caddy assumed to be Blue, stepped out of the trailer in a white undershirt and dark jeans and started waving around a pistol. Even with the sound of the motor running, she could hear his threats, telling Boom he was some kind of crazy son of a bitch showing up at his woman's place. Boom put his hands up, stepping back into the dirt road, but Blue, a short black man with gold teeth, was not standing down, moving right for him.

The gun went from being held down at his leg to pointing right at Boom's chest, and Caddy didn't even think about it. She knocked that beat-up truck into gear, hit the lights, and punched the gas. She must've knocked Blue Daniels five or six feet.

As the dust cleared in the headlights, she threw open the door and walked to where Boom was standing over the man. She saw a gun in the road and picked it up, trying to give it to Boom, but he shook her off, making sure she kept it.

"Not smart, Blue," Boom said. "I told you to check yourself."

"Motherfucker," Blue said, head lolling, eyes looking hazy in the dust, gravel marks on his bloodied face where he'd landed. "Goddamn."

Boom squatted down to look at him. He had big bug eyes and gold teeth, white tank top covered with dead grass, dirt, and blood. He had one ear that looked as if it had been chewed on.

"I'm gonna kill your ass, Boom Kimbrough."

"You been promising that for a long time," Boom said. "Guess my truck got in your way again."

"Motherfucker."

Caddy stood back from them, closer to the truck, holding the pistol in her hand, not pointing it but keeping it close and at the ready. She'd already shot one man in her life and she had no desire to do it again.

"Need to ask you a question," Boom said.

"You run me over and now you want to talk?" Blue said. "What's wrong with you, man? What's wrong with you?"

152

"You were running two girls," Boom said. "Mexican girl named Ana Maria and a little black girl named Tamika Odum."

"What you mean 'running'?" Blue said, his teeth shining a bright gold in the headlights, lip busted and bleeding.

"Pimping," Boom said. "You had those girls down at Cho Cho Porter's juke last month. She wouldn't let you inside and you were selling out some time in your truck. Go ahead, man. Go ahead and say I lie."

"You gone crazy."

"But I don't lie," Boom said, stepping up close and laying his big boot on Blue's chest, pushing him down on the road. A woman appeared from the mouth of the trailer, yelling for them to stop, to leave Blue alone or she was going to call the police. She was screaming and carrying on and seemed to be every bit as crazy as Boom had promised.

"I'll call the sheriff," Caddy said. "Fine by you?"

"What'd you say those girls' names was again?" Blue said. "I know a lot of girls."

"Tamika and Ana Maria," Boom said. "A couple of damn kids, man."

Blue swallowed and wiped the blood from his face, still lying down in the center of the road, looking up at the big full moon, Caddy, standing back, obscured from his view behind the hot headlights. "They tole me they was eighteen."

"So you were running them?"

"They ask me," Blue said. "Goddamn. You know I'm in the life, player. Pussy is what I do. Some little girl want to throw it at me, it ain't something I'm thinking on. I drive them to where they go and get paid."

"How much you get paid?"

"What's it matter?"

As Boom stepped down hard with his boot on the center of Blue's narrow chest, Blue let out a long whoosh of air and started kicking his legs in the air like he was riding a bicycle.

"How much?"

"Forty dollars."

"Girls were fifteen," Boom said.

"I ain't their goddamn daddy," he said, spitting out more blood. "They a couple damn hos. Not worth shit."

Caddy felt a little nudge somewhere down deep in her chest and she stepped out from behind the lights and ran for him. She kicked Blue hard enough in the ribs that he turned over, his face back down in the dirt.

"Why you coming at me like this, Boom? You want to eat off my other ear, you sick son of a bitch?"

"Where are they?"

"Don't know, man."

"You pimping them," Boom said. "That means you keep on pimping them until they knocked-up. Or dead."

"Aw, c'mon."

"Let me call the sheriff," Caddy said. "I'll call him right now."

"And what?" Blue said. "You tell 'im you call me out and run me down with a truck?"

"Where are they?"

"Help me up," Blue said. "I want to see who you got with you? Who that little white lady? So damn tough. You tough, little girl? You want to play some? Get on down in the dirt with ole Blue?"

"You move another inch and I'll bust you fucking wide open, man," Boom said.

Boom reached down and yanked the man up by his belt, setting him down on the ground like he was nothing but a bundle of sticks. The sudden movement of it, the big burst of the strength of Boom Kimbrough, threw Blue off and he had a hard time standing and keeping his feet. All bloody, his head swimming.

"Those girls are gone."

"Where?" Caddy said.

"Don't know."

From down the dirt road, Caddy heard the deep rumbling of a big engine and flashing lights from the front of some kind of truck. A siren sounded, **woop-woop**, a couple of times, a spotlight beam flashing to where they stood looking down at Blue Daniels. His girlfriend had called the sheriff's office down to the Ditch.

"Talk quick," Boom said.

Blue looked down the road at the truck stopping, the sound of gravel crunching under boots as someone walked toward them. Caddy saw the tall shadow and heard the voice of Lillie Virgil telling them to all stand still, stay where they are, show their fucking hands. They all did as they were told.

"I sold them," Blue said under his breath.

"What?" Caddy said.

"I sold their ass to that white lady," Blue said. "That madam at the truck stop. Fannie Hathcock."

12

"Anyone moves," Rick Wilcox yelled, "and I'll shoot 'em right in the pussy."

Nobody moved. Especially the old women. Everyone was silent, kneeling in the middle of the Potts Camp bank, hands on top of their heads. It was the next morning, after shooting pool with the boys, and they were at it bright and early. Sixty miles from Memphis, a little town right up on the Holly Springs National Forest, more than two hundred thousand acres of rolling hills, dense forests, and a good green swatch of Mississippi pines. They had the Kawasakis gassed and ready to go not five minutes from the bank.

Opie worked the drawers that morning, Wilcox on overwatch, keeping the four tellers and two loan officers honest. Only one customer this morning, an elderly black man in oily coveralls making a two-hundred-dollar deposit. Wilcox told him to put his money in his pocket and get down on his knees. "We're all gonna make America great again," Wilcox said behind the Trump mask, unable to resist.

Opie was quick, maybe quicker than Wilcox, hitting the drawers, and he stayed away from the vault. They'd hit the vault only if they knew it was a target-rich environment. This town wasn't worth tacking on the time. No Walmart deliveries, no local factory payroll. Amazing what you could find out online.

Opie tossed the sack over the drawers and vaulted himself up and over the teller's desk. Wilcox looking at his watch, sixty seconds. Man, he was going to have to hear about that shit all the way back to Memphis. Nobody had done a faster exercise, even during the practice and training phase.

Cord backed up the truck, this time the boys stealing a nice V-8 Tundra with a crew cab. He and Opie were out the door just as fast as they had entered, Wilcox throwing down a dummy IED, saying that if anyone got up within five minutes, they'd be picking body parts off the walls.

Opie tossed the black bag in the truck bed and jumped in the backseat. Wilcox rode shotgun, leaving on the mask until they were well clear of the bank. They drove at a steady sixty miles an hour until they got to the turnoff into the forest. A local policeman passed them, hauling ass back toward the bank.

"How much?" Wilcox said.

"I don't know," Opie said. "Piss-poor. Maybe forty grand. At the most."

"Shit," Wilcox said.

"I'm tired of this," Cord said. "Aren't y'all tired of this? There's only so long we can keep crossing the state line for some pocket change."

"You call forty grand pocket change?" Wilcox said, taking off the mask, putting his gloved fingers through the eyeholes. "You know, these Donald J. masks aren't real."

"Are you in?" Cord said. "Or do you want us to keep fucking around with Mom and Pop?"

"You know I prefer a little resistance," Wilcox said, Cord stepping on the gas a little more, moving that truck up to eighty now. Wilcox watching for the turn coming up soon. "But how the hell can a damn chicken-wing shop have that kind of money?"

"Like I said," Cord said, seeing the turn at the same time Wilcox did and turning the wheel hard and fast. "They're fucking drug dealers. It's a drug house. The biggest fucking drug house in Memphis."

"Says your finger man."

"Yep."

"And who is he?"

"I can't say."

"Then who am I to trust them?"

The truck rocketed down the back road, gravel flying up behind, Cord taking two turns, barely taking notice. "Do you trust me?" Cord said.

Wilcox didn't say anything. He took in a deep breath, letting down the window with his gloved hand, feeling high and light but not as good as he felt during battle. When the bullets were on you and you lived to tell the story, nothing felt better.

"OK," Wilcox said. "Tell me everything you know about these boys."

Opie leaned up between the seats and placed a hand on each's shoulder. "I knew it," he said. "I just knew it. Hot damn."

"Just what the hell did you hope to accomplish?" Lillie Virgil said, hands on hips, looking down at Caddy and Boom in the sheriff's office boardroom. "Y'all should be charged with aggravated assault."

"Against Blue Daniels?" Boom said. "C'mon, Lillie. That's giving the law a goddamn gift."

"Maybe you don't get the law, Boom," Lillie said. "I don't care if you kick ole Charlie Manson in the nuts, it's still assault. The shitbird status of the victim doesn't make it any better."

Caddy's hands were still shaking, now coming up on five hours since she hit Blue with the truck. Lillie had called in Reggie Caruthers to help bring in her, Boom, Blue, and Blue's girlfriend, Dynasty. Lillie driving her and Boom to the jail and not speaking the whole way. That was late last night. And now it was six a.m. and they were no closer to leaving the jail.

"Are you going to tell Quinn?" Caddy asked.

"Goddamn right, I'm telling Quinn," she said. "He's not only the sheriff, he's my boss. I don't tell him and it's my ass. Do y'all know what kind of crazy son of a bitch you're messing with?"

Boom nodded. "Yeah."

"And you?" Lillie asked, looking toward Caddy.

"He was pimping out Tamika and Ana Maria," Caddy said. "No one's seen those girls since he was offering them up for forty bucks a throw at Cho Cho Porter's place."

"You mean **Goddamn** Cho Cho Porter," Lillie said. "When we get a call from dispatch, that's how she says it. What's your address? And the woman says, 'Everyone know where Goddamn Cho Cho stay at.'"

"You going to charge us?" Boom said. "Because I got shit to do."

Lillie just stared at Boom, shaking her head, trying to calm herself but not doing much of a job. She rubbed her temples in thought and started to speak but closed her mouth.

"We went to the Ditch to talk to Blue," Boom said, "and he just went plain crazy. Waving that gun around, threatening me, and then chasing me out in the street, where Caddy accidentally ran over his ass."

Lillie dropped her head into her hand, closing her eyes and rubbing her temples. "Accidentally?"

"That's right," Boom said.

"That's the way you see it, Preacher Colson?"

"I'm not a preacher," Caddy said. "Never have been. Never want to be."

"Is that what happened?" Lillie said. "You and Boom taking a little ride down to Sugar Ditch to talk to Blue Daniels and he went so damn crazy he hopped in front of Boom's truck?"

Caddy didn't speak, thinking. Again, she had the flash of half a dozen Bible verses on each side of things. But she nodded, looking to Boom, not wanting him to get into any trouble. "Sure," she said. "Didn't you find his pistol?"

Lillie nodded.

"Didn't know felons could possess guns," Boom said. "Even down in Mississippi."

"He wasn't even supposed to be within five hundred feet of Dynasty," Lillie said. "She has a restraining order on him after he put her in the hospital last time. Between the shoplifting in Tupelo and the problems with men, that girl needs to be institutionalized."

"So why you messing with us, Lillie?" Boom said.

"You don't need directions to the bad guy. You know where he's at."

Lillie blew out her breath, taking a seat at the table down at the end away from Boom and Caddy. She folded her hands, leaned in, and said, "I can't just let you go."

"Why not?"

"Because you two broke the law," Lillie said. "And now I'm worried about you both. What did you think, that Blue Daniels was gonna have a come-to-Jesus moment and tell you the truth about those girls? I don't care how much Boom whipped his ass or how far you knocked him with that truck. People like Blue won't tell the truth. Shit, they don't know how."

"Nope," Boom said.

Lillie looked to Boom, Caddy nodding at him.

"Reason you can't find those girls is 'cause Blue Daniels sold them," Boom said.

"Wait," Lillie said. "Wait one goddamn second. What are you talking about?"

Caddy caught Boom's eye and nodded again, knowing the only way they were going to find those girls was to get help from the sheriff's office and be-yond. No telling where those girls had ended up.

"Where'd they go?" Lillie said. "Tell me what he said."

"Will you let us go?" Boom said.

"Boom Kimbrough, I love you like a brother," Lillie said. "But, son of a bitch, you put me in a real tight spot. How about simple assault?"

Boom shook his head.

"Come on, that's a bullshit charge."

"Not to Old Man Skinner," Boom said. "He's looking for any reason to fire my ass."

Lillie looked damn tired to Caddy, heavy-lidded and worn-out. But less physically exhausted than just put-out that she was having to handle their mess.

"OK," Lillie said. "What did Blue tell you? And if you try and lie to me, I'll wake up Quinn and tell him to keep y'all here all damn day."

There was a lot of fog that morning, steam rising up out of pastures, obscuring roads, making driving slow. Quinn was behind the wheel of the Big Green Machine, Hondo riding shotgun, with a thermos of black coffee between them in the console. He'd started off making the early rounds, trying to take on many of the same responsibilities of his deputies: early checks of local businesses, check for road conditions after heavy rains, and wellness checks of some of the older folks deep in the county. About the time he'd made sure that Mr. Williams was still alive, Quinn always being surprised by seeing the ninety-two-year-old heavy drinker and smoker come to the door in his bathrobe and offer him some eggs, he was on to running possible escape routes of the bank robbers. He'd been down the same roads time and again since the robbery but kept feeling like he and Lillie had missed something, maybe a patch of that white van showing in a clearing of trees or somewhere down in a creek bed or up a deer trail.

Hondo could've cared less, head out of the window, tongue lolling, while Quinn drank coffee and turned off onto Yellow Leaf Road, dispatch chatter battling it out with a new Sturgill Simpson CD. He could give equal attention to both.

The road ran up from Yellow Leaf, a little hamlet about eight miles northeast of Jericho, into the wilds of the north part of Tibbehah. He wound down broken roads and cleared land, deep patches of second-growth woods, and deep plantings of pines for harvest. The trailers and cabins thinned the farther you drove north, the mist collecting, almost swallowing the truck whole, and then breaking, him running free, following creeks and pastures up into parts of Tibbehah that hadn't changed much in fifty years.

Quinn was recalling this forgotten part of the county where he and his uncle used to take metal detectors to hunt for Civil War relics when he nearly passed a road that had been cut off for years. Sometime long ago it had been the Jenkins place, but that family had died before Quinn's time. It was closed now, with padlocked gates and a lot of NO TRES-

PASSING signs. Quinn had passed it a couple of times already that week, dismissing it as an escape route since the road came to a dead end a mile up the hill.

He parked the truck and whistled for Hondo to get out with him, Hondo already on high alert for a little walkabout. Quinn brought his coffee with him, stretching after the last hour in the truck, feeling the chill coming on from the day, a mist breaking apart into the hills but lingering down below.

Hondo trotted at his side, sniffing the air. Quinn reached down and scratched his pricked ears, thinking the house was somewhere around here. He recalled years ago, back when he'd been a kid, breaking into it and finding a mess of furniture, a piano turned to shit, shattered windows, and a roof caving in. No one had bothered to clean it out after the last resident died.

And there had been a barn. A big, ragged barn filled with two rusted-out tractors and lots of snakes. So many black snakes, grown fat from gobbling up the rats, that it was impossible to shoot them all. Quinn kept on walking, seeing deep into the woods and weeds the old structures still hanging on, although mostly falling down, with rusted roofs and caved-in walls.

Hondo ran ahead, making his way toward the barn. Quinn let him run, catching up with him, getting a call from dispatch that Lillie needed him to call in to the office. He was about to radio back when he noticed the tire tracks, rutted deep into the mud.

There'd been a lot of gravel off the road where he'd parked and a lot of rain overnight. But closer to the barn and into the weeds it was nothing but deep mud. Someone had been down this path recently. He followed his dog and the tire tracks toward the high barn. All around the structure, people had dumped rusted appliances and old cars, tires, and trash. As Quinn walked, he picked up a deer skull and whistled for Hondo.

But Hondo was already inside the barn, barking. Quinn reached into his pocket for a small flashlight as he walked into the leaning structure, praying like hell the thing didn't topple over on him and Hondo.

As he moved past the empty stalls heaped with wood and machine parts, he spotted the vehicle. A newish model white Ford Econoline. **Son of a bitch.** Hiding in nearly plain damn sight.

Quinn reached for his radio and called into Cleotha at dispatch.

"Call Batesville," he said. "We need a unit to head this way pronto. I'm not moving until we get this van dusted and photographed. Park down along the road and follow the tracks. They must've headed up into the Big Woods."

13

"Can I have a beer?" Caddy asked.

"Are you sure that's such a good idea, baby?" Jean Colson said. Her momma stood over her in her newly refurbished kitchen, Caddy seated at the end of the table, tearing a paper napkin to shreds.

"My hands won't stop shaking," Caddy said. "I hadn't had a beer in almost two years. Don't make it a big deal. Just something to calm me down a little bit."

"I have some Valium."

"And how's that any better?" Caddy said. "Anyone who knows Elvis like you do should know that's a horseshit idea."

"Caddy Colson," Jean said, leaning her sizable

backside against the sink, drying her hands, watching her daughter. She had on an oversized gray sweatshirt that said STUNTS UNLIMITED, her daddy's old outfit. Had it been Caddy, she'd have tossed that damn thing in the trash.

"Just pour me some of that god-awful boxed wine," Caddy said. "That'll work fine."

"It's not god-awful," Jean said. "I'll have you know it's a delicate blend of the finest grapes from South Africa. I'll pour you some, but don't act like I'm trying to pour you some g.d. Boone's Farm down your throat."

"Appreciate that, Momma," Caddy said. "Son of a bitch, what a day. Thank you for taking care of Jason and getting him off to school. I haven't had a bit of sleep."

"You want something to eat?"

"No, ma'am," Caddy said. "I'm fine."

Jean poured out a rosé-looking blend into some stemware and set it on the kitchen table. They'd lived in the same house on Ithaca Street her whole life. Quinn had always made a big deal about where they lived. He once called it the address of warriors. Caddy called it middle-class Southern living at its finest.

"Don't worry," Jean said. "I didn't tell Jason a thing. Do you think it'll be in the paper?"

"I wasn't arrested," Caddy said. "I was questioned.

Just thank God it was Lillie and not Quinn. If Quinn had found me down in Sugar Ditch, he would have shit his britches."

"Caddy."

"Well, you know it's a fact," Caddy said.

"I guess so," Jean said. "Did you find those little girls?"

"No, ma'am," Caddy said, taking hold of that nasty wine and taking a big gulp. It may have been the sweetest-tasting swill she'd ever had in her life. "Boom tried to talk some sense into a grown man who'd been using them up."

"Talking some sense?" Jean said. "I've known Boom Kimbrough since he was in diapers. Only way that boy talks sense is to beat the damn tar out of someone."

"I hit him."

"Who?"

"The fella who'd used the girls," Caddy said. "He pulled out a gun, so I hit him with Boom's truck. Got him good, too. Knocked him about five feet into the road. Hell, I thought I'd killed him. And I wasn't sorry about it one damn bit."

"Good Lord."

"And you know what else?" Caddy said. "It worked. We might know where those girls had gone on to next. I'm getting just a little closer to getting them back home. Or as close to home as they can get. Probably have to make room for them at The River. None of them wanted by their families. No one gives a shit for them. No one cares what the hell happens. They're just a couple stupid little girls."

Caddy downed the rest of the wine. She picked up the glass by the stem and pointed it at her mother for a refill.

"I know where you're headed," Jean said. "And I'm asking you for your sake, and for Jason's, to please just take a long breath and slow it down. I know you want to help and do the right thing. I know you have something personal with them. And you're thinking about everything that happened to you and how you got left out alone up in Memphis. But, Lord, Caddy. You're gonna get yourself straight on back in that mess. Can you imagine what that would do to Jason? You'd break that boy's heart. He's finally got his momma back."

"Momma?" Caddy said.

Jean had her arms crossed over her big chest, staring down at Caddy. She'd seen that terrified look about a million times before.

"Please just pour me some wine," Caddy said. "I hadn't showered or slept in twenty-four hours. I spent most of this morning listening to a fucking sermon by the Reverend Lillie Virgil. My ears are starting to bleed."

"I'm not trying to preach," Jean said, "I just want

you to take care of your own. I know you have a good heart. But you've become obsessed with those little girls."

Jean went back to the refrigerator and refilled the glass, only halfway this time, and set it in front of Caddy. Caddy let it sit there by the torn-up napkin, the wine having a little fizz to it, watching the bubbles, so damn sleepy but not being able to close her eyes. "I have to find them."

"Slow down," Jean said. "Those little girls started on that road long before you met them. They were fast, fast children. There'd been something that had poisoned them from a long time back."

Caddy felt her face flush, reaching out for the wine, draining the glass, and pushing back her chair. She stood up, unable to speak, and grabbed her keys. What she really wanted to do was take the glass and shatter it against the kitchen wall.

"Caddy?" Jean said. "Caddy Colson. I didn't mean it. Not the way you're thinking."

Caddy was already out the door and on the lawn, Jean yelling from the front steps as she got in her truck and slammed the door behind her. She took a little pleasure at tearing up a little of her momma's grass as she spun out and headed back to The River.

"If you weren't so good in the sack, I just might be offended," Fannie said.

"Holly Springs was halfway," Cord said. "You said not Memphis. Not Jericho."

"You show up at Vienna's again and the girls will start to talk," Fannie said, sitting across from Jonas Cord at the Huddle House, just off Highway 78. "Those girls are worse than a bunch of hens, clucking away in their cheap lingerie and fake pearls. I expect you're buying."

"I'll even ask for extra cheese in your grits."

"Damn, you're too damn good to me."

"You look good, mama," Cord said. "That a new dress?"

"You ever seen me in an old one?" Fannie said, fumbling into her purse, pulling out a lighter and then putting it away. "Son of a bitch. Do you remember when you could smoke in a place like this? Who the hell got all uppity and offended with a little smoke to cut through all this goddamn grease?"

"The dress suits you."

Fannie touched the red lace along the V-neck, her silver pendant hanging deep between her titties, and smiled. She reached her long fingers around the cheap china mug and leaned into the table, well out of earshot of the hash slingers and broke-ass waitresses, maybe ten years gone from being able to work the pole. "You don't need to sweet-talk me, baby," she said. "I know I'm sitting on the best pussy in north Mississippi. Just tell me where you boys stand."

Cord looked around the Huddle House and then

back to Fannie, all Marine seriousness. He flared his nostrils and nodded. "Yes, ma'am."

"Good."

"But we'll need some time to prep," Cord said. "Do some recon on those Twins. Any chance you know what it looks like inside the counting room?"

Fannie reached into her purse and pulled out the little diagram Ordeen had drawn for her. She'd added a few of her own thoughts and placed it on the center of the orange table. Cord caught it and spun it around, checking all the angles and details. If anything, Fannie knew Cord was a man for details. He fingered the edges, moving his mouth, but not speaking any words, studying each bit.

"This is good," he said. "You trust it?"

"I know it."

"Five inside?"

"And maybe three in the restaurant," Fannie said. "The Twins keep a couple shooters in cars around the back. If you go bust in that way, you'll have to take them out."

Cord nodded, lifting his eyes from the paper and staring at her.

"Will that be a problem?" she said.

"A bunch of black guys with popguns?"

"My man says it may be more than popguns," Fannie said. "They may have some assault rifles. One guy, this one they call Armani, keeps a damn gold-plated Glock."

"Gold-plated?" he said. "You shitting me?"

Fannie shrugged and put the thin little coffee mug up to her lips. The waitress had left them alone after checking on them twice, Fannie giving a cold-ass stare that sent her away with her muff tucked between her legs.

"I promise, we've met lots worse."

"One fights for money," Fannie said. "One for God. In the end, who wants it more?"

Cord didn't answer, the waitress walking back and slapping down some steak and eggs in front of him. She smiled at Cord, gave Fannie a nasty look, and switched her narrow bony ass on back to the cash register. Some old boy by the jukebox punching up one of her daddy's favorites by Kenny Rogers, "Ruby." She recalled him hitting that one on his eight-track, liquor and cigarettes on his breath, a dark shadow looming in the room she shared with her sister.

"When do they make the pickups?" Cord said.

"They pick up every night," Fannie said. "But the best night is Sunday. The Twins come in after a four-hour church service and do the count in their best suits."

"What time?"

"Most deliveries come in before four," Fannie said. "They're elbow-deep in the cash by five. My man says they get real into it, everyone wanting to know the count, some of the boys on the outside getting lazy, coming in for free beer and chicken wings, maybe smoke a blunt and talk some shit."

"Taliban didn't smoke blunts."

"And didn't care about money?"

"Oh, they cared about money," Cord said. "Money means power and control."

"But it's all about religion."

"Seventy-two virgins," Cord said. "Paradise."

"So they're fighting for pussy?"

Cord cut into the steak and eggs, taking a bite of both. He reached down for a napkin and wiped his mouth. He nodded and said, "Yeah."

"You boys," Fannie said. "So damn predictable. Peckers always pointing you right to the fucking grave."

Cord grinned and kept eating. The waitress left them alone until Fannie snapped her fingers.

"Guess you heard about Potts Camp?" Jon Holliday said. "Two men in Donald J. Trump masks hitting the cash drawers and threatening to shoot folks in the pussy. Taking off in a stolen vehicle that they dumped a few miles away and rode off on motorbikes."

"Our boys," Quinn said.

"Only got thirty grand this time," Holliday said. "But they're getting national press on account of their style. The Trump masks, hitting the banks in under ninety seconds. People are calling them heroes. Some say the robberies are politically motivated."

"Bullshit."

"I agree," Holliday said. "But there's so much bullshit going on these days that you don't know where to separate facts from reality. How'd you like to be a goddamn Fed right now? We're swimming in a sea of bullshit."

Quinn sat with Holliday on a green bench outside the county courthouse in Oxford. Holliday looked strange in a navy blue suit with crisp white shirt and red tie. Quinn had on his uniform: starched jeans, Tibbehah County SO shirt, cowboy boots, and Beretta clipped to the belt. They drank coffee from paper cups and watched the cars and trucks around the town square. It still wasn't spring, but the sun had come out, and college students were out jogging and women with lots of makeup and styled hair shopped the local boutiques. Daffodils had started to bloom, adding some green and light yellow to the roads leading downtown, even if the trees were still bare and cold.

"My wife grew up here," Holliday said. "There used to be a hardware store, pharmacy, and a diner called Smitty's on the Square. Now it's all ladies' boutiques and college puke bars. Got some good restaurants, a nice little bookstore, but it's all changed so damn much. Folks from the Delta who can't cut it up in Memphis."

"No worries about that down in Jericho," Quinn said. "Unless you count a western-wear shop or the Dollar Store as a boutique."

"Oh, it's coming, brother," Holliday said. "Pretty soon, you'll have a pretty little Starbucks next to the Sonic."

"I've prayed on it," Quinn said. "It hasn't happened yet."

Three men walked past, two of them in matching red sweater-vests and visors, the other in a fuzzy Sherpa vest and khakis, talking about how Ole Miss needed to fire their football coach. The talker's belly swelled over his belt, toothpick swiveling in his mouth, as he ran down a few things he'd heard on sports talk radio. Holliday lifted his eyes to the three, let the noise pass, and turned back to Quinn.

"How's it coming along with that van?"

"MBI towed it to Batesville," Quinn said. "They gave it a good look but didn't find anything except a couple cigarette butts. Unless one of our boys has donated some DNA to Big Brother, we don't have shit."

"Boot prints?"

"A partial," Quinn said. "The van was stolen up at the Oak Court Mall in Memphis. The plate on it was taken off another van at a Target in Olive Branch. We checked the surveillance at Target, but the guy had parked too far away. Didn't want his van scratched by the carts. We haven't been able to get any security video from the mall folks yet. Only thing we do have is those tire tracks off the dirt bikes. All seem to be the same make. We're checking out Kawasaki dealers to see who might have purchased three at the same time."

"Smart," Holliday said. "I have a few contacts at the VA. Officially, I can't bust in and make inquiries for vets who might have criminal tendencies. But they're checking. We've also been looking for vets in Tennessee, Mississippi, and Alabama who've committed felonies. You talk about a mountain of shit. Just because you put on a uniform doesn't make you goddamn Sergeant York."

"You and I didn't have much experience with regular Army," Quinn said. "But we had enough to make us sick. Young fuckups who had a choice of the recruiter or jail. We put a gun in their hand, teach 'em how to use it, then expect them to be choirboys when they get back home."

"Aren't all who serve American heroes?"

"Hardest part of my job was getting my boys not to kill," Quinn said. "And I worked with the very best the Army had to offer."

"You think these guys might've been Rangers?"

"No way," Quinn said. "Every Ranger has a set of brass balls and a heart of gold."

"You know what I think?" Holliday said. "I think these boys are having the goddamn time of their lives. I don't think it's about money at all. They hit these little towns, make a little dough, and move on to a new target. Some men like to hunt, fish, play golf. These guys can't play golf. They can't relax. Their heads are fried by the danger of combat. Their asses are wound up and this is the only thing that levels them."

"Like coming home and carrying a badge?"

"How'd you like to be a fucking salesman?" Holliday said, leaning back into the bench, watching a crew of young women in tight pants and sports bras. "Or one of those turds who just walked past talking college ball?"

"No, sir."

"These assholes will get bored soon," Holliday said. "I think all these little banks—excuse me, chickenshit targets—are a warm-up. They're going to get bored again and hit something bigger, like a nice, fat First Tennessee in downtown Memphis. Can you imagine that? Assault rifles flying loose on city streets, trying to make a getaway down fucking Poplar Avenue."

"Little more crowded than Jericho."

"Lots of folks will get killed," Holliday said. "And with the attention these fuckers are getting on the cable news . . . **Whew.** Some real shit."

"Well," Quinn said. "We don't have solid descriptions, leads, prints, or any workable evidence other than these boys liking Kawasakis. Damn, we got this all figured out."

Holliday leaned forward, placing his elbows on his knees, and turned to Quinn. "You got any job openings down in Tibbehah County?"

"Are you sure you're qualified?" Quinn said. "You, sir, have perhaps less of a tolerance for bullshit than I do."

"Is it thick?"

"Hell." Quinn nodded, no expression on his face. "You can smell it all the way to Tupelo."

14

"The toughest question I got asked by the judges was 'Crissley, what makes you happy?'" Crissley said, twirling her hair. "It's tough because so many things make me happy, Rick. Sunshine, seeing live music. Hanging out with my family and watching cheesy horror movies. Shopping with Daddy, even if Daddy can sometimes be a real horse's butt about the way I dress."

"What's wrong with the way you dress?" Wilcox asked, driving down Elvis Presley Boulevard behind the wheel of Crissley's white BMW. The car smelled like leather and baby powder. She had a bubbly Taylor Swift CD playing on the stereo.

"Daddy doesn't like me to show too much leg,"

she said. "Or when my boobies are all pushed up. He said it makes me look trashy."

"Daddy sure didn't mind you strutting across that stage in a pink string bikini," Wilcox said. "I've seen the pictures. What were you, sixteen? He was smiling and clapping in the front row."

"You don't understand that world," Crissley said. "The swimwear competition is a celebration of physical fitness. I hadn't eaten anything but rice cakes for a week before I jumped in that bikini. When it was all over, I ate an entire pepperoni pizza from Domino's."

Crissley had on yoga pants and a sports bra, her bleached-blonde hair in a ponytail, since they'd just left the gym. That's where he'd met her, chatting her up at the squat rack, telling her that she had the best form he'd ever seen on a girl. And that's when she told him about her platform at Miss Teen Mississippi, physical fitness. Now she says she would have won outright if she'd picked a sexier topic, like working with old folks or hunter safety.

Wilcox passed Graceland on the left and all the construction for the welcome center and new hotel, no more riding the short bus across the street from that crappy strip mall. He looked at his watch, noting the time, keeping the speed limit, and headed two miles down the road for the Wing Machine.

"Even though I didn't win," she said, "I won't

change what I said. I told the judges the most important thing for me was living by the Golden Rule, to treat others as you would like to be treated. My mom has always told me to go out in the world and let your light shine. Because if you radiate kindness and positive energy, you have the power to turn someone's day around, and, in turn, it'll come back to you. I really feel that way, Rick. You know me, I'm always so happy. Sometimes it's hard for me to keep smiling. I smile so much sometimes it hurts."

"I like the Golden Rule," Wilcox said, idling at a stoplight, checking the watch, timing the light, and punching it at the green. "I always do unto others before they do that shit unto me."

"That's not exactly what I'm talking about, silly."

"I guess we've had different experiences," Wilcox said, slowing down, knowing that the address would be coming up quick on the right. "I had a whole lot of folks want to exterminate me over the years. Bullets flying over your head will wipe a smile right off your face."

"I don't know how you did it," Crissley said. "Honest to God, I believe I'd pee myself."

"Sometimes you do," Wilcox said. "At first. And then you stop caring."

"You stop caring about people trying to kill you?"

"You stop caring about yourself," he said.

He glanced over at Crissley. She looked confused. But Crissley often looked confused, with that big, beautiful smile on her face. Wilcox grinned at her and winked.

"Didn't you care if you lived or died?"

"I cared if my men lived or died," he said. "That's pretty much it. But if you care too much for yourself, your own safety, it's all over."

Crissley didn't answer. Wilcox saw the strip mall coming up on the right, the wing shop out front and a detail shop behind. A bunch of cars were being waxed and detailed in the parking lot, vintage sedans painted metallic blues and greens, one a flashy orange. Big silver rims, lots of bass shaking the windows, as he turned and moved toward the restaurant.

"How'd you get through it?"

"You just have to make your mind up that you're already dead," Wilcox said. "You think you're going to die, but you keep moving ahead. You react from your training, try to think about the mission. Probably the worst of it for me was before you got into the shit. That would tear out your guts, but once you heard those AKs chattering away, you knew you were home."

Wilcox parked in front of the strip mall but let the motor keep on running. He checked the time and then his chiseled profile in the rearview mirror, still handsome as ever. When he turned to Crissley, he saw she was crying. Big tears running down her cheeks, black from all the mascara.

"Don't cry, baby," he said. "You know what? I see things clearer now than ever before."

Crissley looked up, just now noticing where they'd stopped and parked. "What are we doing here?"

"I want you to go inside," he said, "and get a dozen wings to go."

"Since when do you eat chicken wings?"

"I love chicken wings," he said. "Good protein, after we lift. The spicier, the better. And, baby?"

Crissley wiped her face and looked to him.

"Look around and tell me if that joint has a back door. If you can, take a couple pics with your phone. Just be real cool about it. Tell them you're a tourist coming to see Elvis's pink Cadillac."

"I don't understand."

"You don't need to," Wilcox said, patting her leg. He leaned back in the driver's seat, hitting the RE-CLINE button and shutting his eyes. "Just do it and wake me when you're done."

"How's my sweet baby doing up there in big, bad north Mississippi?" Buster White said in his unmistakable gravelly drawl.

"Oh, you know," Fannie said. Feet up on her desk, speaking into her toss-away cell. "Slinging cold Coors Light and warm cooze for lonely truckers. Raking it in and dishing it out."

"Fine, fine," Mr. White said—always "Mr. White"

186

since he stepped out of Angola running the show. "You know, you've always been a favorite of mine, Fannie. I look at you like I look on my own daughters."

"I do," Fannie said, but thinking that she hoped he'd never asked his daughters to let him grab their titties. Which Mr. White had done one lonely night in his suite at the casino in Biloxi. "**Just one,**" the old man had said. "**Let me just feel it, baby. Whoa! I could wear them things like a damn crazy hat.**" Fannie just said, "I appreciate that."

"Ray tells me you've been helping him out with some real ass ache up in Memphis."

"Yes, sir."

Buster White wouldn't be Buster White if he ever spoke direct about a damn thing on the telephone. When you did a stretch as long as he did in the joint, you got a sly, casual way of talking in code, making sure what you said wouldn't hold up in court even if a Fed was sitting right there in your office.

"Well, we appreciate you, Fannie," he said. "Ray's filled me in some business up there in the piney woods. Sounds like you got some real Bible-thumpers crawling up your ass."

"They want to shut down Vienna's," Fannie said, seeing no reason to hide that fact. "The truck stop is still in play, although I've been asked to add Johnny Stagg's famous chicken-fried steak back to the menu."

"Turning the screws to us."

"Yes, sir."

"Ray told me they didn't want nothing in return."

"Far as I can tell, they want to shut down the girls and bulldoze the bar," she said. "They're going to stop drinking right off. That'll cut me off at the damn knees."

"Mmm-hmm," Mr. White said, voice sounding like he'd been gargling with rocks. "Clean up Tibbehah County. Damn, that's a first. I knew some boys that used to bootleg up there in the sixties, right before things got wild up in McNairy County."

"You know the man I told Ray about?"

"Yes, I do."

"And can you help me with him?"

Mr. White didn't say anything, only hearing his ragged breath over the phone line. Fannie looked out from the office and saw Mingo lingering at the railing overlooking the bar. His back was turned to her, waiting for her to finish up on the phone, standing there and pretending not to listen. He was a thin, wiry boy, as patient and helpful as they got.

"That old boy who's got your panties in a twist is a tough bird," he said. "He's not cut from the same cloth as Johnny Stagg. He actually believes his own bullshit like it's gospel. He wants you gone. And to be honest, there's not a hell of a lot we can do about it."

"If liquor sales stop—"

"Oh, I know it."

"And you can't help?"

"I'd rather not discuss family matters on the phone," Mr. White said. "I'll get our lawyers involved, and there'll be a lot of paper pushed back and forth, but that rotten old man's got some real power."

"Y'all are afraid of some backwater county supervisor?" Fannie asked.

"It's not who he is," Mr. White said. "It's who he knows."

"Son of a bitch."

Mr. White didn't say anything, just kept on with that ragged breathing, coughing a little bit, waiting for Fannie to square the idea in her mind. Mingo glanced back over his shoulder, long Indian-black hair covering part of his face, turning back to rest his arms on the rails and look down into the empty bar.

"I'll handle it myself," Fannie said.

"If you get shut down, I'll see that you're up and running on down the highway right quick. But this fella, don't mess with him. He's got some real juice."

"With who?"

She heard Mr. White swallow. "Don't you worry your pretty little head about it."

"Hold on, hold on," Fannie said, looking up. Mingo still standing there, not moving. She placed a hand over the cell and called to Mingo: "You want to take a seat where it's more comfortable? If not, close the fucking door."

"Someone's here to see you, Miss Fannie."

"They can wait."

"It's a sheriff's deputy," Mingo said. "He's got a piece of paper that says the girls have to put on their panties or they can shut us down."

"I only wish I could see Fannie's face when she finds out," Lillie said. "I bet she about choked on those nasty little cigarillos of hers."

"Oh, we'll see her," Quinn said. "I'm waiting for a phone call any minute."

Lillie nodded, both of them standing outside the sheriff's office, Lillie leaning against her Jeep. "Would you do me a big favor?"

"Anything, Lil."

"Let me take the call," Lillie said. "I have some unfinished business with that woman."

"Fine by me," Quinn said. "I don't think this is going to stop anytime soon."

"So let me get this straight," Lillie said. "You can either serve liquor when the girls wear a G-string or have them buck-ass naked with a dry bar."

"That's right."

"Skinner's call?"

"Nope," Quinn said. "It's an old law I didn't even know existed. He's going to discuss details on Monday night. I don't think there's anyone on that board who'll go against that man or want to be on the side of liquor and naked women."

"What do you think?"

"I don't make the laws," Quinn said. "Only enforce them. I'd just as soon have Fannie Hathcock out of here. I thought we'd wrapped up all this crap when Stagg got busted."

Lillie crossed her arms over her chest. It was a cool, dry morning, bright and cold, wind whipping loose strands of hair across Lillie's eyes. She had her ball cap on, standing tall, while she and Quinn ate some sausage biscuits Mary Alice had cooked up for the morning crew.

"Heard you took that Powers woman for a milk shake at the Sonic the other night," she said. "That's mighty fine community service, Sheriff. Wouldn't have anything to do with the fact that she's hot as hell. Or so I'm told by Reggie and Kenny."

"I knew her a long time back," Quinn said. "When she used to stay the summers with her grandmother. She used to run with me and Boom and Caddy. And sometimes Donnie Varner. We were just catching up, is all."

"Sure thing, Sheriff."

"She's a friend," Quinn said. "Someone broke into her home. We got some ice cream."

Lillie smiled bigger than shit, knowing she'd got to Quinn. Every damn time they talked women, it put him and Lillie on a rough road. Sometimes Lillie acting like he was contagious and keeping him at arm's length, sometimes standing flat-footed in front of him and planting a kiss. You never quite knew, or understood, what you were getting with Lillie Virgil. She loved you or she wanted to shoot you.

"Isn't she married?"

"Separated."

"So she's married."

"About to be divorced."

Lillie nodded. "Uh-huh."

"It was her ex that busted into her house," Quinn said. "I know it. Broke her television, knocked over her bookshelves, and scattered her clothes around. Not one thing was stolen, not even a pretty nice twelve-gauge, a flat-screen TV, and some stereo equipment."

"What does the wife say?"

"She's not his wife."

"She still is on paper," Lillie said. "Like you said, you don't make the laws."

"She doesn't believe it," Quinn said. "Said it was probably some kids. Doesn't want me to investigate or press charges."

"You learn all this at the Sonic?"

"Just catching up on old times," he said. "I hadn't seen her since we were kids. Her parents quit letting her come after what happened to the Taylor boy. I never knew what happened to her and always wondered."

"Spoiler alert," Lillie said. "She went through puberty, got knocked up, and married some shithead with sociopathic tendencies. It's a song played so much the grooves have worn out."

"Damn, you're cynical, Lil," Quinn said.

"But truthful," Lillie said. "It's truth that makes most folks nervous about me."

"I thought it was the big goddamn gun."

Lillie grinned, looking over her shoulder at her fine Winchester .306 in the Jeep's rack. "That goes without saying," she said. "You sure you don't mind me calling on Miss Hathcock?"

"Help yourself."

Lillie squinted at Quinn in the harsh morning light and hugged herself tight in the wind. "Watch yourself out there, Sheriff."

"I don't think these robbers will be back."

Lillie laughed. "That's the least of your concerns, big guy," she said. "Watch your ass, but protect your heart."

Lillie was within a half mile of Vienna's Place when Mary Alice reached her and told her that Fannie had called up, raising hell. "How mad is she?"

"She called me everything but a white woman," Mary Alice said.

"Damn," Lillie said. "It's just about to be a beautiful day in Tibbehah County."

"You need some assistance?"

"And let someone else steal some of the joy?" Lillie said. "No, thank you. This is a private conversation."

It was early for a strip club, only two cars parked outside the big white corrugated-tin building. One of the cars was Fannie Hathcock's, a black Mercedes S550 with tinted windows and shiny chrome wheels. The woman rented a nice house in Jericho but spent a fair amount of time up in Cordova, according to Lillie's friends with the Memphis police. She had some kind of business up there, too, but no one was really sure what it was all about.

Lillie parked and walked into Vienna's, the place oddly bright and airy, front and back doors propped open to clean out the smell of smoke, sweat, and nasty-ass perfume. The houselights had been switched on, beaming down onto the wide, barn-like expanse of the club and up into the cross-beams, where Fannie kept that office perch to look down on her girls and bartenders and count every last dime.

"I didn't call for you," Fannie said. "Get the sheriff over here. I don't deal with hired help."

Fannie was seated on a black leather sofa behind one of the circular stages. She was smoking, a cup of coffee on a little black table in front of her. Everything looked worn and scuffed, under the hard light. The woman had her back turned to Lillie, her face in shadow.

"Sheriff Colson is out," she said. "Heard you had some trouble reading."

"Can't enforce something that's not a law," Fannie said. "It's business as usual until I hear different."

"It is a law. Board of supervisors tells us this is a county ordinance that's been on the books since the fifties," Lillie said. "Getting your girls to cover up their coots or you close down the bar seems reasonable to me."

Fannie, sitting there in a black skirt with white silk top, artfully smoked her cigarillo as if she was a woman of some kind of means. She still hadn't looked at Lillie. "What's gonna happen?" Fannie said. "Some good ole boy can handle his liquor until he sees some wild snatch and then all hell will break loose?"

"I don't make the laws," Lillie said, quoting Quinn. "Just enforce them. You can take it up with the board next week. You know how agreeable they can be."

"Skinner."

Lillie didn't answer, just stood there in the middle of Vienna's, hands on hips, waiting to get an earful from Fannie Hathcock but only getting the smooth, polite version from the woman. She seemed calm, almost resigned to the fact her bread and butter was about to be split down the middle.

"You got to wonder what makes a red-blooded Southern man so afraid of a naked woman," Fannie said. "Got to be something with his momma. Sick fucks are always mistreated by their mommas. There's something seriously wrong with that son of a bitch."

"Skinner says he wants to see Jericho like he did when he was a boy."

"That's bullshit and you know it, doll," Fannie said. "This godforsaken county has been running wild since the white man ran out the Indians. Moonshining, whores, good ole boy reach-around deals. Don't fall for Skinner's so-called morality. I heard when that fucker was younger, he'd have stuck his pecker in a light socket. Just because his equipment ain't functioning doesn't mean he's got to throw on the houselights."

"You'll have time to speak at the meeting," Lillie said. "Starts at six."

"Are you sipping some of that Kool-Aid, Lillie?" Fannie said. "And here I was thinking you weren't like the rest of the shit-kickers around here."

"Shit-kickers come in all shapes and sizes," Lillie said.

Fannie finally turned her head toward her, squashing out the cigarillo in an ashtray. A little wind blew through the club as that boy Mingo came down from the upstairs office. He spotted Lillie and nodded but didn't speak, waiting for his handler Fannie to tell him whatever it is she wanted at the moment.

"I got the call," Lillie said. "But I was coming to see you anyway."

Fannie turned, full body, toward Lillie. Mingo stayed at the edge of the staircase, hand on the railing.

"I'm looking for two girls," Fannie said. "Mexican girl named Ana Maria and a black girl named Tamika Odum."

"I got a lot of girls, Miss Virgil."

"These girls are special," Lillie said. "They're only fifteen."

"I don't hire children," Fannie said. "You got to be eighteen to work that pole. That's a federal law. Figured you know that."

"These girls wouldn't be onstage," Lillie said. "This would be some off-the-books stuff."

"If it ain't here or over at the truck stop," Fannie said, "it's none of my concern."

"I'm hearing different," Lillie said.

Fannie stood and walked up close to Lillie. Lillie smelling that Chanel perfume and seeing those expensive silk clothes and makeup job up close. Every little bit of that woman was as flawless as some high-dollar show dog. "How can you stand it?" Fannie said.

Lillie didn't answer. Fannie's eyes flickered over her lace-up boots and dusty jeans. Lillie stood her ground, not knowing whether to smile without a care or bust the woman right in her jaw.

"This town doesn't appreciate what you do," Fannie said. "They took the word of a goddamn sicko pedophile instead of you. How in the world can you stand it?"

Lillie, hands still on her hips, stepped nearly toe-to-toe with Fannie, standing there in front of the big-breasted redhead like a couple of fighters at a weigh-in.

"Maybe it's because I know who I am," Lillie said. "And I do my job with a clean mind."

Fannie puffed out her lips, almost purring at her. "Hmm," she said. "I don't know those girls or even ever heard of them. If someone is telling you I hire out kids, they're bald-faced lying to you."

"I hope so, Fannie."

"Where did you hear it?"

Lillie stared at Fannie, feeling her mouth twitch a bit. She smiled at the woman but didn't say a word about what she'd heard about Blue and those girls.

"Are you ever going to admit that you and I aren't that different?" Fannie asked.

"Not with my boots in the fucking fire."

"You are a pistol," Fannie said, sort of smiling now. She turned to Mingo, who'd stayed quiet and still in the shadows as the two women spoke. "Well, shit. Mingo, go ahead and make a run to Tupelo for a big ole box of panties. All sizes and shapes, colors and trim. Looks like we're going to have to house-train the fucking help."

15

"This is a beautiful place," Maggie said, sitting on the front porch of Quinn's farmhouse. Her Chuck Taylors had been kicked off, bare feet up on the railing.

"It wasn't at first," Quinn said. "It was a mess. My uncle had left the house in pretty sorry shape. Boom had to help me clear it out. It was packed with nothing but junk."

"You salvage anything?"

"Few pieces of furniture," Quinn said. "Few guns, a coat. And records. My uncle kept a pretty nice record collection. George Jones, Charley Pride. Lots of Loretta Lynn albums. He had a real thing for Loretta Lynn. I think he was truly in love with her."

"What'd you do with the rest?"

"Boom and I made a big fire," Quinn said. "And

we burned it all. That was right after the funeral. And I had no intention of staying. I'm glad I burned it. It needed burning."

"Do you miss the Army?"

Quinn nodded. It was a warm late-winter day, strangely warm weather, with the trees starting to bud and the daffodils in full bloom down the brick walkway to his front door. Hondo had just trotted up from the pasture, covered in mud and cow shit, looking happy and pleased with himself. He lapped up the water from the bowl Quinn had set down. Quinn and Maggie drinking Coors and sitting in a couple of rockers.

"My husband was military, too," Maggie said. "I thought he'd be career. But after his last tour, he was worn out. Said he was ready for other challenges."

"Roger that," Quinn said. "Tibbehah County was maybe more of a challenge than being in the Rangers. At least with the bad guys over there, you knew where you stood. No one promised to be your friend."

"I've heard things about the goings-on about town," Maggie said, tilting the beer to her lips, toes wiggling in the sunshine. "No wonder my grand-mother didn't want me to come back to Jericho. When I was a kid, I thought everything was so damn sweet and wholesome. The town square, that soda fountain downtown. People seemed nicer here, moved at a slower pace. Men tipped their hats at you when you walked past. It was like going back in time."

"Some of those nice fellas on the Square might've been part of the Klan," Quinn said. "Or the John Birch Society. I guess I always knew things were rotten around here since I was a kid. Nothing surprises me."

"But it can't be all bad?"

Quinn shrugged. "Nope," Quinn said. "I wouldn't be here otherwise. There are a lot of good people, my sister being one of them. I have to say, she's always been a damn headache for me. But I really admire what she's doing now. She's all action. Helps out a ton of people who really need it."

"I see some real tough stuff at the hospital," Maggie said. "Lots of illness and disease. People that are broke, malnourished, and just plain worn out. God bless her."

"Not to mention, she's a good mother," Quinn said. "My nephew has turned out to be a great kid."

"Sorry Brandon couldn't come," Maggie said. "He really wanted to fish. But it's his time with his dad all weekend, starting tonight. I hope you didn't think I was too forward by showing up alone."

"I happen to like forward women."

Maggie smiled, kept rocking, and quickly drank some more beer. It was twilight, and you could hear the cows deep in the pasture lowing and the frogs in the nearby creek. Hondo had drained the water bowl and settled between them with a sigh. Quinn reached down and scratched his head.

"You like catfish?" he asked.

"Of course."

"I made some slaw and set out some fillets to fry," Quinn said. "I have a refrigerator loaded down with Coors. And plenty of whiskey, if you'd like some."

"Whiskey and catfish," Maggie said, smiling, looking out into the depths of the pasture and farther out into the rolling hills growing up into the Big Woods. "I may never leave."

"You like Loretta Lynn?"

"Love her."

"Damn," Quinn said. "If you're not in luck, Maggie Powers."

Caddy drove out to Choctaw Lake and sat in her truck for a long time, watching the sun go down over the water. There was a little playground, a camping area, bathrooms, and a boat ramp. Jean used to take her and Quinn out here as kids. Quinn now took Jason fishing on the lake during the summer in his jon boat. Sitting there, she wished she had a cold beer but hated the thought, knowing that Jean was right, excuses and lying to yourself will only lead to blackouts and long backslides that were a family tradition. The gold light shone hard on the choppy waters, wind blowing through the cracks in the old truck.

Another truck, a nice red one, pulled up beside her and a boy got out. He closed the door and came around the back of Caddy's, crawling into the passenger side.

"Thanks for meeting me," Caddy said.

Mingo nodded, pushing his long black hair behind his ears and letting out a long breath. "I didn't even know this county had a lake," he said. "I guess I only go to the truck stop and Vienna's and then back home."

"This county has a little bit of everything," Caddy said. "There are so many little back roads and little corners I sometimes discover. Funny how you can live in a place your whole damn life and not know it."

"That's like the Rez," he said. "Of course, the Rez isn't like when I was a kid. The casino gave us a lot of money but took more away. Most of what's happened makes me sick."

"That's where you and the Hathcock woman met?"

Mingo nodded. "She took me in when I was young," Mingo said. "I ran errands for her. Helped clean up the trailers she had down there."

"Running girls."

"Mostly in Airstreams," he said. "We had a couple double-wides. Lots of business. She and the chief were big friends until they weren't."

"Why y'all had to leave?"

He nodded, hands fumbling around in his lap, playing with a set of car keys. Caddy kept on looking out on the water, sometimes thinking this was one of the prettiest spots she'd ever seen. The cypress coming up on the edge of the water, the big crooked oaks and wild pines glowing with the final light of the sun. She didn't know why she didn't come out here more often, to get a break from packing food boxes, washing towels and sheets, and running down lost children.

"Does your boss know you've joined the church?" Caddy said.

He shook his head. "Who's playing this Sunday?"

"Mr. J.T. and the boys plan on 'Jesus, Don't Give Up On Me' and 'I'll Fly Away.' And we have a group coming up from Ackerman," Caddy said. "A family group that I hear puts on a hell of a show, lots of old-time stuff that gives you goose bumps."

"I'll be there."

"Have you heard anything?"

"No," Mingo said. "But Lillie Virgil came by this morning, asking about those girls. She said she knew about Miss Fannie running them, but Miss Fannie lied and said she'd never even heard their names. Mainly, they talked about some folks wanting to shut down Vienna's. Fannie sent me to Victoria's Secret in Tupelo to buy three hundred dollars in women's panties. The folks there didn't know what to make of me. I think they thought I was some kind of pervert or a serial killer."

"So the girls are gone?"

"Yes."

"When did you see them last?"

"Miss Caddy," Mingo said. "I'm not real proud of who I am and what I do. But I do owe Miss Fannie a lot. She's been real good to me."

"These girls were fifteen."

"Yes, ma'am," he said. "I understand that."

"And they may be in bigger trouble than you can ever imagine."

"I couldn't afford to eat when I was a boy," Mingo said. "My mother was a meth head. She took our government check and spent it on crank and booze. I was supposed to have a little sister, but she died when my mother was still pregnant. Sometimes I slept on my uncle's sofa. Sometimes I slept in a car. Miss Fannie may be a lot of things, but she's been good to me."

Caddy nodded, reaching up, touching the steering wheel, feeling those worn, familiar grooves from the previous owner and probably the owner before that, the truck broken in just right. She didn't say anything for a while, letting Mingo sort all this out on his own.

"Sometimes I can't sleep," Mingo said, "thinking of what I've seen pass through that place."

Caddy turned to him and smiled, trying to reassure him, watching him playing with those keys in his hand, flipping them around his worn knuckles. His black eyes were filled with a lot of pain. "You don't have to keep it to yourself," she said. "He'll take it."

"It's a lot."

"Nothing is too much for Him."

"You ever seen a bunch of scared-looking girls staring at you from inside a tractor-trailer?"

Caddy shook her head. The light was nearly gone over the trees on the other side of the lake. The gold waves had now turned silver and the air blowing through the windows had grown cool. **"Come unto me, all ye that labor and are heavy laden, and I will give you rest."**

"Damn, I'm tired," he said. "I'm just so damn tired."

"Lay it down," she said. "You know what to do."

"Does it really work?" Mingo said, sad eyes turned on Caddy.

She nodded. "Damn straight."

"Zoo's about to close," Opie said.

"They can wait," Wilcox said. "This is the only time worth a crap to see the big cats. They sleep all damn day and get up at dusk. Look at that jaguar. He's just starting to stretch and pace like crazy. You know he wants back in the wild to hunt, but instead he's waiting for some son of a bitch to toss him a rump roast."

"They don't know how to hunt any more than a

house cat does," Opie said. "Born in captivity. But that jaguar sure is pretty. Black as midnight."

"Can you hear them start to make noise?" Wilcox asked, leaning onto the post, looking through the mesh fence at the jaguar. Folks already moving toward the Memphis Zoo exit after the second warning over the loudspeakers. "It's in their blood. They're flippin' hunters. They can't stop hunting and killing any more than they can't stop screwing. It's who they are."

"Hey, Sarge," Opie said. "You want some peanuts? They're making me sick. I had a barbecue sandwich on top of that ice cream. I feel like I'm going to puke."

"Suck it up, buttercup," Wilcox said, pushing away from the jaguar and moving up the path to the snow leopards, who were jumping around a few logs tossed into their concrete world. He took the peanuts and cracked one, tossing the shell on the ground. "Now, these guys are pretty. Almost as pretty as me. Natural trackers. They love that rocky terrain, blending in as they hunt. You know I saw one when we were at FOB Golestan?"

"Bullshit."

"Seriously, man," Wilcox said. "I got up one morning to take a piss and smoke a cigarette right by the fence line. I saw that big cat and it saw me. Our eyes kind of met, like we were kindred spirits."

"Maybe it just wanted to eat your pecker like a hot dog."

"Maybe," Wilcox said. "But there was a show of respect. The thing growled and ran off back into the mountains. Hopping from rock to rock. I'll never forget it."

"I saw a lot of mangy-ass dogs," Opie said. "Fucking goats. And too many flies. Those damn things in my ears and my mouth. Yuck. Come on, let's go, or we'll miss the lions. And the gift shop."

Wilcox walked with Opie, heading down the path, passing more leopards, cougars, and a big pack of tigers snoozing by a waterfall. It was nice to be away from Crissley for a while, not having to listen to her yammer on about pageants, her damn faggoty daddy, and shopping. She and Wilcox spent half their days at shopping malls, when he wasn't out robbing banks or killing beers with the boys. You could land a fucking Osprey in her closet.

"So you're good with Cord's plan?" Wilcox asked.

"Yes, sir," Opie said. "That's our speed."

"It's different than banks," Wilcox said. "Way different. Folks will get shot. You can damn well bet on it."

"God, I hope so," Opie said. "I'm getting tired of telling old ladies to get down on their faces. The only real challenge about hitting those banks is the speed. You did see the clock on that job down in Potts Camp?"

Wilcox nodded, smelling that big-cat scat in the wind. All those animals marking their places in their little fake habitat. "These are bad hombres," Wilcox said. "Doing bad things. Might even make us heroes again."

"We shut down the Wing Machine first," Opie said. "One inside, two to neutralize the fuck nuts around back."

"That's the plan."

Wilcox cracked another peanut, watching tigers wake up, stretch, and take a little stroll at the little compound all dressed up to look like a jungle in India, with rock carvings of dudes with a lot of arms. "The speed ain't enough," he said. "You got to know that violence cuts both ways."

"Better than sex," Opie said.

"Then you're doing it wrong," Wilcox said. "Or just using your hand."

"I had a nice country girl the other night," Opie said. "Even if she was a whore, she told me she would have screwed me for free."

"She's lying."

"I know," Opie said. "But it still sounded good."

"We make a dry run Sunday. Just like the day of the hit," Wilcox said. "You need to follow that boy Shortbox, see how long it takes on the pickups. Cord and I can check out what the shooters outside look like. Getting into the count room is second tier. We got to take out those boys outside."

"How long?"

Wilcox shook his head. Opie kept on watching

the tigers, saying he really liked the white one and telling Wilcox all about seeing a couple of white tiger cubs when he was a kid. "They were with the damn circus," Opie said. "Maybe it's the same one? You know? Why not?"

An announcement came over the loudspeaker letting everyone know the zoo was now officially closed and to please head for the gates. They walked away from the tigers, out of Cat Country, and rounded the corner at the lion exhibit.

Wilcox whistled for his son to get going, the kid up on his tiptoes, studying the male with the big mane standing tall on a big rock.

"C'mon, Brandon," Wilcox said. "Damn. Sometimes I think that kid is just trying to piss me off."

16

Fannie Hathcock drove over to Maxwell Field Air Force
Base and went through security at the federal prison.
It was minimum security, most of the inmates con-
victed of white-collar crimes, spending their days
exercising, tending to the beautiful landscape, and
sometimes working as caddies to the officers at the
airfield. Fannie met Johnny Stagg in the common
room, a place for friends and families to sit around
and drink coffee. No glass between them, just little
orange tables set up like a high school cafeteria. She
brought Stagg a box of Church's fried chicken and a
big sack of his favorite peppermint candy from the
Rebel Truck Stop.

"Today must be my lucky day," Stagg said. "To
what do I owe this honor?"

"Eat your chicken, Johnny," Fannie said. "And let's cut though the bullshit. I got some serious-ass problems down in Tibbehah. Some fucker named Skinner is trying to run me out of town."

"Wondered how long that would take," Stagg said. "He'd all but retired when I took over the Rebel. Never gave me much trouble, but I heard he was back in the game, running the supervisors now, acting like his shit don't stink and that he'd found Jesus. Me and you might have had some problems in the past. But I can assure you, I'm no friend of that man and highly doubt he's changed his ways."

"What's in it for him?" Fannie said.

Stagg grinned, smiling across the table at her, and said, "What's in it for me?"

"What do you want, Johnny?"

Stagg tilted his head, his trademark Jerry Lee Lewis pompadour cut down into short businessman style. His face was red and bumpy, looking irritated from a close shave where he'd missed a few gray hairs. Stagg's craggy face looked like a dirt farmer from a Walker Evans photo. "How about you start with acting like you like me?"

"I do like you, Johnny," Fannie smiled, sweetly. She reached across the table and touched his bony hand, cold as a dead man's.

"Of course you do," Stagg said. "You and Buster White must've wept a biblical flood when the Feds swooped down on me and shut down everything I'd built. How long did it take y'all to get over your grief and snatch up my property?"

"Old news," Fannie said. "I got current bullshit to deal with. Talk to me about Skinner. And I'll help you out any way I can. How long is your sentence?"

"My lawyer's working on the matter," Stagg said. "I've been prisoner of the month two times in a row. I graduated from clipping hedge rows to riding the lawn mower. Funny how you grow accustomed to a different value system. I'm big man on campus now, riding a Toro with a fifty-inch deck. Behind the fence, it's better than driving a cherry-red Cadillac."

Fannie nodded, letting go of the cold hand, wanting to wipe hers on her pant leg. A man she'd recognized as the former lieutenant governor of Alabama sat in the back corner of the room, meeting with his woman and two young kids. The woman was crying. She'd seen him a half-dozen times at the casino in Biloxi. She recalled he had a real thing for blackjack and redheads, the man spotting her but refusing to meet her eye.

"What's ole Skinner asking for?" Stagg asked.

"Nothing."

"Nothing, huh?" Stagg said. "Well, that's something new. Don't you have a few items down at the Booby Trap to meet with his needs?"

"Booby Trap is dead, Stagg," Fannie said. "I sunk

four hundred grand into a new building. It's called Vienna's Place now. Finest girls in the state of Mississippi. You need to keep current on the times."

"Oh, I've heard," he said. "But it'll always be the Booby Trap to me. You should have kept the name. It's what city folks call branding. Every trucker south of the Mason–Dixon line knew where to find the best pussy and chicken-fried steak in north Mississippi. A new name might confuse matters."

"The name wasn't up for debate," she said. "All my places are called Vienna's. Named after my dear, departed grandmother."

"Is that so?" Stagg said, grinning, face splitting into a jack-o'-lantern smile. "Well, she must be damn proud of you for erecting a pussy palace in her memory."

"She's been dead for twenty years," she said. "But you bet your ass she would. She ran two whorehouses down in Gulfport. That woman entertained more troops than goddamn Bob Hope."

Stagg smiled. "Bless her heart."

"Skinner," Fannie said, spotting a muscular black guard by the back door and lowering her voice. "What's his game?"

"You hadn't figured it out?" Stagg said. Fannie wanting to knock that smug smile off his craggy face. "Damn, Fannie. Come on. How long you been up in the piney woods?"

"He says he wants to return to old Southern values."

Stagg started to laugh, nearly choking on a peppermint, catching it and cracking it with his back teeth. "Lord, Lord," he said. "It's funny how you can be forgotten. You're only the second person from Jericho who's come to see me in the last year. The last man was a fella named Jason Colson, famous Hollywood stuntman back in the day. Doubled for Burt Reynolds and Lee Majors. We had a little shared history."

"Any kin to the sheriff?"

"Would you believe it's his daddy?" Stagg said. "But cut from very different cloth. Jason Colson is what I'd call a reasonable man."

"And his son?"

"He's more like his late uncle," Stagg said. "Has what I call a John Wayne complex. If I'd been in charge a bit longer, I might've made him see the ways of the world. Just like I did his uncle."

"You and his daddy good friends?"

Stagg shook his head, reaching for a piece of chicken, seeming to debate between a thigh and a leg. He took a bite of the thigh and opened up a little container of baked beans. "He came to me for help, too," Stagg said. "And if he'd been able to follow through instead of shagging ass, things might've turned out different for all of us."

"How so?"

Stagg swallowed and spooned into the beans, taking a big bite and closing his eyes. "Mmm-mmm," he said. "Sure do love that Church's. Well, his daddy was going to front me some land down the street from the Rebel. If he'd laid hands on that piece, you'd never even known the name Skinner."

Fannie waited while Johnny Stagg finished with the chicken, gnawing it down to the fucking bone.

"Why do you think Buster White and those Syndicate boys sent you to Tibbehah?"

"No one sent me," Fannie said. "I saw an opportunity to get off the Rez."

"Bullshit," he said. "I know, same as you, that Tibbehah is a hell of a little poker chip, a fateful little county that sits just about perfect in north Mississippi. Close enough to Memphis, far enough from Tupelo, riding right on the highway headed down to Mobile and up to Nashville. Skinner isn't your fucking problem, Fannie. He's no more in charge than you are. He's making sure your ass is gone and everything I built is churned down deep under the earth."

"He wants the Rebel?"

"They want it all," Stagg said. "There's grand designs on Jericho. Ever heard anyone talk about the Tibbehah Miracle?"

"Never heard those words put together."

"How about the name Vardaman?" Stagg said, raising gray eyebrows, breaking into a full-out smile, his veneers looking two inches long in the fluorescent light. "I know you know him. If that ole boy gets what he wants, you and I are fucked five ways from Sunday. He'll be skipping his sorry ass right into the governor's mansion."

"I don't like this," she said. "All this hopscotching is making my teeth hurt."

Stagg closed up the Church's fried-chicken box and drummed his fingers on top. He wasn't smiling now. "I'm getting tired of fetching golf balls for flyboys and cutting grass," he said. "How about you and me make some plans for the future?"

"Fine by me," she said. "But I need to know one thing straight off."

"Yes, ma'am?"

"I need that chicken-fried steak recipe," Fannie said. "Damn truckers are starting to riot."

After all the wait and bullshit with the mall's lawyers and Shelby County DA, you can't see shit," Lillie said. She and Quinn hunched over a sheriff's office computer screen together, rewatching the same ten seconds of grainy, faraway security video. "It looks like a goddamn shadow stealing that van. We got much better video from the fucking bank."

"At least he's not in a Trump mask," Quinn said.

"That is a major improvement," Lillie said. "But now we've got just some blurry white dude in sunglasses and a ball cap down in his eyes. He looks like half the fucking contractors eating lunch at the Fillin' Station. Maybe a plumber or electrician. Too healthy to be a roofer."

"It's definitely the same guy," Quinn said. "The tall one in the bank who was giving orders? We could get the folks in Batesville to work out a sketch."

"You can only see half his face."

"He's wearing Carhartt pants and work boots," Quinn said. "He's got some kind of ink on his right arm. Stop it right there and zoom in."

"Sure," Lillie said, playing around with image on the monitor. "I see it. It reads 'Fuck you, Tibbehah County.'"

"You got sharp little eyes, Lillie."

"This may be something," Lillie said. "But it still ain't shit. It's not evidence."

"I thought you couldn't jack cars with a screwdriver anymore?"

"He's got some kind of computer override in that backpack," Lillie said. "It's a little handheld device. Fifteen-year-old kids buy 'em off locksmiths and mechanics. Hell, you probably can get one off eBay."

"So we got a white man, a little over six feet and somewhere around one-ninety," Quinn said. "I'm guess he was somewhere in his early to mid-thirties?"

"Say, just where were you at the time of the robbery, Quinn Colson? That shitbird kinda looks like you."

"Dealing with Fannie Hathcock," Quinn said. "Remember how she beat the shit out of a customer with a framing hammer?"

"Oh, yeah," she said, "that's right. She claimed to be protecting her girls."

"You know what?" Quinn said, studying the frozen image on the computer screen, two empty paper cups of coffee next to it. "I think I'd know that shitbird on sight."

"I wouldn't know that boy if he walked right into the sheriff's office and tried to grab me by the pussy."

"God help the man who tried to do that."

"God couldn't help him," Lillie said. "I'd splatter his fucking nuts from here to Toccopola."

Rick Wilcox figured he'd open up with a real rouser, something like "Beer for My Horses," talk a little bit after about being in the Corps, love of his country and all that bullshit. And then he'd take down the room a bit, "Till My Dyin' Day" by Brooks and Dunn, get everyone on their feet, slow-dancing, maybe singing along with Bic lighters in hand. By the third song, he'd really have them with "Buy Me a Boat," one of Crissley's favorites. It was going to be a real win-win tonight down on Beale Street. The gig coming late, Crissley having to work the bar anyway with the American Honey Team, the girls giving away free shots of sweetened Tennessee whiskey, wearing tight gingham shirts, tied up over their bellies, matched up with the tiniest pairs of Daisy Dukes.

Wilcox had on a black T-shirt, a pair of snug Levi's with split legs to work with his mud boots, and a green baseball cap with a Marine Corps insignia. Any night he wore the hat he didn't have to pay for a single drink, although Crissley assured him that the band drank for free.

"Jesus, Rick," Crissley said, marching up to the stage. "You can't bring a kid in the bar. The manager about shit two bricks when he saw Brandon. Can't he just sit around and play Xbox with Opie and Cord?"

"He's tired of games," Wilcox said. "Besides, he said he wanted to see his daddy play some country songs. You know, he's never seen me up on the stage. I think it would be good for him, always wondering what his daddy did besides shoot bad guys."

"Well," Crissley said, hands on those slim hips, "he can't stay here. Go send him to the movies or something. I got to work."

"Work?" Wilcox said, plugging in his Gibson, tuning it at the top of its neck. "Since when do you call showing some skin work?"

"You sound just like Daddy," Crissley said. "Goddamn you, this is marketing. We're the fucking American Honeys. Do you know how hard it was to get this job?"

"Only thing hard was in your bossman's pants."

Crissley's face turned red as she poked out her jaw and gritted her bleached teeth.

"Aw, shit," he said, setting the guitar in its stand and jumping down off stage. He placed a hand on Crissley's warm back, not a speck of fat on that waist. He pulled her in and whispered, "Don't fuck up a night with my family, babe. I can replace your ass in two seconds and get every American Honey in this room to jump in my truck."

She swallowed, teeth still on edge.

"But it won't come to that," he said. "Will it? Now, go get me a Coors Light. And a Coca-Cola for Brandon. This is a damn family night. Look at that boy. He's already having the time of his life. I told him I'd buy him a big-ass plate of ribs later at Blues City Café. This is awesome. Meat City, baby."

Those cool blue eyes settled on Wilcox, standing tall in her cowboy boots. "I should have stayed with my old boyfriend," she said. "You know, he played point guard for the Grizzlies."

"Sure, baby," he said, arching his eyebrow. "Sure."

Wilcox looked down at Brandon playing on an iPad on a barstool. The kid looked up, still wearing the Memphis Zoo T-shirt he'd bought him yesterday, and he gave the boy a thumbs-up. **Daddy's got it.** The boys in the band climbed onstage, checking the equipment, bar filling up with a few folks wandering in from the neon lights on Beale. At that very moment, Wilcox called an audible and switched up the set. He slid on his sunglasses and launched into "Buy Me a Boat," putting a real country-ass twang in his voice, although the only country he'd ever known was when he visited his country-ass relatives in Adamsville.

A half-dozen folks dancing now, all women, shaking their butts. Wilcox looked back to the bar and saw Crissley talking to the bartender, both knees up on a barstool, her narrow ass mocking him even as he had control of the whole room. Wilcox knowing he could turn it back around once again. and huddled up with the boys at the end of the song. Skip Toby Keith and go right on into "Something About a Truck," one of Crissley's favorites, the song they'd played when they spent those five days together going out to her daddy's lake house, blasting music and drinking tequila and screwing like rabbits, not wearing a stitch of clothes the whole time.

Soon as he strummed that steady guitar melody, she heard it, recognized it, and turned around from the bartender to look at him. She shook her head and smiled, tapping her cowboy boot and leaning back slow, elbows on the bar, chest poking out big and proud, and smiled.

He smiled back and looked down from the stage at Brandon, who had on earphones and was thumbing through his iPad. Not giving a good goddamn that his daddy was a country music god who could make things happen with a guitar pick. Sometimes he wished he could shake some sense into that boy. But Wilcox only shrugged it off, enjoying that familiar neon light, all that flesh, and the sweet taste of that free bourbon.

"**Something about a kiss gonna lead to more**," Wilcox sang, stomping his boot and getting everyone to follow. Tonight was his damn night.

"Maybe we should slow down," Maggie said, she and Quinn kissing now for an hour straight on his sofa. Loretta Lynn on his kitchen radio singing "How High Can You Build a Fire." "Good Lord, Quinn. This is moving fast. **Way** too fast."

"I always wanted to kiss you."

"It's not the kissing I'm worried about," she said. "Would you please hand me my shirt."

Quinn smiled and picked up the flannel shirt that had fallen to the floor, Maggie wearing only a black bra and a pair of Levi's, shoes kicked off as soon as she walked into the door. Tonight was the second night in a row she'd come out to the farm, with Brandon up in Memphis. They'd already had dinner, Quinn cooking a couple of deer steaks with sweet potato fries, and watched nearly five minutes of a Western, before things got interesting.

"You didn't like the movie."

"I'm not into Westerns."

"OK," Quinn said. "I can work with that."

"And when you said you always wanted to kiss me," Maggie said, "then why didn't you? You had plenty of chances. Remember when we ended up together in that culvert by the ball field? It was just me and you, playing a game of truth or dare."

"Maybe you got too close to the truth."

"Maybe you don't even remember what I'm talking about."

"There was a little bit of an age difference," Quinn said. "You were just a kid."

"And how old were you?"

"I was a grown-ass man," Quinn said. "I was nearly fifteen."

Maggie laughed and buttoned up her shirt nearly to the top button. "For you, I'll keep watching the movie," she said. "But I need to check back in with Brandon. I haven't heard from him since my ex took him to Chuck E. Cheese's for lunch."

"Are you worried?"

"When he's with Rick," she said, "I'm always worried."

"You know, that's the most you've ever mentioned about your ex," Quinn said. "I didn't even know his name."

"I've wasted enough time with that idiot," she said. "I'd rather not clutter up your mind with him, too."

"I'm going to have to meet him sooner or later," Quinn said, clearing off the plates, walking back to the kitchen. He started to run some water in the farm sink to get it hot, Maggie behind him, checking her phone. Loretta Lynn now on to women who were "Rated X."

"That son of a bitch."

Quinn put the stopper in the sink and added in some soap. He rolled up his sleeves and looked back to Maggie, who was now seated at the table, running her hands through her hair and looking down at her phone as if she couldn't believe what she was seeing.

"He brought Brandon to a bar," she said. "Is he crazy? Well, of course he's crazy. I've known he's crazy for a long time, but I keep thinking something is going to change. That maybe he'll start making some smart life choices. But you can't bring a six-year-old to a bar. Is that even legal?"

"Talk to your lawyer," Quinn said. "I'd get Brandon to take a few pics. You can use them with the judge."

Quinn cleaned the plates and set them in a wooden rack. He reached for two more bottles of Coors from the refrigerator and set them down on the table, popping the tops. Maggie looked up, crying. Quinn pulled up a chair and reached for her hands, holding them in his, staring right into her light green eyes.

"I've got to go."

"Where?"

"Memphis," she said. "He's somewhere in Memphis. I'm not letting my son stick around a bar. Rick will be drunk. He's always drunk. And reckless as hell."

"Can I drive you?"

Maggie wiped her face, mad and determined. She shook her head. Quinn reached over and placed his hand on her freckled cheek. He smiled at her. The room had grown quiet and still. Somewhere out on the hill he heard Hondo barking.

"That might make things worse," she said, reaching over to the chair and grabbing her keys. "I had a beer before dinner. Can you make me some coffee?"

Quinn got up and filled a blue-speckled pot with cold water. He didn't speak, only listened to Maggie run down a long list of continual fuckups by her ex. **Rick. The son of a bitch.**

"I need to know something."

Quinn nodded.

"Are you just playing with me?"

Quinn shook his head. "No, ma'am."

"Because if you are, please stop it right now," Maggie Powers said. "Because I don't think I could handle it."

Quinn leaned down and kissed her, long and hard, on the mouth. He felt swelling in his chest, everything dimming around him. He broke away and looked into those pale green eyes staring right through him. They waited for the coffee and he poured her a good amount in a tall tumbler.

Maggie smiled. "I'll be right back."

Quinn walked her out and watched her drive away, her car kicking up dust from the gravel road. Hondo trotted up and sat by Quinn's side, exhausted from chasing deer out of the garden.

Damn, he hated to see her go.

17

"What's so insane about the situation is that she's mad at me for spending quality time with my own kid," Wilcox said, two minutes after K-Bo and Shortbox headed into some shitty apartment building off Central Ave. "Can you fucking believe it?"

"Look at that guy," Cord said. "Fat shooter by the car? All he does is stand around and try to look tough while eating Cheetos. That must be the one they call Johnny Snacks."

"Wasn't like it was a titty bar or something," Wilcox said. "It was just a regular family-style bar on Beale Street. She knows I don't sing in church. This is how I get people to hear what I'm doing, where I shake some hands, drink some beers, and sell some CDs of 'Semper Fi.'"

"So we got two shooters," Cord said. "Johnny Snacks and that black dude with the gold gun. Armani."

"Damn that woman," Wilcox said, seeing the Twins come back out of the apartments and into their black Expedition, Johnny Snacks behind the wheel. "She about tore me a new asshole when she drove up to Memphis. Do you know it cost me more than a hundred bucks to take that kid to the zoo Friday? We spent all fucking day with him Saturday, too. I only did two sets at the bar. Hell, we got home before midnight. Bought him supper at the rib place, just like he wanted. She didn't have to drive up in the middle of the night like some kind of looney tunes."

"The Twins will head into the count room with Armani," Cord said. "But Johnny Snacks is the one who'll stick around, being a pain in our ass at the car wash. Got a piece in his saggy-ass jeans while waxing vehicles. Watch out for him. He scoping shit all the time. I'm pretty sure he spotted me when I turned around yesterday."

"She drinks," Wilcox said. "She parties. Hell, that's how we met. She just has it in for me. She's always looking for me to make bad decisions, to fuck up. She's always asking me, 'Is this the way you want your son to turn out?' And I say, 'What's so wrong with winning a Silver Star?' I think Brandon can sleep just fine knowing Big Daddy did his part in the war against terrorism. North at Airways?"

"They're going to make a last run in Orange Mound," Cord said. "Into that convenience store by the railroad tracks. Damn, these boys have been busy. To get their stash, we'll have to kill 'em. No other way."

"Lot of trouble," Wilcox said, "just for a cut."

"Trust me, man."

"That's what men say to each other in prison," Wilcox said, "before they bend over for the soap and get cornholed. This is my city. I should make the plan. Where the fuck are you from anyway?"

"Kansas."

"Somewhere over the fucking rainbow."

"We got to get clear of Elvis Presley Boulevard fast," Cord said. "We can head back to me and Ope's place or over on South Main. Drink a few beers at Earnestine and Hazel's and dump this piece of shit."

"Maggie's trying to get custody terms reworked," Wilcox said. "She's using pictures of me and Brandon at the bar as proof of me being a bad dad. I told her him holding that cigarette and the Bud was just a fucking joke. I mean, laugh once in a while. Chill the fuck out."

Wilcox drove down South Parkway past the Liberty Bowl, remembering hanging out at Liberty Land as a kid, the fucking Zippin Pippin, still pissed at hell at Maggie for turning him into some kind of bad guy. She hadn't even let him speak to Brandon after she got him in the car and reamed him out in front of Crissley.

"They got to be bagging at least a hundred grand a week," Cord said. "And they don't use some bank. All of what they got is at that count room at the Wing Machine."

"You want to know the truth?" Wilcox said. "She never loved me. She got knocked up and figured she was stuck. The one and only time I ever saw she was proud of me was when I came home after the last tour, with the fucking bands and WELCOME HOME signs. She wanted to be with me then. But when things got tough, the drinking and shit, it wasn't the same. Now I'm a fucking asshole."

"Damn, Rick," Cord said. "Are you listening, man?"

"She's seeing someone else," Wilcox said, now heading south. "I know it. I smell it on her. She's moved on. She's trying to kick me completely out of the family photo. It's not a wise decision to poke the bear. You know?"

"Listen, man," Cord said. "I'm more worried about Opie. I think he's gone soft."

"Not to mention she's going to turn my boy into a damn pussy," he said. "With all her artsy-fartsy nonsense. Black nail polish and magic spells. I told that woman a long time ago that she can have ice cream or steak. But she can't have both. What did you say about Ope?"

"Come on," Cord said. "You got to let that shit go. Listen, can we do this whole thing with Opie?"

"Huh," Wilcox said. "What? What are you saying? Ope's my chicken-wing man. He's taking down the cash register and everyone in the restaurant while we hit the car wash. Cool?"

"I don't like this," Cord said. "I don't like any of it. It all smells like dog shit."

"Maybe we should see a counselor?" Wilcox said. "Talk it out. Make some changes. There's still a chance, right?"

The bullshit might've been easier to take without the forty-minute discussion on pest control at the courthouse, the supervisors genuinely perplexed by whether bids should include indoor and outdoor spraying or just be limited to the confines of the building. But, damn, if things didn't really get serious, Fannie knowing that Skinner was just fucking with her now, moving the pussy debate until last, when the county road manager, a slow-talking pud son of a bitch named Danny Corbitt, asked the county to approve a purchase of a shit ton of a gravel for unsatisfactory roads. After serious consideration, Skinner finally opened up the meeting to the public for comments.

"I understand one of our constituents would like to speak on enforcement of existing laws," Skinner said. "There's been some confusion about nude dancing on premises where alcohol is served."

Fannie stood up and approached the lectern, feeling all those eyes on her Jezebel ass, packed tight in a black pencil skirt. She nodded at Skinner and the two porky men sandwiching him, in identical blue suits and dark mortician ties. On the far end was a black man named Dupuy, a frequent customer of Vienna's, and on the other was a man named Sam Bishop, Jr., who she only knew from the newspaper as some kind of local do-gooder, Boy Scout troop leader and the like.

Fannie introduced herself as the proprietor of the Rebel Truck Stop, the Golden Cherry Motel, and Vienna's Place, to which she added, "I recognize many of my best customers in this room," but not specifying which business. She turned to scan the crowd, several heads dropped behind hands or ball caps tugged down into eyes. A few contractors in dirty boots snickered, not giving a good goddamn.

"Miss Hathcock," Skinner said, fluorescent light shining hard off his bald head, pearl-gray Stetson turned crown down on the dais. "While we recognize your right to speak here in public, I hope you know this is a county law we've had on the books since 1953 when a predecessor of yours, a spot called the Bamboo Club, offered whiskey and female companionship on the county line."

"Maybe it's unclear exactly what you're enforcing," Fannie said.

Skinner looked down onto some paper, flipping through a few pages, half-glasses down on his bulbous nose. "The law states a few things," he said. "First and foremost, your entertainers must be at least five feet from customers at all times. The other is that your performers must cover their lower extremities if alcohol is being served."

"Excuse me if I don't have a law degree," Fannie said, placing her hands on each side of the lectern and bringing her mouth close to the microphone. "You want us to cover the cooch or cork the bottle?"

Several folks in the meeting room started to laugh, Fannie spotting Betty Jo Mize from the **Tibbehah Monitor** scribbling down some notes she could never publish. Skinner's face turned a bright shade of red, still pretending to read the ordinance. But the old man didn't waver, just answered back. "Yes, ma'am," he said. "That's the way the law reads. And it will be enforced starting now. I guess I had been under the impression you had legal counsel with you. And might I remind you, you're under the clock for public comment. This isn't up for debate."

"I was under the impression you were about to tack on a few more laws."

"The current law is under discussion," Skinner said. "We'll let you know when the board has made a decision about further action."

"That's damn kind of you, Mr. Skinner," Fannie said. "But if you want to shuffle the deck, you need to do it right here. There are public meeting laws even in a sorry-ass state like Mississippi. You want to discuss updating that county ordinance, let's do it now."

"There's a lot to consider," Skinner said, turning his head and listening to one of the porky men, stuffed into his navy blue suit, whisper into his ear. "We are studying the problem. You are welcome to bring it up at the next meeting."

Skinner quickly announced the end to Fannie's time and she vacated the dais, which was turned over to a black woman from Sugar Ditch who said she had drainage backing up into her front yard. As Fannie hit the back door out of the room, she heard the woman talking about the smell being worse than a truckload of mule farts. Fannie pushed out in the hall, getting a little water from the fountain and waiting for the good ole boys to wrap up so she could brace Skinner.

Twenty minutes later, the two doors busted open and Skinner waddled out with the two porky little men in tow, both of them also wearing American flag lapel pins.

"Me and you need to talk," she said.

"No, ma'am," Skinner said. "Not tonight. You have a problem and you can set up a meeting with the county secretary."

"Don't bullshit me," she said. "Just when are y'all planning to take out my knees?"

"There's the consideration of granting a license for your club," Skinner said. "And issuing licenses for your girls by the health department."

"Don't you think I know if my girls have crotch crickets or the clap?" Fannie said. "I run a class establishment, Mr. Skinner. Haven't you seen the billboards? 'The Finest Southern Belles and the Coldest Beer'? I know what I got and what I sell."

"They will still need to be tested," Skinner said, looking both ways down the hall, his two little toads in tight suits heading on out the front door without him. "And licensed. Our goal is to protect the safety and health of the people of Jericho."

"Except for when one of you runs the establishment," Fannie said. "It sounds like you boys want to slap a ban on nude dancing now that a woman is in town. Might want to check with your lawyer first. That's a violation of a girl's free speech."

"If you don't like Tibbehah County values," Skinner said, "no one is forcing you to stay. You can leave town as easily as you arrived from down with the Indians, Miss Hathcock. This is a town of schools and churches. You want to practice your type of business, you might be relegated somewhere farther out in the county and away from children and places of worship."

"That sounds an awful lot like a ban to me," Fannie said. "Extorting money from me and my girls, telling us how we can express ourselves. Telling me that I may need to relocate or be run from town. Have you discussed all this with the sheriff? Because you're dropping a whole truckload of cow shit on my head at the moment. Don't you know my heaviest hour of business starts in twenty minutes?"

"We know the type of people you attract," Skinner said, looking at Fannie over his half-glasses. "College boys and chicken haulers. I think our county is just fine without their support."

"And you might remember a time when the Rebel and what used to be the Booby Trap were the only reason anyone would ever come to visit this backwoods shithole."

Skinner stared at her, placing a couple of fingers to his withered mouth, trying to control himself and keep down that anger that Fannie knew was there. "I will ask you not to speak to me with such filth," Skinner said. "And I will be the first to say Tibbehah County and the town of Jericho did fine before the days of the repugnant Bamboo Club or Johnny Stagg's barnyard establishments. We are quite serious about this, Miss Hathcock. You've been advised. Look for the sheriff to start enforcing our laws immediately."

Fannie ran a hand over her red silk blouse to make sure her black bra wasn't showing and giving a free show. "I've dealt with better men," Fannie said. "And so has my high-dollar lawyer up in Memphis. He doesn't make five hundred dollars an hour just to jack his thumb up his ass and cry to Momma."

"I like a woman with spunk," Skinner said, grinning with his yellowed teeth. "Always a pleasure, Miss Hathcock."

Fannie collected her Birkin bag from the hallway bench, snatching a cigar from her little case and plucking it into her mouth, walking out of the building and into the parking lot. She hit the UNLOCK button on her Mercedes as that newswoman, Betty Jo Mize, trotted up behind her like a little dog.

"You think you might be able to repeat some of those same things in English?" Miss Mize asked.

"Just what didn't you hear?"

"Nothing," Miss Mize said. "Eavesdropping is one of my true talents."

Fannie liked the old woman, smiling at her as she lit her cigarillo and leaned against her open car door. "Wish I could I could tell you mine, Miss Mize. But I don't think you'd print such trash in a family newspaper."

"I've known Skinner his whole life," Miss Mize said.

"Is he who he says he is?"

Miss Mize thought about it, watching Fannie smoke there in the parking lot. She shook her head.

"No, Miss Hathcock," she said. "He's something far worse."

The old man lived at the edge of the Skid Bucket, a gathering of busted-ass trailers not far off the Big Black in east Tibbehah. Most of the trailers were empty, since sweet potato picking time had come and gone, pickers heading into central Florida for strawberry season. Caddy found the ramshackle trailer at the front of the park. The old man named Manuel had been there for years. She heard he was a pretty good bricklayer when he wasn't drunk.

Caddy got out of her truck and walked over to the old man. He was cooking a whole chicken over a split oil drum held up by concrete blocks, a mess of other chickens pecking around in the dark. None of them seemed worried their friend was dinner.

"Manuel?"

He looked up from the spit, knowing someone had driven up but so damn drunk that he didn't seem to give a crap. A woman at The River had told her that Manuel knew something about Ana Maria's father but to make sure to bring tequila. "He talks when he drinks," the woman had said.

When Caddy pulled out the tequila bottle from the paper sack, the old man looked up and licked his lips. "My name's Caddy Colson," she said. "We've met before. I brought you some blankets and a heater last winter."

He nodded, bloodshot eyes trained on the bottle. Pepe Lopez in a screw-top bottle.

"I'm looking for someone," she said. "A girl named Ana Maria. Her father was a man named José. He did odd jobs, like you. He was a roofer, sometimes hung Sheetrock. He had a tattoo of the Virgin on the back of his neck."

"Is that your bottle?" he said. The man was small, dark, and shriveled up. He wore a threadbare pair of overalls with a worn-out green flannel shirt and an orange trucker cap that read WALLS FLOORING.

"It's yours, if you help me," she said. "Do you know José?"

"José?" He laughed. "I know fifty men named José. Say, open the bottle. Let's drink, pretty lady. Did anyone tell you you're so pretty? Even with that short hair like a boy. I'll feed you some chicken, lady. I just killed it. I wrung its little neck and boiled it today."

It had gotten cold, a hard wind shooting through the maze of trailers. White feathers swirled under the single bulb by the trailer door. Caddy had on a mackinaw coat Boom had left down at The River. She thanked Manuel but said she'd already eaten.

"I know just as many Ana Marias," he said. "My mother was Ana Maria. Who did you say you were again? I know you. I know your face."

"Caddy Colson," she said. "I've brought you blankets. And meals sometimes."

"Oh, yes," he said. "Oh, yes. You are a nice lady. So very nice. Sweet and kind. A true saint. God bless you. God bless you. Would you like some chicken to go with that tequila? Fine bottle. And it's such a cold night for an old man."

"You don't look so old."

He smiled, lots of teeth missing. And those that remained looked brown and loose. "Not more than sixty," he said. "But I've lived a very long and hard life. I'm a bricklayer. Do you know anyone who would hire me? I'm the best in north Mississippi. A man just fired me for being drunk. But I lay the bricks better drunk. It helps me see the patterns and shapes."

"This girl," Caddy said, pulling a picture of Ana Maria from her pocket. "She's fifteen. She's with a girl about the same age. A black girl named Tamika."

Manuel nodded, taking the photograph, really staring at it a while, before handing it back. "I know her," he said. "She's a nice little girl. She lived with her father. Sometimes her father would come here and get drunk with the other men. She would help get him home. Nice girl. Very nice. Like you, my friend. Are you a nice lady?"

"Where is she?"

"The girl?" he said. "Oh, she's gone. They're all gone. It's the end of the season. And I'm too old to travel with them. I live here. I've lived here for fif-teen years. I'm from Nuevo Laredo. Do you know that place? This town is much nicer. This home I have is a mansion to me."

"Do you think she's with her father?"

"May we open the tequila?"

"Do you have answers?"

"I have answers," he said, shaky hands reaching for the bottle. Not looking up. "But you won't like what I have to say. Is this girl your friend?"

"Yes."

He cracked the seal and poured the tequila into a red Solo cup. Lifting the cup to his lips, he drained the tequila and poured another. "I'm sorry," he said. "So sorry. Would you like some? Such a pretty lady needs a drink. Where are my manners? I can be more forward as an old man. You don't have to be afraid of me."

Caddy looked at the bottle, shiny in the firelight, and swallowed. She shook her head and waited while the man drank some more.

"Her father came back for her two weeks ago," he said.

"Did you see her?"

"No," Manuel said. "He owed some men a lot of money. He left the girl and then came back."

"But he left with her?"

"The girl was gone," he said, face flushing with the tequila. "When he demanded his daughter be returned, two men with lead pipes came for him. They beat him very badly. I had to help him stop the bleeding and wrapped his ribs with duct tape. The next day, his truck was gone."

"Where?"

"Back to wherever they go."

"Do you know his name?"

"Like you said," Manuel said, "José."

"A last name?"

The old man laughed, sticking a fork in the chicken and turning it over onto the spit. The meat sizzled as he poured more tequila into the red cup and savored it a long while. "Will you take the bottle when you leave?"

Caddy shook her head.

"These people here," he said, "they don't have names or addresses. This man was illegal. So was his daughter. The men who beat him reminded him that he was less important than some stray dog."

"Who were the men?"

"Anglos," he said. "In a new white truck. I pretended not to see them."

"Who had his daughter?"

"I don't know," he said. "I'm very sorry. He only complained and cried. José told me he'd done a terrible, awful thing."

"He should have gone to the sheriff."

"The police would do nothing but arrest him," Manuel said. "Who is this man? Who is the girl?

243

Who am I? We don't really exist. Not here. Not now. In this time . . . Are you sure you'll leave the bottle?"

"Where's their trailer?"

"Over there," Manuel said, pointing into the darkness. "It's a green trailer without a door. A small truck has been parked outside without wheels."

Caddy thanked the man and walked toward the dark gravel road lined with empty trailers. She turned to see Manuel sitting in the ragged easy chair, lifting the tequila and smiling into the smoke.

18

Early the next morning, Skinner barged into the sheriff's office, walking by Mary Alice and the Coca-Cola machine to stand right before Quinn's desk. Quinn was on the phone, talking to a police chief down in Ridgeland about transporting a fella named Herrin J. Arnold back to Tibbehah after he'd been pulled over for speeding. Quinn wanted Herrin back in his jail after he'd ditched Jericho and broke into two more houses up in Yalobusha County. The police chief said Arnold smelled like a gosh dang rancid goat and would be more than happy to FedEx his ass, if possible.

Quinn hung up and looked up at Skinner. The man stood before him, plaid shirt with a pocket full of pens, khakis, and the Stetson. His face red and breathing labored.

"Don't y'all speak English?" Skinner said. "I said I wanted Vienna's shut down and locked up tight."

Quinn didn't answer the old man. He leaned back in his leather chair and crossed his arms over his chest. His ball cap up on the hat rack, .45 locked and loaded on his desk. He figured he could shoot Skinner, but Lillie always reminded him about the damn paperwork to follow. Quinn hated that paperwork.

"Before we shut it down, we've got to make a case."

"What kind of case do y'all boys need?" he said. "They got live cooch shows going on twenty-four/ seven down there. Doesn't take Dick Tracy to see decency laws are being broken."

"We sent a deputy by last night," Quinn said. "Girls had on their G-strings, keeping five feet away from customers. Isn't that the law?"

"You know gosh dang well they put on their britches when they saw y'all drive up," Skinner said. "Don't you boys know anything about undercover work? I seen a TV show, on that **Cops** program, where a man had a tiny camera in his hat. Surely y'all can figure something like that out."

"Mr. Skinner," Quinn said, giving the old man a little more respect than he deserved. "I have three deputies on at night. We have more than five hundred square miles of county to patrol. Between the family squabbles, the filling station thieving, and in general drug-induced mayhem over the weekend, we stay a little busy keeping people safe."

"Do your job, Sheriff," Skinner said. "That place is a disgrace to any decent person in this county. Or are you afraid of Miss Hathcock?"

"I'm not looking out for Fannie," Quinn said, "if that's what you're saying. But that place was never built to cater to this county. That's why it sits outside city limits near the highway. In an effort to protect and serve, I don't give a shit if a traveling salesmen from Starkville gets his pecker pulled."

"I don't have time for that kind of filthy talk," Skinner said, face growing even a deeper shade of red. "I knew you'd hide behind the excuse that that Hathcock woman engaged in a victimless crime. Do you know she threatened me before the board of supervisors with some Jew lawyer up in Memphis? And then started to talk about crotch crickets and her girls' wild cooters. We had just been speaking to our county road manager about buying some gravel and he's an ordained minister."

"Yeah, I know Jerry," Quinn said. "I knew him back when he loved Jäger shots more than Jesus."

"You're making us look like fools," Skinner said. "I made a pronouncement in front of the supervisors and Betty Jo Mize. She has it right there in the paper, in Betty Jo's weekly column, next to that chili recipe. If that repugnant, vile place is still open by

247

ACE ATKINS

the end of the week, you better start looking for other employment."

"And how are you going to fire me?" Quinn said. "Sheriff is an elected position, Mr. Skinner."

"Wasn't when your uncle ran things," Skinner said. "He knew where his bread was buttered and how that jam got slathered on. Hamp Beckett was a practical man and knew who really ran the show."

Quinn stood up so fast Skinner took a quick step back. "Don't lecture me on my uncle," he said. "Ever. I had to scrape his brains off the wall of my farmhouse because he couldn't take the bullshit."

"You're a tough young nut," Skinner said, running a hand over his weak jaw and sort of grinning. "Think you got things figured out, know the way a watch works. But, boy, you got no dang idea how things really work. Or the mess you're in if you don't go and take out the trash."

Quinn stared at the man with the long monkey arms and skinny potbelly. The light blue eyes behind the gold-rimmed glasses, the ridiculous LBJ hat, and the loose skin hanging from his neck like a prize tom. He didn't say anything, knowing that the man only wanted to load up on some gossip to spread around the Square.

"How can any Christian man stomach what goes in that place?" Skinner said. "You call it victimless? What about the lives ruined? Families broken up?

248

Those heated-up harlots, panting and sweating, make men do things they wouldn't in the real world."

"Last I checked, Fannie Hathcock wasn't holding a gun on anyone."

Skinner grinned, planted his feet, and shook his head. "**Be sober, be vigilant,** young man," Skinner said, "**because your adversary the devil, as a roaring lion, walketh about, seeking who he may devour.**"

"Appreciate that, preacher," Quinn said, sitting back down. "But I got work to do."

"You did what no one thought you could," Skinner said. "You ran Stagg out of town and opened up a world of possibilities for Tibbehah County. This is a time for miracles, Sheriff Colson. Business and jobs returning to our little county. Why would you even risk that for one moment?"

"I got the ordinance," Quinn said. "I'll enforce it."

"A tough, tough nut."

Quinn nodded. Skinner touched the brim of his Stetson and tromped, splayfooted, from the room.

"Who'd they send?" Fannie asked.

"Reggie Caruthers," Mingo said, wiping down Vienna's bar. "He stayed for a while and watched the girls dance. I gave him a Coke and he insisted on paying for it. I figured he just kinda got bored and left."

"And the girls had on their G-strings?"

"Yes, ma'am," Mingo said. "All of them but Vernice wore what I bought in Tupelo. Vernice wanted to wear some kind of homemade shit she'd made with some red satin, a glue gun, and glitter. She thought it looked sexy, but I thought she looked like she was dancing with a damn cookie on her muff."

"Tell her the Victoria's Secret gear is now the uniform," Fannie said, setting an elbow to the bar and dropping her forehead to the heel of her hand. "Skinner wants all the girls to be registered. I hear a license may be two hundred dollars. That's a night for most of my girls."

"Can't you just pay it for them?"

"Of course," Fannie said. "But that's not the point. Skinner wants to monetize our little skin game. He claims he's holier than thou and doesn't want to get his hands dirty, but that's proof right there."

"Any man buttoned up that tight has issues," Mingo said, slicing up an orange and placing it in the glass with some cherries and gin. "Either that or his pecker doesn't work. Probably makes him mad as hell thinking about all the sweaty gyration and releasing going on down on Highway 45. Man only wants to join in the show."

"As sorry as I am to say it," Fannie said, "the VIP room is closed until further notice."

"No lap dancing?"

"Five-foot rule," Fannie said. "I'll playing Little

Miss Fucking Sunshine until we get all this business straightened out. I'll be honest, I thought we would have shut this bullshit down right quick."

"Why don't we?" Mingo said, placing a little cocktail napkin down and then serving up her Dirty Shirley. "You've dealt with a lot worse."

Fannie took a sip, nodding. "Our boys are afraid of him," Fannie said. "Do you believe that shit? I was told no one wants to mess with Skinner. They won't tell me who's behind him, but I've got it on rock-solid authority it's our buddy Vardaman."

Mingo let out a long breath. "Where'd you hear that?"

"Johnny Stagg."

"Shit," Mingo said. "You spoke to him?"

"Spoke to him?" Fannie said. "I saw his broke-down ass in an orange jumpsuit. That's where I went the other day. Drove all the way over to Montgomery to have a face-to-face. I found out there's no love lost between him and Skinner. Way I hear it, this shit's been boiling over for decades."

"Vardaman's a creep," Mingo said.

"That's the best word you can come up with?"

"At the moment," Mingo said. "I never liked going out to his place. He's almost never there. And when he is, you never see him. All those handlers and ass lickers."

"With this shit show that goes on at that hunt lodge, would you want anyone to see your face?"

"He's got real specific tastes."

"So did Hitler," Fannie said. "He liked women to piss on him."

"We've seen worse," Mingo said.

"I told you when you came on, there's more excitement working for Fannie Hathcock than joining up with the Ringling Brothers," she said, taking a sip of the cocktail. "But they both have about the same smell."

"What do we do?"

"Wait 'em out," Fannie said. "I got my lawyer jamming up these fucking hillbillies until kingdom come. I don't think we'll see any registration or permitting for a long while. But in that long meantime, we play nice. We're straight titties and likker. Got that? If the girls want to put out on the side, let 'em take it across the street to the Golden Cherry. But here at Vienna's, we're going to be cleaner than goddamn Main Street at Disney World."

"Two girls are out today."

"Who's that?"

"Vernice and Skylar."

"What's wrong with them?"

"Vernice says she has a cold," Mingo said. "Skylar says she's just real tired and staying home to watch **Days of Our Lives.**"

"When I worked the pole, I never missed a chance to make money," Fannie said. "I had those boys from the base just begging me to take their wallets. Hell, I

had a steady rotation of a dozen or so flyboys sending me money from bases all around the world. They
thought we'd get married when they got home. Or
else they said they'd leave their wife and they'd set
me up in some crummy apartment by the airfield.
Not for me. Not for the best piece of pussy in the
state of Mississippi."

"I wouldn't know," Mingo said, leaning by the bar
taps, towel thrown over his shoulder. Lean and hard,
with all that black hair, he looked just like Jeffrey
Hunter all made up in **The Searchers**.

"And you never will, kid," Fannie said, toasting
him with her cocktail. "You're about the closest thing
I'll ever have to a son."

"You raised me right, Miss Hathcock."

Fannie winked at him and took a long, cold drink.

"Two men came for Ana Maria's father and beat the
tar out of him with lead pipes," Caddy said. "What
is this, Russia? You can't pull that kind of crap in
Mississippi."

"Try being black," Boom said.

"You get any names?" Lillie asked.

"Manuel didn't know them," Caddy said. "They
were white men, a couple roughnecks from the way
he was talking."

Boom nodded, all of them sitting in the far back
room of the Fillin' Station, a little section of the

diner cut off from the rest of the restaurant with an accordion partition. The walls lined with photos of Little League teams from all the years gone by who'd held their end-of-season celebrations there. Sometimes couples had anniversary parties, others rented out the space for after funerals. The Fillin' Station pulling out the catfish and fried-chicken buffet with swampy green beans and crisp hush puppies. The room always smelled like grease and cigarette smoke, Caddy knowing she'd have to wash her clothes when she got home.

"Manuel is a crazy-ass drunk," Boom said. "Hangs out at that pool hall up in Yellow Leaf, where they got tables in that shed. What's that man's name who owns it?"

"Bruce Nichols," Lillie said.

"Who the hell is that?"

"You know him," Lillie said. "Used to run the meat department at Piggly Wiggly. Got busted a couple times for selling pain pills."

Boom nodded. "Oh, yeah," he said. "Sure. Cut me some mean T-bones."

"I'm pretty sure Manuel knows more than he's saying," Caddy said. "I don't think he would have told me those men's names if I'd backed up a tanker full of tequila."

"That motherfucker can down some tequila," Boom said.

Caddy looked up at Lillie, who was inspecting the

wall of fame, pointing to a junior high basketball team, Lillie in her uniform, standing a good head taller than most of the girls. "Don't think he'd talk," Lillie said, searching for more. "Even drunk."

"How about Fannie Hathcock?" Caddy said. "What'd she say?"

"She claimed she'd never heard of the girls and that Blue was lying."

"Bullshit," Boom said. "His ass was highly motivated to tell the damn truth. Those girls were sold to Fannie. She had them for at least a few weeks."

"How do we know?" Lillie said, turning back from the wall, hands on hips, full attention back on Caddy. "I mean, really? We're taking the word of Blue Daniels? And finding out about some shadow peckerwoods from a Mexican drunk? Y'all got to get me a little more."

"I know," Caddy said, almost whispering. "Someone saw them, but I can't tell you who. They were there and then they just disappeared."

"Maybe they went back home," Lillie said.

"These girls don't have a home," Caddy said. "Nobody's left out at Skid Bucket besides Manuel. Tamika's mother won't claim her. If we can find these two men, maybe we can find out what happened."

Lillie set her eyes on Caddy. "Who do you know inside Fannie's place?" she said. "One of the working girls?"

Caddy shook her head. "Doesn't matter," she said.

"If they knew where to find them, I'd know. Lots of girls come and go from that place. Some girls who never even see inside Fannie's bar. She runs girls from Houston through some people in Biloxi and New Orleans. They get sent to work up north in roadside jerk shacks. Most of the girls are illegals, can't say shit."

"Wait a second," Lillie said, holding up the flat of her hand. "Hold the fucking phone. You think they got shipped off?"

Caddy looked to Boom and back to Lillie, nodding. "But why would two teenage girls be so almighty important to Fannie Hathcock? She's the kind of woman who does as she pleases and gives the rest of the world the finger."

"She cares," Lillie said. "That woman gives a great goddamn what we think about her. I think she's scared to death Skinner is going to shut down her show."

"Fuck that guy," Boom said.

"No thanks." Lillie pushed off the wall and sat down with them at the head of the table. "Y'all are now getting me into Deep Shit City. Not only has this become a missing persons case but now you've thrown in assault, possibly attempted murder of Ana Maria's father and human trafficking with Fannie. I'm glad to sit down with you both and chew the bullshit anytime, but it's high time we bring in Quinn. We drove way past church camp."

"Nope," Caddy said. "Not yet."

"Jesus Christ," Lillie said. "These girls might be dead. And if there're more girls, Quinn's got to talk to his bearded stranger bud up in Oxford. This is some serious bullshit y'all have stirred up. As if we didn't have our own fucking problems."

Boom looked up from his big-ass Mountain Dew. "Y'all caught those bank robbers yet?"

"Nope," Lillie said.

"Got any leads?" Boom said, grinning.

"Not a fucking one," Lillie said.

Boom looked to Caddy and then over at Lillie. "Well, looks like we all in the same boat," Boom said. "We all don't know shit about shit. I'm for bringing in Quinn. Ain't no telling where those little girls went. What Blue did, selling them into that world, just grinds my goddamn teeth."

"You want another shot at him," Lillie said. "Don't you?"

Boom smiled and stood, reaching for his cap with his hook hand. Caddy amazed how he could set it down on his head without cutting himself.

19

They'd been over and over it. Cord had sketched out the interior of the count room and Opie had run through all the photos Crissley had taken inside the Wing Machine. Opie said he'd studied the pictures so many times he could recount all thirty-one flavors on the menu, from Cool Breeze to Super-Bad Mothers, the real ass burner of the bunch. Crissley had bought a dozen to go, a batch somewhere in the middle called Down and Dirty, and they weren't half bad, eating them in the parking lot to Graceland with a six-pack of Bud Light. Cord was back at the wheel today, Wilcox riding shotgun in a navy blue GMC Yukon he'd checked out from the lot and would return for an executive detail from his boys in maintenance. Their watches had been set, plans made, and it would all go down like this if the dumb shits complied.

1. At the set time, Opie would take down the Wing Machine. He'd get them all into the cooler and bolt their ass inside before locking the front door and turning out the lights. No shots. No mess.

2. At the same moment, Cord and Wilcox would roll into the detail shop out back. The detail shop was closed on Sunday, but they'd act like they were confused. Get the boys talking, cool and relaxed, and then put an assault rifle up their ass. They could get shot or they could relax and let it happen.

3. The shooters taken outside would lead them into the count room. The main problem being two cameras inside the Wing Machine and a camera in the alley where they washed cars. But being hit at the same time, double-teamed, would split the Twins' attention. It'd take some time to drop handfuls of money and flutes of champagne.

And if the Twins locked down the count room, Wilcox had packed a few surprises. A door-busting shotgun and a few flashbangs. This crew may be the baddest motherfuckers in Memphis, but no one could clear a fucking room like Bravo Company. And this time there were no snipers, no IEDs out-side the compound, and they had the wonderful gift of surprise. If these boys kept to schedule, they'd be popping the champagne right now, making sure not to spill a sip on those funky Sunday suits. **Hallelujah, motherfuckers.**

"I don't like the split with that woman," Wilcox said. "It doesn't seem fair."

"It's what we agreed," Cord said.

"Everything's negotiable," Wilcox said, grinning, checking over the AR-15 in his lap and putting his hand on the Colt .45 on his waist. "Especially after we have the money."

"What we said is what we said," Cord said.

"Redheads always had a way to mindfuck you, brother," he said. "Haven't you read **The Art of the Deal?**"

Wilcox had on a black Under Armour hoodie and a pair of utility pants with Merrell boots, pant pockets loaded down with four extra clips. After the deed, if they'd fired the weapons, which Wilcox hoped would happen, they'd dump the guns in the Mississippi, burn their clothes, and lay low for at least a month. Maybe go down to the beach with Opie.

Wilcox passed out the Trump masks to Opie and Cord.

"Goddamn it," Cord said. "We've been over this. Why risk the Feds tying us to this shit show?"

"It's our calling card," Wilcox said. "We'll Make the Mid-South Great Again!"

"You're a crazy motherfucker," Cord said. "You know that?"

Opie leaned up between the seats and smiled. "He knows it," Opie said. "Everybody knows it. You just catching on, Cord?"

"Do you really want someone else to get the credit?" Wilcox asked. "Christ on a stick."

"What pisses me off is that you two have all the fun," Opie said. "I just walk in and say, you know, the line—"

"I want you to say," Wilcox said, "'Get down, you disgusting fat pigs, or I will shoot you in the pussy.'"

"We've already done the pussy thing," Opie said. "I'd rather do something new. That guy says stupid shit every fucking day."

"Like what?"

"Like 'I'm not a crook,'" Opie said, big freckled face beaming as Wilcox turned to see if he was serious.

"That was Nixon, you retard," Wilcox said. "Our CEO in Chief would never say he's not a crook. He'd look at the camera, lick his lips, and say I just ass-raped you and what are you going to do about it, losers?"

"How am I supposed to know Nixon?" Opie said. "Shit, man. I wasn't even born yet."

"Say it quick and mean," Wilcox said. "You hit it hard and fast when you walk in that door and those folks will go stone-cold fetal on you."

"Yes, sir," Opie said. "But next time, we go to a different president. Maybe Teddy Roosevelt or

Ronald Reagan? These masks are starting to smell like ass."

"Sure thing, Ope," Wilcox said. "Just do your job and knock on that connect door when they're in cold storage."

"Just save a few for me," Opie said.

Cord looked up in the mirror with some concern in his eyes, turning in front of the Wing Machine, Opie pulling down the mask and jumping from the car, slamming the door and walking with speed and purpose into the shop. Wilcox just caught the beautiful sight of five or six folks with their hands raised behind the plate-glass window. **Yes, yes, yes.** Wilcox's heart was a damn jackhammer in his chest.

"Attaboy," Wilcox said.

"Still don't like it," Cord said. "One of us should be with him. He's still just a fucking kid."

"So was Dennis the Menace," Wilcox said. "But he sure could fuck stuff up."

"People are going to start to talk," Maggie said.

"Let 'em talk," Quinn said. "Never bothered me."

"We were spotted together at church," she said. "Everyone saw us. A few old ladies looked at me weird between the hymns."

"That's because they are weird," Quinn said. "And they didn't know you. A new woman in town is big excitement at Calvary Methodist. If we'd sat down together, then there would a lot of gossip."

Quinn had brought out three Coleman camp chairs to his pond. He'd gotten out Jason's cane pole, a pole his nephew graduated from a long time ago, and placed it in Brandon's hands. The kid watched the bobber, a live cricket on the hook. The rhythm of life, Quinn starting out the same way with his Uncle Hamp until he got a .22 for his sixth birthday. He still preferred fishing to hunting. Maggie unpacked a folding chair, watching Brandon keep on checking his hook, patience something that would come much later. Quinn set up beside her, placing a bucket full of ice, beer, and water between them.

"We did sit together," Maggie said.

"I sat with my mother and nephew," Quinn said. "You just happened to find a seat next to us. I didn't invite you."

"Jason's a sweet boy," Maggie said. "He passed the hymnal to me when he saw me sharing with you on 'Blessed Assurance.' Does he know who I am?"

"Nope."

"And your mother?"

"She knows," Quinn said.

"How's that?"

"As soon as you sat down, she cut her eyes over at me," Quinn said. "She saw something pass between us. She knew. After the service, I walked her and Jason to their car and she said, 'She's darling, Quinn. How about you bring her over to dinner sometime?'"

"And what did you say?"

"I told her I'd never seen you before in my life, but you had a cute little ass."

Maggie laughed and leaned back into the chair, tugging a ball cap down over her eyes. Quinn reached for a Coors in the ice bucket and tossed her a can. She caught it in midair without even looking.

"Wow."

"Shit," Maggie Powers said. "You don't know the half of it. I'm full of surprises."

"I told you, man," the fat black dude called Johnny Snacks said, orange Cheetos dust on his mustache. "We fucking closed. You gonna have to rub your own motherfucking ride today."

"I've rubbed my ride too many times," Wilcox said, turning from him, pulling on the mask, and leveling the AR-15 at his fat ass. "But it just doesn't give me the same satisfaction."

"Oh, fuck," the thin, ugly dude called Armani said. He tried to reach inside his coat but saw Cord had already leveled a rifle out the driver's window. He pulled down the mask and stepped out toward the two men, Wilcox following.

Johnny Snacks's stomach hung loose over his

dark blue jeans and he wore an XXXL T-shirt reading GRIT & GRIND. Wilcox snatched the Glock off his fat ass. Armani looked sharp with the black suit, gold tie, and gold-plated Glock hidden beneath his threads. Cord admired it for a moment before tucking it into his hoodie pocket.

"Fuck me," Johnny Snacks said.

"Yes, sir," Wilcox said, marching his big butt to the back door of the count room. "Fuck me. Fuck you. Fuck everything. Fuck that shit."

Wilcox whistled a bit, "Who's Afraid of the Big Bad Wolf," as they moved. Cord looked up at the camera at the roofline and shot out the lens without missing a step. Cord, as always, showing off.

When they hit the door, Wilcox heard a quick double pop of a pistol. Cord turned quick to Wilcox, Wilcox nodding **Move! Move. Fucking move! Keep to the plan.** He pressed the barrel into Johnny Snacks's ear and said, "Knock, knock."

Snacks swallowed and knocked. The door flying open, a tall black man with a shaved head and wearing a canary yellow suit looking out at them. "Goddamn," he said. "Wing Machine being robbed."

Wilcox pushed Johnny Snacks into the room so hard that the fat man tumbled to the concrete floor. "Nope," he said, aiming the gun at one of the Twins. "You boys are being robbed. Hands up or I'll shoot you and your zoot suit twin in the fucking head. Now."

The black dude and his identical twin brother, that man wearing the same fucking suit only in bright purple, nodded and raised their hands. But, damn, if they didn't look mighty pissed about it. Cord covered the room, Wilcox looking over at the bank of flat-screen TVs mounted on the cinder-block wall. "Goddamn it," Wilcox said, not seeing Opie, only black folks scattering.

Cord nodded at Wilcox, letting him know he had control of the room. Wilcox tried the door to the Wing Machine, but it was locked. He stepped back and kicked it wide open, seeing two bodies down on the ground and a lot of blood, and someone's spilled Coke.

He checked the corners, searching for Opie, as more shooting came from the count room. He heard Cord yell "Fuck" and start unloading his weapon.

"Can you stay for an early dinner? I have to go on patrol in a little while."

"We didn't catch anything," Maggie said. "Besides two limbs and a stump."

"I need to get that stump out of there," Quinn said. "Jason lost half his tackle box on that damn thing."

They took the worn deer path from the pond through the woods back to the farmhouse. Maggie had gone home after church and changed into frayed jeans and a black Reigning Sound band T-shirt. She'd worn a ball cap and a pair of flip-flops, Quinn offering her a pair of rubber boots that Anna Lee Stevens had left at his house last summer. They were a little too small, but she made them work.

"You never did ask me about last weekend," she said. "When I had to leave so quick and get Brandon in Memphis."

"I figured you'd tell me if you want me to know."

Quinn carried the folding chairs and Maggie carried the bucket, now empty except for a couple of crushed beer cans and empty water bottles. She was smiling and pink-faced from the sun, and kept on knocking the bucket against Quinn's leg as they walked.

"He's shacked up with some woman in a loft downtown," she said. "He told me he was living out in Cordova, which was lie number one. Then he came out with Brandon, standing there telling me that he hoped I was happy waking everybody up on such a lovely night. He said Brandon had the time of his life at the zoo and watching his daddy play his shitty country music down on Beale Street."

"What's shitty about country music?" Quinn said.

"You ever heard of Florida-Georgia Line?" Maggie asked. "Or Jason Aldean?"

"Nope," Quinn said. "My record collection stops

in the early eighties. But I do like some of the new stuff. Jason Isbell, Jamey Johnson, Chris Stapleton. There's also a woman named Margo Price who understands the beauty of outlaw country."

"I knew you were a Waylon man."

"If you got to tell people how country you are," Quinn said, "then you ain't country."

"I know," Maggie said. "I'm got so goddamn sick of hearing Rick singing songs about his dog, his pickup truck, and how much he loved his goddamn mother. First off, his mother is a real queen bitch. Second, he doesn't even like dogs."

"Hate the guy already."

"And he's a Marine."

"Damn."

They watched Brandon ramble on down the hill, through the deep woods in tall rubber boots, with Hondo trotting alongside. Quinn and Maggie remained in the depths of the woods while Brandon headed on into the house with Hondo. The light was nice in the woods, flickering and mottled, through the sprawling bare branches, purplish pink flowers showing on the redbuds. You could smell spring coming up from the heated earth and in the little bits of green on the rocks and new grass.

"Your old girlfriend had small feet," Maggie said. "These boots are starting to hurt like hell."

"You don't like shoes," Quinn said. "You don't like

bro county, and you can catch a can of Coors out of midair."

Maggie dropped the bucket and wrapped her arms around Quinn's neck, lifting up her legs and hanging there. "I only ask one thing from you."

"Whatever you want."

"Don't let me talk about that stupid shit anymore," she said. "He's been headed down the toilet since he got discharged and I'd like to do my best to keep clean of it all."

"He can't be all that bad."

"Wanna bet?"

Maggie kissed him hard on his mouth, dropping her feet to the forest floor and leaning in, arms holding him tight. "My mother told me all the best ones were taken."

"Your momma was wrong."

"I'm just finding that out," she said. "Now cook me some dinner, Ranger. We don't have much time."

"Yes, ma'am."

Wilcox shot them. He shot both those zoot suit motherfuckers right in the chest. He'd been watching them for more than ten days and still didn't know Shortbox from K-Bo, but whether they came from Orange Mound or Kandahar, they dropped the same. Opie came in behind him, locking up the rest of the Wing Machine in the freezer, and shot those boys again. **Bang-bang-bang.** They were just as dead as the others. As were Johnny Snacks and Armani, wide-eyed and open-mouthed and bloody as hell, down where Cord had shot them against the wall.

"Son of a bitch," Opie said. "More of 'em. That cook I shot is dead, too."

Cord was down, bleeding like a bastard from the stomach. Wilcox pulling up Cord's hoodie to see the wound. He ripped off the Trump mask so Cord could fucking breathe.

"Kill the cameras," Wilcox said. "Fuck up that hard drive."

"Sir," Opie said.

Wilcox pressed a wadded-up T-shirt into Cord's abdomen, looking for something he could use as a tourniquet and seeing some duct tape. He called out to Opie and Opie brought him the roll, Wilcox wrapping Cord as tight as possible while allowing him to breathe. The breath was raspy, a bullet or two probably having ripped through a lung.

Opie shot up the hard drive and computer monitors, knocking them off the wall and sending them crashing to the ground. There was blood all over, on the walls and on the floor, all running toward a drain cut in the center of the floor. Cord looked up at Wilcox from the ground and mouthed something, like a guy with dying breath wanting to send his love back to his family. But as Wilcox pressed an ear close to Cord's mouth he heard "Get the money, fucknuts. The money."

On a long table by a far wall—lined with a bunch of posters for rap shows around Memphis—**Al Ka-pone, Rick Ross, Ying Yang Twins / Brought to You by Double Trouble Productions!!!**—lay stack upon stack of money, neatly bundled and shrink-wrapped after being run through the counter. The Twins so damn business-like and organized that they had the bricks of cash stacked at least three feet high.

"Holy crap," Opie said. "Holy crap."

"I got the money," Wilcox said. "You back up the truck."

Opie ran out to the Yukon as Wilcox lay Cord down on his back. Cord stared up into the lights, breath ragged, cussing while Wilcox tossed stacks into their big black bags. It wasn't like the banks. All that money filled the bags after a few armloads. He grabbed a couple of champagne boxes, put them on the floor, and loaded up the rest of the money bricks. Opie was back now, standing in the doorway with his weapon as Wilcox dragged Cord into the SUV and snatched up the boxes and bags.

Opie hit the gas of the Yukon as soon as Wilcox had slammed the door, fishtailing fast away from the Wing Machine and heading east on EP Boulevard, toward Raines and up around Airways, where they'd hit the interstate.

"Where the hell can we go now?" Opie said.

"Drive south."

"Then what?"

"How the hell do I know?" Wilcox said. "I'm making this shit up as I go along."

20

"Something's wrong," Quinn said.

"A woman brings you a barbecue plate from Dixie-land and you've got complaints," Lillie said. "George even added in some extra sauce and double coleslaw instead of all those beans. I know how much you don't give a shit for baked beans."

Quinn opened up the Styrofoam lid and looked at the beautiful half-chicken plate she'd delivered along with a cold bottle of Coke. He'd eaten a couple of hours ago with Maggie and Brandon but always appreciated Dixieland's barbecue. Still, Lillie was prone to tolerance but seldom generosity. "You want the week off?"

"Nope."

"Someone rear-end the Big Green Machine?"

"Nope."

Quinn opened the Coke and leaned back in his office chair, waiting for Lillie to get on with it. She wore a coy little smile, sitting on the edge of his desk, turning down the radio and waiting a moment to deliver whatever bad news had brought her in after seven o'clock, already fully dark outside.

"You know, you should have more of an open-door policy with your baby sister," Lillie said. "That way, the Colson family wouldn't stick my ass right in the middle of the Shitstorm of the Week."

Quinn closed the lid of the barbecue chicken and folded his arms across his chest. He realized he still had his hat on and took it off and tossed it down on the desk.

"You know those two teenage girls that went missing?"

"Of course I do," Quinn said. "I've got a statewide alert on them. I interviewed the one girl's mother. She was a mess, strung out as hell. Didn't know what happened to her baby and didn't care."

"Caddy's been looking," Lillie said. "Roped Boom into their search. A couple weeks ago, they kind of got sideways with Blue Daniels."

Quinn stood up. Lillie motioned for him to sit back down. He didn't. He kept on standing, waiting for her to get to the meat of the situation. He already could feel his temples throbbing.

"I may have arrested them the other night."

"You 'may have'?" Quinn said. "Either you did or you didn't."

"They weren't charged," Lillie said. "Caddy claims that ole Blue walked in front of Boom's truck and she struck him. Blue says that Caddy was trying to kill him."

"Which is it?"

"Complicated situation, Sheriff," Lillie said. "You need a napkin and a fork? I thought George had packed some supplies for you."

"I already ate dinner. Plus, I just lost my appetite," Quinn said.

Mary Alice opened the door with a big smile on her face and eased out fast after seeing Lillie's and Quinn's expressions. Lillie smiling even bigger at Quinn.

"What's Blue Daniels have to do with those girls?"

"Well," Lillie said, "that's the interesting part. It seems Boom's truck knocked some goddamn sense into the man. Before he started getting pissed off and said he wanted to beat the crap out of your sister, he admitted to pimping those two little girls."

"And what brought Boom and Caddy to Blue?"

Lillie looked uneasy. Lillie never looked uneasy. "Would you believe Cho Cho Porter?"

"Blue Daniels and Goddamn Cho Cho Porter," Quinn said. "Man, this gets better and better. No wonder you brought me Dixieland."

"You'd probably already know this," Lillie said, "if you hadn't been spending all your time with that hot little piece of tail. You gonna drop by and see her on another call later?"

"She's got work early in the morning," Quinn said. "Same as you."

"What is it with you and married women?" Lillie said. "You sure as shit got the fever for it. Is it the temptation or the danger that gets your blood boiling?"

Quinn searched around the desk for his box of cigars, reaching for an Undercrown, his go-to smoke, and snipping off the end. He kicked open his Zippo, banged up by other Rangers before him, from Vietnam to Somalia to Iraq. But damn if it still didn't work fine. He sat back down and took a sip of some cold coffee, his temple still throbbing, now at a persistent but easy pace.

"Blue Daniels," Quinn said. "Cho Cho Porter. And Caddy and Boom doing our jobs for us. What the hell's happening, Lillie? I don't care for what they're doing. And I sure as hell don't like my assistant sheriff keeping secrets."

"I didn't want to piss you off."

"Since when?" Quinn said, blowing smoke up into the ceiling fan.

"I was looking out for you as much as I was Caddy," Lillie said. "Boom is just being Boom. He was watching out for your baby sister because that's what he does."

"Did Blue Daniels do something to those two girls?"

"He's part of it," Lillie said. "But, signs and wonders, he's changed the fucking story he told me. He doesn't know those girls now. He doesn't know Cho Cho Porter or even his own fucking name."

"He say where they went?"

"He told Caddy he'd sold them."

Quinn smoked down the cigar. He played with the cutter on his desk, watching the smoke lift up out of the ashtray and scatter in the blades. Outside, in the jail yard, he spotted a couple of prisoners washing Lillie's Cherokee, hosing off all the soap bubbles under the bright lights.

"Blue was pimping them out. And when he got tired of that, he sold them to Fannie Hathcock."

"Shit."

"Hold up, hold up," Lillie said. "Fannie and I had a little heart-to-heart the other night and she denies every word. She says she doesn't know Blue or those girls. She said she doesn't put underage girls on the pole or out on the lot. Of course she said no prostitution ever happens out at the Golden Cherry."

"You believe her?"

"Fuck no."

"Then what do we have?"

"Nothing," Lillie said. "But I came to you because I'm sick and tired of Caddy's bullshit. I've run interference for as long as I can, more for you than her. But she's got someone inside Vienna's Place whispering in her ear about what goes on out there."

"Caddy feels a kinship with those pole dancers."

"Don't get negative, Sheriff," Lillie said. "Doesn't suit you. Besides, she's trying to do the right thing. And she's gotten a shitload farther down the road with this disappearance than you and me, two supposedly professional law enforcement officers. What bothers me isn't just these girls but the other rumors Caddy passed on about Fannie."

Quinn waited.

"According to Caddy, Fannie's been running illegals through the truck stop since she got to town," Fannie said. "Girls coming in from the Coast, Vietnamese and Mexicans. She's been working some kind of fucked-up way station sending these girls to big cities. From there, nobody knows what happens, but I sure as hell can use my imagination."

"Christ."

"We're gonna need him. And some help from the Feds," Lillie said. "You still got that tattooed weirdo in Oxford on speed dial?"

"Yes, ma'am."

"Well," Lillie said, "eat your barbecue and get ready. I have a feeling that this shit show is just getting revved up."

"**Oh, holy fuck,**" Cord said, gritting his teeth. "Jesus."

"Don't be a pussy," Wilcox said. "You've been shot before. And you'll be shot again."

Opie had pulled off at a Love's truck stop somewhere thirty, forty miles south of Memphis. They'd pulled around back, behind the safety of all the tractor-trailer trucks, where they could get a better idea of the wound. It wasn't pretty. Two big holes through Cord's stomach, one nasty exit wound in his back. Wilcox had ripped open the QuikClot with his teeth, packed the front and rear wounds, and rewrapped Cord's midsection with lots of gauze and more duct tape. "Motherfucker," Cord said, breathing hard, wheezing, but awake and wild-eyed.

"Better?" Opie asked, laying Cord on his back, the Yukon's seats pushed down flat, with the bags and boxes of money stacked behind the driver's side.

"Sure," Wilcox said. "That'll slow it down. But he's lost a fuckload of blood. Doesn't matter. Cord is ninety percent tequila and cold beer."

Opie covered up the bags and boxes with a blanket and went around the side to push his hoodie under Cord's head. He slammed the door and walked in front of the Yukon to where Wilcox was smoking a cigarette. His hands covered in blood.

"You need to get cleaned up."

"So do you," Wilcox said. "Anyone asks, tell them we were cleaning fish."

"Never seen a fish bleed like that."

"This is the Delta," Wilcox said. "They got god-damn catfish in the river bigger than this truck. Red-necks go out into the little coves and catch them with their bare hands. I shit you not."

"Your people are crazy."

"Not my people," Wilcox said. "Like I said, this is the Delta. These people are born fucked-up."

Opie shook his head, taking a cigarette from Wilcox. The kid's hand shaking as he held it to his lips, Wilcox lighting the end. "He's bad."

"Yep."

"And he's going to die if we don't get him a doctor."

"Damn straight."

"Those motherfuckers," Opie said. "I wish they weren't dead."

Wilcox just stared at the crazy kid and blew smoke out of his nose. In the distance, the lights clicked on over the big diesel pumps. "Why?"

"So we could go back and kill their asses again."

"We better stay out of Memphis for a while."

Opie nodded, waiting for directions, orders, a fucking action plan that didn't exist.

"His woman," Wilcox said. "We call her. Tell her the situation and get her to have a doctor waiting on us out at that airfield."

"You think she'll do it?"

"Hell," Wilcox said. "You've showered with Jonas Cord. He's hung like a barnyard donkey."

Opie nodded, seeing the logic in the explanation. Wilcox looked down at his hands, wanting to wash up, get clean and straight before moving on, but he knew there wasn't much time. They needed a little gas, maybe just a half tank, to cut across the state to Tibbehah County.

"You know how to reach her?"

"Cord does," Wilcox said.

"Is he going to die?"

"Hell, I don't know, man," Wilcox said. "Don't ask stupid fucking questions like that. Cover up that blood and get cleaned up. I'll fuel up the truck and talk to Cord."

"Change the plates before you do."

"Who the fuck are you talking to, kid?" Wilcox said. "I didn't get you boys in and out of the Wasteland by sheer luck. Jesus."

"How much money is in there?"

"Boats, titties, and champagne dreams until your goddamn dick falls off."

Opie covered his hand with his hoodie, walking in the cold in his black T-shirt, looking like any other All-American fuckface with freckles and jug ears. Goddamn Archie Andrews of the Marines. At one time, a million years back, Wilcox wanted to call him Archie, but Cord started the whole Opie thing, always whistling the **Andy Griffith** theme when the boy walked up.

Wilcox got in behind the wheel and headed to the pumps, lights shining down, the sun, orange and big, being swallowed by the endless flat land over the Delta. He'd been all across the world and deep in the armpits of the earth, but he'd never felt a chill like this. His heart beat fast, not from excitement or danger but from feeling absolutely alone. He had finished another cigarette and started a new one, when he glanced down and saw the blood spotting the tip of his boot with a steady drip, drip.

It was the first time he knew the gunshot was that bad. He didn't have time for it. He'd worry about it later after they got Cord safe and sound back to the backwoods whorehouse.

"Get up," Fannie said.

Wrong Way lay asleep on a pool table in the Born Losers' club house, some skinny bitch under the blanket with him. He was on his back, eyes closed, with a cigarette still burning between his lips, a bottle of half-empty Jack Daniel's in the corner pocket, along with the girl's panties.

"Up," she said. "Get up, Lyle. Jesus, wake up."

Wrong Way opened one eye and looked up at Fannie. "Don't call me Lyle."

"Get your woman dressed and gone," she said. "We need to talk."

"I thought you were still pissed at me," said Wrong Way, skinny, with a long black beard and long black hair. He looked like Hollywood's idea of what a pirate might've been. Central casting for a fuckup. The man only had on a pair of black underwear and black riding boots. Tattoos all over his arms and chest, most of them saying the Born Losers MC were the baddest motherfuckers in the Mid-South.

"How'd you get that idea?" Fannie said, plucking the cigarette from his lips and tossing it on the floor.

"I don't know," he said, pushing up off the pool table, waking the girl and looking around for something. "Maybe 'cause you told me and the boys to get the fuck out of the Golden Cherry or you were going to burn the motherfucker down?"

"Oh, yeah," Fannie said. "Boy, was I in a mood."

"You see my Levi's?" he said. "Me and this little lady had a bet and she kind of lost. What's your name again, girlie?"

"Fuck you, Lyle," the girl said. She was pale and skinny, bony, and buck-ass naked. She fingered her panties from the corner pocket and scooted her ass out of the room. She had some kind of fucking dream catcher tattoo on her upper back. Young girls will ink anything on their bodies these days. When she hits forty, that dream catcher will look like an old catcher's mitt.

"I tried calling."

"I ditched my phone," he said. "Threw it in the fucking river. Been meaning to get a new one."

"I need help."

"Of course you do," he said, finding his jeans and a black T-shirt and wandering over to the makeshift bar in the corner, which was nothing but concrete blocks and two-by-fours with a cardboard cutout of some Mexican model holding a six-pack of Corona. Wrong Way unscrewed a new bottle of Jack and poured a good half glass in a jelly jar. "Goddamn Breakfast of Champions."

"You still know that doctor down in Eupora?" she asked. "The one who lost his license for drinking in surgery?"

"Sure," he said. "Why? One of your girls need a quick abortion? Because he's more of a bone doctor. Patched some of the boys when they lay down their bikes."

"Gunshot wounds?"

"Sure, sure," he said, throwing back the rest of the whiskey. "He does it all. Took a shit ton of buckshot out of my back one time. You can barely see it."

"And he won't go to the police?"

"The police?" he said. "Fuck no. He hates the police maybe more than we do. He only has about eighteen DUIs. What's your issue, Miss Hathcock?"

"I need you to sober up fast and scoot on down

to Eupora," she said. "I need that doctor out at that airfield in less than an hour."

"Fuck me," he said, laughing, hacking a little a little cough. "I can barely see. We stayed up for three days straight and I got fucked up and stoned to Jesus and back. Last thing I remember was my sweetie back there sticking a pool cue up my ass for a little fun."

"Does this help?" Fannie asked, reaching into her bag and tossing down a wad of cash. "Sorry I didn't have time to go to the fucking Hallmark store."

Lyle smiled, playing with the gold hoop in his left ear. He walked over to the rat's nest of his pool table bed and picked up the cash. "Well," he said. "Sure, then. OK."

"And whatever bullshit problem that passed between me and the Losers is now done."

"Didn't figure it was forever," Lyle said, and reached for Fannie's ass and pinched it. "We got ourselves a mutual admiration society."

"In your fucking dreams," she said, knocking his hand away. "But don't worry. I'll get that skank back to wherever you found her."

"Hell of a ride back to Tulsa," he said, thinking on it. "Or was it OK City?"

"Hope she likes riding Greyhound," she said. "Get your shit on and go."

"How bad is your friend?" he said, face serious,

as he pulled on his shirt and kicked off his boots to slide on the jeans.

"Haven't seen him yet," she said. "But it's bad."

"Man or a woman this time?"

"Man."

"Is he important?" Lyle asked, buttoning up. "Or hired help?"

"Important."

Lyle got dressed, reached for the key to his Harley, and whistled for a couple of the boys asleep in the back. They wandered out, slit-eyed and sniffing like coyotes from a burrow. Fannie stayed at the bar, pouring herself a shot and saying a little prayer. The skank looked at her and asked if she was OK.

"Even better if you'd just fuck off."

21

"You won't catch anything if you come inside," Caddy said.

"Appreciate it," Quinn said, looking to the mouth of The River's barn, bright light and music spilling out. Tons of cars and trucks parked all along the road and down by the garden. "But I didn't come for the fellowship."

"Then why are you here?" Caddy said. "It's third Sunday. We always do a night service on the third Sunday. Hell, even you know that."

"Y'all sure do love some church."

"Maybe you would, too, if you had the damn Blackwood Brothers performing."

"I thought the Blackwood Brothers were dead?" Quinn asked.

"Since you asked, the last surviving member of the original Blackwood Brothers, James, went home to be with the Lord in 2002. But his son Billy continues the family tradition with Wayne Little, Butch Owens, and Mike Helwig. Some of the best old-time gospel around. When Momma found out Billy used to play drums for J. D. Sumner and The Stamps, she about lost her mind."

"Of course she did," Quinn said. "She once said Sumner had the voice of God Himself."

"But you didn't come for the service," she said.

"Nope."

"How about some supper?" she said. "We're feeding about a hundred folks tonight after the show. Can't you smell the chicken in the pit?"

The gospel music rattled the wood of the barn, a man taking the lead in a deep bass that brought a lot of clapping and hollering from inside. If Quinn didn't know any better, he'd've thought J. D. Sumner had come back to life, Quinn never forgetting Sumner's voice on his mother's Elvis record, "Precious Lord, Take My Hand," that she played over and over. Caddy looked back at the barn and then at Quinn, growing impatient. The light over the river and down in the cotton fields, now bare, had turned a bright orange and deep black.

"I know what you and Boom have been up to," Quinn said. "Why didn't you just come to me straight off?"

"I did," she said. "And where'd that get me?"

"I tried my best," Quinn said. "But Tamika's own mother said she'd just run away. I didn't hear a word about them being damn snatched and sold off."

Caddy swallowed, slipping her hands deep into her dusty jeans pockets. "Well," she said. "I just learned that myself."

"Been a good thing for the sheriff to know."

"You and Lillie start kicking around and the bad guys might get spooked," she said. "Boom knew some folks."

"Goddamn Cho Cho Porter."

"Yeah, he knew Cho Cho Porter. And she told us some things about the girls," she said. "You think she would've talked to you?"

"Nope," Quinn said. "But Blue Daniels would have. And I wouldn't even have to have hit him with my truck."

"Listen," Caddy said, holding up the flat of her hand. "That was an accident."

Quinn studied his sister, her cropped hay-colored hair, wrinkles forming at the edge of her eyes, looking older than she should. "He ran out in front of Boom's truck?"

"No," Caddy said. "He was trying to shoot Boom. He was waving around a gun and I was trying to get the gun away from him."

"OK," Quinn said. "That makes sense. But that's how you got Lillie into this mess. If it had been anybody else but Lillie, I would've fired them. Y'all should have at least been charged with a hit-and-run."

"Not really." Caddy narrowed her eyes. "We didn't run."

"Jesus Christ."

"What is it?" Caddy said. "What do you want me to do? You want me to tell you that I'm gonna quit looking for those girls? Because that ain't gonna happen. They came to me looking for answers and help and I did all I could. Blue Daniels should have his damn pecker chopped off in the town square."

Inside the Barn, the Blackwood Brothers did a slow rendition of "What a Friend We Have in Jesus." "That's some real Old Testament shit you got going on," Quinn said.

"You want to lecture me after all the men you killed?"

Quinn nodded. "We all got a notch in our belts," he said, regretting it as soon as it slipped from his mouth.

"I know who I am," she said. "And what I've done."

"Doesn't matter much now," Quinn said. "That's all chickenshit. You really think Fannie Hathcock is trucking women through Tibbehah without anyone noticing?"

"I know it," she said. "And they're not women. These are little girls. Most of them can't speak English. Coming up from the Coast and over from Texas. Vietnamese and Mexican girls. She's part of some kind of fucked-up pipeline to big cities where they get to work off their passage."

"And how do you know this?"

"I know."

"You need to do better than that."

"Not until Ana Maria and Tamika are home," Caddy said. "You start kicking around and shooting folks and I'll never find them. These folks will make sure they damn well disappear."

"I've been sheriff, off and on, for about five years now," Quinn said. "I may have picked up a few things about how to run an investigation."

"You do what you need to do," Caddy said. "And I'll do what I need to do. If we meet in the middle, so be it."

The Blackwood Brothers had moved on to one of Quinn's favorites, "Jericho Road," making him think of being a kid and believing the song had been written about his hometown. The words always making more sense to him in that context. Caddy rocked back on forth on her feet, hands deep in her pockets, looking at Quinn and waiting for him to get on with it or let her go.

"They sound pretty good," Quinn said, "for a second act."

"Why don't you come on in and take a listen?" she said. "We can talk later."

"Who do you know at Fannie's?"

"Oh, no."

"Can I meet them?"

"Nope," she said. "Not now. I'm not sure if ever. It might get them killed."

"Or save their ass."

"They trust me to do the right thing," Caddy said. "This is something that's weighed heavy on them for a long time. They came to me to help them with their burden, not get them in trouble."

"You might consider that the sheriff's office and the Feds might do a hell of a lot better than some crazy woman and a one-armed mechanic."

"Do I need to remind you these girls are fifteen, cast off like damn pieces of trash by their families? They're being ripped inside out every damn day, making what you did at Ranger school seem like child's play."

"Is your contact inside the barn?" Quinn said. "Listening to the Blackwoods and ready for a plate of pit chicken?"

Caddy looked up at Quinn but didn't answer.

"Bring 'em out," Quinn said. "Right now. I'll protect them. Make sure no harm comes their way."

"Not up to me."

"But you'll ask?"

It was on to "Why Me," and the band really leaned into it, heavy drums with wailing guitar, the entire barn seeming to sing along. **"So help me, Jesus, my soul's in your hand."**

"Can't beat the classics," Quinn said.

"Jamey Dixon once told me that there was no re-placing real gospel music," she said. "He said all that new praise music wasn't worth two shits."

"He was a pistol."

"It's not what you think," Caddy said.

Quinn didn't answer but knew where she was headed. He just looked at his kid sister and waited.

"Momma believes I can't let this go because of what happened to me."

"And what do you say?"

"I say I got to do a lot of good to make up for a lot of bad."

Quinn shook his head and turned to a ditch to spit. He walked toward his sister and wrapped her in his arms, pulling her in close and kissing the top of her head.

Wilcox waited up most of the night, knees drawn up to his chest, sitting on a pile of bricks, smoking end-less cigarettes and looking for the doc to finish with Cord. Opie had wandered out into the woods around the airfield, knowing and expecting the worst. Wil-cox not believing it, thinking Sergeant Jonas Cord was Kevlar-plated and bulletproof. Sometime after midnight, the doctor, a rangy old man who smelled of gin, walked outside the Quonset hut and placed a hand on the redheaded woman's shoulder. Wilcox watched them sort it all out as shadows cast by a bright light shining from a pole in the alley between the hut and another building.

The redheaded woman, Hathcock, crushed a cigarette under her foot and walked toward him. Wilcox stood up, cold outside in his T-shirt, blood dried across it and his forearms.

"Cord's dead," she said. "What do we do with him?"

"Maybe say a few words or sing some songs," he said. "Goddamn, woman, you got a way with words."

"No need to sugarcoat it," she said. "Don't you Marines like it straight? I would've arranged for a band to play 'Stars and Stripes Forever,' but I got shit to do."

Wilcox moved up to Fannie, lifting back his hand and wanting to slap that smile off her face. But he stopped himself, seeing her face had grown wet, her teeth in a wild grin, but she was crying all the same. Her upper body was shaking, lip quivering.

"Oh, fuck it."

"That all you got, Marine?" she said. "'Fuck it.' Isn't this what you wanted? Cord told me all about the feeling of battle and brotherhood that y'all miss so much. You know damn well that he'd have rather died shooting it out with some bad motherfuckers than towing cars and busting fat women for sticking jewelry up their coots. He wasn't right in the head. And, if I can be honest with you, neither are you."

"Where's the money?"

"It's safe," Fannie said, wiping her face. "We'll talk about that later. But right now we need to get you stitched up and cleaned up and down the road. I got friends. I can get Cord FedExed wherever you like."

"Damn, you're a cold-ass bitch."

"Yes, sir," Fannie said. "Now come on inside with me and get that leg stitched up before our doctor drinks another pint of gin. We ain't got his ass long."

"Get me a new car, level the split, and we're gone."

"Shit," she said. "What did you hear about a fucking split? Y'all got twenty percent. None of you could've found that honeypot without the help of my friends. They got paid. I got paid. Don't worry, there's enough to keep you knee-deep in pussy for a long while."

"You got him killed," Wilcox said. "I didn't want to do it. He couldn't say no to some redheaded snatch. How long did you have to suck his peter before he said yes?"

Wilcox heard a rustling in the woods and reached for his gun but saw it was only Opie walking toward them. The kid had his black hood up, arms around his waist, looking just still and dead-eyed. His pale skin looked damn near blue in the artificial light.

"How'd it go?" Opie asked.

Wilcox shook his head. Opie pulled the hood off and walked over to a big pile of bricks and kicked the shit out of them, making noises somewhere between a choking sound and a cry. If he still felt something,

Wilcox might've been upset himself. Instead, he felt so damn numb he could stick a knife through his hand.

"Shut the fuck up," Wilcox said. "Control yourself."

"What do you want?" Fannie said.

"We want our money," Wilcox said. "All of it."

Opie stopped making noise. He looked to Wilcox and swallowed, pulling his .45 and marching toward the Hathcock woman. But she didn't look scared, not one goddamn bit, just shaking her head like she thought both of them were stupid as hell coming all this way from Memphis with a half-dead Marine and a GMC Yukon splattered with so much blood it looked like triage.

"You get what you get," she said. "I don't change my deals. You should have asked Cord."

"You want me to ask him right now?" Wilcox said. "I can't. Because he's fucking dead in some kind of stupid-ass shit show that you laid out for him with his cock down your throat. You must've made it all seem like a cakewalk through goddamn Candyland."

The Hathcock woman was shaking, Wilcox not sure if it was from grief or the cold. She had on a thin black dress, already looking the part of the grief-stricken widow, lace around the tips blowing in the wind. "I'll get you a car fueled up and the trunk packed," she said. "Then y'all need to leave."

"Opie?" Wilcox said. "This woman wants to fuck us both in the ass. And I'm in no mood."

"What's the plan, Sarge?"

"We take this bitch, kick in a few doors, and get back what we took," Wilcox said. "She doesn't do a damn thing for me. I ain't into red snatch."

"Yes, sir," Opie said, snatching up the woman by her right arm and marching her back toward the huts.

Wilcox heard a big rumbling of engines and a dozen or so ugly motherfuckers on motorcycles came riding, slow and easy, down the busted road from behind one of the hangars. The light shined so bright and hard in Wilcox's face that he lost sight of Opie and the big hut where Cord had died, the Hathcock woman twisting away from Opie and running off toward the bikers. A big, ugly, long-haired motherfucker dismounted his scooter, came up and caught the Hathcock woman with his hand. The other holding a shotgun. Wilcox and Opie leaving their damn rifles in the Yukon.

"Damn, that woman's one tricky bitch," Wilcox said.

"I'm not leaving without Cord," Opie said. "They'll have to kill me."

"Don't let them have the pleasure," Wilcox said. "Remember that time back in Zamindawar? Those Taliban fucknuts in the rocks?"

"We killed 'em."

"Why?"

"'Cause they thought we'd left," he said. "They fucking cleared out and went back to the compound."

"And what did I do?"

"You pulled out the javelin and smoked all their asses," he said, the men walking side by side through the darkness. The growling engines covering their conversation.

"Damn, that was fun," Wilcox said. "I never saw Cord laugh so much in his whole goddamn life."

22

"Do you get the Memphis news at your farm?" Jon Holliday asked. "Or are you too far in the damn sticks?"

"Another bank?" Quinn said.

"Not a bank," Holliday said. "A little mom-and-pop restaurant run by some drug dealers. Place got shot to shit. They've got five dead, one man wounded. I think it may have been your boys."

"Team Trump?"

It was nearly eight, Quinn back home at the farm, going for a short run up in the hills with his fifty-pound rucksack, feeding the cows, and eating bacon and eggs straight from the skillet. He was showered and shaved when his cell buzzed. Hondo made a lot of racket munching his kibble from his

ACE ATKINS

bowl, looking up at Quinn, staring with those mismatched eyes.

"A masked man took over a wing shop on EP," Holliday said. "Shot the cook when he didn't move fast enough into the cooler. Second man ran in from the back door of the restaurant to help out. Both men, mind you, armed with AR-15s. Then folks heard what they said sounded like a war zone coming from behind that back door, which was the dealers' count room. Memphis PD has a damn bloodbath in there. Only money left was on the dead."

"Whew."

"Couldn't have happened to a nicer crew," Holliday said. "Twin brothers by the name of Shortbox and K-Bo and couple of their shooters. Witnesses made the news last night. All of them talking about men in Trump masks."

"Video?"

"Nope," Holliday said. "Those boys knocked out the cameras and shot the server. Police think they maybe can rescue some of it. But descriptions match, beyond just the MO and masks."

"Vehicle?"

"Some women in a wig shop next door saw a black Yukon hauling ass," Holliday said. "Police are looking for it. But, damn, you know how that goes. Needle in a shitstack."

"Our boys are branching out."

"And getting bolder," Holliday said. "What did I

say? Five dead? Hate to say it, but it will be lots more to come unless we catch 'em."

"Sounds like a fucking mess."

"Just spoke to a buddy in Memphis homicide," Holliday said. "He's pretty sure that the Twins took out one of our boys. There was a nasty blood trail that dragged all the way from the count room into the parking lot."

"A lot of blood?"

"Too much blood for anyone to live," Holliday said. "Or, at least, so I was told."

"You want me to drive up?" Quinn said, checking his watch. Setting down the half-empty skillet for Hondo. "Will take me an hour or so."

"Not much to see," Holliday said. "Or do. I just figured you'd want to know."

"Listen, man," Quinn said. "Something else has come up. I may need your help on a situation down here."

"I'm not exactly Tibbehah County's favorite son."

"With the beard off and those tattoos covered with one of those government-issue suits," Quinn said, "nobody'll know who you were. You look half-way respectable, for a Fed."

"Down there?" Holliday said. "Now, that's saying something."

"How much do you know about human trafficking?"

"Enough to make me want to puke," Holliday

said. "Worked a case a couple years ago where we found twenty undocumented girls working a motel down by the airport. Some shitbags had it set up like a real rabbit factory, each of the girls turning over a few dozen johns a day."

"Shit."

"Sound familiar?"

"I have a friend down here," Quinn said. "She does some community outreach and came in contact with two teen girls. The girls went missing and my friend did some digging without letting us know. These girls might have been forced into something like your Memphis deal."

"This connected to the Hathcock woman?"

"What do you think?" Quinn said.

"Y'all have a CI in that place?" Holliday said. "If not, that would be damn nice to have. When I worked Stagg, I picked up on a lot. But probably only knew half his business. Expect Hathcock to be cut from the same cloth."

"My friend has a source."

"And who's your friend again?"

"No names," Quinn said.

"What about the source?" Holliday asked.

"Inside the titty bar," Quinn said. "I suspect it's one of the dancers. But they won't speak to me. They're scared shitless of that woman."

"Anyone see the two missing girls at her place?"

"Nope."

"Anyone seen these girls taken against their will?"

"Nope."

"Damn," Holliday said. "Call up the DA. Y'all got a hell of a case."

"I do have a local pimp I can turn," Quinn said. "He's made statements to my friend that he sold the girls to Fannie Hathcock. Guy named Blue Daniels. As mean as he is ugly."

"That isn't much," Holliday said. "But something. How can I help?"

"Talk to some of your close and personal shit-birds about girls coming up from north Mississippi," Quinn said. "If my county is being used as some kind of way station, I want to know. I'll keep on working to bring this dancer in and get close to Fannie."

"From what I heard about Fannie Hathcock, she's twice as smart as Stagg."

"Stagg had the disposition of a shithouse cockroach," Quinn said. "But he wasn't dumb."

"I hear Fannie's got better friends."

"Like who?" Quinn asked, reaching for the front door. He let Hondo run free down the steps into the field for his morning duty.

"You heard of the Syndicate?" Holliday said. "Some real peckerwoods from New Orleans who came in after Katrina? Real old-time Dixie Mafia shit."

"I thought all that was long gone."

"No, sir," Holliday said. "I just wondered how long it'd take to move up your way. And just what would make it worth their effort."

"Now we know."

"Let me see what I can find out."

Wilcox waited until first light to knock on Maggie's door. He had more class than to wake her up in the middle of the night like she'd done at Crissley's. Sometime around six, smile on his face, and pant leg soaked in blood, he waited for her to answer. Through the door glass, he saw her fixing a sack lunch for Brandon and going about her morning routine in hospital scrubs, hair piled up on her head. Rushing and in a goddamn twirl like always.

"Would you believe I have a flat tire?" he said.

Maggie only cracked the door, giving him one of her special eat-shit looks, but then she saw something in his face and looked down at his bloody leg. She looked back to Brandon, standing up from his cereal, and told him to sit tight. She came outside into the cold.

"What the hell?"

"So damn stupid," he said, already working out the details. Not that she'd believe it, but he knew he should at least try. "I was up in a deer stand and dropped my fucking rifle. Nearly killed me."

"It's not deer season, Rick."

304

Wilcox smiled, showing a lot of teeth and his dimples. "Really?" he said. "I guess I'm doing everything wrong these days."

She tilted her head sideways to look at the bloody pants, the ripped material he'd stacked with Quik-Clot and lots of duct tape. Something passed on Maggie's little freckled face that might have passed for compassion. If she had any of it.

"You need to get to the hospital," she said. "Come on, I'll drive you."

"No," Wilcox said. "I can't do that."

"Why the hell not?"

Brandon walked to the door and looked out through the cracked opening. "Daddy?"

"Go back inside, Brandon," she said, motioning with her hand. "We're having an adult conversation."

Brandon turned and left, leaving the door cracked, used to his parents wanting to have some alone time to chew each other's fucking heads off. Maggie shut the door behind her.

"You don't even hunt," she said. "And what the hell are you doing down here?"

"I'm in a spot, Mags," he said. "I'd go to the hospital. But I don't have good insurance. You know, that goddamn Obamacare and all."

"Bullshit," she said. "You're a six-year Marine veteran. The VA will pay for it."

"The VA, Obamacare," he said. "All of it is such a fucking mess. I just need you to look at this clusterfuck and tell me what I need to do. I don't think it'll take more than a cleanup-and-patch job. Hell, you're better than any pussy doctor at this. You've sewn me up so many times, I can't recall."

"This isn't a bar fight," she said. "Or is it? Christ. You look terrible. How much blood have you lost? Your face looks like a ghost."

"Help me out," he said, "and I'll be good. I promise. I will be on my way and won't cause you any trouble. Not anymore."

"I have to be at the hospital in thirty minutes."

Wilcox flashed the smile again, leaning into the door, the leaning hurting a great deal. But he forced the smile, trying to move in tight into her personal space, knowing he could break down those barriers easier than peanut brittle. "This one time?"

"How many times have I heard that?" she said. "I'll call an ambulance. Or take you to the hospital. But I'm not performing surgery on my kitchen table to get you free from any trouble with the law. What the hell did you do this time? Jesus."

Wilcox looked into those clear, cold green eyes that could either turn him hot or make him want to punch a hole in the wall. She stared back at him, unmoved, unaffected. He shuffled a bit and fell onto one knee, catching himself on a railing. It wasn't an act. He was so light-headed he nearly passed out getting out of the car, Opie waiting for him out by the highway at the Huddle House. Might've been bad manners showing up all shot up with a buddy tagging along.

Maggie helped him up. **Attagirl.**

"Just take a look," he said. "That's all I'll ask."

"What do I tell Brandon?"

"Do what you always do."

"And what's that?" she said, sliding under his shoulder for support, opening the door. She knew the drill, getting him out of all those bars after he'd come home. Dozens of tequila shots and good times.

"Lie to him."

"That's what we're good at," she said, yelling for Brandon to go on back to his room. "Fucking grand prize winners."

Maggie helped him to a kitchen chair and reached into a drawer for a butcher knife. He wanted to make a joke about her finally doing what she'd always fantasized, but he'd grown too damn tired. She ripped into his pant leg and cut carefully all around his thigh, her small hands with black fingernails working far from the flesh, like she was making a pair of shorts.

He didn't look down. He knew what was there. She was on both knees, pulling away all the gauze and cutting into the duct tape, checking the wound.

"Holy fuck."

"Give it to me straight, doc."

"I can't do this."

"Sure you can."

"I can't," she said. "You need to get to the hospital. Right fucking now."

"Don't do it," he said. "Don't do it. I only got one thing left. Don't take that away. Don't take it away, Mags. Please."

"What's that?"

"I've always been Brandon's hero."

He got the words out just about the time he passed the fuck out. The last thing he saw was goddamn Maggie rolling her eyes.

"You didn't have to bring biscuits," Mingo said. "But I appreciate it."

"We feed folks every Monday," she said. "There was plenty extra."

"You make all this?" Mingo said. "From scratch?"

"Oh, hell no," Caddy said. "Frozen biscuits from Walmart and Jimmy Dean sausage. Heavy fuel to start your week. Lots of migrants. Folks on work crews who don't take breaks."

"No work today," Mingo said. "Vienna's is closed. And Miss Fannie's gone. I'm supposed to ride over to Tupelo to pick up some bathroom supplies for the truck stop. Toilet paper, Lava soap, and lightbulbs. Keep things moving. You should see a bathroom after a long-haul trucker gets done with it."

"Where'd she go?" Caddy said. They both sat in her truck at the landing of Choctaw Lake, no one in the parking lot, too early for fishing boats and for families at the little playground by the water's edge. She used to come here all the time with Jason. But Jason had grown too old for playgrounds, begging her for a .22 rifle like Uncle Quinn's.

"Not sure," he said. "Must've been some bad shit because she called up Wrong Way and crew. She had told me she was sick of all them, made them get the hell out of the Golden Cherry. It took me six weeks to patch up all the holes and replace the carpet for all the cigarette burns in the floor. We had to fumigate the whole damn place before a decent person could stay there."

"Any word on the girls?"

"No, ma'am."

"Don't you 'No, ma'am' me," she said. "I'm not old enough to be your momma."

She sat with Mingo and let him finish his second biscuit. She drank from a big plastic cup of sweet tea and watched the gold light out on the lake. Geese had gathered far out in the center. There were a few wild ducks in the weeds and a single blue heron standing on one leg by the boat ramp. Mingo crumpled up the tinfoil and placed it in the bag, wiping his mouth with the back of his hand. He was a strong-looking, handsome kid, reminding her a little of Lou Diamond Phillips about the time of **Young Guns**, that film being one of the few she and Quinn could agree upon.

"I wanted you to know I can't do this anymore," Mingo said. "If you want me to stop coming to Sunday service, I understand. But this? Meeting you out here like we're a couple sliding around? I can't do it. Miss Fannie's been too good to me."

"She's using you."

"That's where you're wrong," he said. "She looks out for me. Always has. If I hear something about those girls, I'll let you know. I want to see Tamika and Ana Maria home, too. But I'm not going to spy on Miss Fannie. I told you I know who I am and what I do. Maybe one day I'll make amends for it and become a good person. But right now—"

"You are a good person," Caddy said. "You're a man of faith. I know you. Fannie Hathcock doesn't see that side of you."

"You see?" he said. "You understand. Right?"

Caddy nodded. A truck drove in from Jericho Road and circled down into the parking lot, passing by the back of Caddy's truck and moving toward the landing. It had a big eight-cylinder engine and growling dually pipes. The heron lifted its wing and rose up into the morning sun, Caddy losing it in the harsh light.

"Did you talk to them when they were at Fannie's?"

Mingo didn't answer, eyes focused on the rearview mirror and the white truck backing up and then

310

turning toward Jericho Road and town, the growling motor fading into the distance.

"Yes."

"Were they working?"

"No," he said. "Not at the club. They were too young, didn't know what to do onstage. Couldn't dance worth shit. She had them clean the toilets, wash the girls' G-strings, straighten up things before we opened up."

"How long?"

"Not long," he said. "Ten days. Maybe two weeks."

"And that was it?"

"Come on, Miss Colson," he said. "I don't want to talk about this. Not anymore. That's why I wanted to see you. It doesn't feel right. I feel like even a worse person than I already am."

"You're a believer," she said. "You came to me when those girls disappeared. You told me that you wanted to make things right."

"I was worried."

"And now?"

"I was worried because of other things," he said. "I think they may have gotten into some trouble. And maybe that's why Miss Fannie sent them away. They didn't last long. Not as long as the others."

"As the dancers?"

"Thank you for breakfast," he said, reaching for the door handle.

"Who else?"

Mingo didn't speak for a long moment. Caddy caught sight of the heron turning and surveying the pond, headed back to the landing, the fishing spot. It fluttered its wings and went back to standing on one leg.

"Miss Fannie runs these parties," he said. "These girls worked some parties."

"When you say 'work'—"

"Yes," Mingo said, combing his long black hair behind his ears. "All of that stuff. Men with certain kind of taste in young girls. What Fannie calls farm fresh."

"Shit."

"I drove them," Mingo said. "Didn't ask any questions. It was a big hunt lodge up in the hills, lots of men drinking whiskey and smoking cigars. They played poker and cooked T-bones. I didn't know anyone there and no one spoke to me. I dropped the girls off at night and picked them up the morning. This was twice. They looked very tired. Ana Maria had been hurt. You know, as a woman can get hurt. Down there."

"Between their legs?" she said. "Yeah, I do."

"I'm sorry," Mingo said. "I didn't know the men. And I didn't know the place."

"Could you find it again?"

"I could," he said. "But I won't. If it wasn't for Miss Fannie, I'd be dead. She cleaned me up, got me some school, took care of all of my pain when I was a kid."

"Mingo?"

He looked at her, with his flat impassive face and brown eyes. She patted his slender leg.

"Fannie ain't Mary Magdalene."

"And, Lord knows, I'm not Jesus," Mingo said. "I'm a sinner and have a long-ass road ahead. Just do me one favor."

"Anything."

"Pray for me," Mingo said, opening the truck's squeaky door. "One day . . . One day, I'll go all the way with this. Just not now."

Caddy sat behind the wheel and watched Mingo drive away in her rearview mirror. She smacked the wheel hard a few times and started to cry. Goddamn it. She was so fucking close.

23

"Now isn't a good time," Maggie said, meeting Quinn on her porch.

"I dropped a prisoner at the hospital," Quinn said. "They told me you were sick."

Maggie was dressed in her scrubs, reddish brown hair piled on top of her head in a bun, a little blood on her shirt.

"I'm feeling better," Maggie said. "I still may go in."

"You don't look good," he said. "You have blood on you?"

Maggie blushed, looking down at the streaks of dried blood, and said, "Oh, Brandon cut himself this morning," she said. "He's fine. We're fine. We're all fine."

Quinn nodded, already feeling strange for just

showing up there. He wasn't her boyfriend—really, not anything, not officially discussed anyway. He took a step back and nodded, not wanting to spook the girl when it had been going so well. A long time back, his dad, drunk on Miller High Life, told him that catching a good woman was like catching a wildcat. You had to do it slow and easy or you'd scare 'em off. That was it. Maggie the Cat.

He'd parked behind a strange car out on Stovall Street, a maroon Chevy Silverado with Tennessee plates. He didn't think much of it, as the street was lined with little white houses just like Maggie's. But something was off, all rushed and jittery movements, great surprise when she opened the door. Take it easy, Quinn.

He touched the bill of his cap and made toward the steps, a man's voice calling from inside the house. "Mags?" the man said. "Who the hell's that?"

Maggie bunched up her face with a wince, teeth gnashed together. Quinn smiled and continued to walk.

"It's nothing," she said. "It's OK. My ex stopped by and we were working through some custody details while Brandon was at school. It's just gotten really complicated, you know. You understand what I'm saying?"

"No problem," Quinn said, feeling his heart up in his throat and hating the goddamn feeling.

"I'll call you."

As Quinn was about to turn for the second time, the door opened and the man, about Quinn's height and build, looked out. He was eating a green apple, eyes flicking down to Quinn's cowboy boots and up to his high and tight. He grinned, leaning against the door, glassy-eyed and almost drunk-looking. "Well. If there isn't another fox in the henhouse."

"This is Sheriff Colson," Maggie said, putting a real emphasis on "Sheriff" just in case the dumb bastard didn't spot the silver star on his chest. "I had a break-in at the house."

"Oh, yeah," the man, Rick, said. "I heard about you. Service with a smile."

The man took another bite of apple, leaning into the doorjamb as if he owned the place. "Don't let me get in the way of you two doing your thing," he said. "I'm about to hit the road."

He stumbled forward a bit, thrusting out his hand. "Rick Wilcox."

Quinn grabbed his hand, the man trying to put some force into it but not making much headway with Quinn. Quinn nodded back, noting a blot of ink on the man's right forearm. CAMP LEATHERNECK.

Wilcox, glassy-eyed and sloppy, noticed Quinn looking and peered down at the tat, calling it a relic from his time overseas. "Got loaded when we got back," he said. "Promised the boys I'd get one done. You got the look. You in the service?"

"Yep," he said. "And spent a fair amount of time at Leatherneck."

"You in the Corps?"

"Ranger," Quinn said. "Third Batt."

"I heard you Ranger boys couldn't squat and piss without a command?" Wilcox said. "Is that really true?"

"Maybe," Quinn said, wanting to knock that green apple down his goddamn throat. "But I gave the orders."

Wilcox laughed, reaching back for the doorjamb, finding some stability. Maggie stood away from them, arms around her waist, a pained look on her face. Her face was bloodred, her teeth clenched, Maggie Powers not one to hide her emotions. Quinn being a little better at it, as he'd love to have taken Rick Wilcox, Marine motherfucker, and tossed him far off her porch.

"Good meeting you," Quinn said.

Wilcox grinned, biting into the apple one last time and tossing it into Maggie's hedge. He walked— more, hopped—into the house, Quinn spotting a bandage wrapped around his right thigh. Quinn looked up at Maggie and said he was sorry for stopping by.

"I'm sorry, too," she said. "I'm so sorry."

"Don't think about it," Quinn said. "Glad you're feeling better."

"I'll call you," she said, reaching out to touch his hand. "OK?"

Quinn nodded and headed back to his truck. It was a bright, gold day in Mississippi. No clouds, lots of sunshine in the chill. Why the hell did he feel like he had a rock in his stomach?

He started his truck and headed back to the sheriff's office.

"This is absolute fucking bullshit," Fannie said. "No touching. Patrons five feet from the dancers and no snatch with a beer chaser. We've made less than half this week than we did the week before. And don't you dare tell me that it'll get better. I hear the CB chatter. I know what those good ole boys are saying: 'Vienna's isn't worth the trip. Ain't the same place it used to be. If you want real companionship, keep on trucking up to Memphis or down to New Orleans.'"

"Maybe your lawyer will set the supervisors straight," Mingo said.

"Don't hold your breath, kid," Fannie said. "Did you pick up the soap and toilet paper?"

"Yes, ma'am," Mingo said. "Got the rubbers machine restocked, too."

"French ticklers?"

"And the Genie De-Lite and the horny goatweed pills."

"Shit," Fannie said, sitting at Vienna's bar, spewing smoke up into the air. "That's all those bastards need. If truckers were any hornier, they'd be fucking their hot tailpipes."

"I'm sure some have tried it."

"I don't like this," Fannie said. "I don't like any of it. I've never been good at laying idle and the old wait-and-see. It's my ass either way. If this place continues to shit the bed, they're gonna want to shut us down. And if I go after Skinner, they won't like it."

"How would you go after him?" Mingo said, setting out the bar glasses, cute pint ones with a redheaded pinup girl sitting atop the Vienna's Place logo. Coy Bettie Page bullshit. "He doesn't seem to like the usual bait."

"You mean pussy or likker?"

"Sure," Mingo said. "Or money."

"Who doesn't like money?" Fannie said. "Anyone says that money doesn't buy happiness has never owned a gold Rolex or a Birkin handbag. Only way to change your life, your outlook, is with some cash. Do you think I run this goddamn cinnamon-scented skin palace out of my respect for the golden pole? The pole means money. Ain't no way around it."

Mingo kept on washing out the beer glasses, setting them on a dry towel, taking the dry glasses, and stacking them behind the bar. "We got any off-site parties coming up?"

"No," she said. "We did that big one on New

Year's, but folks seem to get a little stingier the first of the year. Why? You getting tired of all that mess?"

"No, ma'am," he said. "I'm just looking ahead."

"I hate those goddamn things," Fannie said. "But they sure as hell make some money. I can charge some rich ole coot nearly six times what one of my girls makes in a single night. Not to mention the payment for transportation and our agreed flat rate. That's why I let the girls keep whatever tips they make, God love 'em. You think truckers are bad? Think about some gray-headed coot, high on ten-year-old scotch and hard-pecker pills. You'll love this. One guy last year made a girl tug his pecker every time Ole Miss scored a touchdown. She'd have to pull it like a rickety doorbell and say, 'Hoddy Toddy.' Ain't that some sick shit?"

"Whatever happened to that Mex girl?" Mingo asked, shutting off the water, drying his hands on a towel. "Ana Maria? I used to drive her and another little black girl around. Never saw them again."

"Ana Ma-what?" Fannie said, eyeing Mingo across the bar. The damn kid too smart to act like a love-struck teen, especially over some jailbait tail.

"Ana Maria," he said. "Other girl's name was Tamika."

"Sorry, kid," Fannie said. "Too many girls to count. Too much ass to name. I got too many problems without worrying about the talent. Son of a bitch, what the hell am I going to do? You know if you sit around and gaze at your goddamn navel, you're going to get hit by a fucking Kenworth."

"You want to go against those boys on the Coast?"

Fannie ashed her cigarillo. "Sure as shit thinking on it," she said. "What do you think?"

"What could it hurt?"

"Depends on how big that fucking stick is up Skinner's ass," she said. "If it's poking into his brain stem, then we might have a problem. He might accuse me of bribery and I might end up losing everything. Let me tell you something, kid. I look fucking terrible in orange. It doesn't look right on a redhead. Besides, can you see me chatting it up with a bunch of bull dykes on the inside? I don't swing that way. Especially not for jailhouse hooch and cigarettes smuggled up some woman's bunghole."

"Goddamn, Fannie," Mingo said, laughing. "You know how to talk straight."

"Either sit on my ass and get cornholed," Fannie said, tapping her long red nails on the onyx bar top from Kansas City, "or force that Crypt-Keeper to show his hand."

"You always said money and pussy make the world go around," Mingo said, topping the last glass to form a nice pyramid by the beer taps.

"Did I really say that?"

"Yes, ma'am," Mingo said. "You could copyright it."

Fannie ashed the cigarette again and pressed it

321

into her lips. "Sometimes I'm so fucking smart I amaze myself."

"I love you, man," Wilcox said.

"You're drunk and on painkillers," Opie said.

"That's doesn't change anything," Wilcox said. "You're my brother. My fucking brother. We're goddamn Marines. Ooh-rah."

"I think you need to lie down," Opie said. "Take it easy."

"Where's Crissley?" Wilcox said.

"In the kitchen, cooking dinner."

"How'd I get home?"

"You drove back to the Huddle House and I drove to Memphis," Opie said. "Damn, don't you remember, Sarge? You picked a fight with that guy at the Whataburger Drive-In."

"Whataburger?" Wilcox said. "We had Whataburger? What the fuck, Ope? I thought you had more respect for me than that. At least take me to a fucking Burger King. Say, where's Crissley? Baby? Baby? Where you at? Come see Daddy. Take me to bed or lose me forever, Goose."

"Shit," Opie said.

"You think I'm drunk?"

"No, sir," Opie said. "I think you are stone-cold, one hundred percent fucked up."

Wilcox wavered on his feet, moving fast, or seeming to move fast, in the big, open space of Crissley's big, fancy-ass warehouse apartment with its view of the Bluffs. All industrial windows and brick walls. He stood toe-to-toe with that freckle-faced, jug-eared, brush-cut orange-ass carrottop and said, "I love you, man. I really do. Now, help me get off this fucking bum leg. And get me a beer. Wait. Fuck beer. Fuck beer in the ass. Say, does Crissley have any tequila? I would fucking love a shot of tequila right now."

"You drank it all," Opie said, slipping an arm under his shoulder and walking him back to Crissley's bedroom, laying him down on that big four-poster bed, with all its lace and flowers and shit. Stuffed animals. She was a grown-ass woman and still had fucking stuffed animals and called her father Daddy. There was some sick shit going on there.

"All of it?"

"Yes, sir."

"Can you get more?"

"Sure," he said. "But how about we wait until morning."

Wilcox grabbed the front of Opie's shirt, his breath seeming to nearly knock out that Florida swamp boy. "Are you screwing my woman?" he said. "Because someone sure as shit is screwing my wife. I can't take both. You know? Someone screwing both my girlfriend and my wife. That's just not proper. That's just plain-ass wrong."

"No," Opie said. "I'm helping her make a spinach salad. We're boiling eggs."

Wilcox closed his eyes. "Eggs?" he said. "You sick fuck."

"Good night, Sarge."

"We're going to get that bitch," he said, closing his eyes and then opening them again. "Set it straight. Set it all straight."

"Who?"

"You know," he said, "fucking Fannie Cock Whosis. We're taking that bitch down. We're taking her downtown and going to spank that ass. She fucked us. She fucking fucked us. She did it. She killed Cord. She talked him to go deep into Spadestown and fuck up some shit, only it didn't get fucked up. Cord got fucked up. He died. Did you know that? Cord is dead. He's fucking dead."

Wilcox tried to raise up, damn room kaleidoscope-spinning, and lay back down among the fallen, dead, glassy-eyed animals and frilly-ass, girly stuff that smelled like rotten apples and baby powder.

"I know."

"But you're in?" Wilcox said. "Right? You are in. So fucking in that you're way past Flynn. You know what pain is, Ope?"

"Weakness leaving the body."

"Yes," Wilcox said. "Yes, yes, yes. Where did you hear that?"

"From you, sir."

"We're going to get that bitch," he said. "We're going to go back in country and kill, kill, kill. We're going to get Cord back, and we're going to get back our fucking money."

"Yes, sir."

"She took Cord."

"She said she'd take care of it," Opie said. "When you asked what that meant, she told you not to think too much on it. Goddamn, that woman doesn't know us. What we do. What we're fucking about. Ain't no way we're leaving his body to be buried in some ass-stinking shithole like Jericho, Mississippi."

"No way."

"No, sir.

"Ooh-rah."

"Ooh-rah, sir."

24

The rain had come again that afternoon, Quinn pulling into the shelter of the County Barn to find Boom working on Lillie's Cherokee. Lillie sat on the backseat to some truck Boom had converted into the garage sofa. She was drinking some of Boom's bad coffee and smoking cigarettes, a habit she'd been wanting to kick since Quinn had come home. Lillie looked up at him in that cool, casual way that said don't even think about judging me.

Boom waved his free hand—his good hand—sitting on an inverted bucket and pulling off the right front rotor of the Cherokee. He whistled, showing the ground-down wear to Lillie, who didn't seem to care a bit. "Y'all both need to update your vehicles,"

Boom said. "Not that I don't mind working on 'em. But they spend more time in the shop than on patrol."

"Can't get rid of the Big Green Machine," Quinn said.

"I told you," Lillie said. "What did I fucking say? There has never been a man born of more routine that Quinn Colson. He'll drive that big truck until the wheels fall off."

"I was happy to help rebuild that truck," Boom said. "But seeing what y'all do and what you need from these vehicles, it ain't practical no more."

"She's a beast."

"You ain't pulling nothing," Boom said. "You just like it because it's a big fucking truck."

"True," Quinn said, helping himself to some of that motor oil coffee under last year's **Playboy** calendar. "But I pull my jon boat. Sometimes I get to pull that trailer loaded with ATVs."

"That ain't shit," Boom said. "New F-150s got all the power you need. And that EcoBoost is faster."

"You asking him to drop down to a six-cylinder motor?" Lillie said. "Those are fighting words."

"If y'all are in hot pursuit," Boom said, "don't you want a turbo under the hood?"

Quinn looked to Lillie as he leaned against the tool bench, the inside of the County Barn cool and comforting, rain tapping the puddles outside the bay door. "Did he say 'hot pursuit'?"

"I don't think anyone has said hot pursuit since 'seventy-eight," she said. "Maybe we should bring it back. Make it official."

"Fuck y'all," Boom said, taking off the caliper, using the screwdriver inserted into his prosthetic hand to loosen the bolt. "Y'all sure know how to beat the shit out of a vehicle."

Quinn sat down next to Lillie on the makeshift sofa and stretched out his arm behind her. Lillie stubbed out her cigarette and put about a foot between them. Quinn shrugged, drank some coffee, watching the rain, not in any rush to get out in it. Jean had made some chicken pie tonight and told him to stop by if he hadn't eaten. There were only so many Sonic burgers you could eat in a week.

"You need a ride?" Quinn said.

Lillie shook her head. "Already got keys to Kenny's cruiser," she said. "Not a bad ride, except it smells like barbecue and farts."

Boom got up from the bucket and walked over to the tool bench. He sliced open a box and pulled out a new rotor, an identical box waiting nearby. Quinn turned to Lillie, warming his hand with the coffee mug, and asked, "You see the news?"

"You mean, the great Wing Machine Massacre?" Lillie said. "White dudes in Trump masks with assault rifles. I might have taken notice. What's wrong with you people?"

"Ain't my people."

"But you suspect they're ex-military?"

"So does Holliday," Quinn said. "He also thinks one of the three who hit the First National is dead."

"How's that?"

"Blood trail out the back door of the Wing Machine," Quinn said. "Got a few witnesses who saw a vehicle hauling ass on EP Boulevard."

"Yeah," Lillie said. "I heard. Late-model black Yukon. Got some fancy-ass rims, too. Want to make a wager that it's stolen and dumped somewhere down and deep?"

"Holliday says the Feds are checking hospitals," Quinn said. "Got most of north Mississippi looking for that car."

"What about a tape?" Lillie said. "That place have a camera?"

"It had a lot of them. But those boys shot them out and shot up the server."

Boom walked back to the Cherokee and sat back down on the bucket. He watched Boom add a shiny new rotor and spray it down with something from a can to get the slick surface rough enough to grip the pad. He'd seen him replace brakes at least a hundred times, but Boom could do it better than anyone in half the time.

"The shoot-out wasn't in the restaurant," Quinn said. "Cops haven't released the names. But two of the dead guys were those twin drug dealers, K-Bo and Shortbox."

Lillie set down her coffee and gave a low whistle. "Oh, fuck."

"Yes, ma'am," Quinn said. "And the restaurant was just a front. The back room, with the four dead guys, was a count house. Whatever they had, Team Trump took off with all of it."

"Gutsy move," Boom said.

"Or fucking stupid," Lillie said. "Those guys have friends. Ain't nobody getting out of this bullshit alive."

Quinn nodded, slipping off his ball cap, wet from the rain, and glancing back and forth to Boom and Lillie. Lillie caught his eye, smiling just a bit, and he knew it was as good a time as any to share his theory. He took a breath and said, "Leader of the group is a white male about my size and age."

Lillie nodded.

"I believe, and the Feds believe, he has some military training."

"So does my mailman," Lillie said. "But I'm not hooking his ass up to a polygraph."

"Do you recall that tattoo?" Quinn said. "The one that you claim reads 'Fuck You, Tibbehah County'?"

"Sure," Lillie said. "I imagined it plain as day."

"I think it read 'Camp Leatherneck,' in black ink," Quinn said. "Dead center of the right forearm."

"And how do you know this, chief?"

Quinn reached into his shirt pocket and pulled out two sheets. He unfolded them and passed them on to Lillie. Lillie reading as Boom finished up the right front brake and tightened the caliper. She lifted her eyes to Quinn. "Who the fuck is Richard Wilcox?"

Quinn ran down the basics: his age, height, weight, where he was from, where he'd served, and recent run-ins with the law. Numerous assault charges, public intoxication, and a domestic violence in Memphis.

"OK," Lillie said, "so he's a fucking turd. What makes him special?"

"I met him today," Quinn said. "Looked like he'd been shot in the leg."

"And where was this?"

Quinn took another deep breath and then chased it with a gulp of coffee. He looked Lillie Virgil right in the eye and said, "Maggie Powers's place."

"That freckle-faced girl you been mooning over?"

Quinn didn't answer, playing with the warm mug. Boom looked over his shoulder at Quinn and Lillie. He just shook his head and reached for another tool to insert into his hand.

"And what's the connection?" she said. "Or do I want to know?"

"He's her husband," Quinn said. "About to be her ex. They've put it in motion. It just takes some time."

"Hold on," Lillie said, holding up her hand. "Hold the fuck on. You got to be fucking kidding me."

"Nope."

"Maybe he was paying off his future child support in blood money," Lillie said, grinning. "Real ole-time Robin Hood shit. Yes, that's it. That makes complete fucking sense, Quinn."

Quinn looked to Boom, but Boom only shook his head again. The big man got up, reached for a nearby pack of cigarettes, and walked out of the barn and stood under the slanting tin roof. Quinn could see the shadow of his broad back, smoke scattering out into the rain and fading gray light.

"Do you want me to tell you what I really think?" Lillie asked.

"Maggie's a nurse," Quinn said. "I believe he needed some medical attention."

"And why the fuck did he rob the First National?" Lillie said. "You know one of my first rules of investigation: good crooks don't shit where they eat. I mean, so to speak."

"Wilcox robbed that bank to impress her," Quinn said, standing up and stretching. "He made a big show of trying to show me he was still in charge. Pissing on his territory."

Lillie stood up with him, standing nearly the same height. She placed the flat of her hand to his chest, almost as if she was trying to feel his heartbeat. "Listen to me," she said. "You are a good man. And you've become a hell of an investigator in the last few years. But you have one major flaw, something I like to call the Achilles' pecker. It damn well leads you in directions you have no business going. I just don't want you making a fool out of yourself."

"This isn't about Maggie."

"And your coming home was never about Anna Lee, or Luke, or their damn kid you stuck in the middle of your afternoon delights," Lillie said. "I don't want to talk about this. In fact, I'm not sure I even want to do this. Not anymore. A woman can only be crapped on so many times before she looks up and realizes it's time to move on."

Quinn swallowed and took Lillie's hand. Her face had a little sheen to it. Breathing hard, jaw set. "Calm down," he said. "Listen to me. Listen to what I'm saying."

Lillie shook her head and walked toward the open bay doors, brushing past Boom and heading out into the rain. Quinn followed her, finding Boom grinding out a cigarette. He lifted his chin and looked at Quinn. "That shit went well."

"She's the most stubborn person I've ever met."

"Damn, Quinn," Boom said. "Can you fucking blame her?"

"For what?" Quinn said. "What the hell are you talking about?"

Some dumb shit had left the truck running, a good-looking black SUV with shiny rims, parked outside Chowtime, a soul food and Chinese buffet down on Hacks Cross Road. The kid had just come out, swiveling a toothpick in his mouth, his belly loaded down with greens, fried chicken, wontons, and crab Rangoon. It was a cold night, a little rain starting to fall, and the last thing he wanted to do was walk two miles back to his apartment or call his goddamn sister to leave the nail salon and pick his ass up. She'd want to know just what the fuck was he doing spending twenty dollars for all-you-can-eat buffet when he owed her fifty for a new pair of pants.

The kid thought about it for a minute, his boy Mario following him, wanting to know what the hell he was looking at. The kid shrugged, tried the SUV's door, found it was wide-ass open, and slid behind the wheel and into all that buttery-soft black leather.

"You gonna get your ass shot," Mario said. "Come on, man. Let's go."

"Be cool," he said. "Check this shit out."

"Ain't your ride."

"You want to get wet?" the kid said. "Or you want to ride in style?"

Mario climbed in. The windshield wipers were going, stereo playing some loud white boy music, the kid dialing it to Hot 107, finding DJ Rax playing that new one by Tyke T, "Come Up," bass thumping. **"You can't stop my destiny."**

"If you gonna roll," Mario said, "fucking roll. Before they come back."

The kid was only fourteen but knew how to drive. He knocked it into reverse, backed the fuck out, heading up toward the barbershop in the strip mall, checking out his boys, stuck talking about the Griz and pussy they ain't getting. He honked the horn, knowing none of those boys could see his ass and Mario riding in style behind smoked glass.

Mario, a big man at sixteen, fired up a blunt and passed it to the kid, the kid heading onto the road, under the overpass, toward Winchester in the opposite direction of home. The kid cranked up the radio, pumping his fist as Tyke T got that shit rolling hard, maybe liking this one better than the first one that hit, "C'est La Vie."

"You crazy," Mario said. "You goddamn crazy."

"Ain't my fault some motherfucker left the goddamn engine running," the kid said. "I mean, shit. That's dumb as hell."

"His ass must've been wanting that moo shu pork," Mario said. "Don't give a fuck about his ride. Man got to eat."

The kid took a hit of that blunt and passed it back to Mario, turning left at the Costco onto Winchester, all that bullshit rolling by the window, Red Lobster, Toys-R-Us, super fucking Walmart. His momma worked at that Walmart for ten years and he still got lost in that place. She was probably there now, wanting to know later if he hit those books, just about the time she put her feet up and opened that big box of wine.

"You smell something?" Mario said. "Smell like ass in here."

"That's your weed."

"Ain't my weed, bitch," he said. "Somebody done shit in this car."

"I don't smell it."

"Well, I do," Mario said. "What's wrong with you, man? Your nose broke. Crack a window or some shit."

"Call Lashika," the kid said. "Ain't she the one with that fine-ass sister?"

"Come on, man," Mario said. "Her sister nineteen. She got two damn kids."

"Tell her we'll pick 'em up," the kid said. "Take 'em down to Beale Street and party a little bit. Say, how much weed you got?"

"Not enough to block that funky-ass smell," he said. "Oh, shit. You better slow the hell down. See that? See that shit? You got the fucking police coming up on your ass."

"Fuck the police."

"Police gonna fuck you right in the ass," Mario said. "You forget you in a goddamn stolen vehicle?"

"Come on," he said. "Come on. Be cool. We ain't done nothing. Not yet."

The kid smiled, putting his hand out for the blunt,

as the cop hit those blue lights in the rearview. **Oh, shit.** He mashed the pedal and headed up to sixty and seventy, weaving in and out of the traffic on Winchester, looking for a place to pull in where he and Mario could get out on foot and run like hell from the fucking police and this ass-smelling car.

"Over there," Mario said. "By that church with the statue holding up that big-ass cross."

The kid knew the place, the World Overcomers Outreach Church, biggest damn church in south Memphis. He figured he could pull around the back of the sanctuary and he and Mario could run deep into the woods. Goddamn Mario would be pissed, but at least they wouldn't get busted for stealing the truck.

The kid skidded around back of the big church, running up and over a curb into the grass by the treeline. He didn't have to say a word to Mario, who already had the car door open and was running like hell from the two, now three, cops that were on their ass. Damn, the kid felt like puking up all that Rangoon crab shit he'd been eating. He put a fist to his mouth, going right for the trees and then seeing the chain-link fence. If he hadn't eaten that last egg roll, he might've made it. But some big-ass black cop grabbed him by the seat of his pants and tossed him to the ground, standing above him like he was goddamn John Henry. "Don't think about it, youngblood."

Youngblood? Shit. The kid was on his back, pushing himself onto his elbows, just catching the back of Mario's red jersey deep in the woods and long-ass gone.

"Who was that?" the cop asked.

"Nobody."

"Nobody?" he said. "Sure. OK. This your truck?"

The kid shook his head. A bunch of cops parked around the black SUV, headlights shining on those tall rims, opening doors. One white cop threw open the hatch like he was sure they had a bunch of weed or some shit hidden in back.

"Keys were in it, engine running," the kid said. "Come on, man."

The big black man just shook his head, reaching down, grabbing his skinny arm, and yanking him to his shoes. They got about ten feet from the cars, blue lights flickering, when he saw two of the cops turn away from the truck and head out into the wide parking lot. All the big lights shining up on the Statue of Liberty holding that cross. One of the men looked at the cop holding him and shook his head before tossing his damn cookies on the asphalt.

"Goddamn," said the kid. "Shit."

"What is it?" the black cop asked.

"We got a body," the white cop said, hands on his knees, spitting on the ground. "Damn bloody-ass body under some blankets. Smell about knocked me out."

The men looked like cops, or some kind of security guards, with their khaki pants and cheap blue sport shirts, camo ball caps, and sunglasses. One of the men wore a pistol on his waist, below his big belly, walking as if holding a bowling ball between his knees. The other man was a little leaner and older, with close-cropped graying hair and leathery skin. He smiled like a preacher ready to spread the Good Word.

Caddy had first noticed them while leaving the barn, the men getting out of their truck, a two-door white Chevy with lots of mud thrown up on the grille and splashed on the windshield. They came up on her as she carried a big box of canned goods.

"You Caddy Colson?" the fat man asked.

"We're closed," Caddy said. "Join us for service on Sunday. The Brannon family from Senatobia will be our special guests. Real authentic bluegrass gospel and a fried-chicken lunch to follow. Tell your friends."

"You looking for some nigger girl named Tamika?" the older man, somewhere in his early fifties with red pockmarked skin, said. His breath smelled like an ashtray.

"I don't acknowledge people who use that word," Caddy said. "Y'all best move on."

"Some nigger girl and some spic poon ain't worth

339

your trouble," the fat one said, hitching up his kha-kis and placing a hand to the butt of his gun.

"You think of that all by yourself?" Caddy said. "Or did it just come to you?"

The man shuffled his bowed legs, trying to look tough but looking only weak and fat. The older man spit on the ground, crossing his arms, standing right between her and her truck. The box had grown heavy in her arms and she had grown tired of their shit. She set down the box in the dirt.

"Be a smart-ass," said the fat one. "We'd just as soon burn this fuckin' place down."

"It's been done before," Caddy said. "Didn't change a thing."

"I don't think she's hearing us," said the gray-headed man, still wearing that big dumbass grin. "Listen up, girlie."

"You listen up," Caddy said, hands on her hips, staggering her stance. This was her place, her ground, and these men couldn't do a damn thing to her that hadn't already been done. "You can tell Fannie Hath-cock she can go straight to hell."

They didn't answer. They didn't move, just star-ing and watching. Her friend Diane Tull, who'd stopped by to deliver some fertilizer and seeds from the Jericho Farm & Ranch, walked from the barn and called out to Caddy, wanting to know if every-thing was OK. Caddy called back that she was fine, that she'd back in a moment, and waited for them to get down to it. "You boys trading some muscle for a free lap dance?" she asked. "Let me tell you a secret. Those girls don't give a shit about you. And they'd really appreciate it if y'all would brush your teeth sometime."

Nothing. The men didn't show anything. They just stared, looking at Caddy from behind their sunglasses like she should pee herself and run off with her tail between her legs. Funny thing about being in the shit most of your life, it deadened you from being scared. Caddy had once ridden out an F-4 tornado in a shelter the size of a broom closet.

"Oh, wait," she said. "Y'all been talking to Manuel, haven't you? You're the ones who beat the hell out of Ana Maria's father when he came for her. Same white truck, same ugly faces."

"Those girls are gone," the fat man said, his face swelling big and red like a balloon. "Nobody gives a shit about them. Not their families, not the men pumping them. They ain't nothing but trash. Just like you."

Caddy just cocked her head, kind of curious where they were headed with this, wanting to know who had sent them. They didn't look like boys who were in charge. They looked like a couple of country yard dogs kept on a tight leash. The older one had a little tuft of white hair poking from his sport shirt, a gold cross around his neck.

"You don't remember me," said the older man.

The smile on his face crawling up over his crooked, tobacco-stained teeth. "Do you?"

She didn't answer.

"Oh, baby," he said. "Baby. That just hurts my feelings. Me and you had a real time together. About five years back out at a fishing cabin on Sardis? One of those long weekends with scotch and bloody steaks and whatever kinda pills you were popping. Damn, I rode your young ass like a thoroughbred."

"Get your trashy ass out of here."

"Tell me I'm lying," the old man said, absently adjusting his crotch. He turned to the fat boy and they smiled at each other, happy their dirty little trump card was out in the open. "You had the finest, sweetest little goodies I ever tasted."

"Sorry," Caddy said. "I don't recall. Either it didn't happen or your dick must be the size of a sewing needle."

The fat man laughed, the leathery dude didn't move. His smile dropped, eye twitching.

"Y'all got two seconds to get the hell out of here," she said. "If you know who I am, then you know who my brother is. And he's never taken very kindly to men insulting his family. Southern pride and all that."

Caddy could hear the blood rushing in her ears and her own breath short and raspy in her chest. The fat man walked away. The older man stayed.

"Little blue heart," he said.

"What's that?" Caddy said. "What did you say?"

"Little blue heart with some funny little stars around it," he said. "On your right hipbone right by your coot. You didn't wear much clothes that weekend. Lord, you did things to this man that still makes his toes curl. You done dressed up like a cheerleader with nothing under that little skirt."

Caddy turned and called out to Diane Tull, who'd been watching the whole thing from the mouth of the barn and emerged with a twelve-gauge, racking in a load with a sharp snick. "Called the sheriff," she said.

"Damn good to see you," the old man said, licking his lips. Not seeming to be in a hurry despite a pissed-off woman coming up with a gun. "Sure hate to pass around town all the things you done. Not with all this Jesus camp you got now. Might hurt your business."

"I know who I am and what I've done," Caddy said. "How about you, asshole?"

"Yes, ma'am," he said. "Yes, ma'am. Surely do."

The man gave the preacher grin one last time, turned, and walked away, the fat man already behind the wheel and cranking the engine. The leathery man got about halfway there when Caddy couldn't stand it anymore. She reached down and picked up a big handful of mud, forming a tight ball, and threw it right at the man's back.

The wad caught him in the neck and he stumbled a little bit but only turned and smiled, getting in the car and leaving the compound with a gentle little wave. As the truck disappeared, Caddy felt her knees buckle and her hands shake. She had to take deep breaths, watching the empty road until she felt like she could move. Her heart still thumping in her chest, vision tunneled, with everything muffled around her. Breathe. She needed to breathe.

"You OK?" Diane asked.

Caddy nodded, placing a hand on Diane's strong shoulder. The older woman rubbed circles on Caddy's back, telling her to keep her head up and breathe deep.

"What the hell was that?" Diane asked as they walked back to the barn.

"Came to spook me away from asking about the girls."

"Do any good?" Diane asked, smiling.

"Not a damn bit," Caddy said. "But, damn, I sure feel like I need to take a shower."

25

"Hold the fucking phone," Fannie Hathcock said. "You did **what** with the body?"

Wrong Way shrugged, licking the edge of the rolling paper and sealing the joint. "Got rid of it," he said. "That Yukon, too. Just like you said."

"But you left the body inside the truck?" Fannie said.

Lyle was chilling on a lounge chair by the Golden Cherry's empty swimming pool. He had his shirt off, catching some winter sunshine, dirty jeans and boots seeming to be molded to his body.

"Yeah," Wrong Way said. "Sure. I guess. I don't know what the fuck the boys did with it. I told them not to make it some kind weird-ass **Weekend at Bernie's** situation and fuck around with that body. I told them to drive that truck up to coon town and let the blacks have it."

"And now the cops have him, shit for brains."

"Hey," Wrong Way said, lifting his sunglasses from his eyes. "Come on."

"Some black kids boosted that car and went for a joyride," Fannie said. "Got stopped by Memphis police. One of them got busted and claims to have found it outside some goddamn Chinese buffet with the engine running. They haven't ID'd the body yet. Does that sound familiar?"

"Yeah," Wrong Way said, sliding the glasses back down, leaning back into the lounge chair and crossing his boots at his ankles. "Sort of. But I guarantee no one is pointing their fingers at you. Local police probably got that black kid jammed up a million ways to Sunday. Didn't you say those boys had shot up those fucking Twins? Detectives probably think this kid fucking whacked your soldier boy."

"Shut up," Fannie said. "Shut the fuck up. And hand me that joint."

Wrong Way lifted up the joint and she snatched it from his hand, taking out her little Colibri lighter to set fire to it. She took a good long hit, not caring if his nasty-ass spit was on it but trying to calm down, be cool, and think this thing through. The cops had the stolen car, Jonas Cord, and whatever kind of DNA shit show had been left inside the vehicle. No guns, though. That cocky son of a bitch Wilcox had told her they'd dumped all that shit deep into the Mississippi River.

"OK, mama?"

"I ain't your mama, Lyle," Fannie said, handing back his joint, staring across the street to Vienna's. The marquee outside advertising two-for-one drinks and a ten-dollar cover, damn half price for the half-ass action she could now serve.

"I thought you'd be happy."

"I thought you were going to burn the body," Fannie said. "And take the truck to that son of a bitch in Olive Branch to cut it up in a million pieces."

"Thought about it," he said. "But there was a lot of blood and shit in that car. I thought a little bit of misdirection from Tibbehah County, where the living is slow and sleazy, wasn't a bad thing. Didn't you say the cops nailed some dumb-shit kid? I mean, come on. That's funny as hell. Kid jacks a fucking car with a body inside."

"I don't care about that kid," Fannie said. "But I wanted the body long gone."

Lyle had to arch his back and neck to look up at Fannie's face, she seeing her reflection in his dark sunglasses. "That boy meant something to you."

"Nope."

"Sure he did," Lyle said. "Didn't he? Damn, I knew you had a heart down there somewhere deep in those big ole bouncy titties."

"And you call me mama."

"Just a word, baby," he said. "Why don't you come riding with me sometime and I can show you a hell of a time? You'll forget all about that muscled-up Marine. We're no different than them. We're a damn family, too. **Ride to Live. Live to Ride.** Only we have less rules and sleep more. You'll like it. Did you know Ann-Margret used to ride motorcycles? I read that in a **People** magazine one time."

"Well, you fucked up," Fannie said. "But what the hell did I expect?"

"No," Wrong Way said, stretching out, making a show of placing his hands behind his head, joint between his teeth. "We did good. You'll see. You'll see. Just trust me."

"Jesus Christ."

"Just say the word, mama, and you and me will ride down to New Orleans and party till the money's gone," he said. "I got a pair of tight leather pants and an American flag helmet from an old girlfriend that would fit you just right."

"Never."

"Come on," Lyle said. "One day, you'll be begging me to take you away from this fucking Petticoat Junction and blow your pipes clear out."

"Why do I keep you boys around?"

Lyle handed her the joint and pushed himself up to the sitting position. He flipped the sunglasses up on top of his long, greasy black hair and stroked his beard. "I guess 'cause we beat the fuck out of people who give you trouble," he said. "And make sure that no one gets even an inch from that honeypot you named after your dead grandmother."

"Oh," Fannie said, taking a puff, holding it for a long while. "Right."

"Why do you think it's Manuel?" Quinn said.

"Who else could it be?" Caddy said. "These white guys aren't the kind of company Blue Daniels keeps. And how would Fannie Hathcock connect us?"

"Your friend at Vienna's?" Quinn said. "Whoever it is maybe isn't as honest as you think."

"It's not them," Caddy said.

"How do you know, Caddy?" Quinn said. "You're not exactly dealing with class folks here. You're talking about someone who would work at a truck stop strip club."

"I'm well aware," Caddy said.

"And maybe your blind spot."

"Oh," Caddy said. "I know, big brother. But how about we just see what Manuel has to say. When I mentioned his name to those two men, one of them looked like he'd swallowed a lemon."

"And you never saw them before?" Quinn asked.

Caddy shook her head as Quinn glanced over at her from the wheel of the Big Green Machine, heading on into the trailers in Skid Bucket. Caddy had called him not long after the two men had shown up, saying they'd threatened to burn down her barn if she didn't back off the missing girls. Quinn had talked to her and Diane Tull for a time, taking some notes, before deciding to head on out to talk to Manuel. Caddy was right. Might as well find out what the old man knew, if anything.

They found him in front of his trailer, burning a scrap wood fire that was surrounded by a little circle of bricks. He was humming and singing to himself, well on his way with the tequila, chickens wandering and pecking all around him. He and Caddy were up on the fire now, fast-moving clouds up in the sky lit up by a big moon. Everything wild and eerie.

"Sheriff," Manuel said. "Hello, Sheriff. You're a good man. You know that? You have respect. Fucking respect."

Manuel looked at Caddy. If he recognized her, he didn't show it in his face, only lifting the cheap tequila up to his lips and tilting it back. He wiped his mouth with the back of his hand, eyes shiny in the firelight. "Yeah, yeah," he said. "OK. Good man."

"Two men," Caddy said, getting right down to it. Quinn standing back, listening to his sister being direct, and in a way being damn proud of her. "You told me they came and beat up Ana Maria's father. And then her father went back to Atlanta. Correct?"

"What?"

"Ana Maria," Caddy said, saying it in a spot-on way that Lillie might have punctuated with "fuckhead."

"Sí," Manuel said. "Sure. Yes. Hey, hey, hey. You want to drink? I get some glasses. We drink. It's a good night. Not cold. Everything is soft and quiet. Big moon above us. Everything is so bright. Shining. You know?"

"Who were these men?" Caddy said.

Manuel shrugged, reaching at his feet for a cheap Mexican blanket, the kind they sell at truck stops for five bucks, and pulling it over his legs. "I don't know. But who are you?"

"I'm Caddy Colson, Manuel," she said. "I was here the other night. You warned me about the two men in the white truck. You said they were dangerous. They came to see me tonight and threatened me."

"I don't know," Manuel said, trying to hand off the bottle to Quinn. "I'm not sure. So many people. So many people come through this place. They move in, they work, they live, and they are gone. They are ghost people. You know? We don't exist. We are not really here. Right?"

"And if you weren't here," Quinn said, "half the lazy assholes would have to do the real work. Instead of sitting in their trucks and smoking cigarettes."

"Yes," Manuel said, lifting the bottle again and trying to pass it to Quinn. "Yes. See? The sheriff, he is a big man. He understand. He understand the situation out here."

"Who were the men?" Caddy said.

Quinn squatted down on his haunches and warmed himself by the fire. Caddy continued to stand, wrapping her arms around herself and waiting for Manuel to get straight. The man took another swig and swallowed, knowing they weren't going away without answers. And also knowing Quinn wasn't the kind of man who would threaten or beat him to get what he wanted. Manuel looked Quinn in the eye, knowing he had to answer in an honorable fashion or he'd lose face. "Who is this?" he said, pointing the bottle to Caddy. "To you?"

"My sister."

"**Tu hermana**," Manuel said. "OK. OK. I know. I see it. Oh, yes. Shit."

Quinn didn't answer but waited, feeling very much like he was in some part of a craggy shitsville in Afghanistan waiting for the local chieftain or the village elder to realize Quinn was OK, that maybe the Taliban assholes weren't the village's friends and maybe he'd point the team in the right direction or show Quinn where to find the weapons cache. You drank tea with them. You smoked with them. You offered them cigarettes, vouchers, whatever you could to gain their trust.

"They wanted to harm her," Quinn said.

"Burn my barn," Caddy said. "Our church."

"Church?" Manuel said.

"We help people," Caddy said. "Remember? I bring you food when you have no money. You're no ghost to me, Manuel."

"Yes, yes," Manuel said. "Shit. Yes. OK. I understand. I know these men. And they are terrible men. Bad people. They bring workers up into the hills. When they work them too hard and the men complain, they get beat more. Sometimes they pay the workers. Sometimes they bring them back here."

"They're foremen," Quinn said.

"For who?" Caddy said.

Manuel held up his hand, drinking more, breathing in, looking very sad and tired in the firelight. "If I tell you," he said, "will you tell them about me?"

Caddy looked to Quinn, and Quinn lifted his chin in agreement, being able to speak easy with Caddy, almost communicating as close as he could with Lillie. But not as good, not the same. Quinn told Manuel what he said would stay here with them.

"Those men come down into the Bucket to round up workers," he said. "Take them up in the hills to that big house."

"Where?" Quinn said.

"That big house," Manuel said. "You know? The one that looks like a fort with all the logs and big stone. The big man lives there. The politico."

"Politico?" Quinn said. "Are you talking about Vardaman?"

Manuel smiled big, proud of himself that they'd been able to communicate, pass over a little bit of information by the firelight. He nodded. "Yes," he said. "Vardaman. But these men. They do what he says. They treat us like pieces of shit. You know? We are nothing. We are just like those ghosts. They want. And **whoosh**. We are gone. No one knows. No one cares. This place isn't us."

"Manuel?" Quinn said.

He looked up, wild and glassy-eyed. "Yes."

"You're sure they work for Vardaman?" he said. "In the big stone house. The politico with the long hair and the black eyes?"

Manuel nodded. He was sure.

Quinn shook the old man's hand, who again offered the tequila. "Sometime you will drink with me," he said.

"When there's time."

"Soon," Manuel said. "There will be a time when you can no longer refuse."

"How much?" Opie asked.

"Does it matter?" Wilcox said. "We're not exactly in a bargaining position here. I told him I'd give him three grand for two guns. And another three grand for an RPG."

"You're kidding," Opie said, watching Wilcox to see if he'd bust out laughing. But he didn't. Wilcox was drunk and high, minutes ago walking out of Uncle Sam's Army-Navy Store on Summer Avenue. The storefront closed for the night, a vertical neon sign reading ALL-WEATHER GEAR, GUNS, BOOTS.

"Name a better weapon," Wilcox said.

"Maybe a fucking tank?" Opie said. "Come on, man. We don't need that. We get caught with that thing and it's a federal violation."

"So are bank robbers buying a couple clean AR-15s from the back door of Uncle Sam's," Wilcox said. "But, what the fuck? We've gone this far, might as well add in some extra protection to make sure no one follows us."

"You could take out half the damn downtown."

Wilcox smiled at Opie, making the skin tighten on the back of his neck. "Yeah, we could," he said. "Couldn't we?"

"That wasn't a suggestion, Sarge."

Wilcox looked wrung out, stretching his hurt leg out in front of him, his blue jeans cut off at the knee. He hadn't shaved in a while and looked dirty and greasy, Opie wondering if he shouldn't try to slow this shit down. Talk to him about reevaluating the mission, taking some time to plan it out. Nobody clearheaded bought a backdoor RPG for sport.

"I don't know what's in that titty bar," Wilcox said. "But Cord told me stories. He said that woman keeps a bunch of nasty-ass bikers watching the door.

He said they're all heavily armed and meaner than a horny rattlesnake."

"How many?" Opie said.

"I don't know."

"Maybe we let this one go," Opie said. "Finish out those banks we scouted. Come on down to Florida with me for a while, switch up our routine, and maybe ride up into the Panhandle. See what's cooking there."

"You don't see it?" Wilcox said, leaning back into the passenger seat, head dug into the headrest. "Doesn't have a damn thing to do with money, Ope. We could quit right now and have enough money to live on for a few years. And live like we want. This is about Cord. That woman bundled him up and stuffed him in the back of that vehicle. Treated a U.S. Marine like trash. We can't stand for that. We stand for that and we're nothing. All this would just be for bullshit."

"We won't get his body back."

"No," Cord said. "Police have it. They'll find his family. Deliver him in a wooden box without honor."

"And if they find his family," Opie said, "how long until they get to us?"

"Ah-hah," Wilcox said. "Yes, sir. Now you're getting to the Tootsie Roll center. We don't have long to wrap up this son of a bitch and disappear for a while. We don't have time for more banks. We have time for one great act of violent fucking retribution."

Opie swallowed, reaching down for a Coke bottle in the console. Wilcox had taken a nice Ford Expedition, white with gray leather interior, from the last row of that big parking lot at IKEA. He said they may need to live in it, maybe camp some, for a while until they figured out a plan on getting the money they were owed and how they would be hitting that bitch right in the coot.

"You going to kill her?"

"I'd like to," Wilcox said, but then going full into Citizen Trump again. "But I have great respect for women. I love women. Nobody has more respect for women. Nobody."

"Are we going to wear the masks?"

"Why not," Wilcox said. "All this has gone prime time."

"How's the leg?"

"Hurts like a son of a bitch."

Opie watched a dopey-looking tall dude with a long Moses beard locking up the front door of Uncle Sam's, pointing for them to follow him around back. It was night now and not much going on down Summer Avenue, lots of warehouses and junk stores closed up for the night. Opie started the car and followed.

"You going to take Crissley with you?"

"Don't know," Wilcox said. "I hadn't had much time to mull it over."

The bearded man lifted up a rolling door to a big

garage and motioned for them to drive on inside. The garage was filled with bright light, a lot of boxes, and strewn with flags hanging from the crossbeams. A crazy-looking life-sized statue of a World War II GI motioned for them to follow him into battle.

Opie killed the engine and hit the button to lift the hatch. "I miss Cord."

"Me, too."

"Woman shouldn't have done that," Opie said. "A man like Cord should go off in a goddamn Viking funeral, with fire and shit."

"Yep."

"Retribution?"

"Damn straight." Wilcox smiled, staring straight ahead. "Big-time."

26

On Lillie's day off, Quinn found her outside her little bungalow near Jericho Square doing some yard work. The day was warm, one of the warmest on record for early March, and Lillie sat on the steps up to her front porch, drinking Gatorade, the front of her Indigo Girls T-shirt soaked around the collar and cut off at the sleeves. She didn't say anything to Quinn, who took a seat beside her, holding his half-full thermos of black coffee, on the job since six a.m., running down two shoplifters at the Dollar General to their home up in Fate, where they'd been divvying out the big spoils. Hamburger meat, dog food, and razor blades.

Quinn poured a little coffee into a silver cup as Lillie slid on a pair of leather gloves and headed back into her front flower beds. She pulled dead weeds and chopped up the soil with a hoe. They hadn't spoken since he'd told her he suspected Rick Wilcox robbed the banks.

"Looking good," Quinn said.

"It better," she said. "I'm putting it up for sale next week."

"You were raised here. And it was your grandmother's before that," Quinn said. "You said you'd never sell this place."

"I put in for a job back with Memphis PD," Lillie said. "I did it online and they called me the next day. They have openings in robbery and sex crimes. It's good pay, with lots of room for promotion. They told me I could make lieutenant in less than a year."

Quinn nodded. "This have anything to do with Maggie Powers?"

Lillie stood up from where she was working and wiped her brow with her forearm, keeping it there to block the sun. "Some," she said. "There's no getting around you being a lovestruck dumbass. But the truth is, I've overstayed my time here. I never expected to stay here long. I came back for my mother, then Sheriff Beckett died, and then you showed up. I think I've done the best I can showing you the ropes. You're not just a fucking lunkheaded Army jackass."

"Appreciate that, Lil."

"You're a good investigator," she said. "You don't need me anymore."

Quinn took a sip of coffee as Lillie went back to gardening. Her daughter Rose stumbled out onto the porch, squinting like she'd just woken up from a long nap. He put down the coffee, walked up onto the porch, and lifted her up. She was dark, with big brown eyes. The kids in her class called her Dora the Explorer with respect and admiration.

"You hungry, sweetie?" Lillie asked.

Rose nodded.

"I'll make you lunch," she said. "Give me and Mr. Quinn a second."

Quinn set Rose down and she ran back into the house. He moved back down to the steps and leaned against the brick railing, watching Lillie continue to work as if she was mad as hell at the plants, ripping them from the roots and tossing them in the yard.

"You really serious about this Memphis thing?" Quinn said. "Or just pissed?"

"Don't give yourself too much credit," she said. "I'm more serious than a fat man's heart attack."

"Come on, Lil," Quinn said, smiling. "I can't offer you much. But you're second-in-command down here. Damn, sometimes you're first."

"That's like being king of the fucking trailer park," she said. "I've put in my time for this place. Tell everyone to leave the flowers and notes of appreciation in the county jail shit stalls."

"I appreciate you," he said. "You know that?"

Lillie eyed Quinn and reached for the Gatorade,

downing the rest. Her shadow fell over him, hair tied in a tight bun on top of her head, the sun behind her shining on lean muscular arms shiny with sweat. She didn't answer, eyeing him as she drank, still as trim and in shape as when she'd been a college athlete at Ole Miss.

"But you're not quitting today?" Quinn said. "Right?"

"You're stuck with me for the next two weeks."

"I've been spending the last two days trying to run down those pieces of shit who threatened Caddy."

"You said they worked for Senator Vardaman."

"They do," Quinn said. "But no one out at his hunt cabin would say anything. I found one guy who used to cook for Vardaman acknowledge the descriptions we have. He said they did security work for some outfit in Jackson."

"What about Vardaman?"

"Strange thing," Quinn said. "Some fancy lawyer from everyone's favorite law firm in Ridgeland called me yesterday. He told me that if I continued to make accusations against the senator, or trespass on his property, that he'd have to file a major lawsuit against Tibbehah County and me personally."

"What's so strange about that?"

"I never called Vardaman or anyone close to him," Quinn said. "My inquiries at the cabin were done off premises, speaking to local folks I know."

"Damn," Lillie said. "Word gets around. You got

to love these creeps. Just what exactly did these men say to Caddy?"

"They told her to quit looking for Ana Maria and Tamika or they'd burn down her church."

"Fuckers."

"Did Caddy mention to you she might've seen one of these fellas before?"

"No," Quinn said. "Why do you say that?"

Lillie shook her head, crawling out of the unturned earth, keeping something to herself. She took off her gloves and tossed them on the brick steps. She motioned her head up the steps, the front door open, TV sounding through the screen. "I got a PB and J sandwich to make," she said. "Can you believe that kid won't even eat tacos? So much for genetics."

The sun was high and bright behind Lillie. Quinn had to squint one eye to look at her. "It's just getting good, Lil," he said. "Everything we've been fighting for. All those people who want to turn back the clock to the bad ole days. The users, the racists, the peckerheads who praise Jesus but loot our land and people. We got 'em."

"You really think so?" Lillie said.

"C'mon."

"It's over, kemosabe," Lillie said. "Those fuckers had us beat before we even got started."

She patted Quinn on the back and brushed past him and up the steps. The screen door to the bungalow slamming shut with a hard thwack.

"Money's in the trunk," Fannie Hathcock said, taking a seat in a little alcove down the steps from the casino bar. She set down her key chain on top of the table.

"We appreciate what you did," Ray said, raising a Gibson at her. "Those boys had become a real pain in the ass for all of us."

"And now they're dead and y'all have their money and Memphis," Fannie said. "Wasn't easy. One of my boys got killed."

"I know," Ray said, taking a sip of the drink and snapping his fingers for the waitress. "We were sorry to hear it. Was he someone to you?"

"Nope," Fannie said, taking a breath, stretching her arms from the long ride. "Just another man."

"What's your pleasure?" Ray said.

"Same old," Fannie said. Ray ordered the gin with the grenadine, cherries, and an orange slice. A thick woman with bleached-blonde hair in a wrinkled white shirt and black vest took the order and walked off. A lot of clinging bells and beeping sirens. If she had to work in a casino again, she'd tear her goddamn hair out.

"You look tired."

"Appreciate that, Ray."

"Like maybe things are wearing on you down in Mayberry."

"It's only Mayberry if Andy was a trigger-happy ex-soldier and Barney was a bull dyke in blue jeans with a bad attitude."

Ray laughed. He fiddled with his drink, wanting to say something but unsure of the way to say it.

"They're killing me down there."

"I know."

"And Buster White wants me to play nice."

Ray nodded. He took another sip of his drink, finished the sucker, and looked to the waitress, snapping his fingers and pointing to his empty glass. He leaned into the table and shook his graying head. "It's complicated."

"What's complicated?" she said. "I do something for you. You do something for me."

"This old guy," Ray said, shrugging. "He's connected, you know."

"I figured Buster White for a lot of things," Fannie said. "A liar, a thief, a killer, and possibly the catcher during his time at Angola. But never a damn pussy."

Ray's face reddened and he waved the flat of his hand at her. "No, no, no," he said. "Not here. Don't talk about White here. We don't need that crap."

Fannie shrugged as the waitress brought back her drink and set it down with an arthritic Bunny dip. Ray spotted it, too, and cracked a little smile, as he'd spent plenty of time at the Playboy Club in Miami. He used to talk about it all the damn time.

"That's all chickenshit," Ray said, reaching for her

keys and pocketing them. After they spoke, she'd play a few hands of blackjack, eat a late lunch, and drive back to Jericho. Her cut would be cleaned and stacked in the trunk of her car. No fuss, no muss.

Fannie took a sip of her cocktail, too much gin and too much grenadine. It tasted like Robitussin cough syrup. She coughed a little and placed her fingers on her chest, turning her head and making a yuck face.

"Someone inside your club is talking to the locals."

"Bullshit."

"Maybe," Ray said. "But you know better than me how those girls can be. They'd sell out their own families for a twenty-dollar bill and a baggie of crank."

"Maybe so," Fannie said. "But hired help doesn't know what goes on up in my roost. That's why it's built that way. I'm the eye in the sky. Fucking Queen Supreme."

"What about your guard dogs?" he said. "What's that long-haired ape's name? The one who beat that Klansman into retardation with a lead pipe."

"Wrong Way," Fannie said. "And that fella deserved it."

"What did he do?"

"The Klan parked too close to the boys' bikes," Fannie said. "Someone scratched Wrong Way's baby blue Electra Glide. He got a little annoyed and took out some aggression."

"Maybe he's going straight," Ray said. "Or trying to cut you out of the show? Don't you think those boys believe they could run that titty bar better than you?"

"Nope," Fannie said. "Why would they do that when they get all the beer and cooze they want for free? They cut out my redheaded ass and they'd have to actually man the store. That's not on the agenda for boys like this. They party all night. Sleep all day. Work isn't exactly on their résumé."

The waitress brought Ray a fresh drink and he reached down and picked up a little onion. He took a bite and chewed, waving over to a couple of high rollers in Ed Hardy dragon shirts, taking a break from getting raped in the ass for a free upgrade on their room. They waved back, aging men with spray tans and hair transplants.

"Be careful, Fannie," Ray said. "Buster White called me up this morning and chewed my ass out. He's thinking your people may be turning to the locals, trying to kick up some controversy. I told him you didn't accept disloyalty from anyone."

"That doesn't even make fucking sense," Fannie said. "Why would I make trouble for myself?"

"Do you know anything about a couple missing girls?" he said. "Some local preacher woman trying to make a big thing of it?"

"Sure," she said. "I may have heard something about it."

"That all needs to end," he said. "You know where all that leads, and it would be a huge embarrassment to Mr. White, a possible legal clusterfuck for you, and no freakin' picnic for me."

"Nobody knows anything," Fannie said. "Who cares anyway? Just a freak show of schoolgirl skirts and dirty cotton panties."

"Couple underage whores could smear some shit on a friend of the family."

"Come on, Ray," Fannie said, taking a sip. "I know all about Buster White and Vardaman. That's why y'all won't let me fuck with Skinner. He's Vardaman's local monkey."

Ray smiled, placing a finger to his lips. He twirled the cocktail glass by its thin stem.

"Let's get one thing straight," she said. "I run girls. I clean money. And I help out you boys as needed. However, I am not, nor will ever be, the fucking Mother Superior of north Mississippi. If Vardaman has been sticking his dick in an electric socket, don't go and blame me if the light starts to dim."

"Can you find out who's been talking?"

"Nobody," Fannie said. "Nobody knows my business. And nobody sure as hell knows about all those ass parties in the woods."

Ray took a long breath and shrugged. He reached for his drink and drained the second martini in a quick few gulps. "That's good," he said. "You have no idea how relieved I am to hear it, kid. It's been giving me the indigestion and a true ass ache."

It had been a long time since he'd called her kid, going back to the days at that roadside motel on Beach Road. Back then, he'd picked out bikinis for her, little short shorts. They had laid out by the pool and ate Chinese food, watched movies until he passed out. **Kid.** Fannie hadn't thought about those times for a long while. Funny how she'd always called Mingo the same damn thing.

After Quinn made the kids return the stolen crap back to the Dollar General, negotiating a warning instead of jail, and bargaining out a long day pressure-washing the store's parking lot, he got back to the sheriff's office. When he walked inside his office and took off his hat, he found Jon Holliday sitting in front of his desk, feet up on the edge.

"Make yourself comfortable."

"I looked for some cigars," he said. "Where do you hide your humidor?"

"At home," Quinn said, opening his desk and finding two loose sticks. He tossed one to Holliday and sat down.

"Long day?"

"Big heist out at the Dollar General," Quinn said. "Two pounds of hamburger meat and some Gillette razor blades."

"We've put the word out on those girls," Holliday said. "Lot of that crap going on down South. Even worse than I told you. I've got some people looking into Tibbehah County, also circulating photos."

Quinn chopped off the edge of his cigar and placed the cutter next to Holliday's lace-up dress shoes. Holliday did the same and the men lit up about the same time, Quinn walking to the office door and peering out to see if Mary Alice was at her desk. If she smelled smoke, she'd get all over his ass.

"Jonas Cord," Holliday said.

"Who's that?"

"One of our Trump bandits," he said. "Memphis police found his body stuffed in the back of that GMC Yukon. Police matched blood samples from the shootings and sent the bullets from the Twins' guns to the state. Don't think anyone needs to be holding their breath whether or not it's a match."

"What do you know about him?"

"Like we figured, ex-military," Holliday said. "A Marine sergeant. Did four combat tours in Afghanistan. Served with honor and then entered civilian life two years ago."

"But still a Marine."

"Always a Marine," Holliday said. "Same as an asshole. Once an asshole . . ."

"Where'd he live?"

Holliday rolled the cigar in his mouth, nodding. "Memphis," he said. "Ran security at Oak Court

Mall. Had some issues a few months ago with management and got fired. Lived in a corporate apartment down off Winchester. Neighbors said they saw another man living there, too. But no one seemed to have spoken to either of them."

"Get any prints off the truck?"

"Most belong to the dumbasses who stole it," Holliday said. "Looks like whoever boosted the car and left it running wiped everything down with 409 and Armor All."

"What about the apartment?" Quinn said.

"How about you ride back up with me and check it out?"

"Beats protecting the Dollar General," Quinn said. "And I wouldn't mind tracking down the other two before they roll back down here."

"What makes you think they're coming here?" Holliday said.

Quinn let out some smoke, setting his cigar on top of his coffee mug. He reached into his right-hand drawer and pulled out a small file he'd started on Richard Wilcox: military records, property records, credit report, criminal file with details from MPD, and a mug shot. "My assistant sheriff is about to quit on me because of this," Quinn said. "But I got my reasons."

He slid the file over to Holliday, who snatched it up and read, leaning back in the chair, both feet off the ground.

"Both Marines," Quinn said.

"How come you like this guy?"

Quinn nodded, picking up the cigar and taking a puff. "Maybe just wishful thinking," he said. "His wife and I have become good friends. He showed up at her place Monday with a bad limp, some kind of injury."

"Oh, no," Holliday said, setting all four legs on the floor. "It's a lot more than that, bud. Looks like Wilcox and Cord served in the same unit for two tours."

"Bravo Company?" Quinn said. "Camp Leatherneck?"

"Yep."

"Son of a bitch."

"I'm sure you saw Wilcox won a Silver Star."

Quinn nodded.

"Killing folks doesn't make you a hero," Holliday said. "You and I know that better than anyone."

"Sometimes it's luck."

"And sometimes," Holliday said, pointing the end of his cigar at Quinn, "it's 'cause they fucking well like to shoot folks."

27

"I've been waiting on you," Maggie said, sitting on the porch swing at Quinn's house. He walked up on her, sitting there in the shadows with Hondo, her feet tucked up under her.

"Had to head up to Memphis," Quinn said.

"You want to sit down?" she asked, Hondo wagging his tail.

"I'll stand," Quinn said. "Been in the car most of the day."

"Everything OK?"

"Dandy."

"Damn, I'm so sorry, Quinn," she said. "I tried to call you later, but you didn't answer. Rick needed some help and wanted to talk. I should have let you know."

"Things have moved faster than they should have," Quinn said. "That's my fault. You don't owe me anything. I don't know anything about your personal life and had no right to think you were with me."

"I **am** with you."

"I don't think so," Quinn said. "Not now. I think we better keep separate for a while. I'd also advise you to stay as far away from your husband as possible."

"He's not my husband."

"Legally," Quinn said, "he is. And emotionally he is, too."

"I'm not with him," she said, standing up from the swing and reaching for Quinn's hands. Hondo hopped down from the swing, too, and looked up at Quinn. "Goddamn it. Look at me. Listen to me. He's a bad guy. He's always been a bad guy. Something happened to him the other night, I don't know what, but he'd been shot in the leg. I'm so sorry I didn't tell you. I didn't know what to do or how to say it."

"Maybe you could let me know you cut a bullet out of his leg."

"I don't know what he's up to," Maggie said, letting go of Quinn's loose fingers. "But whatever it is, it's pretty damn bad."

Quinn looked down at Maggie, standing there with her hair covering one eye, her brushing it back and waiting for Quinn to answer. She had on a men's white tank top, frayed jeans, and cowboy boots. With her hands on her hips, he could make out the faint trace of a tattoo under her arm. He recalled what it read from the other night: BE HERE NOW.

"Just what did he tell you?"

"He said he was deer hunting and fell out of a tree stand," she said. "His rifle went off and shot him in the leg."

"Deer season's been over for a while."

"I know," she said. "And it wasn't any deer rifle slug I took out of his leg. I was raised with two brothers who hunted. I dressed plenty of deer. And, for too long, I was a goddamn Marine wife. I know my ammo."

Quinn unlocked the front door and walked into the dark house. Maggie and Hondo followed him. "You know a man named Jonas Cord?" Quinn said, turning on the hall lights and walking into the kitchen. He reached in the refrigerator and pulled out a couple of Coors, popping the tops with his key chain.

"Sure," Maggie said. "He's Rick's best friend."

"He's dead," Quinn said. "Got shot up by some drug dealers in Memphis. Looks like he and Rick and one other fella decided to go after their hidey-hole of cash. Five folks got killed."

"Oh, shit."

They sat across from each other at the kitchen table, a thin beam of light cutting in from the hall and lighting up part of Maggie's freckles. She leaned on the table with her elbows, the cold beer in one hand. "I'll tell you anything you need to know," she said. "I'll help in any way. And I swear to Jesus Christ I will never lie to you, withhold information, or misdirect you in any damn way, Quinn Colson."

Quinn reached out and touched the fingers of her right hand, with its alternating blue and black nail polish, a gathering of leather and metal bracelets at the wrist. He felt her warmth and said, "Who'd be their third guy?"

Maggie nodded, taking a sip of her beer, then setting it down and lifting her long hair off her shoulders and combing it back with her fingers, thinking on it. "You think they've done some other bad stuff?"

"Rick ever talk to you about robbing banks?"

"Oh, hell," she said. "You think he's part of those guys in those Trump masks, robbing all those banks around here?"

"I do," Quinn said. "I think he's the leader."

"You know, I'd like to say I'm surprised," she said. "But that sounds exactly like the kind of bone-headed idea Rick would get excited about. After he got home, he couldn't ever get his shit straight. He was always on to the next thing, country music or selling cars. Just last year he wanted to compete on that show **American Ninja Warrior**. He was just wild, going from one thing to the next."

"Well," Quinn said, "he's found his calling."

Maggie buried her face in her hands, wiping her eyes with her fingers, and looking up while taking a deep breath. "I know who the third man is," Maggie said. "And, goddamn, I like him so much. He's really the best of them by far. But so damn loyal to Rick. He told me he'd go straight into hell with Jonas and Rick and piss right into the devil's mouth."

"What's his name?"

"Sam Pryce," Maggie said. "But everyone just calls him Opie. He's such a good kid. I once set him up with my sister."

"I've done some bad things, Big T," Wilcox said, sitting with the fat man in the Ford Tough Café at the dealership in Southaven. The Vicodin-and-tequila mix making everything seem sharper, brighter, and a hell of a lot better. He really liked the neon around the Mustang clock and the smell of stale popcorn. "Yep. I've screwed the ole pooch."

"Well," Big T said, "everybody has, Rick. No need for you to make apologies. I consider myself a good Christian man, but I'm already on my third wife. Does that mean I did something wrong? Well, I may have made some mistakes. But those mistakes turned out to be a good thing. You know, I have seven kids, five with women I married. Christ forgives. All you got to do is pray on it. Whatever it is you've done, you will be saved, washed in the blood of Christ."

"I don't think so, Big T," Wilcox said. "I've done bad things my whole life, but I'm just starting to see it. Hell, maybe it's all the pills and booze that's put it in focus."

Big T chuckled as if Wilcox were joking, his hands shaking on top of his shaking big fat belly. "You're a great man," he said. "An American patriot and gosh dang war hero that's killed how many of them Muslim folks?"

"I don't know," he said. "I didn't keep score."

"'Keep score,'" Big T said. "Ain't that funny. Would you like some coffee? It was just brewed a few hours ago. Got some kind of hazelnut flavoring it in."

"No, thanks," Wilcox said, stretching his injured leg under the café table. "What I really could use is a car. That last one didn't really work out."

"You ain't kidding, sir," Big T said. "I about jumped out of my shorts when I heard some blacks had stolen our truck and left a gosh dang dead body in back. At first I thought I don't want that thing back, but you know how that goes. We can make that truck as clean as a whistle and send it on down the line at the auction. No one will be the wiser."

"Well," Wilcox said. "That was kind of my fault, too. That was my buddy in the back of that truck."

Big T's chin recoiled back into his fat neck, his mouth open. "What's that?"

"The dead man," Wilcox said, not giving a good

goddamn about Big T, this dealership, or ever set-ting foot in this place ever again. "The dead man was my buddy, Cord."

"Them blacks killed your friend?"

Wilcox shrugged. "A couple black guys," he said. "Twins. But how about we just leave race out of the picture, Big T? I'm a real open-minded kind of guy. Served with a lot of them. But, yeah. Some blacks killed my buddy. I tried to get help. I tried. They shot me up, too. That's what's wrong with my leg."

"You said you fell off a riding lawn mower," Big T said.

"I was fucking with you, sir," Wilcox said, grin-ning. "Mainly because it's so damn easy to do."

Big T chuckled some more, a real Santa Claus belly working under his striped shirt and wide blue tie. **Haw, haw, haw.**

"A vehicle?" Wilcox said. "I could use one."

"Sure," Big T said. "Whatever you need, Rick. You're family here at Big T Southaven Ford. If I can't help out a veteran, then I just don't deserve to wear this American flag tie clip. Or salute the flag every morning when I get here at eleven. It's what I do, sir. It's who I am."

Wilcox stared at Big T through hooded eyes, the older man looking like a squat, golden-eyed fucking toad. He took a long breath and moved to salute him. Big T stood up from his desk and returned the gesture. "How about we go see what's on that lot?"

he said. "I'm real sorry to hear about your friend. I didn't know they shot at you, too. I thought them folks just jacked y'all."

"It's complicated, Big T," Wilcox said.

"Well, if we confess our sins, He is faithful and just to forgive us our sins and to cleanse us from all unrighteousness," Big T said, walking through the showroom, waving to a redneck family dressed in matching camo duds, looking inside a brand-new Shelby. "You know who said that?"

"Mickey Mouse."

"Come on, now," he said. "Work with me here, son. Jesus. Jesus said that."

"The way I feel," Wilcox said, "and the things I done, I'm pretty sure that Jesus might think I'm still just a real asshole."

"Don't talk that way, son," he said. "Come on. I know you and your buddy went through some hard times. I didn't know he'd been killed. That's the first I'm hearing what happened to y'all. Memphis isn't a good place. I stay away from the city much as I can. You just need some time by yourself. Think on things, pray on it. He will forgive you for whatever you done. You know, if Charlie Manson had a change of heart and asked God to forgive him for all them things he done, Jesus would do it. I know that just the same as I know my name is Big T."

"Hallelujah, sir."

"How about that Chevy Silverado over there,"

Big T said, pointing as soon as they hit the fresh air. "Woman just traded her in last Tuesday. Got leather seats, navigation, and a moon roof. You could take Miss Crissley down to the Tishomingo Park and go camping, if you know what I mean. Lie on y'all's backs and count the stars. You'll feel better in no time."

"How about the Shelby?"

"You sure do love that Shelby."

"Big T," Wilcox said, placing his hand on the man's shoulder more for support than friendship, "I believe that little red car would drive me right to the heart of Jesus."

"You mean it, Sergeant?"

"You bet," Wilcox said. "Not to mention, if the law starts riding my ass, I can leave them in the fucking dust."

"Damn, you make me laugh," Big T said. "You Marines sure got some dark humor about you."

"You've got no idea."

Fannie spent the night in Memphis and was back at Vienna's for the Friday night rush. The parking lot, thankfully, jam-packed with pickup trucks and semis, the inside of the bar filled with tons of sweaty, horny drunk men ready to separate themselves from their cash. Ordeen working the bar, Fannie barely having time to wave as she passed across the floor and headed up to her office. Mingo was up on the railing, watching the floor, and he opened up the office door with the special key only he kept.

"How did it go in Tunica?" Mingo said.

"Like shit."

"Can I get you a drink?"

"Nope," she said. "Let's get on with the count. Bring up the cash when the shift changes over. Looks like some of the night crew is running late."

"Delta called in sick," Mingo said. "And Capri has a flat tire."

"That's bullshit," Fannie said. "She took a job at the Pink Pony just as soon as we shut down the Champagne Room. Can't blame her. That's missing out on a lot of cash. How's it looking?"

"Bar's fine."

"How far are we down?" Fannie said. "Don't sugarcoat it, kid."

"From last month?" Mingo said. "Probably four grand. It'll go up as we get into the night."

"Once the lap dance got introduced, it's hard to go back," Fannie said. "That's like taking away the color from a TV. Or the sugar out of your sweet tea. Once you get used to something, that old way won't do."

"We got four rooms working now at the Golden Cherry," Mingo said. "I expect to have a full house around midnight. Girls are working hard to sell private shows, but I told them the law might be around.

I told them if they touched any of the customer's peckers, their ass was gone."

"And what do the customers say?"

"Oh, you know," Mingo said. "They're all about 'Come here, baby' and 'No one will know if I pull it out. Pet my willie.' Typical shit."

"But you got the girls scared."

"Yes, ma'am."

"Mingo, please shut the door and come here," she said. "I have something very personal to ask you. Something between us."

He nodded and shut the door, the rap music shaking the catwalk, the floor under their feet, and the surveillance screens on her left-hand wall. She watched each little island of action on the screens. One girl, upside down, legs wrapped around the golden pole, spinning on back to earth. Another girl, spreading her legs wider than the Grand Canyon, stashing some bills in the garters on each fat thigh, probably some up her ass.

"Has anyone been asking you about those two girls we got from that shitheel Blue Daniels?"

"No, ma'am."

"I shouldn't have done it," Fannie said. "Too clumsy to work the floor and not experienced enough for the Golden Cherry. But that nigger owed me money and getting those two girls was about as close as I'll ever come to collecting. So damn glad we sent them on down the line."

"Yes, ma'am."

"You know if either one of them got close to our girls?"

Mingo shook his head. "Like you said, they never worked the floor," he said. "Mainly, they just lived at the Golden Cherry, watched soap operas, and ordered pizza and fried chicken until you needed them. They did one or two private parties and then you wanted them gone."

"They were smart-asses," she said. "Both of 'em. They talked back to me, wanting to know about the money they'd earned. And when I explained they still owed me for what Blue Daniels owed me, they turned on me. That Ana Maria called me something in Spanish and I know it wasn't 'ma'am.'"

"She was a real pistol."

"Someone's talking, Mingo," she said. "Someone at Vienna's knows we had those girls here and knows they worked some nasty shit up at the hunt lodge. Goddamn, it's put me in a rough spot with Buster White. I never knew that country-fried Louisiana poon hound was so in tight with a Southern gent like Vardaman."

"You saw Mr. White?" Mingo said. "What'd he say?"

"Oh, hell no," Fannie said. "He wouldn't leave Biloxi if two virgins were playing 'The Night They Drove Old Dixie Down' on his scrotum. I met with Ray. He said some of the boys had some real concerns about the trouble these little twats could cause their good buddy."

Mingo nodded, staring dead-eyed serious at her. Fannie glad as hell to have someone like Mingo to listen when she talked, clean up the shit she needed, and run the place when she had to run up to Memphis or over to Tunica like some lapdog in heat.

"Where are they now?"

Fannie was watching one of the monitors, spotting one of her girls getting real cozy with some young dude in a ball cap and sunglasses. It never stopped amazing her how married men thought they needed to pull some real cloak-and-dagger stuff just to look at titties. Their wives probably damn glad to get them out of the house and keep 'em from humping their legs.

"What's that?" Fannie said, seeing the girl grab the man's hand and lead him across the floor. Fannie watching it happen from monitor to monitor.

"What happened to the girls?"

"Shit," Fannie said, "I don't know. I gave them to some of those MS-13 boys over in Batesville. I assume they put them to work at some chicken ranch up in Tennessee. I just couldn't stand them yammering at me. I sure as hell bet that one Mex girl would be calling me Miss Hathcock right about now if someone's peter wasn't shoved down her crawhole."

Mingo got up and stood behind her, watching the monitors, while she pointed out the man in shades and hat leaving with one of their girls. They watched the man leave by a side door and the girl follow right behind him.

"Make sure you check every one of her orifices for the money," she said. "Those clever little bitches are going to rob me blind."

28

"I'd like you to meet Sparrow," Opie said. "Sparrow, this is my friend I told you about."

"And what's your name?" Sparrow said.

"Woody Woodpecker," Wilcox said.

"And what would you like tonight, Woody?" Sparrow said. Shaggy brown hair with a pink streak, tiny titties under a thin purple T-shirt, and a smart little mouth. "Your buddy paid up for the next hour and you can pretty much do anything you can think of. But don't touch my butt. I really hate that stuff."

"I don't want your butt, Sparrow," Wilcox said. "In fact, how'd you like a little shot of tequila? Me and my buddy just like to party and talk. We get real lonely sometimes."

"You want me to talk about how I used to mud-wrestle my sister?" she said. "Or that time I tore my dress in school and had to see the principal?"

"Damn," Wilcox said. "I really wish we had more time. That last one sounds like a real winner. But we just want to know about Vienna's Place. It's fascinating. What's it like inside there?"

"Why don't you just come in and see?" Sparrow said. "I took your buddy to the Champagne Room. Only the Champagne Room ain't what it used to be. I had to dance five feet away from your buddy's dick. I was real careful about it. At first I thought he was a cop, with the baseball hat and sunglasses and all. Are y'all cops? Because I can't stand to be busted tonight. I got two babies waiting at home to see their momma. **Wait.** Hold on a second. Didn't you say something about tequila?"

Wilcox pulled the bottle of platinum Gran Patrón from beneath his seat and handed it to her. The stripper knocked back a good few gulps and spilled a little on her thin purple T-shirt. She had no bra on under the shirt and small white booty shorts with big plastic heels.

"Something a-matter with you?" Sparrow asked. "Your buddy just gave me five hundred dollars cash to come out here on my smoke break. And all you want to know is what's it like inside Vienna's. I mean, it's a titty bar. What else do you want to know? We spin around on gold poles and smack our ass. It ain't high art."

"I'm shy," Wilcox said, laughing. Taking another swig of the tequila, finding a nice healthy glow between the liquor and the Vicodin. "I don't like folks looking at me."

"You don't want me to grind your big ole peepee?"

"Maybe later," Wilcox said, looking into the rearview at Opie, smiling big and enjoying every damn minute of it.

"OK," she said. "And what song would you like?"

"What's that, baby?" Wilcox said, eyes fluttering a bit. "What did you say?"

"When I give you a lap dance, what song do you want to hear?"

"You know that song 'Buy Me a Boat' by Chris Janson?"

"Oh, hell yes, I do."

"That's what I want," Wilcox said, going into song. "**Wish I had a rich uncle that would kick the bucket. And that I was sitting on a pile like Warren Buffett.**"

"You're gonna make me cry," Sparrow said. "That was our senior-class anthem. Damn. Are you a professional singer or something? You sound just like him."

"As a matter of fact, I do sing a little," Wilcox said in his corny radio announcer voice. "Got me a band. Now, sweet baby, before we get down to the ninnies and pecker pulling, how about you tell me about those mean creeps who watch the door?"

"You mean the bikers?"

"Yes, ma'am," Wilcox said, "I **do** mean the bikers. Who's around tonight?"

"Well," Sparrow said. "Let me think. You got Lowrider working the door. I think Jack Straw and Bubba Bear and Tinker are at the bar. They're pretty fucked up tonight. Miss Fannie came downstairs and blessed them out for drinking too much and leaving her bottles all around. The girls like 'em, though. Bubba Bear is the sweetest man I think I've ever met in my life. He brings me roses every Thursday."

"How many?" Opie said from the backseat.

"Wait?" she said. "You said y'all weren't cops. Why do you want to know?"

"We had some problems with those biker boys last time," Wilcox said. "Just want to watch my back."

"Oh," she said. "Well. That makes sense. Can I get another hit of the tequila before we go back inside? Miss Fannie takes shots out of our cashout. Can you believe that shit?"

"You said Miss Fannie came downstairs," Wilcox said. "What exactly is upstairs?"

"The Nest," Sparrow said. "We're not allowed up there. Only Miss Fannie, Wrong Way, and this Indian kid who works the bar named Mingo. It's where they lock away the money from thieves and all that."

"Goddamn," Wilcox said. "Learn something new every day. How about we all go back inside and say hello to the other little birdies. I think we're all about to have a hell of a time."

"Woo-hoo," said Sparrow. "But I still get to keep the money, right?"

"Yes, ma'am."

"And y'all won't make no trouble?"

"God forbid," Opie said, all of them crawling out of the Shelby. Opie opened up the Mustang's trunk for the two rifles with slings, extra ammo, and his RPG. Wilcox took the RPG in both hands and slung it into the passenger seat for safekeeping, following some wobbly stripper on six-inch plastic heels.

Between stopping off to judge the Rotarian's annual wild game feast and then having to run back downtown from the sheriff's office, where some drunk numbnuts had driven his '89 Impala into the local tanning salon/coffee shop, Lillie had gotten little rest. She'd been on the Square for almost two hours, watching work crews remove the broken glass and jack up support beams by the smashed porticos and shaky overhang. Kenny working traffic alongside of her, not shutting his mouth the entire time.

"The driver said he had a fainting spell," Kenny said.

"Happens when you're two points over the legal limit."

"You think?"

"Either he was cracking open a fresh beer or he was texting his sweetie," Lillie said. "But I bet the final words he typed were 'OH, SHIT.'"

"I can see it," Kenny said. "Destroyed two brand-new tanning beds. Tonya Cobb is going to shit a golden brick."

"Better be gold," Lillie said. "That woman spent enough time in the sun. Her skin looks to be the color of an old belt."

"How was the Rotarian dinner?" Kenny said.

"Lucky me," Lillie said. "I got to judge all three categories. Deer, fish, and wild hog."

"Damn," Kenny said. "I bet that was some good eating."

"To be real honest," Lillie said, "I thought all of it tasted like shit warmed over. Any asshole can dump some fucking Ro-tel on a piece of fried bluegill and make it taste decent. Mr. Benedict sure was thrilled about his recipe for venison nachos. But, I swear to Christ, Kenny, I'm going to be shitting for a week."

"You want me to stick around till Tonya gets here?" Kenny said. "You can head back to the office. I know you got shit to do."

"I always got shit to do."

Kenny nodded, watching the boys fit a four-by-four up under the overhang, propping up the tin roof. He was a short, plump little guy with a heart bigger than an Indian elephant. He'd been in gunfights well beyond his skill set, found his momma impaled with a metal gutter after a twister decimated his family's house, and been shot in the leg and left for dead in a ditch by a crew of thieving pecker-woods. And every day he came to work with a big smile.

"Heard you were quitting," Kenny said. "Boom told me."

"Not for a few weeks," Lillie said, a couple of county workers sweeping up the broken glass litter-ing the street.

"Good money up there?"

"Could be worse," Lillie said. "It's been coming for a long while. I told Quinn I never intended to stick around. Shit got serious when Sheriff Beckett died. Made it hard to leave."

"Or if these turds would've made you sheriff."

"I don't dwell on that stuff," Lillie said. "Things happen for a reason. If I'd been elected, I would've been the Tibbehah County janitor way past my prime. Up in Memphis, I can work as a detective, get a retirement going, and maybe do some good."

"You've done real good around here," Kenny said, smiling at her. "Hope you know that. I ap-preciate you."

For some reason, the fat little bastard getting all serious was breaking her heart. Lillie smiled back and punched him in the shoulder. "I may be work-ing vice," she said. "I'll call you if we need an undercover john to help us out at those jerk shacks by the airport."

"Thanks, Lillie," Kenny said. "You're too good to me."

"How else would you ever get some?"

Lillie's phone rang and she stepped away from the sound of drills and hammers so she could hear whatever the fuck Mary Alice was screaming in her ear. "We're still at the scene," Lillie said. "What is it?"

"I didn't put it out on the radio 'cause it may be a prank," she said, "but we just got a call from a woman claiming to be an exotic dancer over at Vienna's Place. She said she's hiding under the bar and having to be real quiet because two men just burst into the place with machine guns."

Lillie said, "They didn't happen to be wearing Donald Trump masks, did they?"

"Sure did," Mary Alice said. "Just like those damn bank robbers who made such a mess at the First National and broke poor Mr. Berryhill's nose."

"Son of a bitch," Lillie said.

"You think it's real?"

"Can't take a chance that it's not," Lillie said. "Put it out, Mary Alice. Right now. I'll call Quinn."

"What's the matter?" Maggie asked, pushing herself up on the iron bed. Quinn had come over after

Brandon had gotten to bed and things had gotten a little heated.

"It's trouble when Lillie says drop your cock and grab your socks."

"She's a strange woman."

Quinn found his jeans and kicked into them. Maggie walked across her bedroom to find his shirt and holster hanging on an antique ladderback chair. She handed him both. The moonlight coming through thin white curtains, Maggie not having a stitch on, a silver slash across her small breasts and flat little stomach.

"Lillie thinks your husband is back."

"Goddamn it," Maggie said. "He's not my husband."

"Sheriff's office just had a call that some boys in Donald Trump masks are robbing Vienna's Place. Sound familiar?"

"That strip club out by the highway?"

"Could be a copycat thing," Quinn said. "Or it could be those Marines out for some action."

"He wouldn't come here."

"Why not?"

"What reason would he have?" Maggie said. "He doesn't know anyone here but me. And why would he be robbing some strip club if he's been robbing banks? The banks I could believe."

Quinn pulled on his cowboy boots and started to

button up his shirt. Maggie walked over and tried to help him. He pulled her hands away and said it was fine, he could get it, and threaded on his belt with holster and Beretta.

"I didn't do this," she said.

"I know."

"I can't control what that moron does."

"If it **is** him," Quinn said, "maybe it'd be a good idea if we kept a little space. At least for a while. This could be a big embarrassment to me. And my deputies."

Maggie nodded but didn't speak, looking small in the moonlight, barefooted and working on a cuticle in the corner of her mouth. Her being naked seemed to be least of her concerns.

"I'll call when I can."

"Do what you think's best."

"He's crazy, you know."

Maggie dropped her chin and set her jaw, her hands on her hips and her small breasts jutting out. "I need you to tell me this?" she said. "You're getting to the show a little late, Sheriff."

29

"Is this some kind of fucking joke?" asked the fat biker working the door.

"Yes," Wilcox said through the Trump mask and shot him right in the chest.

He and Opie moved on into the room, all of it coming back to him so nicely, the narrowed vision, the deafening shit music pumping around him. The way the bad guys would stand up while the good guys dropped to the floor to make themselves smaller. A big bald guy with a wispy beard stood up at the bar, reaching for the gun on his belt, and **boom**. Point and shoot. Man down. Opie crossed the floor, jumping up onto the circular stage, a buck-ass naked black chick covering her knockers, sweeping his weapon over the room, shooting another tough guy in one of those black leather vests, the earring and long hair spinning as he dropped to the ground. **Two in the chest.** Wilcox rounded the bar, checking for more heroes. The two boys from Bravo Company flowing like damn water through all the stink and sweat, twirling colored lights and half-naked women screaming and yelling, dropping to the floor or running backstage. **Eliminate, dominate, control.**

A black kid at the bar raised his hands up high while a goofy-looking motherfucker with a ponytail popped up by the toilets with a shotgun. He and Opie shot the son of a bitch at the same time. The shit music still pumping, fucking lights twirling. A DJ up onstage held his hands high, not looking like trouble other than the crap he was playing. Some bullshit about **"Started from the bottom now we're here. Started from the bottom now my whole team fucking here."** Wilcox raised his gun and shot the DJ and sprayed his laptop until everything went quiet.

Wilcox crawled up on the bar, long and wooden like something you'd see in an Old West movie. "The beauty of me is that I'm so fucking rich," he yelled.

He checked the big space from the floor to the catwalk that looney girl told them about. Opie didn't even need comms, watching the floor, just waiting for some heroic motherfucker to stand up and volunteer to get shot. Wilcox had that catwalk, waiting for someone to bust out of that office with the safe, the redhead, and the cash they were owed. One man, maybe two, watching the woman. Wilcox knew that redhead would never get small. She'd stand right the fuck up from that desk and start firing.

All the screaming had stopped. The girls and the customers getting used to the movie they were in, Wilcox telling everyone to keep their fucking hands on top of their heads. "Don't even think of scratching your ass," he said. "No matter how much your crack itches."

He looked at Opie, the kid in all-black with the Trump mask on crooked, eyeholes askew, yellow hair all wild, and nodded at him. Opie would control the floor while Wilcox got up to the catwalk and into the office. So far, they'd taken control in less than a minute. And, in another minute, they'd be out of that office, down the fucking stairs, and running from the room, only that much richer.

He skidded down off the bar, not wanting to make his leg worse but being so damn high on codeine and Vicodin that he couldn't feel a goddamn thing. Watching the catwalk, he headed toward the steps just as a big fugly dude greeted him with a shotgun. "Drop it, boss."

Wilcox shot him three times in the throat, his fat

body sliding down the stairs, Wilcox stepping on his bloated stomach, rocketing his way up to the money.

Drop it, boss. Damn, these guys were dumb.

Twenty minutes later, Quinn and Lillie, over the hood of Lillie's Jeep, watched the front of Vienna's Place in flickering blue lights. The Big Green Machine parked right next to the Jeep, where he'd skidded up five minutes before. Lillie saying no one had made a move since the call. All she knew was that there'd been a fuckload of shooting and lots of folks screaming. Kenny and Reggie directed traffic, flares lighting up the darkness, sending folks well away from Vienna's and the Rebel Truck Stop. A mess of truckers up and out of the dozens of tractor-trailers parked nearby, curious and watching, waiting the same as Lillie and Quinn. Highway Patrol on the way to shut down traffic and deputies from Choctaw and Lee counties coming in to lend a hand.

Reggie Caruthers walked up as soon as they'd blocked traffic, squatting down behind Lillie's Jeep, wanting to know if anyone had heard back from the stripper who called in.

"Nothing."

"What she'd say to Mary Alice?" Reggie said.

"Said two men dressed as Donald Trump were shooting up the joint," Lillie said. "And several folks had been shot."

"Not good."

"No, sir," Lillie said, her Winchester .306 in hand, lifting the scope to her eye, waiting for that front door to open. Two deputies, Cullison and Watts, watching the exits toward the rear.

"They must've fucked up," Quinn said. "Can't see them taking this long."

"They had plenty of time," Lillie said. "Took me eight minutes from when I got the call. Kenny got here first. Nothing happened. No one has come out of there."

"If we got some kind of Waco situation," Quinn said, "maybe we should try and call 'em up."

"Vienna's house phone."

"Unless one of you has Rick Wilcox on speed dial," Quinn said.

"Yep." Lillie lay the rifle down beside her. She looked hard at Quinn and nodded. "Takes a big girl to admit when she's wrong."

"Appreciate that, Lillie."

"I didn't say I was wrong," she said. "I just was slow to see the evidence on that shitbird."

"Of course."

"We just wait?" Reggie said.

Quinn had out his cell phone, punching in the number he had for Fannie Hathcock and letting it ring. After it rang twice, a woman picked up. "Hello, Sheriff," she said. "Would y'all please come on in and shoot these motherfuckers?"

———

Fannie was behind her desk when they came for her a few minutes earlier. She'd heard them shoot Bubba Bear on the stairs, the heavy thud and roll that followed, knowing that all the Losers were down. She told Mingo to drop his g.d. gun and put his hands up.

"No way."

"I look bad in black, kid," she said. "These boys would like nothing better than to spray your brains all over my glass-top desk."

Mingo swallowed and nodded, Fannie putting down the shotgun she always kept right by her desk. She heard a lot of girls screaming and yelling, a few more shots and the thudding steps of someone racing upstairs. Fannie reached to her little cherrywood box and pulled out a cigarillo, lighting up and leaning back into her chair. Wasn't a damn thing that could stop them now. Might as well see how the whole show shook out.

The door burst open and one of Cord's buddies, wearing one of those ridiculous Trump masks, rushed inside, holding an assault rifle high to his shoulder, aiming it around the room and telling them to put their fucking hands in the air.

"His hands **are** in the air," she said. "Damn. You Marines sure can hold a grudge."

"Shut up," the man said. Fannie knew it was the

guy they called Wilcox. "And stand up. I don't want to shoot a woman, but, in your case, I'd do it with pride."

"I didn't kill Cord."

"You knew where you were sending him," Wilcox said. "And that you'd polluted him with your crazy pussy."

"It ain't so crazy," she said. "But it's so goddamn good."

"On your fucking feet."

"Safe is unlocked," she said, standing. "Help yourself. No heroes here."

"Smart."

"Not so smart," she said. "It's not my money. You boys are really gonna kick yourselves in the nuts when you find out who you've really robbed."

Wilcox told them both to stand and face the corner, like a couple of grade school dunces, while he loaded up a black bag. It wasn't a bad haul, two hundred and fifty grand before the night's take. If the man had any goddamn sense, he'd have hit them later when the girls tipped out and left tens and twenties smelling like cherry perfume and baby powder.

"On the floor," Wilcox said. "Hands behind your back."

The son of a bitch hog-tied her and Mingo with duct tape. Mingo looking more scared than she'd ever seen him, eyes bulging, as they shut his mouth and wrapped his head tight with silver tape.

Wilcox strapped the ruck to his back, reached for his AR, and headed fast from the office, right on time and right on schedule. He and Opie would leave with a final little warning, about the bar blowing up if anyone moved, and by the time the law figured it all out, they'd be halfway down to Mobile, switching cars at that motel in Starkville. His mouth felt dry and his face sweaty under the rubber mask as he made his way down from the catwalk and toward the floor, Opie sweeping the room with the gun, looking up at Wilcox, and both of them telling everyone to shut up. One of the strippers was on her knees, pressing a bikini top to a bearded biker bleeding out by the stage.

Wilcox got down nearly to the floor when that girl, Sparrow, walked out from the one room they couldn't check, the dressing room, and asked, "What the fuck are y'all doing?"

Wilcox barked for her to lie the hell down. Opie firing off a couple of shots. But both of them struck by the fact that their own personal little lap dancer, Sparrow, would turn on them like that. She had on her purple T-shirt and little white panties, smacking gum and aiming the tiniest pistol he'd ever seen in his life right at him. The girl had some grit, that was for sure, calling them a couple of motherfuckers for shooting Bubba Bear and the boys and said she would damn well rather walk on a lake of fire than to give either one of them a lap dance.

"Now get down on your face before I blow a couple new holes straight through you."

The girl spit some gum right at him but lay down like she'd been told, facedown, hands on the back of her head. Wilcox made it down to the last two steps when he heard the shooting start up again and felt a quick, hot pain in his damn good leg and a chunk being eaten out of his shoulder, making him drop the gun and sending his ass twirling and tumbling down the stairs.

Whoever shot him was dead. Opie jumped off the stage and set Wilcox upright, yelling for everyone to quit screaming and for someone to bring him some goddamn towels.

"How you feelin', Sarge?"

"Like a hundred dollars," he said. "Now let's get the fuck out of here."

Those Marines had done a shitty job of taping up Mingo or maybe he used some Choctaw trick to push his butt and legs through his arms and start gnawing on the tape on his wrists like a beaver. He had his hands loose in less than a minute, unwrapping his ankles and cutting Fannie free with a letter opener from her desk. She pulled the tape from her mouth and around her head, taking a good chunk of red hair with it. Fannie breathed in a long breath, hearing the screaming and yelling, the commands going on down on the floor, wanting to run toward it but not excited about being shot.

"What do we do?"

"We wait and pray," Fannie said.

"You don't pray."

"Oh," Fannie said, picking up the still smoldering cigarillo and plucking it in her lips, "that's right."

"That son of a bitch took my gun."

Down the steps, they'd heard more firing and yelling. Someone was up and started shooting with those boys again. She sure as hell hoped that they'd taken out those bastards. If they did, she'd kiss one of those nasty, stinky, scooter-riding miscreants right on the mouth.

Mingo had edged to the door, making his way close to the stairs, listening. He looked back to Fannie and nodded, inching back toward her. "They got one," he said. "Someone is calling for more towels and tape to wrap the man's leg."

"You hear any of our boys?" Fannie said.

Mingo looked right at her and shook his head.

"Dead?"

"No one's talking or shooting."

"'Cause they're dead," Fannie said. "Goddamn it."

"Maybe they'll get gone and leave us alone."

"They're not getting out of here with that money after busting up Vienna's," she said. "I want to nail their fucking nuts to the wall."

"You got a gun?"

She shook her head, looking back to the chair and seeing the dumb son of a bitch had left her damn Birkin bag. Just as she turned back to her desk and snatch it up, her cell phone started to ring, playing a playful little jingle.

She accepted the call real quick—on the second ring—before anyone heard it.

"What did she say?" Lillie said.

"Said she thinks her boys are dead," Quinn said. "And wants us to take out those motherfuckers as soon as they walk through the door."

"I don't like that woman," Lillie said. "But it's a solid idea."

"They're not going anywhere."

"Nope," Lillie said. "They're going to sit on their ass and hold all those good churchgoing folk hostage until we help get them the hell out of there and on down the road."

"How far can they get?"

"Not far."

"Maybe I could go in," Quinn said. "Try and talk

some sense in them. See if they might respect the tactical situation here and cut out some heartache for everyone."

"That's a grand idea, Colson," Lillie said. "How long do you think it'd take for Rick Wilcox to put one right between your eyes just for screwing his damn wife?"

"He doesn't know that."

"Sure he does," Lillie said. "Everybody knows it."

"I think they're going to snatch a couple girls and try to get to a vehicle," Quinn said.

"How do you know that?"

"That's what I would do," Quinn said. "The longer they stay inside that barn, the more people we can get out on the roads and less chance they can get where they've stashed a switch car."

"You think Fannie can get Wilcox on the phone?"

"I don't see why not," Quinn said.

"Try and work out some kind of deal," she said. "Be your normal charming self. And when they come out with a couple working girls on their arms, I'll put a stop to all this bullshit. Just how many do you think they've killed?"

"Fannie said at least five of her boys," Quinn said. "Maybe more."

"I think we're on some solid as fuck footing here, Sheriff," Lillie said, reaching for her Winchester rifle and heading away from the flashing lights, through the roadblock, and across the street.

"Where the hell's she going?" Reggie said, coming up to Quinn, who was squatting down on his haunches and watching the entrance to Vienna's. The sign reading THE HOTTEST LADIES IN NORTH MISSISSIPPI.

Quinn just looked over his shoulder and pointed to the Golden Cherry Motel, the U-shaped building and the chain-link fence surrounding the swimming pool in the center. The red arrow curved under the yellow cherry sign, flashing on and off, directing weary travelers to color TVs, exhaust fans, and air-conditioning. Reggie and Quinn watched as Lillie bypassed the office and mounted the steps up to the second floor of the motel, disappearing for a moment, only to reappear on top of the building, finding a nice spot on the roof to lie down and position her weapon.

"Lillie Virgil."

"Yep," Quinn said.

He picked up the phone and called Fannie back.

Opie had stopped the bleeding on what had been his good leg, where he'd been putting more of his pressure, trying to run and hop up on and down off bars. Now he lay on his ass on the stairs, his thigh filled with QuikClot and closed up with a lot of gauze and medical tape. He downed some more goddamn Vicodin with a bottle of tequila they took from the bar. They'd heard the sirens a few minutes back but couldn't see a damn thing in the windowless barn. Folks started to forget where they were, trying to talk, moving their hands, and Opie had to fire off some shots to get their minds straight. Workers in flannel shirts, frat boys in button-downs, women in bikinis, two-piece lingerie, and one dressed up as Pocahontas, all lay still on the floor again.

They hadn't had time to check any of the prisoners for pistols or cell phones, Opie just trying to keep everyone honest with hands on their heads. Or in the case of the bikers, they were either shot up and bleeding out or already on the way to Harley Heaven. It couldn't be helped. You couldn't talk sense to men like that.

"I can cover you," Opie said. "Can you drive?"

"Shit."

"You don't think we can beat the damn Mayberry PD?"

"I can drive," Wilcox said. "But by the time we hit that door, it might as well be the fucking Bolivian Army out there."

"We walk with a couple girls," Opie said. "You mind if I take Sparrow?"

"Have you lost your goddamn mind?" Wilcox said. "That dumb bitch is the one who got me shot."

"Her feelings were hurt, is all," Opie said. "She thought we were friends."

"Anyone who comes to a titty bar to make friends is a fucking loser."

"How many hostages?"

"One."

"One?"

"We don't need any fucking cover," he said. "Only an attention grabber."

Wilcox reached for the ruck full of cash and thought about that lovely RPG waiting in the Mustang. "Hit 'em right in the fucking mouth," Wilcox said. "By the time the smoke clears, we'll be halfway across the damn state."

Someone yelled "Sergeant" and Wilcox turned to see that Hathcock woman standing at the top of the stairs, loose and free, holding out a goddamn cell phone. "Before you bleed out on my carpet," she said, cigarillo hanging from her mouth, "the sheriff wants to have a word with you."

30

"**Wilcox is walking out,**" Quinn said.

"How long?" Reggie Caruthers asked.

"We didn't exactly set an exact time," Quinn said. "But I expect soon."

"Do we shoot him?"

"I'd rather not," Quinn said. "Too much paper-work. Maybe an inquiry. Lillie and I hate those inquiries."

"How will you know?"

"Whether to shoot him or not?"

"Yes, sir," Reggie said.

"You'll know," Quinn said. "We got seven folks with weapons on him and his buddy as soon as he hits that door. He won't make trouble unless he wants to die."

"Maybe that's what he wants," Reggie said. "Have you considered that?"

"I've considered about everything I can imagine about this situation," Quinn said. "And none of it looks good."

Quinn picked up his Remington tactical shotgun, loaded with seven rounds of buckshot, pumped and primed, and effective from the hood of Lillie's Cherokee to the front of Vienna's door. If he couldn't make 'em cease and desist within seven shots, he still had his Beretta 9 on his hip to put everything in perspective. He just prayed that they didn't walk out with hostages. He was willing to take the buckshot to Wilcox, but not with a couple of civilians in the middle of things. Wilcox had breathed hard on the phone, listening to Quinn, and just said, "It'll be good to see you again, Ranger," and hung up. Kind of like a threat, but the man sounding dazed and confused, maybe even wounded.

Reggie crouched next to Quinn, with four more deputies waiting and watching in the dark, not counting Lillie up on the top of the Golden Cherry, ready and willing to shut off their lights in two quick and effective shots. Nobody, including snipers in his own Ranger company, was as calm and effective as Lillie Virgil.

"Lillie told me you'd just as soon see this one guy on the cooling board."

"I've got no personal issue," Quinn said. "Other

than he's robbed the town bank and now probably killed a few bad folks."

"She said he was married to that Powers woman," Reggie said. "The one who got her home broken into?"

"I know who she is."

"Would you rather have him alive?" Reggie said. "All things being the same?"

"Not my call."

"Who decides?"

Quinn nodded to the front door, which cracked just a bit and then opened wide, two men in black tactical gear and rubber masks, hoods up on their heads, headed out into the parking lot. Quinn spotted Wilcox as the taller of the two, holding an AR-15 in one arm and Fannie Hathcock in the other. Son of a bitch, here they go.

"It's his call," Quinn said.

"Are you sure?" Reggie asked. "Just doesn't seem fair."

"You goddamn fucknuts," Fannie said. "I hope you get your head shot off."

"Shut your filthy mouth," Wilcox said, walking and talking despite being shot to shit.

"Ever seen what a shotgun can do to a watermelon?"

"You don't think I've seen folks shot?" Wilcox said, moving with her, but more leaning into her for support. "You don't think I've walked straight through sniper fire?"

"These people aren't a bunch of goat fuckers with hundred-year-old weapons," Fannie said. "That head of yours probably looks as big as a silver dollar."

"Don't make a fool out of yourself," Wilcox said. "I know I got a bunch of butt-hurt dudes just itching to kill me. So what? That's why I got your ass as my escort."

"How's that leg?" Opie said, walking astride them, keeping the gun trained on all those lawmen hiding behind their cars.

"No pain, brother," Wilcox said. "No pain. Let's walk on through this parade of losers and blow this shit."

"You can't keep me forever," Fannie said.

"Lady," Wilcox said. "I wouldn't want you for more than the next fifteen minutes. Whatever Cord saw in you is completely lost on me. Fucking a redhead ain't like fucking Strawberry Shortcake with freckles and that nice smell. Even if you do have a big set of titties."

"You make me sick," she said. "You're a low-class douchebag with a spray tan and plucked eyebrows. A real American hero with a two-dollar ding-dong and a ten-cent brain."

"I think under different circumstances," Wilcox said, gritting his teeth, leaning in hard to the woman, "we just might have been great friends."

"I doubt it."

"Oh, come on," Wilcox said. "We have so much shit in common."

"Damn," Fannie said. "God sure did phone it in when He made you."

"Lady, God made Marines so folks like that Ranger would have a hero."

Lillie had a clear shot.

She told Quinn to have the boys light up Vienna's Place with their headlights, making the entire front of that tin-roofed shithouse look as big and grand as an opera stage. She could set up and get to work in less than a second, picking off those shitbirds as easy as a covey of quails flying from the field. Barbecue smoke flowed free and loose from the brick chimney of the Rebel, blowing over the big trucks and the parking lot. All of it deep blackness, white-hot light, and flowing gray smoke. A lovely place to work.

"Hold it," Quinn said over the radio.

Left eye closed, right eye trained through the scope, Lillie said to herself, How about we leave your dick out of this?

"Wait," the crackly voice said.

Those two assholes walked with goddamn Fannie

Hathcock between them through the bright light and smoke into a parking lot with dozens of parked cars and trucks. Lillie still had their dumbass masks situated in her crosshairs. She relaxed herself, breathing slow and easy, eye soft on the two targets, moving into the maze of cars, still about twenty yards from where Quinn and Reggie waited behind her Jeep. The blue lights flashing and the neon from the titty bar sign and the motel made her think of a carnival midway.

"Goddamn it, Quinn," she said. "Shoot 'em."

She watched as taillights flashed on the back of a cherry-red sports car, maybe a Mustang, and one of the boys pushed Fannie inside, where she disappeared. Lillie was about to put down her weapon, ready for the chase that would surely follow into the night, when one of those bastards hoisted what looked like a goddamn torpedo on his shoulder and aimed right for the deputies. The crazy son of a bitch had brought a goddamn RPG to the party.

Lillie got off a shot about the same time that fucking thing blasted to life, lighting her scope way the fuck up and dissolving Quinn's Big Green Machine into a halo of bright orange light and a shit ton of smoke.

She kept watch over the parking lot, through the scattered smoke and flames kicking up from the truck, and spotted the taller of the two men holding that RPG and hobbling toward the waiting Mustang, driver door waiting wide open. Red taillights lit in the dark.

Lillie didn't smile, only took in a slow, easy breath and pulled the trigger. Wilcox stumbled and fell like some kind of crazy-ass marionette. The other bastard ran and Lillie squeezed off two more shots, losing the guy among the cars and trucks, the guy hiding down low.

Son of a bitch. She almost had 'em both.

Quinn was on Wilcox immediately, headed around the fire and smoke that had once been his truck, keeping his shotgun up to his right shoulder, waiting for the second man to pop up and start shooting. He'd heard the shots from up at the Golden Cherry and saw Wilcox knocked off his feet and down next to the red Mustang. The car still running as he got up on it, Fannie sitting in the passenger seat, looking pissed off and bored, and pointed to the other side of the sports car, where Quinn found Rick Wilcox, bloody and beaten, lying on his back on the crushed stone.

His eyes were open and his Adam's apple worked up and down, as if swallowing some cool water or trying to speak. Quinn, ears ringing and mouth tasting like soot, kicked the AR-15 well free of Wilcox's hand and saw the rocket launcher laying, empty and useless, at the man's feet.

"Aren't you gonna chase the other little bastard?" Fannie said, leaning in the driver's side. "I told you, they shot up six of my boys inside. Most of them are dead. Damn, you waited long enough. That piece of shit blew the fuck out of your vehicle, Sheriff."

Quinn squatted down, scanning the rows of cars, checking Wilcox's pants and hoodie for more weapons. He found a black pistol and a couple more magazines for the AR and tossed them away. Wilcox was bleeding from old wounds on both his thighs and his shoulder, and Lillie's shot had opened a real nasty bit of bleeding across his chest. Wilcox tried to lift his head but couldn't, his mouth opening and closing, working like a fish set upon land.

Quinn pulled off his jacket and pressed it hard against the chest wound, yelling for the deputies to get ambulances rolling.

"He's not worth saving," Fannie said, getting out of the car, slipping one high heel shoe off her foot, the other lost when coming out of Vienna's. "Just let him die. I won't tell anyone."

"He made the call," Quinn said.

"You're a funny man, Quinn Colson," Fannie said. "But, I swear, that kind of Boy Scout shit is going to kill you one day."

Quinn looked up at Fannie, the woman leaning on the side of the sports car like some kind of spokesmodel, not a trace of humor or irony on her face. She rested one manicured hand on the hood, tapping at it with those long red nails, while Quinn heard the sound of the ambulances coming up from the highway.

He pressed his jacket harder into Rick Wilcox's chest and waited.

"You know I'm right," Fannie said.

Opie crawled under a half-dozen cars, tearing his pants and cutting up his back on the gravel drive, until he saw a path through the barbecue smoke haze and truck stop lights under a Dodge Caravan, helping himself up and out. He had twenty, maybe thirty meters to clear between the titty bar and the trucks and he could make it in a dead sprint if some motherfucker didn't shoot him in the back. Sergeant Wilcox bringing the weight of the world on them, knocking out those vehicles with a goddamn rocket launcher. Wilcox was down. He knew it. If he were to survive and fight another freakin' day, he better move on down the road and put some space between him and the flaming world of shit behind him. He ran for it, getting maybe ten meters before the shooting started, feeling a hard-ass sting in his back but still breaking for it, assault rifle slapping his back, the money Wilcox had divvied up in his rucksack. **Damn, so fucking close.**

He didn't think he'd make it, more shots coming from behind him, thinking, son of a bitch, here it goes, goddamn back in the shit, running from that **pop-pop-pop** of the Taliban, those prehistoric motherfuckers trying to take his head off. But, damn, if a long-ass tractor-trailer didn't ride right between him and Vienna's, giving him a long bit of living, breathing diesel cover, and he could rest a bit. He looked from left to right, thinking, son of a bitch, where could he go now? He could steal a car, hop a truck. Hop a truck. Fuck. Yes, sir. Opie jumped up between that sweet spot of the truck and the trailer, down by all the air brakes and hoses and shit, and held on for all he could as the truck hit the gas and moved on out, wheeling and turning through the brightly lit red flares and all those cops directing traffic. He made himself crouch down, keep against the cab, holding on to the rifle and the money and praying like hell that no one in this shithole saw his face.

He'd ride it out. Keep on riding until this rig slowed down and he could hop the hell off and pay his way back to the beach.

Goddamn, a margarita and sand between his toes sounded pretty good right about now.

He'd ride it out in the darkness. Keep on riding until there was nowhere else to go.

Mingo made his way from the catwalk down to the floor and all the crying and yelling. Girls barely old enough to show their boobies and too young to see bearded old fuckers shot to shit not making sense of the whole thing. He tried not to look, seeing a lot of the Born Losers dead or dying, gasping for air, bleeding out, asking for penance from topless women covered in streaks of blood. **Yes, sir. This is how it all goes.** Mingo wasn't sure what to do. Did he walk out with his hands in the air or did he sit tight until the law came inside and told him that Miss Fannie had the top of her head blown off by the local sheriff? All he could think to do was keep walking, try to figure it out, maybe find a way to step away from this. **Holy hell.** What a fucking mess.

A young girl he knew sat on the floor with a pony-tailed piece of shit known as Crabs. Crabs looked to be dead, or damn near on the way. He was drained of color, eyes open, mouth working, kind of pleading for some kind of help. But, damn, what could Mingo do? Pour him a drink and wish him **"Vaya con dios"**?

"Help me," the girl said.

"Help's coming," Mingo said.

"He's dying," she said. "Goddamn, don't you see it? Can't you do something?"

Mingo just looked at her. She was a portly little girl with small tits, a big stomach, and a bigger ass. Her hair in a ponytail, receding chin quivering. Some bullshit tattoo across her stomach that read TRULY BLESSED.

"What good are you?" she said. "What the fuck good are you?"

She pressed the biker's chest and held out her hand, covered in blood, and showed it to him, Mingo's heart dropping into his belly as he headed to the door and the artificial light in the parking lot.

He didn't give a good goddamn if he got shot or arrested. He just needed to breathe. He'd been in that airless hell for too damn long. He needed to breathe.

"What's the matter with you?" the girl said.

Mingo looked at her.

"Do something!" she screamed.

Quinn and Lillie watched the EMTs load up Rick Wilcox and drive off fast toward Tibbehah General.

"What a shame," Lillie said.

"Hell of a shot."

"Yeah?" Lillie asked. "I was aiming for his goddamn head. A kill shot."

"No you weren't."

"How the hell do you know?"

"Because you would have made it."

Lillie tried to look humble, but did a shitty job at it. Quinn watched the ambulance head on down the road and turn onto the highway. He sighed, moving on toward Vienna's, knowing what they'd find inside wasn't going to be pleasant. The barbecue smoke floated and scattered across the parking lot as half-naked women and shell-shocked men wandered from the mouth of Vienna's. Art and Dave pushed them back in. They'd need to be interviewed. The scene photographed. The damn dead bikers tagged and bagged. Order needed to be restored to this fucking carnival.

"I'm done, Quinn."

"I should have shot him myself."

"And you could've saved your fucking truck."

"I tried to do it right."

"Like I taught you."

"Yep," Quinn said. "Like that. I never felt he was going to shoot any of us."

"Probably not."

"That was a hell of a shot," Quinn said. "From up there, in the smoke, and through all that crazy bullshit."

"When this is all over . . ." she said. "I mean, all of it . . ."

Quinn nodded. "I know."

Lillie nodded in agreement. She handed Quinn her warm rifle and stepped back, Quinn already moving toward the club to start the long night's work. They walked together, the rifle heavy in his hands.

"What's this?" he said, holding the gun.

Lillie grinned. "A goddamn wedding gift," she said. "Don't you know where you're headed?"

"Nope."

"Sometimes it really pains me being so fucking smart."

"I'll miss you," Quinn said.

Lillie cut her eyes over at him. "No fucking shit, Ranger."

31

Nearly a month after the attempted robbery at Fan-nie's, Quinn found himself on the Jericho town square watching Senator Vardaman step up onto the gazebo and glad-hand a bunch of north Mississippi politicians, two beauty queens, and the owner of a John Deere tractor dealership. There was a lot of smiling and good ole boy backslapping, news crews down from Tupelo and up from Jackson to cover what was billed as a major announcement for the working men and women of north Mississippi. Quinn already knew what Vardaman was ready to crow about, a piece of land nearly a square mile, just a half mile off Highway 45, where construction would begin that spring. Most of the land had been pieced together in private acquisitions. Quinn's own father had tried to be part of that very jigsaw puzzle, and, damn, if it hadn't finally happened. There was talk of several factories moving back from overseas, a new high school and hospital, regional airport, and a return to old-time values and a work ethic down South.

Jericho's mayor, a mealymouthed white-headed man named Jimmy Alton, promised bright hope and a renewed energy on the Square, before offering Vardaman the classic two-handed handshake and making room for the state senator who'd done so much to bring hope and prosperity to his hometown. There were plenty of red, white, and blue balloons. Punch and cake from the Piggly Wiggly. Skinner was there, too, watching all the action from the shadows under his pearl-gray Stetson.

It was an overcast spring day on the Square, Quinn wearing his ball cap and rain slicker, as several storms had blown in from Texas. He stood under a large, sprawling oak, listening to Vardaman's little speech, wondering if he'd have anything to say about a couple of girls who'd come to his hunt lodge, got used up, and then shipped on down the line.

"Learn anything new?" Reggie Caruthers asked, walking across the Square, carrying a couple of tall coffees.

"Apparently there's nowhere finer to live than Tibbehah County, Mississippi," Quinn said.

"Anything else?"

"Looks like Vardaman's making his play," Quinn said. "That son of a bitch wants to be governor, and what happens to Tibbehah will be his platform."

Vardaman looked like money, tanned skin and graying hair worn long as some Civil War general or fading country star, swept back from his high forehead and brushing his shoulders. His face was oddly defined, as if molded from clay, something from a sepia-toned photograph, with dimpled chin and small, mean black eyes. He had on khaki pants, a checked dress shirt under a woolly-looking fleece vest, reminding Quinn of half the men he had seen on football Saturdays at the Grove at Ole Miss the couple of times Anna Lee made him go. He spoke of world-class businesses excited about relocating to a county of scenic beauty that embraced conservative and Christian values. He repeated at least twice that Tibbehah's proximity to both Memphis and Birmingham made it special, calling it the perfect partner with a vibrant workforce and a short drive to international airports, major modal facilities, and both the Mississippi River and the Tombigbee.

"You think it'll happen?" Reggie asked.

"New jobs, factories, a boom for a local economy?"

"Sure," Reggie said, handing Quinn the coffee. "That stuff."

"Time will tell."

"Sounds like bullshit to me."

"Lots of big money riding on this little show," Quinn said. "They've been talking about this deal since I came home."

"You ever seen Vardaman here before?" Reggie said. "I never even knew he was from Jericho until yesterday."

"First time I ever laid eyes on him."

Quinn took a sip of black coffee, watching the man basking in the applause, more backslapping, and being led down the steps by a couple of state troopers, who flanked him. Skinner shook the man's hand and slapped his back as he headed out. As Vardaman made his way to a black SUV, he looked over at Quinn, caught his eye, and smiled just a little.

Quinn nodded back, the man disappearing into a SUV just in time for J.T. and his Good Ole Boys to strike up a nice rendition of "Sitting on Top of the World."

"How's that witness coming?" Reggie said.

"Scared," Quinn said. "But ready to talk. He's not sure what happened to those girls. But he'll help get warrants on the men at Vardaman's hunt camp. Maybe we start something federal, with the trafficking."

"It'll make for a short campaign."

"I hope so."

"You don't believe the implication will ruin him?"

Quinn shook his head. "People believe what they

want to believe," he said. "No one cares what a man does, or actually stands behind, only what he jaws about."

"Ain't it the truth."

"Come on," Quinn said. "I want to show you some new land I'd like you to patrol. Show you some new routes, parts of the county."

"Business as usual?"

"Until we hear different."

Caddy spotted the white truck after she'd turned out of The River and headed to the Jericho Farm & Ranch before they closed up for the night. At first, she thought she was being paranoid, watching everyone around her ever since Mingo found her and said he wanted to come to Jesus and give his life some meaning. But even though it was just a white Chevy, like dozens and dozens around the county, it just happened to keep pace with her and turned where she turned, even after the turning and cuts didn't make any sense, taking the back roads to the feed store, Loretta Lynn on the radio as the first bits of rain smacked her windshield.

She hit the main road from town, turning into the Farm & Ranch, knowing that if there was any trouble, Diane Tull would be more than happy to show off that twelve-gauge again. But after she parked by the loading dock, Caddy watched the white truck follow and then just as quickly U-turn back onto the road and scoot away.

Caddy turned back a couple of times to make sure, stepping inside the building filled with about everything a woman needed to survive. Diane, and her stepfather before her, sold everything from blue jeans to penny nails to shotgun shells to fishing poles and cowboy boots. Diane's little Sheltie ran out from the register to greet Caddy, sniffing her leg and smelling Hondo, who Diane referred to as the love of her dog's life.

"No planting tomorrow," Diane said. "Supposed to rain all weekend. A real shitstorm blowing in."

"Did you see that truck that drove in with me?"

"Sorry," she said. "Working on inventory. Folks from the fishery stopping by next week. Do you know if Quinn still wants that order of bluegill?"

"I think it's them."

"Who?"

"Those boys who stopped by The River," Caddy said, heart pumping fast. "Damn, I feel like I can't breathe."

"Easy does it," Diane said. "I've been there. You want me to call Quinn?"

"No," she said. "I'm not sure who they were or what they wanted. I just need a moment. Son of a bitch. When are they going to leave me the hell alone?"

"Folks like that won't quit until they shut you

down," Diane said. "I know that for a fucking fact. They got small minds and black souls."

Caddy nodded, watching the rain come down on the Farm & Ranch parking lot. Everywhere looked clear and she took a long, deep breath to steady her nerves. "I need a couple pair of pants," Caddy said, looking at a little spiral notepad from her purse, "thirty/thirty-twos. A couple large T-shirts, and a pair of a size-ten mud boots."

"Boy, that Jason sure is growing."

"It's not for Jason," Caddy said, half listening, watching the parking lot to see if those sons of bitches had doubled back.

"Caddy?" Diane said. "Are you sure every-thing's OK?"

"I've lived here most of my life," Quinn said, "and I'm still discovering new parts of this county. Lillie liked to patrol up here. Not much on this road, but it gives you a nice perspective on the valley."

Quinn was driving a newer F-150 Boom had found for him with the V-6 turbo, four-wheel drive, and off-road suspension. A lot of improvements over the old truck, only it was flat gray and not green. Boom said he might be able to help with the color if Skinner allowed him to stay on at the County Barn.

"You think Lillie's coming back?" Reggie asked.

Quinn took the slow, gentle curves, the big tires gripping the mud and gravel, passing a couple of abandoned trailers and an ancient barn leaning hard toward the ground but refusing to quit altogether. "I don't think so," Quinn said. "Hard to argue with what she got offered in Memphis. More money. Better schools for Rose."

"My wife wants to move," Reggie said. "She said Tibbehah is no place to raise a child. Tornadoes, gunrunners, crazy-ass bank robbers, and bikers. But, hell. Me and you were both born and raised here. We turned out OK."

"My people have been in this county since the Choctaws sold it," Quinn said. "My mother has Choctaw blood, so some of them were here way, way before that."

"My people were from Louisiana," Reggie said. "They didn't have much of a choice where they landed or what they did."

"You know where they were from?"

"Africa," Reggie said. "That's about it. My great-grandfather moved to Jericho for my grandmother. Some family land. He was a farmer down in the Ditch. Did some moonshining."

"Our people probably did business together."

"Wouldn't that be something?" Reggie said, looking off the road and down into the valley, which was turning a bright green, a mist rising up off Quinn's pasture dotted with cattle.

"Ever think about heading on?"

Quinn drove with one hand, thought about it a moment. "Nope," he said. "I got too damn much to do. Between the cows, my family, and the criminals around here, my dance card is pretty well punched."

He slowed the truck and knocked it into park with the engine running. He and Reggie got out and stretched their legs, running the patrol for the last couple of hours since the Vardaman rally. It was getting dark, with long black clouds rolling in from the west, wind picking up in the pine forest, quick flashes of lightning. You could sense more rain coming, the fertile spring earth, and the clean smell of the pine needles. Quinn took a long breath, looking down on his little farm, thinking about Maggie Powers coming over later that night. He'd cook supper for her and Brandon, maybe show him a movie like **Shane**, and talk a little bit about those next steps. Both of them had braced themselves for a trial, but Wilcox had gratefully copped a plea from his hospital bed. Maggie saying that maybe all that good blood they pumped in made him a little bit smarter.

"Good a reason as any to stick around," Reggie said, nodding at the view.

"Yep," he said. "There's still some good country left."

"And people?"

"Them, too."

Caddy sat next to Jason, Boom on the opposite side with Mingo, and Jean at the head of the dining room table. Jean had made meat loaf, despite Jason's protest, and served it with mashed potatoes and gravy and a big green bean casserole topped with lots of French onions. Jean promised her grandson if he would just attempt to eat that meat loaf, she'd serve him a huge slice of chocolate pie with whipped cream.

Jason cut his eyes at his mother and scrunched up his face. Caddy nodded back at him as Jean looked to Boom and Mingo, tented her hands, and said a short prayer, thanking God for the food, family, and wonderful new friends. You could hear the heavy rain on the roof and the back porch.

After she opened her eyes and everyone began to serve themselves, Elvis singing "Such a Night," a track that, Jean explained, was recorded sometime soon came after Elvis had returned from serving his country in Germany. Elvis the King. Elvis the American Hero.

"Do you like Elvis, Mr. Mingo?" Jean asked.

Boom, stabbing a big slice of meat loaf and slapping it onto his plate, lifted his eyes to Caddy but didn't say a word.

"It's just Mingo, Momma," she said. "It's a family

name. And if he didn't like Elvis, he sure wouldn't admit it in this living shrine."

Mingo smiled, not offended, wearing the stiff new jeans, T-shirt, and boots she'd bought at the Farm & Ranch. He hadn't been able to change his clothes since he'd walked away from Fannie Hathcock three days earlier and asked God for forgiveness, being baptized in a cattle trough that very Sunday.

"Did you just get to Jericho?" Jean said, waving off the mashed potatoes as they came around, saying earlier she was on a low-carb diet she'd read in **Oprah** magazine.

"No, ma'am," Mingo said, taking the potatoes and adding a sizable portion to his plate. "I've been here for two years."

"And what brought you here?" Jean asked.

Mingo looked to Boom and then Caddy, shrugging. "Work."

"And where do you work?" Jean said, taking a bite of green bean casserole.

"He didn't like his job," Caddy said quickly. "He's helping me out at The River, helping work some odd jobs down at Boom's place. Right, Boom?"

Boom met Caddy's eye and nodded. Boom, as a grown-ass man, still had a hell of a hard time lying to Jean Colson.

"Where do you live?" Jean said.

Caddy looked over at Jason, who was trying to hide the slab of meat loaf under the potatoes and beans and doing a poor job of it. Jean looked down and gave her grandson a hard eye. Jason looked up with a little grin and took a bite of a single green bean.

"I'm staying with Mr. Kimbrough tonight," Mingo said. "I have been down at The River, but Caddy thought it best I find a new place."

"What was wrong with the church?" Jean said.

"Jesus Christ, Momma," she said. "What is this, **Jeopardy?**"

Jean shot Caddy a look, a real sour-faced momma look, and reached for her big glass of white wine, taking a good sip. Caddy could almost hear the refrain in her head: always give yourself a moment to think before you speak. **Slow to speak, slow to anger.** If Caddy had heard that once while growing up, she'd heard it a thousand damn times.

"Just trying to be friendly," Jean said. "No harm in that."

"Mingo is just sorting a few things out," Caddy said.

"And he's staying with you, Boom?"

Boom nodded. "We're old friends," he said. "Right, Mingo?"

"Right now, I'll take all the friends I can get."

"Well, I hope everything works out," Jean said. "Would any of y'all like some more gravy? I believe I made a gallon of it, for some reason."

After supper, Mingo joined Caddy in the kitchen. Jean was in her easy chair watching **Dancing With** the Stars with Jason and Boom. Boom, full of meat loaf, potatoes, and two slices of pie, had passed out on the couch, his big arm and long legs splayed across the whole thing.

"Appreciate your buddy putting me up," Mingo said, reaching for a dish towel to help dry as Caddy dipped another plate in the sudsy water.

"I felt it was safer," she said. "He can watch out for you. And nobody knows where Boom lives."

"You expect some trouble?"

"Some men in the same white truck followed me today," Caddy said. "Nothing happened. And they took off after a while. But it was them. They wanted me to know they were there and make sure and scare me good."

"I don't think you scare easy, Miss Caddy."

"Just 'Caddy,'" she said. "And bet your ass I do. I'm scared right now. I'd actually feel better if you'd talk to my brother again, go ahead and maybe stay at the jail until he gets this all worked out with his friend in Memphis. Would you do that for me?"

Mingo reached for another washed dish and dried it, setting it in the rack. He shook his head, long black hair scattering across his face. "I don't trust those people."

"But you're going to have to talk to them," Caddy said. "Quinn has someone special coming down tomorrow to meet you. Without you, we won't ever find Ana Maria or Tamika."

Mingo swallowed and put a hand to Caddy's fore-arm. He smiled at her. "What if there was another way?" he said. "If the law comes down on this, the girls are as good as dead. You know that."

Caddy nodded, pulling the plug in the sink and hearing the gurgling sound of all that dirty water starting to drain. The hard rain tapping the roof above them.

"What if I could guarantee a way to get both of them back to Jericho without getting into all this mess?" he asked.

Caddy looked at him, hands on hips, waiting for the kid to tell her just what the hell he had in mind.

"And how would that work?"

"You just need to trust me," Mingo said. "I want to make everything right."

32

Quinn had stayed a while at the Fillin' Station that morning, allowing himself a fourth cup of coffee with the locals, a longer talk with a group of old farmers. Luther Varner had stopped by, asking a lot of questions about how Lillie had made that shot on Rick Wilcox. Varner, an ex–Marine sniper, had taken a lot of pride in Lillie, always proud of her in a way he'd never been with his own children. Luther shook Quinn's hand and went for the door, the rain coming down hard now, and he tugged down his SEMPER FI ball cap and headed out to his truck. Within a couple of seconds, the bell jingled above the door and Skinner walked into the nearly empty diner. Quinn was sitting at one of the tables in the middle, all the booths and tables in back cleared of breakfast.

Skinner nodded to Miss Mary and walked toward Quinn's table. Quinn nodded at the man but didn't stand. Standing would have implied respect.

"You mind if I take a seat?" Skinner said.

"Thought we had a meeting at one."

"Good a time as any," Skinner said. "Work crews starting early. Didn't have time to eat."

Quinn pushed away his empty plate and wrapped his hand around his coffee mug. He motioned to an empty chair across from him. Miss Mary took his order and headed off to the kitchen, afterward opening the front door, leaning against the jamb while she smoked a cigarette.

"OK," Quinn said. "I'm ready. Let's use whatever laws we got to shut down Hathcock."

Skinner's clear blue eyes and drooping face looked uneasy. He set his wet Stetson crown-side down on the seat next to him and brushed his fingers over his bare scalp in thought.

"Isn't that what you want?" Quinn said. "If we don't do it, the Feds will come down here and embarrass us all. How will that look to your big-shot investors?"

Skinner cocked his head. "The way I understand it is that Miss Hathcock is now following the county ordinance," he said. "Far as I know, the girls are wearing proper attire and not touching patrons. As long as they comply."

"Fannie's running girls out of there," Quinn said, quicker than he meant to. "They've got hookers going all night at the Golden Cherry."

"Whew," Skinner said, shaking his head. "That's a hell of an accusation. That's the first I'm hearing of any of it."

"Folks have been running whores out of the Golden Cherry since long before I was born," Quinn said. "It's been as regular as folks pumping gas at the Rebel."

Skinner looked hard at Quinn, breaking into a smile as Miss Mary delivered his sausage biscuit and set down a complimentary glass of prune juice. Skinner toasted Quinn with the prune juice and finished it in a couple of quick swallows.

"Well," Skinner said, "how about you address the board next session? You can lay out all your concerns. But you can't go all willy-nilly with this stuff. You're going to have to show us some proof."

Quinn shook his head and laughed. "Or how about you and me drive out to the Golden Cherry right now?" he said. "Knock on a few doors and see how many county workers come crawling out of their holes?"

"Some might call that slander, Sheriff Colson."

"Some might."

Skinner worked on his biscuit, his jaw muscles

like big balls flexing as he ate. He wiped his greasy mouth and set down the rest of the biscuit. "Board appreciates you making Hathcock follow the law," he said. "But after that Wild West show out there, we'd like things to cool down a bit. We get in the news any more and it might scare some folks off. We had to really reassure some important men after what happened out there."

"Sorry to inconvenience y'all with a hostage situation," Quinn said. "And four dead bikers."

"The others pulled through?"

"Afraid so," Quinn said.

"Well," Skinner said, "y'all did an outstanding job. I know Sam Bishop is working up some kind of citation for y'all. You think you can get Miss Virgil down here to accept it?"

"She said she'd rather bathe in a river of shit than see the board again."

Skinner nodded, eyes flicking up to Quinn as he chewed, mouth slightly open and greasy. "Well," he said. "I'll take that as a no."

"I really thought you wanted Fannie Hathcock gone before y'all cut the ribbon on the Tibbehah Miracle."

"No, sir," Skinner said. "We just want to enforce what's on the books. Rome wasn't built in a day. And it may take me a bit longer to get Tibbehah looking like it did when I was a boy."

"You sure miss those times."

Skinner leaned back in his seat, reached for his Stetson, and nodded. "I sure do," he said. "Folks out there are fed up."

"Vardaman's kind of folks?" Quinn said. "The real working man. The rednecks for change."

"If you want to put it so crudely."

Quinn shook his head. Skinner stood, reached into his pocket, and pulled out a few loose dollars and lay them on the table. "Look forward to seeing you next week," he said. "I think that citation is going look real nice hanging in your office."

Caddy drove out to Sugar Ditch in the rain, the wind blowing so hard it buffeted and rocked her truck, rain leaking through the busted passenger window and spilling onto the floorboard. The worn-out windshield wipers didn't do much good and the glass had fogged up, Caddy having to reach up and clear her view until she found the dirt road and the turnoff into the endless acres of farmland. During the harvest, Boom liked that he lived in the middle of a snowy field, cotton for as far as you could see.

She drove another mile past nothing but open, muddy fields, hitting potholes, jarring the truck and splashing up brown water as she drove through little ravines the rain had made. When she finally got to Boom's, she saw that the front porch light was on, his house a small shotgun shack that had been in his family for almost a hundred years. It barely looked big enough for Boom, but he always said it had once been good enough for his great-grandfather and eight kids. He could make do.

She parked her truck up next to his and raced through the rain up onto his porch. He had a string of colored Christmas lights dipping from the tin roof, two rusted green chairs on the uneven porch slats. But the door was open, floors swept clean, the interior smelling like bacon and kerosene.

Boom came to the screen door, filling it up with his huge frame, lifting the hook lock, and walking on out. He had on a pair of blue jeans, a white undershirt, and no shoes. He'd yet to put on his prosthetic hand, as he often didn't at home, and the nub of his arm was puckered and pink, hanging down by his big chest.

"How's the road?" Boom said.

"Looks like shit," Caddy said.

"Supervisors said they're gonna pave it next year."

"You believe 'em?"

"They just cut me down to three days a week," Boom said. "I'm not in a position to argue."

Caddy took a seat, watching the rain hitting all the dead cotton stems and currents of water flowing off the higher land down into the ditch lining the gravel road. Boom sat down next to her, rubbing his face with his good hand, looking like he'd just woke up. She wasn't sure if he'd been drinking, but his eyes were bloodshot and he had a haze about him.

"Have you heard from Mingo?" he asked.

"No," she said. "You?"

"I tried to stop him, Caddy," Boom said. "I really did. But he's a quick little bastard. He had his own vehicle down here. I could've shot at him but didn't think you'd like that."

"Good call."

"What the hell was he thinking?"

"Mingo told me he had a way of getting the girls back," she said. "He said he didn't trust the police or the Feds. Fannie had polluted his mind that they were all corrupt and dirty and he would only get the girls killed."

Boom nodded. He watched the endless land his people had been working for generations, looking more tired than she'd seen in a long time. "We both got to face it."

Caddy turned to him.

"Those girls are dead," he said. "They were probably dead before me and you ever talked to Cho Cho Porter."

Caddy started to cry. She hadn't felt it welling up inside her, but slow, gentle tears just spilled out. She felt her eyes fill up and wiped them with the back of her hands. "What a damn waste."

"They didn't mean nothing to nobody."

"Except us."

Boom nodded.

"I just wish like hell that Mingo trusted me," Caddy said. "I tried to talk him out of whatever he was planning and he promised me he'd sit tight. He was supposed to talk to that federal agent up in Oxford about what he saw, with all those immigrant girls being moved through Fannie's place."

"He could have shut down that show."

"And shut down Fannie for good."

Boom stood, walking to the edge of the porch and leaning into a post. He looked at Caddy with sad eyes, not saying he was sorry but expressing as much.

"I heard that woman raised him from a kid," Boom said.

"He's still a kid."

"He won't leave her," Boom said. "That's where he went. He couldn't turn on that evil woman any more than he could his own momma."

Boom and Caddy sat there for a long time until, without a word, Caddy got up and hugged the big man, then got into her truck to head back to The River. There were more people to clothe, mouths to feed, and ministry to do.

The next morning, leaving Vienna's at four a.m., Fannie drove Mingo down toward Picayune, Mississippi, for a reunion with those two girls he'd been wanting

447

to find. Ana Maria and Tamika had been nothing but a pain in Fannie's ass since they arrived at her club, but Mingo was determined to see this through and get straight with Fannie and she'd promised to help.

"Who are these men?" Mingo said, the only light coming from the glow of her Mercedes dashboard as she hit eighty on the interstate.

"I didn't ask," she said. "But I agreed to pay the freight. So here we go."

"Are you mad?"

"Kid," Fannie said, "I could never be mad at you."

"I've seen a lot of things," he said. "But I couldn't live with this anymore. These girls were about the same age as my little sister. I figured something bad might have happened to them."

"Mingo, your heart is too big to be in this racket," Fannie said, punching the lighter in her dash and cracking her window. "I've always been worried about that."

"No, ma'am," he said, looking meek and humbled as he sat in the passenger seat, a faint blue light coming from the east. "I understand women do what they want to do. I know the girls that work for you have families, kids, and need to make some money fast. But these two girls. Well, you know. They're just kids. Both of them just turned fifteen. When I drove Ana Maria, she used to bring a damn stuffed dog around with her like a little girl."

"You do understand that some folks are born into

things," she said. "No matter what Blue Daniels did or I did, these little girls would've been whores. If anything, I did them a favor getting them out of Tibbehah County. If you're going to be a whore, it's not good to do it in your hometown. Give these girls a chance to make some money, pay off their debt, and maybe they'd come back as women."

"You get started early?"

Fannie drove the Mercedes, loving the way it handled with just a slight touch of the fingers, the way the dash lit up like the inside of a spaceship, the rich smell of the black leather. She nodded, knowing she'd worked for everything she got. Every quiver, every grunt, every drop of sweat. Fannie had risen from the damn stinking cypress swamp to run the show. "Yeah," she said. "I got started early."

"How early?"

Fannie turned her head slightly as she sped south on the highway, the radio station they'd been following out of Jackson now replaced by some screaming preacher talking about the devil walking among us, looking for the many ways to provide us with a shot of evil in our lives. She reached down and turned that bullshit off. A new day dawned in south Mississippi, the grayish blue light spreading across the wide pastures and beaten red barns, the small brick houses and double-wide trailers.

"You really want to know?" Fannie said.

Mingo had on a navy blue T-shirt with cut-off

sleeves and slim Wrangler jeans, his black hair tied back in a ponytail, looking more and more like he should be riding a fucking painted pony and carrying a spear. He nodded.

"My daddy took to me when I was in the first grade," she said. "He didn't back off until I was in junior high and I stabbed him in the ribs with a pair of sewing scissors. Didn't stop him, but it sure slowed him down."

"I'm sorry."

"I told you, don't be sorry, kid," Fannie said, turning off the interstate, following the directions she'd been given. "My daddy wasn't the worst of it. It was being passed around to his buddies, having him wait in the car when he drove me out to shithole motels in Biloxi or towns in Louisiana with a bunch of oil riggers. Guys with skinned knuckles and greasy hands no matter how many times they washed them."

Mingo didn't speak for another ten miles until dawn was full on them. Fannie turned down a dirt road through some property that had probably been a farm at one time. Now it was only cleared land and an abandoned trailer up on blocks. She kept on driving through a thicket of young pine trees and came up to a levee and small pond. Two trucks were parked by the berm, a red Dodge and a white Chevy. Fannie knew she had the place and shut off her engine.

"Where are they?" Mingo said.

"With those fellas," Fannie said, reaching into the backseat for a canvas gym bag, stuffed fat and full. "Give 'em this. And they'll give you the girls."

Mingo looked at Fannie, squinting his eyes, not so sure about what was happening but trusting her all the same, as he always had. As he reached for the door handle, Fannie reached across the console to give him a quick hug and a kiss on the cheek. "You're a good kid," she said. "You've done good."

Mingo looked up at the levee, at the four men standing up by the water looking down at him and Fannie. In the faint morning light, Fannie couldn't make out their faces or who'd come down from Jackson. She'd rather not know.

She sat back in her car and watched Mingo walk toward them. He turned back only once, now knowing just exactly what his errand was but moving ahead just the same, following a little footpath up to the men. He was an inky figure in the purplish blue light, looking like an old-time silhouette drawing, holding out the bag. Two of the shadow puppet men grabbed him from behind and fitted a pillowcase over his head. Another reached around with some type of wire, pulling so tight it knocked the kid's legs out from under him.

Fannie started the Mercedes. She was crying now, crying hard, watching the man twist the wire until the kid collapsed. Another man walked up on him and aimed a gun at the back of Mingo's head. She heard two quick shots and it was over.

Fannie turned her car around, sobbing now, barely able to see, surprised she still had this kind of emotion in her, not knowing it would affect her like this. She wiped her eyes, a clutching hand on her heart, until she got back on the interstate and then pulled off a mile down the road.

She walked from her Mercedes, hazard lights flashing, bent at the waist, and threw up over and over. Her perfectly styled hair fell loose, some of it catching the bile and spit and scattering in her eyes as the sun rose.

33

"I brought back the records you loaned me," Maggie said. "The George Jones and Tammy Wynette and the Jeannie C. Riley. I really dug her voice, but the album was kind of different versions of 'Harper Valley PTA,' which is cool because I love it. But a little repetitive. I really liked the Porter Wagoner version, such a happy way of singing about some really dark shit."

Maggie stood on Quinn's porch, her car running with Brandon in the back, Brandon seeing Quinn and giving him a big wave, them lowering the glass and yelling. "Hey, Mr. Quinn," he said. "Where's Hondo?"

Quinn whistled for Hondo in the house and pointed to Maggie's car, Hondo running out to greet

Brandon. The kid got out of the car and hugged the dog, hunting for a stick to toss him. Maggie gave Quinn a nervous smile, handing him the records. Her hair worn long, nearly down to the waist of her cut-off jeans. She wore a bandanna print shirt with thin straps, her face scrubbed clean of any makeup, making her green eyes and freckles stand out even more.

"Y'all want to come in?"

"Planned on heading up to Nashville to see my sister over Easter," she said. "Get my head sorted out. I was thinking we might want to slow things down. At least for a little while. With everything that happened, us being together is only gonna embarrass you. You know how people can be."

"Let 'em talk."

"You say that now," she said. "But if it got out that you were seeing Rick Wilcox's wife—"

"Ex-wife."

"Almost," she said. "Maybe we should keep a little distance until the divorce is final. I haven't spoken to him since he was arrested and don't care to ever again. My lawyer is working it out."

"I'll wait."

"Good."

"But I don't want to wait," he said. "I don't want you and Brandon to go anywhere. And I don't give a damn what anyone whispers behind my back or says to my face. I'm looking forward to a long time of being together and I'd rather not put off another day. Does that work for you?"

Maggie brushed the hair off her face, her translucent green eyes looking through him and then over her bare shoulder at Brandon running on the old Indian mound with Hondo, the kid finding a deer rib to toss him, the dog having fun but trying to herd the boy at the same time, playfully nipping at his heels. The sun was high and bright over them.

"Think about it," Maggie said. "We can talk when I get home."

"I don't have to think about it," Quinn said, pushing the front door open wide, the screen door at the back bringing in a lot of light and air into the musty house. "Come on."

"My sister—"

"Long drive to Nashville."

"This won't be easy," Maggie said. "Right now, nobody knows. But if it gets out, they might try and vote you out. That's all this town needs right now is for everyone to give up and quit."

"Let 'em try," Quinn said. "They've done it before. Come on in. Have y'all had breakfast?"

"We were going to stop at the Sonic on the way out of town."

"You ain't going anywhere," Quinn said. **"'Pick up your money. And pack up your tent.'"**

"One of my favorites," Maggie said, smiling.

"Pretty sure I have that Dylan album inside,"

Quinn said, smiling, reaching for her hand. "How about I put it on while you make some coffee?"

"You haven't made coffee?" Maggie looked suspicious.

"Could use another pot."

Maggie peered around his shoulder into the old house, stepping inside, running her fingers over the familiar grooves of the beadboard. The heartwood floors, the wide-open rooms painted white and left as empty and bare as when he and Boom had stripped out all of Uncle Hamp's junk. "Ever think about hanging up a few pictures?" she said. "Maybe getting a stick or two more furniture?"

Quinn nodded, sliding his hand around Maggie Powers's waist and kissing her for a long while. "I could use a little help."

"This isn't going to stop," she said, slow and quiet into his ear. "Is it?"

Quinn shook his head and called for Hondo and Brandon to come on in. "No, ma'am," he said, reaching for her hand and closing the door behind all of them.

Caddy wasn't used to seeing a lot of nice cars coming down the dirt road to The River. But one day, not long after Mingo had gone missing, she watched a black Mercedes roll up into the dirt parking lot by the barn. Caddy was inside the trailer where she kept her office, sorting expenses for the past month, running through donation checks and bills, trying to put both in some kind of balance but not having much luck. She was curious about the car, wondering just who was going to show up next: a battered woman, a homeless family, a sinner seeking redemption through volunteer work, or some asshole from the county wanting to shut them down for lack of a permit. They'd tried twice that month, but public outcry after Betty Jo Mize wrote a column in the **Tibbehah Monitor** about their need of a better sewage system had saved them. By later that day, she had three companies ready to help for no charge whatsoever. Once you got Jesus on the main line, few folks could stop your mission.

Caddy got up from her desk and walked out of the trailer, shielding her eyes from the sun, watching the car door open and seeing Fannie Hathcock crawl out. The woman was wearing an expensive-looking black dress layered with lace and showing off a lot of leg with tall pumps that weren't meant for walking through the mud. She got about halfway to Caddy before she stopped, waved, and Caddy, dressed in a T-shirt, Levi's, and mud boots, tromped out to see what the hell she wanted.

"Service isn't until Sunday," Caddy said.

"Don't think I can make it," Fannie said, wearing

a little smile. "My titty bar stays open to three a.m. Sunday morning. I plan to get drunk and sleep until late afternoon."

Caddy nodded.

"I guess you're wondering what brings me out to your own little slice of the Holy Land."

"It had crossed my mind," Caddy said. "I know who you are but don't think we've ever met."

"I know your brother."

"Sure you do."

"I like him," Fannie said. "Hell of a sense of humor when his jaw's not set."

The wind kicked up a bit of grit from the from the newly plowed fields, blowing it up to them, into their eyes and mouths. Fannie made a sour face and spit out a few grains. "Lovely spot."

"What do you want?"

"I know you don't like me," Fannie said, "and don't approve of how I make my living. But I do pride myself in being a member of this community. I want you to know I sincerely appreciate the work you do here for the real outcasts."

Caddy leveled her eyes at the woman in the frilly dress, looking so painfully done up that she just might melt into a puddle of wax down in the dirt. She waited for Fannie to get to with whatever it was she was wanting.

Fannie reached into her purse with fumbling hands and brought out an envelope. "Here," she said, thrusting it toward her. "A little appreciation from me and the girls from Vienna's. You're a gutsy little towhead, ain't you?"

"Keep it," Caddy said. "I don't take bribes."

"It's not a bribe," she said. "Don't y'all take up an offering on Sunday? Just throw it on in the basket and buy yourself a few chicken coops and a tanker truck full of grape juice or whatever floats your boat."

Caddy shook her head, placing her knuckles on her hips, thinking how the old Caddy would've launched right at that bitch, with her thousand-dollar heels, and beat some sense into her. But the new Caddy was calm, finding strength and compassion in the Lord. This woman was a child of God. Someone special and valued. Caddy steadied her breath and, without putting a lot of thought into it, just said, "Ana Maria and Tamika."

"What?"

"They're dead, aren't they?" she said. "That's why you're here. You knew I was looking for them."

The woman's face shifted a bit behind all that makeup, eye twitching a bit. She looked uneasy on those tall heels, shifting a little, like that spring wind might just knock her on her ass.

"I wouldn't wipe my ass with your money."

"Dumb."

"Where's Mingo?" Caddy said. "He missed this past Sunday's service. You must've scared him into not going."

The woman took a long breath and swallowed, still holding the envelope and shaking her head. She bit her lip and started to speak, kind of choking on it, but nothing would come. A lot of sadness on her face like she just might break apart. "Here," she said. "He'd want you to have this."

"Where is he?"

"I don't know."

"Lady," Caddy said. "You damn well do. Why won't he call me? What'd you do to him? Where are those girls? You can't buy me off. You think you can get clean by tossing a check down at my feet like I'm some kind of mangy dog. You need to stand here and listen. Where are you going? Listen to me. Listen to me."

But Fannie had already turned and marched back to her car, Caddy still screaming at her as she put on a pair of sunglasses and raised the driver's-side window, leaving The River in a little plume of dust and disappearing on down the road.

"Looks like you got it made down here," the man said, watching Opie make a margarita at the tiki bar. "Good job right on the beach, plenty of good-looking women in bikinis. And, damn, you don't even have to wear shoes."

"I'm pretty lucky," Opie said, placing the two

margaritas on the server's tray. "Got a great girl, too. You see her there under the umbrella?"

"The one in the red string bikini?" the man asked, smiling. He was a medium-sized guy in a blue polo shirt and khaki shorts, lots of tattoos on his arms, his head shaved nearly bald. Like a punk rock business-man.

Opie nodded. "Sometimes I can't believe it my-self," he said. "She doesn't brag about it too much, but she was runner-up for Miss Teen Mississippi a few years ago. She ended up taking the crown for half the year. The winner got involved in some kind of Internet nudie thing. I didn't ask a lot of ques-tions."

The man finished up his grouper sandwich, push-ing it away, drinking a Coke on the side. "You live here on Treasure Island?"

"Yes, sir."

"'Yes, sir'?" the man said, smiling. "You must be a military man."

"Marine," Opie said. "Best years of my life."

The man kept on admiring Crissley, sitting under the palm frond umbrella, sipping a mai tai, waiting for Opie to get off in an hour and go for a walk on the beach until the sunset. It was her favorite time of day.

"Always liked Marines."

Opie glanced down at the man's tattoos, seeing

some things he recognized. Daggers and such, a map of parts of Afghanistan. "Army?"

"Sure," the man said, real noncommittal, drinking a little Coke and checking his watch for the time. "Things sure slow down when you're back."

"You have no idea," Opie said. "I love all this and appreciate having a great-looking girlfriend, the beach, and all, but sometimes . . . Well, you know."

"The brotherhood."

"That's it," Opie said. "That's fucking it. You know? Hey, don't you want a beer or something? On me."

The man shook his head. "Other people can't understand," he said. "At first it's scary as hell, but once you get over that sick feeling, it's a lot of fun. Don't you miss the fun?"

"Yeah," Opie said, grinning. "Damn straight."

"The mission, the brotherhood," the man said. "Being part of something bigger than yourself."

Opie nodded some more, this tattooed Army guy understanding what the fuck things were about, really getting it. Maybe he could invite him to dinner with him and Crissley. Not often you get to talk to folks who really get what you've been through, besides some of the Vietnam bikers who stopped by on Sundays. Those guys knew all about the shit.

"Kind of like being a bank robber," the man said.

"What's that?" Opie said, feeling like his temperature just dropped about twenty degrees. He looked to Crissley, who was talking to some muscled-up dude drinking a beer. He looked across the bar to the exit by the front register and back at the bald man, who just gave him a big smile.

"Good to find you, Sam," the man said. "I'm federal agent Jon Holliday. And that man by the railing is with me. And that woman in the Hawaiian dress, drinking the margarita, by the bandstand? That's my friend, Melanie, a U.S. Marshal from north Mississippi. She's rounded up a few locals to join us."

"Shit," Opie said.

"The bad thing about a vacation," the man named Holliday said, "is that it always has to end."

I wondered what it'd take to finally get you down here," Buster White said in his gravelly voice. "I can always comp you a suite, but we got to be a little careful about it. You know how the Feds can be real hard-ons when it comes to elected officials getting special attention."

"I'm not staying the night," Vardaman said. "My wife and I were just driving through on our way up from New Orleans. We had lunch at Galatoire's. You ever had their Oysters en Brochette?"

"No," Buster White said, in his black Ray-Bans with wraparound strap, white hair brushed back, thinning and flowing wild in the salty Gulf breeze. "Rich food gives me the shits."

"It was a lovely day," he said. "Did some antique

shopping on Royal Street. Had a Sazerac over at the Roosevelt."

"Sure you don't want to stay the night?"

"We're in session tomorrow," Vardaman said, crossing his legs like a woman. The men sitting on the casino hotel penthouse balcony overlooking the Gulf. He had on a seersucker suit with a white shirt wide open at the throat. White had on an XXL Hawaiian shirt, red with yellow hibiscus. He was smoking Kent cigarettes and nursing a scotch and water.

"Maybe this summer," White said. "I just booked Reba McEntire for a full week. I'm not crazy about that country shit. But, whatever. I'm pretty sure we may be getting Olivia Newton-John in August. Now, that's something. Woman is, like, seventy years old and you can still bounce a quarter off her ass. Ever seen a woman that age in leather pants?"

"Buster," Vardaman said. "I wanted to thank you for your contribution."

"Oh, yeah?" Buster White said, inhaling long on the Kent. "Sure. What the hell. You're welcome. You're guaranteed to be a better governor than that fuckwad hillbilly we got now. Me and him used to be pals, but once he got in the mansion, he acts like he knows how to wipe his own ass. Between me and you, something's wrong with him. You know, mentally."

"He's been a kind supporter."

"Whatever," White said. "He's a moron. I swear to God, I don't think he can tie his shoes."

"I couldn't be happier with everything happening in Tibbehah," Vardaman said. "I know to you it's just a little postage stamp on a map. But, to me, it's home. Your hospitality made it all come together."

"What can I say," White said. "The world is round."

"I'm glad to know we smoothed over some things with your interests up there," Vardaman said. "I'm always pleased to help where I can."

"Sure, sure," White said, blowing the smoke in the warm breezes, pointing out a couple of seagulls hovering by the balcony. "Goddamn birds. Always fucking wanting something."

"Has Miss Hathcock ever talked to you about this local sheriff?"

"Why?" White said, getting to his feet, knees aching like hell, and tossing the bread from his club sandwich into the wind. "You got some more trouble up there?"

"Getting a little pushback," Vardaman said, sitting fine and dandy in his gentlemanly threads. Long graying hair shining in the sun. He smiled at Buster White and nodded knowingly.

"And whattaya want to do?"

"Might I suggest we start by cutting his fucking nuts off?"